TRIANGLES

"A compelling, explosive story of an ultimate moral dilemma..."
John D. MacDonald
Author of the Travis McGee series

"In a highly entertaining read, TRIANGLES OF FIRE lays bare the little known secrets of the world of arson"
Patricia Highsmith
Author of The Talented Mr. Ripley series

"... Siler is extremely knowledgeable on the subject of arson, and his characterizations of firemen and low-lifes are razor-sharp. And the conclusion to this ironic and neatly plotted tale is compelling."
Publisher's Weekly

"This is a crisp, compelling cat-and-mouse yarn of arsonist vs arson investigator set in the Bay Area that engenders empathy for the good guy and bad guy while detailing the methods and madness of arson-for-hire.
Siler shows great care for his characters, his story and subject area, and his language."
Los Angeles Times

"... As San Francisco becomes blistered by suspicious blazes, the two men are pitted against each other, drawn by a common bond and both faced with classic moral dilemmas. The author draws an authentic view of "the fastest growing crime in America"."
Los Angeles Times/The Book Review

"... a hot summer read...Siler was once an arson investigator, and it shows in his inside stuff about fires, how they start, and how firefighters combat them. The plot is another plus... Siler's yarn crackles like a five-alarm fire."
New York Daily News

"Arson, a fascinating crime for the often darkly psychological motivations of the arsonist, for the utter devastation of lives and property, and for the tons of dirty money being made on it, does not get the attention it deserves from the writers of thrillers. But here, set in San Francisco, is a story far more dramatic than most murder mysteries. ... A compelling, explosive story of an ultimate moral dilemma, according to John D. MacDonald, who knows a compelling, explosive story when he sees one."
Chicago Tribune

"This is an unusual book. Every firefighter will identify with this novel."
Fire Chief (Magazine)

ARSON-FOR-PROFIT

LIFE INSIDE THE WORLD OF CRIMINAL FIRES

STRETCH JACKSON—He torches buildings for a living. Handsome, honest, fresh from the Midwest. Caught in a race more deadly than he ever dreamed. Seduced by the corruption of San Francisco. In love with a woman who wants something more.

TOM FARLEY—The ultimate private investigator. One of the tough new breed dedicated to fighting arson – the fastest growing crime in America.

KAREN CANFIELD—A tarnished innocence. Fleeing a past of abuse, in search of a wholeness her love needed, but fate had denied.

JONAH WEST—The fireman's fireman. Rock solid. A front-line firefighter who discovers that the battle against arson is not only on the fireground.

The first book to expose the respectable men, the powerful money, and the terrifying tricks-of-the-trade that caused arson-for-profit to explode across America and around the world.

A book about those who fight – and sometimes die – to stop that crime.

The real story of their loves, their lives, and their lethal conflict are the secrets hidden within...

TRIANGLES OF FIRE

TRIANGLES OF FIRE

Jack Siler

WILLOUGHBY EDITIONS

First Published 1984 By
Dell Publishing Company, Inc.
New York, NY

Published 2018 By
Willoughby Editions
willoughbyeditions@gmail.com

Print ISBN: 9781625361301
Ebook ISBN: 9781625361295

To Kim—
  and the firemen, who risk their lives to protect the public, and to
  the arson investigators, private and public, who try to reduce that
  risk (with a nod to Rick Schmitt—one of The Best in The West).

1

Late afternoon sunlight filtered lazily through the open doors. It made the big room sparkle with reflections of chrome and candy-apple red. Yet no matter how pretty, how peaceful the quiet made it seem, the calm at Station House 1 always held a subtle undertone of menace, for this was home to the men who wait for the Fire God to breathe.

Behind the glass in the little corner room the man on duty took a call, listened intently, jotted down a note, and immediately pushed the alarm button, which long ago someone had painted with red nail polish. Much of it was still there. A finger on that button always had the same effect—suddenly all hairy hell was unleashed! Above the door, the clapper slammed at the bell in a frenzy, and the deafening result pierced the building with violence and life.

The duty man swept up the microphone and the loudspeakers blared out his message. "Task Force Eleven! Ladder One, Engine One, you're on!"

Men who had been dozing in the upstairs bunk room were instantly wide awake and moving. The tillerman did not even take the time to scrape his change off the card table—he knew it would all be waiting for him when he got back. If he got back.

Oakland's main fire station housed a ladder truck, two fire engines, and a chief's buggy. Jonah West, captain of Ladder 1, and Mannie Rojas, captain of Engine 1, broke their conversation in midsentence and leaped to their feet.

"Okay, let's hope it's worth the trip!" Rojas shouted as both men ran for their units.

Feet were shoved into boots. Fumbling fingers stuffed shirttails into pants with legs already in motion. Flies were zipped, helmets grabbed. Men grasped the glistening brass pole and disappeared through the hole in the floor into the engine room. In a mere thirty seconds the fire station was transformed from a scene of tranquillity into a throbbing cube of chaos.

The engine under the chrome and candy-apple roared to life, belching an embarrassing little cloud of blue exhaust. Red lights began to whip out their warnings and the siren added its ominous wail to the din. In a thunder of yells and flashing color one of American La France's finest hundred-foot ladder trucks moved out of Station House I with Rojas's shining engine right behind.

As quickly as bedlam had come, it left. The concrete cavern was more still than ever. A small puddle of oil mutely testified to the brilliance that had just been parked above it. From the doorway a fireman looked wistfully after the fading siren sound.

* * *

The din in the cab of Ladder I didn't let up. Between the siren, the motor, and the radio's high-pitched cackle an infernal racket followed every zig and zag as the truck weaved through traffic. It was a mobile box of noise.

"Engine Company Four responding," spat out of the. radio. "Ten-four."

"First-due unit reporting. Fireground red! It's a working fire. Give me a second alarm."

Jonah West, captain of Ladder 1, leaned toward the driver and screamed above the furor, "Fireground red and two alarms! It must be a son-of-a-bitch!"

And so it was. An old three-story factory was but a shadow of its once bustling self. A small machine shop still occupied a corner of the ground floor, but most of the rest of the building had been slowly abandoned. Flames were quickly trying to finish what years of deterioration had not yet accomplished. Twilight rapidly turned to darkness as fire gnawed through ancient grease- and grime-soaked floors. The fire's sinister roar was accentuated by snaps and pops as the building's innards gave way.

An organizational relic from the days when army men were the firefighters, every vehicle is a company, and every company has its officer. Since all industrial and commercial buildings in a city are classified by the risk they represent, a report of fire calls out a predetermined task force composed of units that are coordinated to deal with the risks involved. Each task force is drawn from several stations and commanded by a Fire Chief. Once on the fire site, he assesses the need for more equipment. Each call for another alarm brings an additional prearranged task force. The Chief of Task Force Eleven had not waited long to call for a third, then a fourth, alarm.

Trucks, hoses, men, and water were everywhere, bathed in the light of soaring flames. The parking lot and the adjoining streets were blocked with pumper units sucking water from hydrants and rushing it to the fireground nozzles. The top priority at the moment was to keep the fire from spreading to an adjacent building that had managed to maintain an active life as a factory. The owner of Gloria Pump and Suction Equipment, Inc. was frantically trucking everything out of his threatened factory that wasn't bolted down.

Jonah West stood before the blaze like a block of granite, getting a moment of badly needed relief. Above him a pane of glass popped and the pieces tinkled on the pavement a few yards away.

As Jonah watched, a fireman staggered out of the door, gagging from smoke. He bent for a moment, hands on his knees, gulping air, trying not to vomit. A medic rushed up to ask if he was okay.

"Yeah—soon as my lungs cool down. Where's the water jug?" He retched anyway. The medic hurried off.

Jonah moved over to him. "It's a goner."

The fireman looked up. "Sure is. And it's a torch job, the motherfucker—" He halted in a fit of coughing.

"We'll get him," Jonah replied, his voice ringing with determination.

The man straightened up and shot the captain a grim look. "Like hell we will, Jonah," he said disgustedly.

Jonah had to accept the truth with a sigh of resignation. "Yeah. You're probably right. Doing any good at all in there?"

"Not much."

Jonah didn't know the man, but the firefighter knew Jonah. Almost everyone in Oakland knew Jonah. He had often seen his own name and photograph in the newspapers as well as in the fire trade journals. He was one of the leaders of the Oakland fireman's union. Also, in his twelve years on duty he had received three citations for bravery at fire sites, one of which merited the city's highest award and a Presidential Citation. On that occasion, ten children had been trapped on the third floor of a blazing nursery school. Jonah had carried two of them on his 5 foot 11 inch frame while leading the others out of danger. For an on-line fireman he had acquired quite unusual renown.

West looked like a statue whose sculptor had forgotten to chisel in the details. Everything about him was square and rough-hewn. His head, nose, cheeks, jaw, body—all were heavyset and angular. Surprisingly, his eyes were kind. They were the only hint of a gentler interior.

Jonah decided he had better head back to his truck. He hopped aboard three hundred fifty thousand dollars worth of the latest in tractor-drawn, hundred-foot, aerial ladder trucks. As with any semitrailer, the turntable between the cab and the ladder section allowed a short turning radius—necessary for Ladder 1 to maneuver the tight corners of the Berkeley Hills streets. The rear wheels of the trailer had a separate steering wheel known as the "tiller" high up in a cab. At a fire the tillerman doubled at the ladder controls, changing the ladder's direction and height and keeping a close eye on the load indicator so that the men and equipment on the ladder did not become top-heavy beyond the unit's safety level.

The tillerman gave Jonah a wink. "Got it up for the panoramic view again, Captain?"

Jonah replied, "You just make sure I don't tip this baby over," and swung himself upward.

As Jonah moved up the rungs, he stopped for a moment to survey the several hundred spectators who had gathered to watch the blaze. Their number always intrigued him. Even though he was paid to do a job, Jonah knew there was something else that linked him to the gawking onlookers, something that binds every person to fire whether or not he is in one of the fire professions. The link is in some biological, psychological umbilical cord to man's prehistoric past. In the million years since pre-man started heating his caves in southern France, fire may have been domesticated, but it has stubbornly refused to become totally tame. From the fireplace to the blast furnace, the camp fire to the forest fire, the candle to the holocaust, flame feeds both our fear and fascination. Captain West knew that was part of the reason he was on the ladder doing battle—the work was too grimy, too dangerous to be *just* another job. No child, man, or woman is immune to that double face of fire's horror—and attraction.

Jonah turned his eyes away from the people lining the street and stared beyond the ladder to the angry orange flames. Maybe someday they'll get me, he, thought, and maybe they won't. Meanwhile, there was duty. An extra dose of adrenaline surged through him and he moved on upward to take command.

2

Tom Farley's stomach began speaking to him with greater urgency than his drive to continue working. It was, after all, eight thirty and Saturday evening. He heaved a sigh of exasperation at the forces of nature, which demand so much time for sleeping and eating. Resolving his conflict in favor of food, Tom closed the file and stuck it in his briefcase to finish after dinner. He swiveled around, glanced through the office window to the beauty of San Francisco at dusk, then grabbed two more files from a shelf and added them to his homework.

Despite the drive of Farley's mind, everything else about him seemed relaxed, from the loose, easy frame of his body to the round contours of his face. Even his suit usually looked as though the cleaner had forgotten to press it. At first glance, one would have assumed he was the classic absentminded professor, or perhaps a middle-level bureaucrat, forty-five and stuck in a rut. Neither was quite the case.

Farley rose and grabbed his hat. He was not pleased about the thinning of his dark hair in the back, but the hat concealed that. He had an engaging face—not quite plain, not quite handsome, marked by high, round cheekbones, an indelicately chiseled nose, and a firm, relaxed mouth above a remarkable dimpled chin. His eyes had a piercing and effervescent quality that let you know not a single detail escaped them. Tom Farley's overall image was a peaceable facade for a main-frame brain—he was not the easy mark his exterior implied. The Sunday-golfer bearing hid an ex-paratroop captain; the unflappable calm was a mask for the feverish determination that ruled his mind. Farley locked up his office and left for a quiet evening of overtime—although "overtime" was an unknown word in his vocabulary.

In the parking lot he started his black-vinyl-topped white Pontiac, hit reverse, and turned the sixteen-band scanning receiver to the San Francisco Fire Department wavelength. Not much was going on. He pulled smoothly into traffic, heading for home and Oakland, which lay across the Bay Bridge. He switched the radio to the Oakland wavelength. *That* was where the action was. As soon as the dimensions of the fire that menaced Gloria Pump and Suction Equipment became clear, Farley's foot pressed heavier on the accelerator.

San Francisco's twilight twinkle rapidly faded behind him and the lights of Oakland came into focus. When the red glare and the ponderous column of smoke in the industrial area became visible, Tom kicked the car above the speed limit.

A police officer stopped him at the barricade, took a quick look at his I.D., and promptly pulled the sawhorse aside. Wiggling the Pontiac through the clutter as best he could, Farley finally gave up and parked. He opened the car door and stood up, his big six-foot form filling the opening completely. He placed his fist on the black vinyl top and rested his dimpled chin on his hand. Silhouetted against the flames, Tom Farley surveyed with restless, bright eyes the two things he knew best in the world: fire—and arson.

Farley could immediately tell that this inferno was no accident, for he had spent twenty years honing himself into the best private arson investigator in the West—possibly the best in all America. He had a "sense" that most others lacked. What intuition didn't tell him, his scientific knowledge of fire did. What those two failed to ferret out he filled in with what he liked to call "patient, plodding, and persistent investigation"—in a word, legwork. Farley had flair, all right, but as often as not his technique consisted of simply putting one foot in front of the other until he had walked his quarry into the ground.

Obviously, no insurance company had called him to hurry over and check out this fire. Occasionally that happened within an hour of the first spark, but not this time. He might never get this assignment. Like the rest of the people watching, Tom was there because the fire was there. Fire was his profession, but it was also his passion. He had the same prehistoric affinity for flame as everyone else.

After a few minutes, he pulled his priorities into focus, slammed the car door shut, and headed for the Fire Chief's buggy. Tom's relaxed gait contrasted vividly with the search-ing, diamond-sharp concentration of his deep-brown eyes as he sized up the situation.

The Chief looked up at the approaching figure. "Hello, Tom," he said familiarly. "You in on this?"

"No. Just picked it up on the squawk box. Thought I'd have a look-see."

"Well, *some* arson man will get it."

"That's what I figured. It's a standard setup. Started in the rear well on the second floor if they're pros, ground front if they're amateurs."

The Chief's eyes narrowed by a half-millimeter. Farley's uncanny accuracy always baffled him. "The well on two. They're pros, all right."

It was uncommon to have a fire set before dark, even in the industrial area on a quiet Saturday. Tom knew that a nov-ice would have made his light near the front in order to get out fast. A pro would take advantage of the updraft in the back stairwell, where the flames would rapidly be sucked up to the floor above. The second floor would be assured of a fresh supply of oxygen moving up from below—like the principle of grates in a fireplace. The heat buildup on the third floor would consequently be faster, and the ignition of both wood and roofing would be more rapid than with a first-floor light. In addition, the rear well, away from the street, might give the fire an extra ten to fifteen minutes before detection—an important block of time.

Knowledge is the heart of intuition, but since Tom enjoyed his reputation of having a "sixth sense," he was not going to share his reasoning with the Chief.

The inside of the factory was getting risky. All of the firemen were being ordered out of the interior.

"Which were the first-in units?" Tom asked the Chief offhandedly.

"Engine Four. Then Ladder One came in with Jonah West about a minute later. Why?"

Farley shrugged his shoulders. "Hunch," he said. He smiled enigmatically at the Chief and walked off with all the nonchalance he could muster. He knew he would be stopped if he explained the nature of his hunch.

Gathering speed as he approached Ladder I, Tom looked up at the burning structure. Despite the exterior ring of fire hoses and those blasting water inside the beast's belly, it was clearly a matter of time—a short time—before fire would win the battle. As if to accentuate its inevitable victory, a long tongue of flame burst out of a third-floor window above Tom's head.

Jonah, at the top of Ladder 1, caught sight of the figure rushing toward his truck. He knew Tom Farley and he knew Farley would not be waving at him to come down if it weren't urgent, so he turned the nozzle over to his second-in-command and scrambled down the rungs.

"You been in?" Tom did not waste words on greetings.

"Just for entry and to secure the stairwell."

"The back one?"

"Yeah. That's where she started. What are you looking for?"

"A telephone."

"Need change?"

A quick smile fluttered around Tom's mouth and disappeared. "Did you find any kind of accelerant?"

"No, but it went so fast it had to be set."

"Was there a telephone near where it started?"

9

"I didn't stay long enough to look around, since it was moving upstairs so fast, but there are some old offices on the second floor next to the stairs."

"Still many men inside?"

"A few. I think the Chief will pull them back pretty quick. We're just trying to keep it off old Gloria next door there."

Tom set his jaw. "Got a helmet to spare?"

"You go in like that," Jonah chided, "and it'll cost you a pair of shoes and a suit. Here." He reached into a gear compartment and pulled out spare boots, a regulation slicker, a helmet, and a heavy-duty flashlight.

Tom thrust his hat into Jonah's hands, jerked on the gear, and ran for the entrance.

"You've only got about five minutes, Tom!" Jonah called after him. He shook his head and watched Farley duck through the door into the dying factory, uncertain whether his warning was heard or not. Well—he shrugged his shoulders helplessly—that's Tom Farley.

Tom hadn't asked himself exactly why he was doing this. His action seemed perfectly natural. After all, he had a hunch, and the only way to verify his suspicion was to go in and look. If the building ended up gutted and the roof collapsed, no one would take the place apart just to find out if he was right or wrong. If he was right, it was another link in a chain he had been forging for over a year.

Tom had no trouble making a beeline to the rear stairs; the few remaining fire hoses either branched off up the front stairwell or continued to the rear one. The firemen still inside were fighting a rear-guard action, though most of them were headed out.

Acidic water and ashes cascaded down the rear stairwell. Smoke and heat could not get out of the windows fast enough and were backing heavily downward to the ground floor. The acrid smell made Tom wish he had grabbed an oxygen tank and mask—the last thing he wanted was to be overcome by fumes in some dark corner of this blazing furnace. He hesitated, judged that he didn't have far to go, and bounded up the stairs. Keeping his head as low as possible to stay under the level of the heaviest smoke, he followed the tunnel his flashlight pierced in the dark.

At the second-floor landing he passed a crew hurriedly descending, pulling their hose behind them.

"Hey," one of them yelled. "You're going the wrong way! We just got orders to get out."

"Won't be a sec." Tom saw the room he wanted and headed for it, fast. Every fiber of his body was mobilized now. Not one trace of his easygoing self was left.

Only one hose snaked on beyond the office Farley entered. At the end of that hose, farther down the second-floor corridor, was Jonah West's best friend, Captain Mannie Rojas of Engine 1, with two of his men. Mannie, thin as an I-beam and twice as tough, was usually the first in and the last out. A combination of courage and intelligence made him the youngest company captain on the force. He knew where the limits were and could be counted on to play right up to them. The three men were crouched low, working their 2½-inch hose under the smoke layer into a back room. Mannie had one last objective before retreating, and he calculated it would only take a few minutes.

In the furnacelike room Rojas kneeled on his left knee to brace himself against the hose's terrible back pressure. He checked the position of his backup men, gave a nod, and opened the nozzle full blast. A ton of water per minute ripped at the back wall. At close range its force could break a man's bones.

The raging water did exactly what the captain wanted it to do. It knocked holes in the flame-weakened plaster and drove a spray of liquid through to the strips of lath, soaking everything between the studs. Now if he could just get the jet to break through into the next room. . . .

Mannie was melting in his own sweat. Under the mask his face was the color of his fire truck. They'd have to get out quickly. He braced against the hose's force. In a few seconds he'd shut it off and scramble to fresh air.

Mannie's left leg was getting cramped from kneeling so he moved it out just to change position. A long thick splinter of wood from an aging floorboard jammed straight into the tendon of his knee. In itself the wound didn't amount to much, but the instant's painful distraction cost him his grip on the wet nozzle. The maddened snake of hose whipped its deadly brass tip back at him. The metal lashed out, ripped off his mask, lashed again, and felled him with a blow to the temple. Rojas pitched backward without even a grunt, unconscious and bleeding. The backup men yelled and jumped at the flailing nozzle to try to shut it off.

In the room by the stairwell Farley's flashlight had just found the object he was searching for when he heard the yells. He wanted to take the telephone, the bell, and the sound-actuated ignition device out, which would require a few minutes. But someone was in trouble, so he whipped off his tie, wrapped it quickly around the actuator, and shoved the bundle into his pocket. Too bad about the rest. He ducked low and raced out to follow the hose. There was an ominous cracking sound, then a bang from the floor above his head as a roof rafter collapsed.

The arson investigator hit the fire-lit room at the same second that the nozzle swung wildly around in his direction. He jumped back just in time. It was the last swing before the two firemen managed to get the hose under control and shut it down.

Tom instantly got the picture. He leaped to Mannie's crumpled form as one of the men called for a stretcher on his walkie-talkie. Tom and the second fireman cradled the unconscious figure and rushed toward the stairs as another crash above them rattled the ceiling. At the top of the stairs they met the incoming stretcher men and a fire crew.

The medics hustled Mannie's still body onto the stretcher, out of the burning building, and into the antiseptic interior of an ambulance, which formed a stark contrast to the filth their patient had just left. As the white streak fled the fireground, its sirens howling in the night, the driver called back, "He going to be okay?"

The man who was trying to stanch the flow of Mannie's lifeblood yelled back, "Yeah! But that's sure no goddamn way to make a living!"

* * *

As soon as Tom had turned his burden over to the medics, he headed straight for Jonah West.

"I heard on the intercom," Jonah said, worried about his best friend. "How's Mannie?"

"Cut, bleeding, and out cold, but I suspect it's not too serious. He got the nozzle on the hard part of his head."

"That could be anywhere above the neck in Mannie's case," Jonah quipped in relief. "You got more than you bargained for, huh?"

Tom reached into his pocket to retrieve his find. "Yeah, but I got what I wanted, too," he said proudly. "The little item that set it all off. Sound-actuated device. It was sitting next to the telephone bell. First, the guy plants this thing. Later, when he's verified no one's in the building, the arsonist calls. Phone rings. This gadget makes sparks, sets off an accelerant, then the whole place goes. The torch is way off, sipping a whiskey and soda somewhere, safe, clam happy and getting richer by the minute. I just happened to click on the fact that this site and time—late Saturday afternoon—fit in with a pattern of telephone setoffs around the Bay Area. I think I'm closing in on the son-of-a-bitch."

"Well, you took a helluva risk to prove it."

Farley grinned and shrugged off the exploit. "If you don't gamble, you don't win. Incidentally"—he changed the subject quickly—"are any fire marshals around? I'd like to give this to one of your people." Tom figured it was better to leave a fresh piece of evidence in a potential criminal case directly with a fire marshal—one of the fire department's own criminal arson investigators.

"Does it come with or without the tie?"

"Might as well be with, I'm afraid the tie has had it."

"The new guy was here a few minutes ago. He went off to take crowd shots."

"See if you can rouse him on the intercom. I'll go to the car and get a Chain-of-Evidence form."

First, Farley retrieved his hat, then he took off the fire gear. He did not feel right without his tie, but that was compensated for by the warm sensation of success.

As Tom passed the Chief's buggy Task Force Eleven's Fire Chief emerged, torn between dishing out half-hearted hell or profuse thanks.

"I should have known," the Chief said reproachfully. "As soon as you said you had a hunch you lit up like a neon. That was a great piece of work, but you—"

"If I'd said it, you'd have stopped me cold."

"Damn right!" He slapped Tom's shoulder. "Good thing you didn't ask. But next time . . . Jesus, Farley, I never know what you'll do next."

Farley laughed and walked off. When he reached his Pontiac, the car's mobile phone was ringing. He answered and immediately recognized the voice of Vic Whitlock, the Fire Loss Manager of Global Insurance Company. Even though Whitlock was one of his best clients, Tom never could get friendly with him. Vic was too cold fish, too humorless, too frigidly efficient. Fortunately, Tom didn't have to love his clients.

"Where the hell have you been?" Vic demanded. "I've got one going over in Oakland that doesn't sound right. Half hour after it began the insured was already calling his agent and it's his second one this year."

"Tell me the sad story."

Whitlock hesitated, brought up short by the mocking tone of Tom's reply.

"Tell you what, Vic," Tom gently needled, "I'll handle the case if you'll buy me a tie." He knew that would shake up Whitlock's straitlaced way of thinking.

"You got a Saturday night bag on or what?" Whitlock demanded, though he had never known Farley to be drunk.

"No, but I've half-solved your case just for the hell of it." Tom savored the claims man's incredulity before explaining that he was already on the scene. As usual, he left Whitlock reverently amazed.

It did not even cross Tom's mind that if he had played his cards differently he could have quadrupled his fee. Tom Farley did not know how to cheat. All he asked was the pleasure of putting an offbeat item on Whitlock's expense bill: one silk tie, $32.50. It was expensive, but Farley liked nice ties.

When he finished the phone call, he got a Chain-of-Evidence form from his car and returned to look for the fire department investigator. He found Fred Krinke waiting for him.

"Hey," the neophyte fire marshal said eagerly, "I hear you've got an acoustic detonator for me."

"Yep." He handed Krinke the tie-wrapped object. "Ever see one?"

"Just pictures." Krinke took it. He was clearly excited. A fire marshal could pass a lifetime without coming across an acoustic trigger.

Farley had a soft spot for anyone who was really interested in the fine points of his work, so he carefully explained how the device operated. "They're rare, because only a high-class pro would know how to use one. A lot of investigators wouldn't even think to look, but I've had half a dozen cases with the same MO in the last year or two. Probably all the same guy. I don't want to muddy the chain of evidence on this doodad— we may need it in court. If there's any gap in the chain of possession from the fire site to the courtroom, the evidence is useless and the whole case can fold. I've brought the Chain-of-Evidence possession form, so I'll sign it off. You sign there and it's officially yours."

Convinced that the young man would become a useful ally, Tom decided to go on. Careful not to make his tone patronizing, he asked, "Now that we know this fire was incendiary in origin and we've got the trigger, what's the next step you'd take?"

"I'd run it to the lab for fingerprints and try to find out where it came from."

"Okay. The fingerprints are a long shot. This trigger is the same make as the others and I'm beginning to suspect the torch bought a gross of them in Hong Kong—I've checked every dealer in a hundred-mile radius at least six times. As long as you're at the lab, though, check for bits of accelerant still stuck to the exterior. He tends to use magnesium foam rubber and charcoal starter. They should run that through the spectrograph. But the most important place to check out is the phone company."

The young man looked baffled. "Why?"

"I'd bet another new silk tie that this phone was hooked up in the last two or three weeks, just for this job. Who signed the order? Who paid the bill? Ask the installer who let him in. Who showed him where to put the phone? Then there are details. Why did they have a desk in that so-called office, but no files, no chair?"

The novice was staring in bug-eyed admiration.

Heaving a sigh, Tom admitted, "But whoever the torch is, he's no slouch. The insurance companies have been stuck with paying every one of these telephone triggered fires. I may be tightening the noose around his neck, but he's still on the loose. He plants these things, sits at home taking life easy, makes a call at his leisure during the weekend. A phone rings, and *whoosh*. The guy hangs up, relaxed, untraceable. The building owners invariably have some waterproof alibi. This is the first time I've gotten a trigger while it was still warm—the next one I want to get before the phone rings. If you're going to handle the case, Fred, come by the office and check my files—and I can also tell you where you can find a few more cases in other offices around the Bay."

"You're on. Hey!" His eyes lit up hopefully. "I almost forgot to give you the news. Guess who I just photographed in the crowd again. Holy hell, Tom, maybe he's our telephone man, hanging around to see if it worked! Remember the ex-fireman?"

"Marty Martin?"

"You got it."

"Not likely. He's torching, all right, but surely nothing as sophisticated as acoustic triggers."

"Shouldn't I haul him in and ask?"

"No." Tom tugged at his earlobe. How could he make this young buck understand the subtleties of applied psychology without deflating his enthusiasm? "Each time Martin gets questioned he gets nastier and more self-righteous. He feeds on it. Makes him a big shot. Swells his ego."

Krinke persisted, but less surely. "But the more we call him in, the more likely he is to slip up, isn't he?"

"Look, I don't run your department," Tom said patiently. "I'm just a private investigator and I've no business interfering in your procedures. But Martin gets his kicks out of being a suspect on whom we can't get the goods. It may shake him up more if we just let him know we know he's here and then start ignoring him. He gets it off just setting us up. That's why he shows up at fires he *didn't* set, begging to get questioned. I don't only think his 'fire buff' number is phony, I suspect he's psycho as hell—and a public menace to boot. He's the kind that gets a sexual charge at a fire and probably dreams of burning people. If anything will make him goof, it's if we stop playing his game and start pretending he doesn't exist. Point me to the son-of-a-bitch," Tom concluded with pleasure. "I'll go give him a big hello and then walk on."

Heading for where the marshal had last seen Marty Martin, Farley began worrying. It was not the first time he had encountered an arsonist who repeatedly appeared at fires.

He had personally questioned Martin on two cases. More than anything, he was struck by an undertone of violence, by a man seriously disturbed but socially functioning, crudely clever, simultaneously convinced that the world was down on him but that it owed him something special. Marty Martin, in Farley's opinion, probably didn't get big jobs, and it was doubtful that he could even handle a major fire. Yet Tom sensed something inherently dangerous in this suspect.

It didn't take, a major conflagration to kill someone, and to Tom's refined nose Marty Martin smelled of killer.

The blond, blue-eyed, beach-boy type was brazenly standing in front of the crowd. Good-looking son-of-a-bitch, Tom thought. Why doesn't he just get a woman? But the answer was as apparent as the question.

Tom stepped up close. "Hiya, Marty. How are you?"

Surprised, Martin instantly turned, rabid. "You come to bug me again, Farley? I'm an honest citizen interested in fires, like everyone else here. My attorney is going to break your back on harassment charges!"

"Hey, slow down. I just saw you standing here and came over to say hello." Tom relished the confusion on his adversary's face. "It never crossed my mind you had anything to do with this."

"Well, that's a goddamn change," Martin snapped suspiciously.

Tom tied on his best smile. "Maybe, but like you said yourself, a lot of people watch fires. Doesn't mean they light them. See you, Marty. I've got work to do." Tom nodded politely and left.

Martin's perplexed look meant the mission had been accomplished. It was all Tom had hoped for. He knew that he would see Marty again and suspected he'd catch him match in hand one day. Tom heaved a great sigh. He certainly hoped it was before—and not after—someone had paid with their life for Martin's derangement.

Fatigue suddenly caught up with Farley. His muscles ached and he became aware of a slight burning sensation in his lungs. It had not been the quiet Saturday evening he'd expected. Tom wended his way through the thinning mob of the curious. The bastard who rang that number isn't tired, he thought. Suddenly, the best arson man in the West began to wonder if he would ever lay eyes on the telephone torch.

* * *

Finally, the fire was knocked down. The owner of Gloria Pump and Suction busily directed the replacement of everything that had been so frantically hauled out. The last few flare-ups were fought. The aerial monitors came down. The relay pumpers were disconnected and the spaghetti of hoses was rolled up. The firemen talked, sipped coffee, put the bits and pieces back neatly in their compartments. Exhaustion was etched on every face. The pace was slow. Ash, water, and weariness covered everything.

One by one, the engines belched to life once more. Even the candy-apple red and chrome seemed to have lost a bit of luster as the trucks left the fireground and the little cluster of hard-core, curious bystanders behind.

3

Fifteen hundred miles to the east of the Oakland fire, noise, dust, the blue haze of exhaust smoke, and a blazing dome of light exploded into the darkness from the midnight-green farmland of southern Illinois. The usual rural peace was blown apart by a shouting crowd and the guttural scream of engines booming around the Highland stock car track. Gasoline fumes, dry earth, and fine particles of burnt rubber hung in the air.

Stretch Jackson gave a howl of delight, as his bright red bomb hurtled into the final curve. He was about to overtake the lead car on the inside. Stretch's left front wheel clung tightly to the inner rim of the dirt track. The rears were spinning, drifting out. It was just the kind of precarious, split-second action Stretch loved. His mastery of the millisecond, plus a great Chevy engine, made him one of the best drivers on the regional circuit.

"Out of the way, Cuevas, I'm coming through!" he yelled. His voice was a spit in the wind, lost in the roar of the crowd and the growl of engines. He knew every tic of every driver. He also knew that Johnny Cuevas, the driver of the lead car, never gave an inch to anyone.

Just ahead, the driver of Number 20 saw that the two leading cars were about to lap him, so he moved to the outside to let them through. What no one counted on was that Number 20 was about to lose a wheel to the centrifugal force at the curve's far end. The left front tire spun right off and rolled wildly up the track, free and independent. The car's brake drum bit into the dirt and in a flash Number 20 flew 360 degrees around its unexpected pivot. The rear end welded itself momentarily into the front of Cuevas's lead car, then bounced back around its screeching brake. Cuevas was thrown into Stretch's right-front fender, destroying the delicate balance of the red Chevy's drift.

To a man with Stretch Jackson's coordination what followed seemed to take quite a while, but the sequence actually occurred in a mere five seconds. Stretch turned his wheels into Cuevas's side to counter the slippage of the rear end and pumped the brake pedal. He figured Number 20 would spin to the outside and Cuevas would have to cut to the left. Then he could drop back, gun between the two, and leave everyone stuck in the orange flag behind the point of the wreck. It was the last lap; another 100 yards and Stretch would be in easy—the winner.

Cuevas had regained control and—as Stretch had anticipated—moved left. Stretch jammed his wheels to the right and hit the accelerator. But that maneuver allowed the ragged slash of metal that had been his right fender to slice his tire neat as a razor! Even to a driver of Jackson's skill, the disaster was unforeseeable.

Stretch's pride and joy flipped over on its shiny right side, tearing off the neat white letters that advertised his backer: BERT'S FURNITURE. Grinding corners, the red Chevy crashed onto its roof. Stretch managed to switch the key off. With a final jolt the car slammed onto the other side, ripping away STRETCH'S AUTO SALES and grinding to a halt in a shower of sparks. The crowd leaped to its feet, screaming for Stretch to get out before the car blew up.

A warning—FIRE!—clanged in his mind. Before the car stopped rocking, Stretch unbuckled and, cat quick, hoisted his lithe body out of the right window. Fury and frustration flashed through his system as he vaulted to the ground beside the heap of wreckage. The fury went as quickly as it had come—he was too easygoing to ever maintain more than an instant's rage. But the frustration stuck as the full implications of the disaster rocketed through his mind.

"Shit!" he said under his breath as he ran beyond the reach of a possible explosion. Stretch looked back at the pile of torn metal, kicked the dirt, and swore again. Poetry was not his forte. He walked toward his pit, wrapped in a personal gloom, oblivious to all the concern and hubbub whirling around him.

* * *

Stretch Jackson just cleared six-two, not counting the unruly shock of dark hair that topped him off. He was not really tall enough to play center when he was in high school, but he had a way of leaping up and stretching out that made him seem six inches taller, whether he was guarding or flipping the ball through the basket. The gym rafters would vibrate with the rhythmic roar of "Stretch, stretch!" That *stretch* earned him both the center slot and a permanent nickname. The same driving energy and his will to be the best propelled him to the top of the racing circuit ranks.

Stretch's startlingly pale blue eyes, flecked pearl gray, riveted the attention of everyone who looked his way. His face was craggy and angular for a young man, but it tended to crease frequently with an easy grin. All in all, he more closely resembled a cowboy posing for a Marlboro ad than a small-town, small-time Midwestern used-car dealer—which is what he was. A native animal charm made him a real lady-killer, but he was so blind to everything except his work and racing that he had slipped over the hard line of thirty and still hadn't met a woman who made him want to settle down for more than a night or two at a time.

Between races, Stretch arranged for the red Chevy's sad carcass to be hauled into the pits and, as the next heat got under way, headed glumly for the hot dog stand. He eyeballed Marge, who bounced up to serve him. She was all peroxide, chest, and chewing gum.

"Give me a dog and a Bud—in a bottle."

"That was a piece of bad luck, Stretch. Looked like a demolition derby." She forked a hot dog between the layers of a flabby bun and compensated for its tastelessness by slathering on lots of mustard. "You gonna take me out tomorrow night?"

"Can't. Got to fix a car for delivery."

She snapped open the beer bottle. "If you'd spend less time under a car and more under a skirt, it'd be good for you." She plunked his order on the counter.

Stretch couldn't help but snigger.

"You know"—she leaned her treasures right behind the hot dog—"you're the best lay in town!"

Stretch laughed until tears came to his eyes. It wasn't really that funny, but his nervous tension had to break loose somewhere. "You ought to know, Marge. You've got to have tried us all." One good needle deserved another.

"Missed three," she said jokingly. She loved to see a man laugh. "And I ain't telling which ones."

"Hey, Stretch!" Fat Bert Morton of Bert's Furniture— Stretch's backer—came rolling toward them like a runaway locomotive.

Stretch leaned toward Marge. "Bet Bert's one in three."

With a guffaw that almost cracked her pancake makeup she let out a "You betcha!"

Bert Morton had a momentary sensation that he might be the butt of the laughter. He hesitated a second between asking what was going on and ignoring it. He chose the latter.

If obesity is the modern American malady, Bert, now fifty-two, had been one of overweight's pioneers. He had been fat in grade school, fat in high school, and fat ever since. He couldn't conceive of any other condition. Sensitive to the subject of weight, he was delighted to look around and see how many people had come over to his side of the scale in the last ten or fifteen years. Thank you, junk food and anxiety.

"Fat folks are funnier" was Bert's byword. The trouble was, Bert wasn't really funny. He was a bundle of nerves. It should have wasted him, but he warded off that possibility with an awesome input of food.

"What'll you have, Mr. Morton?"

"Sixteen-ounce Pepper." He licked his lips and turned to Stretch. "Too bad about the Chev." Although he had paid half of the cost of the car, Bert seemed strangely indifferent. Stretch could tell he had more on his mind. I'll be damned, Stretch thought angrily. He's perfectly happy to see me in trouble.

Bert pulled out a cigarette. Before the cigarette hit Bert's lips, the flame from Stretch's Zippo lighter was at the end of it. Stretch's eye skipped from the word CONGRIL that was engraved on the lighter to the look in Bert's eye, and for the first time felt a twinge of discomfort about the Zippo.

When Stretch was inducted into the army, flamethrowers had not been entirely replaced by the impersonal wholesale use of napalm from tanks and airplanes. Every recruit received his training in the handling of the devil's weapon, and Stretch mastered the technique faster than anyone. He loved the roar made by the flaming gel when it struck and exploded in a fiery cloud. The blast of flame seemed to shoot right out of his hands. It gave him a feeling of invincibility, a sensation of power that made a rifle seem like a popgun. "Gonna fry their ass!" he would shout with delight. "Zap, zap! I'm the cinder man!" At Stretch's request, the sergeant made him the company's flamethrower operator.

Someone put a sign over his bunk: THE CONG GRIL. That it was misspelled was of no importance, and the sign stayed until they were shipped out. Four of Stretch's buddies solemnly presented him with a Zippo lighter engraved CONGRIL, complete with the misspelling. The ceremony was thoroughly drenched in beer. Ted Bowen, a curly-headed farm boy with glasses, said, "You're the Congril, Jackson! You'll burn 'em up out there!" Everyone howled with laughter, and Stretch was christened "The Company Incinerator."

He pocketed the lighter as Bert jerked his head, indicating he wanted to talk in private, away from the stand.

As they walked to a quiet spot behind the crowd, Stretch's flesh crawled with distaste about the conversation he knew would follow. The crash was going to make it even more unpleasant.

Stretch thought again about last Monday's discussion. It was natural that Bert had called him. They were partners in the car and, in a remote way, they were friends. Bert had given him invaluable tips about advertising and selling when he'd set up the car lot. Stretch had appreciated the help and, almost as much, appreciated the cash Bert had loaned him when a tight spot had come up. As usual, Stretch was loyal to his friends, but that had not softened the blow of what had followed.

Bert had closed his office door after a bit of small talk. "Listen." He had been visibly nervous. "I've got to talk to somebody I can trust. I made a mistake."

Jackson's eyebrows had gone up at the desperate quality in Bert's voice. "Well, you know you can trust me. Shoot."

"Okay." Bert paused for a moment before taking the plunge. "I had a chance to make a quick kill with a warehouse full of furniture from a bankruptcy sale." His monumental frame seemed to tremble just recalling the purchase. "So I went in hock up to my eyeballs. I was sure it would sell fast if it was cheap enough. I was wrong. Even cheap, it's fancier than my customers want. And you know the high-tone trade in this town—if they didn't buy their living room suite in St. Louis, it's not good enough for them."

Stretch nodded in understanding.

"I had a high-interest, twelve-month loan on it, and when almost nothing sold in three months, I was in real hot water. So I found a dealer over in Edwardsville who'd buy the load if I took a bath—and by then I had no choice. But he would only get it off my hands thirty days later and pay thirty days after that. By that time I would have been two payments overdue on my loan." Bert had taken a deep breath. "That's when I made my mistake."

Stretch's brow furrowed. He'd thought Bert's purchase was the "mistake."

"I mean, I knew the Edwardsville guy. I counted on him. I mean, I was into big money and big trouble. I'd already missed one payment. So on everything I sold last month I did a triple paper number." Bert read the confusion on Stretch's face. "Old buddy, sometimes I think you don't know nothing. Look—a customer comes in, wants to buy a bedroom set. Finances a thousand bucks. I type up the contract in three originals. Tell him to sign here, here, and here. Hell, the dummies never notice when I shuffle the papers right. So I lay off each original—two on banks and one on a household finance outfit—and collect three thousand dollars. When the Edwardsville guy pays, I give the two banks a song and dance about a clerical error, pay them off, and it's all okay."

"Well?" Stretch had asked, appalled and suspicious.

"He backed out. And I'm sitting here with forty-three grand's worth of illegal paper I can't explain and can't pay off. I mean, I'm in the shits up to here, friend."

"Jesus Christ, Bert, what are you going to do?"

That was when Bert had leaned in, confidential-like, and driven the spike home. "Well, you know me—honest as the day is long— but I'm in such a bind that there's only one thing I *can* do." He paused for emphasis. "I'm gonna burn the son-of-a-bitch!"

"What?"

"Yep. Burn it. Overinsure it for the amount of the phony paper, collect for the whole lot, and start fresh. I've got no choice and I've got it all figured out."

"Bert, you can't do that!"

"Well . . . I can't do it by myself. That's why I needed to talk to somebody I can trust. I need someone to light it."

Stretch had jumped to his feet. "You're fucking crazy if you think *I'm* going to do it! Not a chance in hell, Bert. I wish to Christ you hadn't even told me about it. You got in it and I'd love to help you out, but don't get me involved in anything like that." Stretch had spun on his heel and stalked right out.

Now, in the darkness behind the stands at the racetrack, Stretch knew exactly the subject his oversize backer wanted to bring up again.

Stretch gazed cheerlessly at the countryside beyond the track. Across not too many miles of rolling land was his hometown, West Alton. A full seedpod of moon scattered brilliant light across the landscape. It was a perfect early-summer picture of pastoral calm. Sweet night dew was forming. The fields stood ankle deep in honey-smelling clover. The corn was up, ready for the home stretch. It was dirt-farm country, good Mid-America—Mid-America being almost everything outside of Metropolitan New York and Greater L.A. Stretch Jackson felt naturally, intimately at one with it.

For all that was right about the night, the setting was wrong, the subject was wrong, and Bert was after the wrong man. Stretch tried in vain to think of a way to avoid the confrontation. Terrible as he felt about the predicament Bert was in, the wreck of the Chevy had just put Stretch in a bind of his own. He felt a creeping sense of vulnerability and hated it.

"There's no use stalling." Bert wheeled on him. "I already told you what I'm thinking about. Well, the damn jig's up. Yesterday one of the bank officers called and he smells a rat. I'm in up to my neck, old buddy. I'm gonna end up in jail for fraud."

"Jesus, Bert."

"Not only don't I have any money to help buy you a new race car, I'm looking at bars. Everything I've spent my life building is about to go down the tubes for one lousy mistake."

"Two."

"Okay, two. But if I can sell out to the insurance, I'm back in business, and we'll buy that new car and move you up to NASCAR class right on schedule. You realize what it means to go to prison? Me. At my age! Man, I lose everything for the rest of my life. You can't start over an ex-con at fifty-five. You're dead! I couldn't show my face in West Alton. My neck's in your hands, Stretch. The game's up. You've got to help me out." His face was turning high-blood-pressure red.

A roar went up from the crowd. Stretch stared at the track. He wanted out of this. "Half-mile Supers. I think old Allister just won that trip to California."

27

There was an awkward pause. Bert studied Stretch, trying to calculate just how much he'd have to give up. He had already overinsured the store by seventy-five thousand dollars. He heaved a convincingly real sigh. "Okay. I've got it insured to cover five thousand extra. I'll give you the five. That'll get you out, and me, too."

"I don't give a good goddamn about the money, Bert!" That was a bit of a lie.

"Jesus H. Christ! I'll cancel your debt. You owe me twelve grand—I'll cancel it!" Bert was getting red right down his hairy arms. "I've got every single thing worked out—the alibis, the gasoline, everything. I just need someone I can really trust to throw the match."

Stretch kicked the dirt into a little mound with his right foot. It *was* a lot of money.

"Goddammit, boy, you're ornery! You need the money and I need a fire. We're buddies. It's an easy seventeen thousand dollars, foolproof and tax-free. What the hell more do you need?"

Stretch looked the fat man in the eye. "I don't know, Bert. I'm not any goddamn criminal."

Bert locked in on the pale-blue gaze. "Well, I'm not either, old buddy." He waited a moment and thought of playing his trump card then and there, but finally held off. "Look, you think it over till Monday. I'll come by your place at four. And I want you to tell me *yes.*"

Stretch watched the broad beam waddle off, kicked the little mound of dust flat, and turned to haul what was left of a bad day home. Not on your life, mister, he decided.

* * *

Stretch's Auto Sales was one of those millions of little used-car lots that huddle together in Automobile Rows or string out along town edges. This one was complete with its minuscule office and a three-bay workshop in U.S. Steel's corrugated finest. Two bays were for racing machines, one was for sale cars. The banner spread across the street entrance said: STRETCH YOUR DOLLARS. It was festooned with the red, white, and blue spinners that twirl in a breeze.

Monday morning there wasn't any breeze. Everything hung limp. The graceless plot was livened up by exactly fourteen highly polished vehicles of varying vintage, colors, and makes. The star was obviously the '79 Seville in metallic maroon that perched on a ramp next to the broken cement sidewalk. After that, the age rose and the quality dropped rather quickly.

Inside the frame twelve-by-twelve office were a desk, four chairs, a phone, an unruly batch of parts catalogs on a bookshelf, and Bob Schmollinger, Stretch's CPA, who resembled an underweight chimney stack. Sixteen years before, it was Schmollinger Stretch had beaten out of the center slot on West Alton's basketball team. After college, Bob had been on the verge of taking a job in Chicago when he picked up Jack Kerouac's forgotten masterpiece, *The Town and the City*. That and a West Alton girl named Cheryl, who stood five-foot-one in pumps, convinced him marvelous things could happen in small towns, so he came back home. Stretch always wondered what a slender five-foot girl and a six-eight pipestem did at night.

When Stretch came back in after talking to a prospect, Bob took off his gold-rims and rubbed the red dents they always left astride his nose. "You're in rocky shape, my friend. You sell enough cars, but there's no profit in them. You spend too much on fixing them up."

"I know that, but a guy buys a car off me, he knows it's right. He'll come back and send his friends. I couldn't sell them otherwise. I can't operate like that creep by the lumberyard."

"Yeah, well that creep by the lumberyard is making money." Sometimes Stretch's naiveté irritated Schmollinger. "We've known each other too long for me to just keep your books. You either get into business or you get the hell out. People in business don't give all their profit away being Mister Nice Guy all the time."

"So you work for a bunch of crooks. Except me. My old man . . ." Stretch began a familiar litany.

Schmollinger jumped up, exasperated. "I know about your old man, remember? You say it all the time—'Do it right. Be the best.' Well, it works in basketball and it works in racing, but it's not the criteria for making money."

"But that's the way I am, for Christ's sake!" The red wreck, Bert, and his NASCAR hopes going down the tubes all flashed through Stretch's head. "I *am* tired of running like hell and not getting ahead. But it's all I know." He waved toward the cars on the lot. "No matter what, I won't go out dead broke like my old man."

"Okay, Stretch, okay." It was no use. Schmollinger didn't want to lose a friend—or a client either. The town was too small for that. "But you'd be money ahead if you took back your old job as sales manager over at Anderson Ford." They stepped outside.

"Go back to Anderson Ford? And give up racing? I'm going to hang in here if it kills me," Stretch said bluntly as they walked to the CPA's car. "I may live on the margin, but at least I'm my own man."

"You win. I guess everyone's got to figure out what's important in his life. Most people seem to think it's money and a family. Or family and money—pick your order. You could get both and you're not interested in either." He climbed into his car and started the motor. "Have to have a few oddballs here and there. I guess you're it." Bob gave a wink and backed the car toward the street.

Stretch flashed his easy smile and waved good-bye.

By lunchtime things were looking up. Stretch had made one sale, which was only mildly marred by the trade-in, a Chrysler that had been destroyed by the gravel road between town and the owner's farm. He decided to go to the Busy Bee for a small T-bone with his usual crowd of buddies. It struck him that one of the good things about a small town is that you don't have to go far to find your friends.

He locked up and jumped into the lemon-colored Camaro—a front-row car. He always took a stick shift if there was one. Working quickly through the gears, Stretch pulled the sleek yellow machine onto South Main and headed up the hill. He found a space on the square in front of the granite Civil War soldier that graced the courthouse lawn. It was said that piles of brass cannonballs had surrounded the statue but were donated to the war effort during World War II. There sure wasn't anything similar for the guys who went to Vietnam, he thought. Just lost their balls and that was it.

Stretch looked up at the light-gray, granite statue as he had done thousands of times since he first toddled around the square. He had always felt some tenuous link bound them together. There was neither decay nor progress in the proud eternal soldier—just a century of solidity. Stretch set his chin. There's no doubt about it, he decided. The gray soldier would never light that fire. Goddammit, I won't either! Heading across the street to the restaurant, he felt bad for Bert, but much better about his own self-esteem.

* * *

From behind the desk Stretch watched Bert park. He was certainly not going to go bounding out to greet him. Sunlight sparkled off the beads of sweat on Bert's balding head. Strangely enough, for all that body, Bert's face was firm—round, all right, but there wasn't anything saggy about it. His body followed his belly through the office door. The fat man's mood was gruff, impatient. "Okay, old buddy—you made up your mind?" He had let the boy stew until four twenty-five.

"Well, sit down, for Christ's sake."

"I got no time." Bert stood there, hovering like a Goodyear blimp. "Well?"

"I made up my mind."

"So?"

"No, Bert, I won't do it. I'm sorry—"

31

"That's okay," Bert interrupted. He shoved a paper on the desk in front of Stretch. "Remember that?"

Stretch got the picture. He didn't even have to look at the note he had signed when Bert had loaned him the $12,000 in December. "Sure, I know it."

"Okay," Bert snapped. "I loaned it to you when I had it. Now I need it back—bad. I want it in the morning. All of it!"

Stretch jumped up. "Goddamn, Bert—you know fucking-A well I don't have it!"

"That's all right, old buddy." Bert's voice was suddenly soothing, reassuring. "Don't worry about it." He placed another paper on the desk. "Just sign that."

"What the hell is that?" Stretch was torn between anger and suspicion. Bert's syrupy tone suddenly sounded dangerous.

"Just read it. It's perfectly clear."

Stretch sat back down. The paper was titled TRANSFER OF OWNERSHIP. It began: "I, R. A. Jackson, hereby transfer the ownership, goods and stocks, equipment and credits of R. A. Jackson d/b/a Stretch's Auto Sales to Bertram Morton . . ."

Stretch, furious, would have jumped up again, but Bert's stomach was in the way. "You gone crazy, Bert? What are you trying to do? I owe you twelve grand, but I won't sign that!"

"Well, old buddy, you don't really have to. That's a pay-on-demand note you signed. It's either you or me. You won't light it, so I've got no choice. Call the wholesaler, fold the sign." Bert pulled out a cigarette. For once, the Zippo did not fly out, so he lit it himself, proud of the trap he'd sprung. "If you can't pay, you sell. If you won't sell, I sell. If you won't sign, I go to the courthouse tomorrow and start proceedings. It'll take a little longer, but you're out of the race, buddy boy." No hayseed was going to get the better of Bert Morton—not in these circumstances.

Stretch was too dumbfounded to reply. He had never been up against anybody downright mean before, and right now everything that was important to him was at stake: his business, his racing, his reputation in town, and his self-respect.

"Stop jerking around, boy! I've got no time left. Either you make seventeen grand or I call the twelve and you close shop. If you think I'm kidding, try me."

Stretch started to protest, but was cut short. "Look, it's nothing personal." Bert's attitude suddenly turned fatherly. "Listen, Stretch, lots of people aren't good enough to hack a business of their own. Folks will understand. You don't *have* to race and you don't *have* to own your own business. Maybe you can get your old job back selling at Anderson Ford." Bert couldn't suppress a nasty little smile.

Twice in one day! The words cut through Stretch like a rawhide whip.

Bert continued. "If you want to think about signing that paper friendly-like, you get in touch anytime before ten in the morning. After that, call your lawyer."

"You haven't got all the aces, Bert. How'd you like me to call the banks?" Stretch attempted to muster a mean streak, too.

The fat man's eyes narrowed to little slits. The look that came out drilled holes in the pale blues. "You short on smarts? That wouldn't get you one damn thing. I'd shut your water off at the tap for sure. If I can get up enough dough, the banks will make a deal. They don't want court cases. They want money. From you—and from anywhere else I can scrape up a buck. Like, I may have to put a squeeze on your buddy, Banning, but I think he can probably cough up the dough without closing his hatchery. You're the one's got his ass in a crack. Meanwhile, you just think how you want to handle it." Bert knew the threat to Banning would be one more weight on Stretch's conscience.

Without another word the belly whirled and led the way out the door. Stretch was left in his chair, crushed like a bug.

* * *

Bert's Furniture was housed in a squat one-story building. It was not in the downtown high-rent area but in a little shopping district on the south side of town. Smack in the workingman's neighborhood, the store got quite a bit of traffic, since one had to take that street to get to the superhighway.

Bert had a truckload of unpainted wood outdoor furniture delivered to the store on Wednesday. On Thursday a twenty-five-gallon drum of white paint, a twenty-five-gallon drum of brown paint, and a twenty-five-gallon drum of paint thinner were delivered from nearby Vandalia. Allegedly the supplies were for painting the new stock of wood furniture.

The outdoor tables, chairs, and benches were stacked in the parking lot. A hundred-foot roll of six-foot-wide black greenhouse polyethylene was on hand to cover the new furniture in case it rained.

Early Saturday afternoon the boss unexpectedly had his men uncrate all of his normal stock in the back storeroom, ostensibly for a sale. To protect the new outdoor furniture from theft over the weekend he had the men bring it inside and pile it throughout the store, on top of stoves, refrigerators, sofas.

After a lot of fervent prayer on Sunday morning, Bert told his wife he needed to check something in the accounts. By the time she had lunch ready, he would be back. At the store he pried the top off the drum of paint thinner. The floor mop was placed next to the thinner.

At five thirty Barry Freedman, salesman for one of Bert's main furniture suppliers, drove in from St. Louis. He was delighted that Bert had decided to sell their living-room line exclusively and delighted that he had been invited to stay at the house Sunday night before they negotiated the deal on Monday morning. The thing Mrs. Morton did best was cook. After dinner the threesome sat down to play dollar-ante poker.

"I thought you didn't drink, Bert," Barry said, surprised.

"Well, I don't usually, but I can't let you drink alone, old buddy. Especially since we're going to become almost partners."

Down fifty dollars, Bert wouldn't let the others quit. He seemed to be getting very tipsy, to the absolute horror of the missus. At one o'clock Bert fell asleep at the table, his nose in the chips. It was all they could do to shove him, mumbling, off to bed.

Very little stirred in West Alton after midnight, even in the summer. The county was dry, and the lack of booze didn't leave much but boredom and early to bed. At 2:30 A.M., even the two policemen in the town's only night-patrol car were snoozing.

Stretch quietly slipped the key into the lock of Bert's furniture store, turned it, and pushed the door open. Bit by bit, the interior was illuminated by his flashlight. His hands were sweaty around the chromium handle. The ray of light spotted the mop, gas, polyethylene roll, linoleum knife, and masking tape. Bert had kept his end of the bargain. All that was left to do was put the black plastic over the windows so that no accidental passerby would see the blaze before it was too late to stop it, slosh the thinner around with the mop, light it, and get the hell out. The place looked like a warehouse for kindling wood. It should burn completely out of control in a matter of minutes and then ignite the flat, four-ply asphalt roofing. Given the late hour and the efficiency of the local fire department, it was doubtful that even the walls would be left standing.

Stretch had painfully agreed to light Bert's fire, since he saw no alternative but ruin, but he certainly didn't like it. He carried the plastic and the roll of masking tape to the front of the store. Because there were already hanging plastic sun shades, no one would ever notice a few extra plastic ashes in the debris.

He laid out the polyethylene, cut it with the linoleum knife, and started to unroll the masking tape. Jesus! He stopped. The tape made such a high-pitched ripping sound as it came off the roll that it seemed even the sleeping cops might hear. Stretch had never been this unnerved when he was risking his life on the track. He unreeled the tape more slowly. Standing on the kitchen ladder Bert had placed by the door, he taped the unwieldy polyethylene over the first window, ran it across the door, and started to cross the second window. The awkwardly pliable plastic kept falling down over his head.

Suddenly Stretch realized that he heard the hum of an approaching car. He couldn't see out. He was stuck there like a window dummy, holding the plastic above him. All he could do was freeze. The sound came up the street. Got closer. His body jerked stiff and a sweat drop burned his eye when the shot came. "Damn," he said softly, feeling foolish as an empty beer can identified itself on the second bounce and clanked right up to the door. The car went by, never even slowing.

Limp for a moment, Stretch wiped his forehead on his arm, then moved on more frantically than ever. He swore when he saw that Bert had forgotten to move a refrigerator that stood only six inches out from the middle of the window. He fumbled the heap of plastic in front of it, but not before three feet came untaped at the top. Finished. He looked at the vent fan above the front door. He was beginning to panic. It took every bit of his basketball stretch to reach from the little ladder to the top of that opening, but he did it. He felt confident, at least, that the store was sealed as tightly as possible from the view of any passersby.

The paint thinner was mopped and slopped over tables, benches, divans, everywhere. Finally Stretch stood by the back door, flooded with relief. Bert had thought of everything, right down to the rolled-up copy of the local newspaper.

Stretch glanced at his watch. It was three o'clock sharp. Exactly as he had planned, despite the little problems. He flipped the Zippo and the trusty lighter flared. As quickly as he lit it, he snapped it shut. Revulsion took the place of relief. *What in God's name am I doing?* His six-foot frame blocked the rear door. He couldn't do it. The odor of paint thinner came to his nostrils. He could not undo it, either. He lit the Zippo again, started the paper, threw it inside, and rolled around the corner of the door. There was a great *whoosh* of fire. Relief came back. He slammed the door, jumped into his car, and fled.

Once at his house, it took him only three minutes to collapse on the sofa, and fall into the sleep of total exhaustion.

* * *

A bit of predawn light was filtering in between the curtains. Bert rolled his bulk onto his right side. He had not been as drunk as he'd pretended, yet the booze certainly had had an effect. One of his eyes fought to surface, then to focus. Slowly the other followed suit. Something had awakened him. He looked at the slumbering lump that was Mrs. Morton. There would be the devil to pay. Maybe his supposed drunkenness would be overlooked in the excitement. Excitement? He grabbed the bedside clock. The location of the hands escaped him, but the daylight didn't. He bolted upright. Under that weight even a Simmons Beautyrest made sounds of protest. He got a fix on the hands—5:20 A.M.

The doorbell rang again. Questions jumbled together in Bert's head as he juggled himself to a standing position.

"I'm coming!" he bellowed. He wanted his alibi, Barry Freedman, to hear him clumping out of bed.

He needed to relieve himself so badly that he stopped at the bathroom door, then decided he had better not take the time. Abreast of the guest room he yelled, "I'm coming!" again, full volume. He straightened a dining room chair in passing and opened the door.

Ray Merrifield was there and another fireman he didn't know.

"There's been a fire at your store, Mr. Morton," the unfamiliar one said.

"Wha . . . Oh, Christ!" Bert shammed shock very convincingly.

Out of Bert's line of vision, Officer Reynolds, of West Alton's finest, was leaning against the wall shaking his head. He stood straight and moved to the door. "Bert, I hate to do this. I got to put you under arrest."

"Jim . . . !"

"A fire needs oxygen, Mr. Morton," Merrifield said unhappily.

"Nobody saw it, Bert, but you sealed it off *too* good," said the policeman.

"Nobody could see it, all right, but it couldn't get no air, either, Mr. Morton," Merrifield added redundantly. "All the stuff's there. Mop, thinner, plastic. Whole thing. Just went out. Suffocated. A guy going to work saw a little smoke . . ."

"Bert," the policeman said, "I've got to tell you your rights."

Barry Freedman suddenly came up behind the shaking form. "What's up, Bert?" Barry asked, giving his new partner a hearty slap on the shoulder.

A thin yellow stream spread swiftly down Bert Morton's white pajama leg.

* * *

Like everyone else in town, Stretch got the news about Bert's arrest early in the morning at work, but only he was thrown into a hybrid state of shock and panic. Run! Run! Run! rang like a broken bell in his head. He thought fast and made an urgent call to a St. Louis wholesaler.

What worried him most was his mother. She would have to stay in West Alton and face it. It would kill her. At any moment the police might come. Would Bert tell? His mind was at the melting point, but getting out—in a hurry—was the only solution he could think of. Also he had to protect the Jacksons' reputation—if they weren't rich, they *were* honest. Stretch gritted his teeth. At least, they had been until today.

Mustering a superhuman effort for the sake of his mom, he lunched as usual at the Busy Bee. Everybody was talking about Bert until Stretch announced his departure. Bad business, the wreck, and the fact that Bert obviously wouldn't be able to help finance a new car seemed plausible-enough reasons. He acted as if he were making the best of a bad situation. "Decided time's come to make a clean break and start fresh."

He tilted the chair back and did his best to look placid. "When I do a thing, I do it fast. Gonna see some of the country." He put his hands behind his head confidently.

He did not dare call Bert—if he'd made bail yet—and he assumed Bert was afraid to call him. At three o'clock the wholesaler came. They struck a bad deal, but Stretch hardly cared—the man wrote out a check. He boxed up all of his tools, unable to bring himself to give them away. At five, he and a surprised Bob Schmollinger got the books straight. At seven he broke the news to his mother, who cried. At nine he sat at his desk and wrote checks to everyone to whom he owed a penny—except for Bert. The fire may have been a failure, but this whole mess was Bert's fault, the son-of-a-bitch.

Anyway, there were not that many dollars left. He dropped the envelopes in the post office and the wholesaler's check in the night depository at the First National.

The odds and ends at the office were boxed, as were the things he could not throw away at his rented house. Everything went into the back of his mother's garage. It was five fifteen in the morning when Mrs. Jackson's son tiptoed into her room, gave her a kiss, and said good-bye. He left a check on the dining room table for more than he kept for himself. He felt her need was greater than his. A note promised more, if and when.

The sun was peeking over the Yankee soldier's granite shoulder. The driver of the yellow Camaro was too ashamed to look up. He slid guiltily past the furniture store, the windows of which were still neatly covered with black plastic.

The only places Stretch Jackson did look were at the road ahead—and in the rearview mirror to see if the police were catching up with him. If they did not, he meant to follow the center line to where the highway met the Pacific Ocean.

4

A little whirligig of wind scudded some crumpled papers
up the sidewalk of Montgomery Street, dropped them in
the gutter, and whirled away. It was Friday. A July fog chilled
San Francisco's morning air. The passing shoppers all glanced
up at Shoreline Office Supply on the east side of the street.
Some even stopped and stared at the windowed front. A few
stepped between parked cars and crossed the street, but the
hardy picked their way along the sidewalk, avoiding the glass
and mounds of burned trash. Above the windows the brick
facade had long tongues of black rising right up to the fourth
and final floor.

On the inside, Shoreline was cool and damp. The calm
was punctuated by a drip that fell regularly into a puddle at
the rear of the main aisle. Its counterpoint, at a higher pitch,
dropped onto the top of a large oval conference table near the
entrance where Tom Farley was standing. The last of the firemen's water was wringing itself out of the upper floors. The
huge oval table stood in what had been last night's inferno.
Its only potential purchaser now was the Phoenix and Foreign
Insurance Company, and they were reluctant buyers. That's
why they had called in Farley.

The even light coming through broken windows provided the only illumination. The lack of glass was of little
consequence—there was no longer anything left to sell, let
alone protect. The walls were charred, the floor was a gumbo
of black, and one of the floor joists was cracked and had

dropped into the basement, making a nice fire vent from the cellar to the showroom. Dante would have been inspired to write a postscript.

Blue coveralls kept the soot from staining Farley's suit. His shoes were slipped into rubber boots. The only piece of clothing exposed to this filth was the perpetual hat cocked back on his head.

When Farley was barely inside the door, his brain had already begun to unreel the program on the Shoreline case.

Shoreline's brick wall masked a building classed "mercantile, ordinary construction" in the fire-rating book. After the great San Francisco earthquake and fire in 1906, everything in the rebuilt downtown area had to have masonry walls to impede the spread of any future fire. The building that housed Shoreline Office Supply was dated 1910. Other than the walls, however, the structure was wood: joists, floors, and studs. It had been modernized with the usual false acoustic tile ceiling on an aluminum grid that was studded with fluorescent lights.

Even in this devastated interior, Tom's expert eye had no trouble picking out the essential lines of the flames' progress. From the front door Tom could already see that the grid was more seriously warped at the back of the store. Following the grid back to the obvious point of both the greatest heat and longest exposure to it, Tom skirted around the area where the joist had collapsed, pulling a chunk of flooring with it. He barely paused by the black hole, but his "sixth" sense made a mental note and underlined it heavily. He doubted that fire alone had broken the rafter.

The path of the heaviest damage led straight to the basement stairs. When Tom looked down a beam of light suddenly shot out of the dark and flashed in his face.

"Hey, Farley—come on down, but use the ladder. I don't think the stairs will hold you."

Tom instantly recognized Fire Marshal Hugh Haferkamp's voice. "What you got down there?" he asked, noticing with surprise as he spoke that a nail was driven deeply into the center top of the basement doorframe.

"Just came down. Furnace room's right here. Might have started with a leak. At least, that's what it looks like—or what it's supposed to look like. Not what it was, though. Check this."

The Marshal pointed the beam of his flashlight at the big rolling blisters of charred wood on the top surface of the steps.

"Burned like hell on top," he said, "but, so far as I know, heat still goes up. If it started at the furnace, it'd be even worse on the bottom side of these steps."

Several of the stairs were burned right through, but those that were not showed a very different, flat, baked char underneath, clear evidence of a less intense fire exposure than the upper side had received. So the furnace was not the culprit.

"Want to saw a piece out and tag it?" Tom said. "I'll get my sniffer."

Tom's "sniffer" was a hand-held, motor-driven unit with an air intake. Placed next to a burned object, it sucked in the air like a portable vacuum cleaner, passed it through a platinum catalyst, and gave a reading if any residual vapors were present indicating combustible gases. With the exception of alcohol, which dissolves in the firefighters' water, most starters that accelerate an arsonist's initial light leave characteristic traces of their particular vapor in the ashes.

"There was an accelerant, all right," Tom said, studying the gauge. "It's not only gasoline, it's leaded gas. That narrows it down!"

Haferkamp raised a doubting eyebrow. "Yeah, sure. That must narrow it down to about twenty percent of the gas sold in San Francisco."

Tom ignored the Marshal's sarcastic tone. Not only did he know now that this was a case of arson and that the fire had been fed with gasoline, but he also might find out if the fuel was Shell, Texaco, or Exxon, since each major gasoline refiner adds a different color of dye to his product. In the event of an underground leak into a sewage or water system, the station with a leaking reservoir can be quickly identified. At the sophisticated laboratory that Tom used for the technically tough jobs, they could often pull those dyes out of ashes. *If* he could find a suspect, *if* the suspect used the same gasoline in his car, and *if* anyone at the suspect's regular service station could remember putting five gallons or so in an individual container—that was a nice web of evidence. A lot of "ifs," but that was how Tom Farley built up a case—and his legendary reputation.

The Fire Marshal began sawing out a section of one of the steps to be lab-checked and held as evidence.

"Here's how he did it," Tom announced from the top of the stairs. "The door sags and the lead edge touches the floor. There's no char at the bottom edge of the door or the floor right under it, so it was open when the fire started. It's the old swinging-gas-bag trick."

Haferkamp agreed, with grudging admiration of Tom's astuteness. A plastic bag of gasoline had been hung from the nail that Tom had spotted in the center of the doorframe at the top of the stairs. A candle had been lit below it and the bag had been swung like a pendulum above the flame. When the swinging stopped and the bag came to rest, the plastic melted, the gas poured out, ignited, and spread across the floor and down the stairs. The torch had had about three minutes to make his getaway while the bag was still in motion.

"Want to scrape a sample from where the candle should have been? The paraffin will be a cinch to verify at the lab." Tom paused a moment. "He was a pro, all right, but he wasn't as smart as he thought he was."

Hugh Haferkamp was more than pleased to have pinned down a clear case of arson, but that was only a beginning for Farley. He wanted the man who did it. He headed for the collapsed beam. In his mind it was not in the right place to have given way. While Haferkamp scraped samples into little cans for gas chromatography, tagged the items, and got ready to leave, the private investigator—without comment to the Marshal—grated ash off the broken floor joist and headed upstairs, where he found a place to sit and went to work.

When the Marshal came upstairs to leave, Tom was at the conference table, gently scraping a bit of the rafter's ash into a test tube. He unscrewed the top from a small, dark blue bottle, shook the last bit of liquid out of an eye dropper, and filled it with the blue bottle's contents. He did not look up when Haferkamp's left boot accidentally connected with a large carton of assorted-sized staples. The shiny objects sprinkled out of their waterlogged prison by the thousands. They were the only thing that sparkled in the whole place.

"I guess they'll have to pay for that anyway." The Marshal shrugged. He would have been the typical bull in a china shop if all the shops he visited had not already been destroyed.

Tom still didn't look up. He was counting drops into the test tube. "Don't be too sure anybody's going to pay for this mess," he said tightly.

A smile broke through Haferkamp's gray countenance. "Okay, Bulldog Drummond. Wish I could stick around and play with that sophisticated stuff like you do, but I have to run off to the next one."

Tom continued counting. "That's the trouble with you marshals." He was matter-of-fact. "You only have time to put away the creeps who completely blow it. You never get the good ones. You guys have to go running to half the fire sites in the city. It's not your personal fault that you're so under-staffed, but if you guys hit fewer of them you'd save enough just in driving time to solve twice as many cases."

That struck a raw nerve. "Those are the regula—"

"I know the regulations," Tom broke in quietly. "I'm talking about common sense."

"C'mon, give us a break. You private guys get paid every hour you lay into a case. The rest of us are just trying to hold down a city job."

"I'm paid to *do* a job, not hold it down." Tom still watched the test tube, but his voice flashed with irritation. "And somewhere out there's the torch who burned this place—counting his money and laughing his ass off."

"Get off my back, Tom. Both of us know we'll never lay an eyeball on him."

Tom looked up. "Well, if I don't, it won't be because I didn't bust my butt trying."

Intimidated, the Marshal started to leave. Tom returned to his factual tone. "Anyway, I've got a good shot at the messy bastard. Nothing I hate more than sloppy workmanship."

Haferkamp stopped in his tracks. "You're weird, Farley." He spun around, his boot crunching a piece of wood ash to powder. "You know, you're weird! You got it in for the torch because his work's shabby. Man, that's fucking bananas!" He headed for fresher air repeating, "Ba-na-nas!" and left.

The investigator poured some crystals into the tube, sat back, and watched the reaction with a grunt of satisfaction. Magnesium hydroxide. "The son-of-a-bitch," he said softly.

Drill a hole in a joint or rafter, stuff it with magnesium hydroxide and when the firemen's water hits the chemical it literally blows up. Not knowing what caused the explosion, the fire officer in charge cannot take further risks—he is obliged to pull the men out and fight the fire from the outside, which is much less efficient. That explained why the collapsed joist was closer to the front of the store than the heaviest fire damage, and why Farley's "sixth" sense had been alerted. Only a professional torch would know about magnesium. Only a few pros would use it. Tom now had a very special MO, because the torch's explosion could also have killed or injured one of the firefighters. Not many pros would invite the risk of killing a fireman.

Tom's clients paid on the policy unless there was positive proof that their policyholder was directly involved in the planning or committing of arson. When a hired torch was involved Tom had two separate quarries to chase—the torch and the policyholder. He had to tie them down conclusively and, hopefully, link them together. In this case the magnesium changed the whole ball game. If Tom could nail down the man who was paid to put a match to the building, it was not the "attempt to defraud an insurance company" that Shoreline's owner might face. It was not the practically insurmountable rules of evidence required to prove arson. Depending on the D.A., it would be a charge of "attempted murder" at best, "to do bodily harm" at least. Those charges were easier to get a conviction on than those governing arson, and promised a much tougher sentence if the torch was ever found—and found guilty.

Tom decided to call his secretary, Charlene. She kept all of Tom's files cross-referenced by accelerants. By the time he got back to the office, Charlene would have whipped out every case he had ever handled that involved magnesium, put them in chronological order, and neatly stacked them for correlating with the Shoreline case. Charlene was the summum bonum of efficiency.

Tom leaned back in the chair, stretched his arms in front of him, and popped his knuckles. He couldn't hide the fact that he was pleased with himself. It showed all over his face. Then his smile left like a passing cloud. He wondered if he would nail the torch before some fireman got blown apart by magnesium hydroxide.

5

Hell hath no fury like the Broadway Game Parlor at full tilt. It was eleven forty in the evening, and Broadway Game—a stone's throw from Shoreline in the rotting zone between the financial district and the North Beach area—was going full blast. Lights flashed, bells rang, sirens howled, guns boomed and cracked, gum popped. The air hockey tables were clacking wildly and, to top it off, the Broadway had a duckpin alley in the corner. It was so noisy the cashier had once threatened to quit and get a quiet job, "like in the testing room of a small arms plant." Tonight the screaming hard-rock music did its best to raise the decibel level but couldn't. The volume had already reached seismic proportions.

Stretch was working over a pinball machine that had more multicolor strobes and produced more noise than any other. His reaction time had won him free games all evening.

The money changer who went around with the sack of coins tied to his waist decided they'd better check the machine after closing. It had to be out of whack. The customer had only paid a quarter for his first round and there were still eight free games racked up.

Suddenly Stretch turned his back on the machine in the middle of a drop. "C'mon, Eddie—let's get the hell outta here."

"But, Stretch, there's three more balls . . ."

"Fuck 'em."

"But—" Eddie realized he was talking to himself. One eye on the machine, one on the receding Stretch, he did a throwaway shot, then hurried off to help his distraught friend. The heels of Eddie's immaculate white cowboy boots clicked on the cement. The boots had elaborate yellow stitching that echoed the color of the gold nugget holding his yellow string tie. EB was monogrammed in lemon-colored embroidery on the pocket of his white cowboy shirt and repeated on the right pocket of his elegant white cowboy pants. Eddie Barker was straight out of west Texas via Neiman-Marcus. To him, July was summer, San Francisco weather be damned.

Right down to the Navajo turquoise watchband and belt buckle he flashed: Texas! Summer! Texas! in alternating symbols. Every single thing about his life-style was simple, low-key, deliberately inconspicuous—everything except the way he dressed. The real Eddie Barker had to come out somewhere.

Lean, tan, weathered skin, a thin, straight nose set on a thin, straight face, Eddie had spent thirty-six years looking like he was sitting on a horse.

A few parking spaces away from Broadway Game's front door, Stretch got into the passenger side of the cowboy's car, a boring '75 Chevy four-door with dull blue paint in an advanced stage of oxidation.

Climbing in behind the wheel, Eddie asked, "Okay, where do you want to go?" His tone revealed concern and understanding.

"I'm starving. How's the Buddha?"

The turquoise watchband flashed in the glare of neon lights. Eddie's sporty three thousand two hundred dollar Audemars Piguet read 11:52. "They're open. Let's head for it." A brand-new supercharged Corvette engine came quietly alive under the faded old hood.

At this late hour the Buddha held the only signs of life on a street full of commercial buildings. It was announced by a yellow neon sign in the classic outline of the master.

Each time Stretch walked through the door of the Japanese restaurant he beheld the place in disbelief. The long, narrow room had a twenty-foot-high ceiling, then jogged to the left into another, identical space. At the end of the first room, suspended in a recess at the top of the wall, was an enormous statue of a seated Buddha painted gold. The ceiling of the front room was covered with an Oriental fresco—not too well executed, but all the stages of the Buddha's life were depicted. Whether the customers could decipher them or not was another question. Black lacquer glazed the walls. On the left were low, lacquered tables surrounded by red cushions on the floor for lounging diners who wanted to socialize and be seen. For those who didn't, the right side was lined with bamboo cubicles. Curtains could be drawn across each opening to provide total privacy. Soft koto music set a peaceful tone for conversation.

The proprietor, Ho, came up to greet them, his arms crossed in the folds of a resplendent silk gown covered with gold-embroidered pagodas and samurai swords.

"Hello, Eddie." He bowed to his regular client. "Hello—" There was a hesitation. "Stretch, no?" Ho was one of those blessed with a memory for names.

"That's it," Stretch said, pleased to be remembered.

"Ah, so. Table? Booth?"

"Booth," Eddie said.

Ho was as Japanese as Southern fried chicken. Two years of being a G.I. in Korea, a bit of shell shock, a lot of R&R in Japan, and he had fallen in love with the country. He refused to leave and return to West Virginia, so he took his discharge there, able to live on his medical disability pension. Fluent in Japanese, he married a girl named Mayumi, made the passage from Shintoism to Taoism to Buddhism, spent six months in a Jodo Shinshu monastery, and converted to Zen. In his own mind Ho was totally Japanese—including the way he spoke English. One winter's day, fourteen years later, something told him to come home and open the Buddha. It was the time of the Flower People and he had prospered.

Before the booth's curtains closed Eddie leaned over to Stretch and whispered, "If you ever need anything cheap, that last guy—the one at the end table—is Benny." He indicated a chubby man in his mid-thirties who sat with an Amazonian blond. "He's the best fence in town."

"Oh." Feigning nonchalance, Stretch tried not to stare. Given what he'd just been through in West Alton, he didn't quite understand how a known criminal could just sit there in public, guzzling sake, gobbling sukiyaki, and laughing as if everything were rosy and right.

When Flower Power wilted into disillusion and the hip clientele faded away, Ho's all-night emporium—which maintained the eccentric hours of eleven P.M. to seven A.M.—began to attract the shorter-hair denizens of the darker hours. The new clientele was a curious mix of artists and other "hourless" creative types rubbing elbows with people whose jobs ended at one and two in the morning: bartenders, musicians, B-girls, and strippers. Sprinkled in were a handful of characters who lived on the fruits of "respectable" crime. Not thugs—none of them would deal dope or carry a gun. They were an odd lot—like Benny, or Sweet Pea, the forger with the squeaky voice, or Gene, whose freckled, boyish face enabled him to sell bonds in nonexistent companies. Gene's constant companion was El wood, whose training as an engraver helped him design and pass artistic and convincing five-dollar bills. Inflation had him working on a new series of twenties. Tony Bertolucci, the gambler—alias Caruso—was a caricature of a musclebound bodyguard. Waldo, the jovial and distinguished older gent sitting under the statue, was always with one beautiful young girl or another. In his prime he had been the finest diamond thief on the French Riviera. Now he was reduced to palming them in jewelry stores.

All in all, it was a colorful crowd. Seventy percent were habitués who formed a family of those riding on the social fringe.

In the booth Stretch studied the menu while Ho arrived and waited patiently. "You gonna order that sushi again?"

"Yep."

"Jesus." The idea of biting into cold, raw fish gave Stretch the shivers. Tempura was his choice for openers, then beef teriyaki.

Ho had explained teriyaki to him. "We slice beef thin, marinate long time and grill—glazed with sauce. That's real way. Cheap cooks save money, cook whole steak, slap sauce on, serve it to customers who don't know any better. Sauce never soak in." He had bowed, beaming righteous pride. Wasn't it his duty to instruct the uninitiated in the ways of the Orient?

"You want a Texas Tranquilizer?" Eddie asked. Stretch nodded. "Two bourbons on the rocks for starters."

Ho backed out and bowed, discreetly closing the curtains.

Eddie leaned back and studied his troubled friend. "You remember what happened to you eight days ago?"

For a moment, Stretch thought back. The sequence of events in the month and a half since he had fled from West Alton was still a jumble. He had wanted a maximum of distance between himself and the mess he had created at Bert's. He also wanted company, yet he had few friends away from home. His ex-sergeant in Nam, Eddie Barker, was one, but his last contact had been a two-year-old postcard giving a San Francisco address.

Stretch's first move on arriving had been to find a cheap motel in the shabby heart of the Tenderloin area. His next had been to search for Eddie. A series of dead ends led to dejection. Stretch Jackson's life seemed to have fallen apart. By accident or intentionally, the one person he wanted to see appeared to have slipped off the planet without leaving a trace.

For Stretch, boredom began to replace worry. Wandering, with nothing to do except ask himself, What next? was more fatiguing than work—especially since no answers came. Stretch had little in common with the winos and drifters who made the Tenderloin their home, which limited human contact to the casual, endless nothings said to the man at the next pinball machine or on the next barstool. His supply of money dwindled.

51

Eddie shook his head and interrupted Stretch's reverie. "You got a memory like a prairie chicken. That's when I almost ran you over."

"Oh, Christ!" Stretch exclaimed in embarrassment.

The Texas Tranquilizers arrived on a plasticized raffia tray. The waitress was authentically Japanese.

Stretch had been crossing Geary Street to go sit in Union Square—again—when a blue Chevrolet in terrible shape honked right next to him. The driver had jumped out yelling, "Stretch! Hey, Stretch Jackson!"

Stretch could hardly believe his eyes. There was Eddie Barker, in person—his old sergeant from the 101st Airborne. Eddie had been the top sergeant at B Company when Stretch had arrived at training camp as a raw draftee, and then his sergeant in Nam. Even though Stretch had been discharged with his own three stripes and Barker had become his buddy, Eddie remained Stretch's superior. They had been together from one end of horror to the other.

After three days of reminiscing, the West Alton firebug had broken down. He had to tell someone, and here, at last, was a friend who knew him like a book, who had given him help without questions the last time he had been ashamed of what he had done. So Stretch had spilled all the details about Bert and the fire across the table in Eddie's apartment. His guilt and his heart tumbled out with the story. The minute Stretch had finished, Eddie had doubled up, roaring with laughter. Stretch had gone pale with shock. When the Texan had finally recovered from his spasms, he had explained how he made his living.

Ex-sergeant Edward A. Barker, decorated from hell to breakfast, cited for bravery under fire by President Nixon himself, and the pride of Midland, Texas, was a full-time, flat-out professional torch. "The best in the business, if I say so myself," Eddie had added.

Stretch had sat there speechless and unbelieving.

Eddie snapped Stretch out of his daydreaming. "Yep, eight days ago at a quarter to five," he said. "And it was five days ago at my house you told me about Bert and your booboo. I don't know how many times it's been since that I've told you to forget it and settle down. It's not like you'd get slung in the pokey for ten years with the key thrown away. Arson's only one to five—and out in an average of ten months. It's just the damn county jail, not Sing Sing or something. Bert can't squeal on you—he'd be admitting he set it up." Eddie took a sip of bourbon and went on. "Anyhow, any attorney that could convince a fox to enter a henhouse could get him off. Arson's easier to get out of than a traffic ticket. They almost have to catch you with a match in your hand and the place on fire."

Stretch heaved a sigh.

"Can't lasso a calf with a rubber band, pardner—come right back at you. You gotta learn your trade."

"It's not my trade," Stretch shot back.

"Don't get touchy. Six years ago, when I was tending bar for a lousy two bills a week, the boss got in a money bind and asked for a little help. I grant you, my first one went off smooth as hand cream. I didn't have any Bert to plan it, so I had to dope things out for myself. You know how I did it?" He could not stop a chuckle of satisfaction. "Steak flambé."

"What the hell's that mean?"

"There was this fancy French restaurant in Midland that used to douse perfectly good meat with cognac and then light it right at the table. It gave me the idea to flambé the whole Old El Rancho Bar. Closed up one night. Faked a short circuit in the lighting near the liquor shelves and doused the whole thing with six bottles of cognac. Threw in a Pink Label rum for luck. Figured the rest of the bottles would break and feed the fire once it got hot enough. Boy, did it work! I lit, split, and never looked back. Had the boss's five grand in my pocket, his girl friend in the front seat, and headed for Frisco. Neither one lasted very long. She ran through the loot and went back to Midland. Well, I thought lighting fires would be a handy way to make a living, so I got into it. Wasn't my trade either, but when I decided to take it on, I had to learn it."

The curtains parted. The appetizers were served. The two men ate in silence for a moment.

"Listen, Stretch, I never been to West Alton, but I know small-town morals. All of Texas isn't six-guns and poker games. When I got in the army I wouldn't hardly roll dice. Well, Nam and the army taught me better. The whole damn thing's just a crap game—till you roll your last pair of snake eyes. If you're scared to take a gamble, you've lost the game before you start. Look. Everybody who goes into business is taking a gamble. Roll 'em and win and everybody looks up to you. The higher the rollers, the richer they are—long as they're winning. Big shots. But they know their business. Torching gets to be like any other job. You need bread? Burn something."

"Eddie, I can't do that." Just thinking about it made Stretch drop a chopstick.

"Yeah, and if a frog had wings he wouldn't bump his ass so much. You do what you do with what you got to do it with. You've got a light and now you've got a connection."

The beef teriyaki came, filling the cubicle with its steamy, sweet-pungent fragrance. Stretch watched the suntanned man in the cowboy clothes. He was curious about the change he saw. Eddie had lost his old, whooping exuberance. Now, despite the flashy clothes, he seemed to be poised, serious. The war had shocked some boys into premature manhood, but Eddie simply seemed solid, sure of himself. He knew what he wanted and went about getting it. Perhaps he was too busy "making it" to ask all those questions that were plaguing Stretch. Or maybe he had asked them and found the answers.

As though he had read Stretch's thoughts, Eddie said, "It may not be legal, but it's a straightforward job. You know how many million people in this country do something that stretches the law or, hell, breaks it for that matter? I don't mean killers or guys who use guns. I'm talking about earning bread doing something a judge would say no-no to if you got hauled into court. Man, they'd have to put half the country in jail.

"Since we hit Nam in the mid-sixties, the times have changed. The Mafia has become part of the establishment. The biggest money crop in California is marijuana, and your friendly coke dealer is welcomed with open arms from Hollywood to Washington, D.C. So what's a little arson? You're not sticking a gun in anybody's ribs. Listen, we did our time. We did everyone else's dirty work in Nam. Seems to me we earned our right to play the same game as the big boys. The way I see it, you'd have to have bad brain damage to try to be a hundred percent straight in this mess."

Stretch followed the implacable logic. He wished to hell it were not so convincing. Had his brother Wayne died in the Mekong Delta, had Ted Bowen gotten his foot blown off, and had he himself wallowed through all those fields of death merely to earn the right to be dishonest? The answer seemed to be a deafening *No!*—until he inspected the world around him. Then suddenly he wondered if he was out of step, trying to win the race with an obsolete machine. Times really had changed. Stretch had been thinking in terms of a tune-up. If Eddie was right, he needed a whole new engine. The very idea made the teriyaki taste sour.

"You know how much I made last year?" Eddie made the question sound innocent. In the face of the ensuing silence, he provided the answer. "A hundred thirty-one thousand." He watched Stretch expectantly.

"You *what?*" Stretch choked.

"You heard it. And it's all free and clear of taxes. That's like making a quarter of a million legit. I'll double that when I move to New York. Okay, so I'm at the top of the ladder, but if you want to stop hustling jalopies and go Ferrari class, you get into it, cowboy. You learn the trade and you'll make out. You're smart and you're honest. Most dudes in this business are bums. A guy with balls *and* brains can make a fortune— like in anything. You've got them both if you'd use them."

Despite the hundred-thirty-one-thousand-dollar figure still reverberating in his brain, Stretch responded without hesitation. "I can't burn somebody, Eddie! And you of all people know why." His voice had a note of desperation.

"Jesus, banjo brain! You don't burn anybody! Idiots burn people. That's a murder rap. The rules of evidence are different, but, more than that, you have to live with yourself." Then the sergeant remembered what the CONGRIL engraved on Stretch's Zippo lighter meant. Eddie cocked his head and looked into the blue eyes across the booth. "You think I'd do that?" It was more an accusation than a question.

Wavering, Stretch stammered, "Well . . . no, of course not." Actually he *had* had doubts.

"In six years I've gotten no more than ashes down a fireman's neck. You say no—N-O!—to that kind of job. You keep your ass away from bums and mob types. Make it respectable, for Christ's sake—you got standards."

Do it right, be the best, flickered through Jackson's mind. "Well, I guess you're proof it doesn't have to get nasty."

"Damn right. There's guys in the East make three fifty, four hundred thousand. I'm going to do just that—*and* keep it a class act." Eddie put his elbows on the table and sighed, relishing the prospect.

"What the hell do you do, list in the Yellow Pages under Torches'? Or buy a fifty-buck license plate that says TORCH?"

"Nah—I just go down the street with a lit candle and a can marked GAS." He couldn't help laughing at his own joke. "There are more guys want fires than there are jackrabbits in mesquite. Some public adjusters will go for it. There's a weekly newspaper that lists bankruptcy proceedings. Lots of those guys are open to suggestion. Once you're in it all kinds of things unravel. Surprise the bejesus out of you. There's one-shotters and regular connections, bigwigs, and desperate guys about to pee their britches they're so scared."

The cowboy mused for a minute, drumming his fingers on the table.

"Hey, pard," he exclaimed, "I got an idea. Three days and I'm off to New York for good. Maybe I can get you out of the bull chute. I had a proposition two weeks ago from a guy. I'm leaving, so I turned it down. It's small potatoes, but it'd give you a chance to learn. Keep you off the streets and put some money in your pocket. I'll give you a crash course tomorrow. You can handle it!"

"Jesus, Eddie, I don't know." Stretch resisted the idea.

Eddie continued, "Okay, you sleep on it, but I'll tell you, it's a damn sight more exciting than racing cars. Hell, you'll probably even quit that stuff. Have to keep a low profile."

Stretch looked at the conspicuous cowboy costume and wondered how Eddie got away with *that*.

"Pardner, I'm leaving the number-one slot in the West open. You think on it, hear? In some ways it's a secret, lonesome life. Yeah, more than anything else that can get to you. I let these guys, like Benny and Waldo, talk about what they do, but there aren't twenty people in the world know my business—outside of clients.

"I told Benny. Once he knew, he'd vouch for me to the others here without getting specific about my line of work. That's all that anyone needs to know. Hell, I'd never even have told you if you hadn't spilled your guts about Bert. I admit it can be lonely. That gets you, all right, but how you gonna take a shot at the big time if you're scared of big risks? Think on it, but get some style in your life, cowboy. We didn't go through all that hell in Nam for nothing, did we?"

6

The burgundy towers of the Golden Gate Bridge climbed out of sight into a fog bank, but Sausalito and Tiburon were basked in sunshine. Alcatraz rose on its menacing rock between Stretch and the north shore towns. From the perch of Eddie Barker's apartment on the bluff above Russian Hill Park there was a dramatic 180-degree view: Ghirardelli Square, Fisherman's Wharf, Treasure Island, the Embarcadero, even the ultramodern pyramid of the Transamerica Building. It was a majestic panorama of America's most intricate city.

"That's Coit Tower over there, sitting on Telegraph Hill. Some rich old lady built it as a monument to volunteer firemen. It'd be better for business if they were still volunteers." Eddie turned away from the breathtaking view. "Strangest town I ever rode into. Koreans, Chinese, Vietnamese, Japanese—you name it from Asia—all mixed up with Irish, Spanish, Italians, French, and what-have-you from Europe. Must of been a helluva place a hundred years ago when they all hit here."

"It's a hell of a place right now, if you ask me."

"Yes, but wait till you get into it. Just make sure the chick you pick up isn't a guy." Eddie was interrupted by a flash of fire on the dining room table. He checked his watch. "There. Just like I told you. Seventeen minutes. You light the cigarette and it takes sixteen to twenty minutes to burn in a horizontal position. Take the pack of matches, put the lit cigarette between the match rows, and put it down. You got, more or less, seventeen minutes before it flares up."

"Okay," Stretch said. "And if there's a draft, fourteen."

"You're learning. When the matches flare, that ignites your accelerant. The matches burn up completely, so there's no evidence. Remember, you're looking for three things." Eddie pushed the ashes off the plate and into an ashtray. "First, you want the right fire for the job. You don't always need to burn the barn to the ground. People want all sorts of kookie things. I had a guy wanted me to burn just one set of file drawers in his accounting office. Had all his tax records in it. He must have been cheating the IRS out of a wad, because he paid a bundle for the job. It had to appear to be accidental, be thorough, and not really disrupt the business." Eddie smiled at the recollection. "I hardly singed the space beyond the file cabinet. Second, you got to have time to get out and be whistling Dixie up the street before the fire starts. The more delay the better, as long as no one can stumble onto your setup before it goes off. And third, you don't want to leave any evidence that could nail you. It's got to seem absolutely innocent and natural—just an accidental fire." Eddie shrugged his shoulders and put up his hands. "Happens all the time."

"Jesus, Eddie, it sounds god-awful complicated," Stretch said, unable to hide his worries.

"C'mon, cowboy—it's not near as hard as fixing up one of your racing machines. You start off easy-like and earn as you learn. Besides"—he eyed Stretch questioningly—"you've got no choice unless you want to hustle cars, do you?"

"At least I already know how to do that," Stretch retorted.

"Man, you're skittish as a mare in heat. Stop worrying. Before the end of the day you'll know all the ropes you need to get you on your way. You've got to quit making mountains out of molehills. Look, just because I fade into gray doesn't mean I don't know what goes on out there. I promise you, before I'm through with you, you'll know as much as most guys in the business. The ones they catch are the amateurs who light a place for revenge or because they're bored or crazy. Not that there aren't pros who are crazy. There are nuts in any business. This one dude, for example, is the opposite of me. Everybody knows him—good-looking, blond stud type, thirty, maybe thirty-five. Wears a fireman's badge on a silver chain around his neck. Used to be a fireman. Partly he's a cuckoo, partly he plays the opposite game to mine."

"How's that?" Stretch's curiosity was aroused.

"I don't hang around a fire site, but this bugger turns up all the time so he'll get mistaken for an honest fire buff. Lots of folks follow fires just to watch. Well, fire marshals sometimes take crowd pictures to see who's there that's suspicious. This character, Marty Martin, gets called in by fire marshals as often as Willie Nelson takes encores. I think he gets his rocks off on it. I hear he's just arrogant as hell when he's questioned, screaming about harassment, him being an ex-fireman and all. Well, its a foxy tactic, but it's for a creep who's got a screw loose somewhere. Probably a guy like him isn't good enough to do a big job, so he makes out on bits and pieces. Means he doesn't come up against the tough P.I.'s."

"P.I.'s?"

"Private Investigators—you know, like private detectives who specialize in arson." Eddie stopped himself. He was about to mention his personal nightmare, Tom Farley. He decided Stretch was spooked enough without throwing that devil in his path. If Stretch got into it, he'd lock horns with Farley sure as hell. The Best in the West half-smiled to himself. *Once I clear out, Farley's going to have a lot of extra time to chase after everyone else.*

Eddie quickly made a hard-nosed reassessment of his buddy. He changed his mind. Stretch was no baby. He was entitled to play with a full deck when he made his decision. "You ought to know up front," Eddie said dryly. "Tom Farley's going to be on your ass."

"Yeah?" Stretch shrugged. "So who's that?"

"When you told me about flipping your Chev in the last race, you said the guy who won was always second in your circuit, always right on your tail. Well, cowboy, you follow my advice, you'll be the top honcho on the torch circuit. Your competition won't be other torches, though, it'll be investigators. I'll tell you from first-hand experience, you fuck up and one dude out there will jump you—a P.I. named Tom Farley. If you're worth a damn, that bastard will be in your ashes while they're still hot. You slip up and he'll get you sure as hell. I don't expect you to goof, but it wouldn't be right if I didn't warn you that there are others in the race." No matter how Stretch took his warning, Eddie felt better. He had respected his obligation to be honest with a friend who trusted him.

Instead of being frightened Stretch rose to the bait. "Wouldn't be much fun running around the track all by yourself, now would it? If this guy comes with the territory, I'll keep it in mind—*if* I light my first match. You ever get picked up?"

"Me? Jesus, no. Farley's poked around some of my jobs, just like the marshals and other P.I.'s have, but I never left enough evidence to give him a lead. He's still scratching his head on my cases. The whole trick is to never get on their books, because if you do, they'll haul you in every time the fire bell rings. Like they do with that son-of-a-bitch, Martin. And one of these days, Martin's gonna end up laughing out of the other side of his loud mouth."

"If you didn't goof, then why did a P.I. investigate in the first place?"

Eddie gave a snort. "The guys who hire you aren't lily white! Sometimes their insurance company is sure something is wrong right off the bat. But if everything looks normal at the fire site, they plain don't have anywhere to go with their suspicions. All they can do is cough up and forget it. Some companies will call in a P.I. automatically if there are big bucks involved. I already told you, arson's tougher to prove than almost anything—and even if they prove it, it doesn't mean they can lay a finger on anyone for criminal charges. Hell, it doesn't even mean they can avoid paying the insurance claim. The insurance company not only has to prove that a place was torched, but that the owner was in on burning it."

"If you're so well camouflaged, how do you know all that?"

"Clients. I collect my bread from a one-shot customer and never hear from him again, but repeaters tell me who's poking

61

around, what they're looking for, what questions they're asking. I get the scuttlebutt that way, sometimes right from the fire marshals, via my customers. If he's a nice guy, sometimes I'll even call a one-timer back just to see if anyone's on the case. He'll tell me who it is, whether they're hot or cold, and almost anything else I want to know. You'll see how it works soon enough. But I promise you, you're about to learn everything you need to know to do the easy ones and stay out of trouble."

Getting back to the practical, Eddie said, "Don't forget that fire hoses push out a lot of water. Evidence gets scattered, things get shoved around. Right off the bat nobody's thinking about evidence. They just want to get the fire out and save the property. That's a hundred percent in your favor. If you can start the fire with materials that are normally on hand—a bin of paper, something like that—so much the better, because it arouses fewer suspicions. If you have to use an accelerant, which you usually do, it pays to cover your tracks by, say, making a short circuit in the electric system. If I remember right, it was always you who fixed the rotten wiring system in the barracks."

"Yeah, I'm pretty good with electricity."

"It'll come in handy. Let me show you a few tricks." Eddie considered giving his pupil his favorite device—the telephone lighter—but he had heard about Farley and the Gloria Pump incident. The client said the insurance company was going to have to pay, but that the phone device was getting too hot to use for a while. The technique might be a poisoned gift, so Eddie stuck to the simpler methods.

"Keep in mind that there are things you shouldn't do, too. An investigator will spot them in a minute and know the fire was set." He looked his reluctant protégé in the eye. "It's like racing—everybody's out to get you. It's a serious business—dead serious. And I mean *literally* dead. Your accelerant can get you, your fire can get you, the cops can get you. Sometimes, even the guy who hires you might want you to disappear—permanently—because you're his most damaging evidence. But all of that's what makes it exciting. Now you listen to me carefully, Stretch. I don't want your blood on my hands."

Stretch heaved a sigh. A vaguely unpleasant little dose of adrenaline spurted into his system. "I read you, Eddie."

The fog burned off and the thermometer rose to sixty-one, but before the two had finished their intense discussion the temperature was back down to fifty degrees and the bridge lights beaded the bay, north to Marin County, east to the home of the Oakland A's.

Ten o'clock had just punched in when the Texan rose, gave his student a playful poke on the shoulder, and announced, "I'm hungry as a bear in March. Come on—I'll take you to a place that'll make you think you're back on Tu-Do Street in Saigon. Unless you want something real exotic—like there's a Moroccan, an Ethiopian, and a Hungarian restaurant in the same block as the Vietnamese place."

"Saigon's strange enough for me." Stretch hesitated. "You think I got it?"

"You got everything you need to start with—except making your mind up." Eddie held the door open. "Come on, lead-ass, let's chow down!"

* * *

Stretch's shrinking resources had made his decision. He slipped the yellow Camaro into the parking spot and pulled the folded paper out of his pocket to check the address. It was a superfluous gesture. He had already studied the name and address twenty times: Moe's Fire Sale and Salvage Company, 3090 Mission Street. He turned the ignition key off, put the paper in his pocket, and sat there—breathing deeply, trying to pump up courage.

Through the big plate-glass windows mounds of goods could be seen. It was one of the two- and three-story buildings that marched down Mission Street to the horizon, housing mostly stores, like this one, and offices, and here and there an old apartment.

He started to put a quarter in the meter, then decided, hell, let them send their ticket back to Illinois.

Once across the street. Stretch stopped, breathed deeply again, and faced the door. Pretend you're in the pit about to start a fifty-lapper, he said to himself. That jacked him up a little bit.

A clerk said Moe, the owner, was upstairs on the right. A glassed-in office stretched across the back of the store on a mezzanine. The room to the left contained several people who looked like bookkeepers and secretaries, all very busy. On the right, the door was open, revealing a cluttered office. Stretch relaxed his face and concentrated on getting up at least a weak smile. A man was writing, his big, balding head bent over the desk.

Stretch stepped through the door. Thick cigar smoke had found a floating level about five feet off the floor—nose height. The office was a memorial to junk. For a moment the man didn't look up, then he leaned back, shifting his dead cigar stub with his tongue.

"Whaddya want, kid?"

Stretch glanced over his shoulder to see if a "kid" had come in the door behind him. Recovering, he asked, "You Moe?"

"Who the hell do I look like—the secretary?"

Actually, Moe looked like a waterlogged paper bag. Not just because he had baggy eyes, baggy cheeks, baggy jowls, and a brownish complexion. No, the chest bagged, the paunch bagged, and no doubt he sagged behind as well.

"How's the salvage business?" Stretch tried to sound cheery.

"Lousy!" The growl was impatient. "It's always lousy."

"Well, I came to help. You buy salvage, old buddy—I make it."

One hustler recognized the other. "Yeah?" Moe said warily.

"Moe, you and I'd make a great match. You need a partner."

Moe was curious, but he couldn't let it show. "Cockamamy kid! I need to split 50 percent of my nothing? C'mon, get out of here."

Faking confidence, Stretch dragged over a chair, sat down, and turned the Zippo between his thumb and forefinger. "Eddie sent me."

A smile like sunshine breaking through creased the fleshy lips. "Yeah? Why didn'ya say so?" He pushed a box across the desk. "Have a cigar."

Stretch Jackson was in business.

* * *

It was almost ninety minutes later when Moe opened the door and let his new partner out. There wasn't even a ticket on the windshield of the Camaro. Stretch slipped behind the steering wheel, pleased but worried. He took out the Zippo, watching the engraved word CONGRIL glint as he turned the lighter in the sun's rays.

It had been a bit disappointing the first several times out on search-and-destroy in Vietnam. With the flame launcher always at the ready, Stretch had converted a couple of bunkers into furnaces—but no enemy was inside. Then, one freezing afternoon, his squad sneaked up on the mouth of a tunnel. They could hear voices inside. I'll get the bastards this time! Stretch swore to himself. His eyes gleamed and he blew hell-fire into the entrance.

Two men came out screaming, covered with flaming gel. One reached out for Stretch, as if begging for help, but he didn't make it. He collapsed at Stretch's feet, shrieking, writh-ing, ablaze, crackling, smoke pouring from burning flesh. Stretch stared an instant, then doubled over and puked out his guts in horror. Ted Bowen was yelling, "There's more gooks in there, Stretch! Hit 'em, goddamn, hit 'em!" But Stretch was paralyzed. That was when a grenade sailed out of the tunnel and blew off Corporal Bowen's foot. Blindly Stretch whipped his weapon toward the hole and burned it—burned it and three more Viet Cong to a smoking crisp, but too late to help Ted Bowen.

"It's them or us, Sarge," Stretch said the next day. "And I'll fight my ass off. I'll shoot them, I'll grenade them, I'll stick a knife in their eye if I have to, but I won't do *that* anymore! It's not human! I want off it." He felt like shit. "I'm sorry."

"None of this is human, cowboy. It's duty." The sergeant studied the young man from the Corn Belt. He liked him. The boy ought to be back where he came from, plowing fields or something—sowing wild oats, at least. None of us should be here, he confessed to himself, though he was too serious a soldier to say it aloud. Sure, he understood the kid. Any front-line veteran in Nam who wasn't psycho would understand.

So it was Sergeant Edward Barker who got the C.O.'s permission to put Jackson on reconnaissance and gave the task of burning fellow humans to death to someone else.

The stench and sight of the soldier sizzling at his feet and the accusing finger of a blood-bathed, curly-headed cripple dominated Stretch's screaming nightmares. On reconnaissance nausea would roll in like a foul-smelling fog and he would have to duck away to hide his vomit from his comrades.

A few weeks later, someone got word that the doctors had been obliged to cut off the mangle that was Ted Bowen's other foot. Stretch closed the door of his mind and could speak to no one for days. Just as he was pulling himself together, he received the letter. His hands shook when he saw the return address.

That it was a delirious wail of rage made no difference. That it was all the fault of remote and famous people made no difference. That the letter should have been written to a senator or to the commander-in-chief—who would not have noticed—made no difference. It also made no difference that the words would scar a man still in his teens who already had been well scarred. The note was as long as it had to be.

Fuck you forever, chickenshit.
I hope you roast in napalm!

Ted

Only three men would ever know the contents of the letter: Ted Bowen, Stretch Jackson, and Eddie Barker.

"What a shitty thing to do." Sergeant Barker pressed his eyes closed with one hand as if that would erase the message. "Stretch, he didn't mean it. Oh, fuck—sure he meant it. But he didn't mean it like you're taking it. He can't hit out at anyone else. What can you expect from a kid who wakes up in bed with no feet? You don't even get good sportsmanship in sports anymore—you're sure as hell not going to get it on a stinking battlefield. Everything we're doing here goes against everything . . ."

Stretch, who was mutely hunkered on the other side of the tent, got another dose of the shakes. The sergeant knew it was useless to go on. By nightfall Barker had arranged for one badly battered psyche to get choppered out for R&R.

When Stretch returned, in shape to fight, the incident was never mentioned. The company had only been in Vietnam for ten weeks, but traumas worse than Jackson's had piled up in his absence. Perhaps to pretend it had never happened, he clung dearly to his CONGRIL lighter. Stretch Jackson was half immune to horror by the time the C.O. called him in to break the news of his brother's death while Wayne was fighting in the Mekong.

Sitting in the yellow Camaro across from Moe's, Stretch had just made a fresh, disturbing pact with fire, and he was not sure that he was proud of it. He held the CONGRIL Zippo out of the window for a moment, then let it drop to the blacktop of Mission Street. He turned the key and started the motor.

A second later he killed the engine. No, it would be better to keep a reminder—not of the Viet Cong, not of the war, but of the terror of a man on fire. He retrieved the lighter and slipped it into his pocket. The best thing about Moe's deal, he thought, is that it's only salvage. Only a store or warehouse in the dead of night. There can't be any people involved. He gained a bit of conviction and considered what Eddie had said he would have to do.

"For salvage, you don't want to burn the place too bad," Eddie had carefully explained. "With hardware, appliances, sporting goods, furniture, you want water stains." He gave a chuckle. "That's the firemen's specialty. Light it on the upper floor or in the ceiling joist—that looks like it was a short circuit—and those boys do your job. They pump it plumb up with H Two O, which then proves the theory of gravity, pissin' down all over everything, full of acid and filthy dirty!"

It had only been a one-day crash course, but if the Best in the West thought Stretch could handle it, Stretch guessed he could—with some luck and bluff.

No one was coming. He started up again, and this time pulled the Camaro out, dared a U-turn, and headed toward North Beach. Sitting in his hotel room was too grim and West Texas had flown to New York, so Stretch went to drown his uncertainty about lighting fires in the electronic pandemonium at Broadway Game.

In the past tomorrow had always appeared to Stretch to be the natural result of today. He was trained to believe that life was controlled by others, from God to Uncle Sam. Boring daily routine punctuated by totally uncontrollable and unpredictable events seemed to have an ironclad grip on the lives of ordinary people. At best one could just flow with it.

However, San Francisco was a radically new and exciting horizon opening before him that would change a lot of things. Stretch suddenly hit the pinball machine so hard it went TILT. No, sir, by damn. Now that Eddie was gone he would get some perspective and think more clearly. The life of a lonesome cowboy outlaw was not for him! No way, he muttered to himself. A few dollars ahead, a few fires for Moe, and he would be able to stop drifting. He would grasp life like a steering wheel and at least have a bit of control. He saw very clearly that it was time for Stretch Jackson to get it together and come to grips with decision.

He felt deep-down good and turned to leave the Broadway flushed with confidence. But it did flit through Stretch's mind that seeing the ring and grabbing it were two different things.

7

The sun scattered a bagful of diamonds across the water. A steady breeze hovered between light and moderate. Little waves without white caps dimpled the long, smooth swells. About a quarter-mile offshore, before the sea became an immensity, the surface creased and made a low hissing sound around the bow of the *Sapphire,* a thirty-five-foot, yawl-rigged Choy Lee. Not for the weekend Tupperware sailor, the *Sapphire* was a magnificent cruiser/racer with teakwood hull, decks, and interior, though today she was in no hurry. The mainsail was reefed down; the jib and mizzen were enough to progress comfortably southward. The day was a lazy sailor's dream.

Given the direction and constancy of the wind, Tom Farley had locked the tiller and mizzen sail on a course parallel to the coast, then sat in the open cockpit to work on a file.

The *Sapphire* was a floating office. The unique miniature desk of Tom's own design sat under a plastic hood. It was only twelve by eighteen inches. A clear glass insert in the hood allowed him to read what was underneath in his files and to write reports. The hood itself kept out minor spray and wind; a flap made the arrangement waterproof if the weather really became heavy. Under the plastic hood was a hook for a plastic stapler, a holder for a pocket calculator, and a magnet for paper clips. The equipment was completed by a cigarette-pack-sized tape recorder for dictating that clipped up under the hood. Its voice-actuated mike meant that all Tom had to do was talk.

Long ago his secretary, Charlene, had learned to ignore the various damns and other curses inspired by unexpected ship-board mishaps.

Farley's two offices—the one on land and the one afloat—were about the only places where he rarely wore a hat. It didn't seem dignified behind his desk, and at sea he liked to tan his scalp. Farley's personal theory was that a tanned scalp concealed the slight thinning of his hair better than when bright white came shining through.

Tom squinted at the brilliant sea. He regretted for the thousandth time that he hadn't discovered the joy of sailing until eight years before. When he did, boats rushed in to become his second passion. Fire was the first, of course. His passion for his wife, Betty, had long been banked (which explained why she was now his ex-wife), and the feeling for his children was more mellow love than passion.

Tom's thoughts were shattered by the ship-to-shore telephone. "Jesus!" he exclaimed, jumping up. The recorder's light clicked to ON-RECORDING.

"Tom?" It was Charlene. "You floating around out there getting suntanned while I'm slaving in the office?"

"What?" he sputtered. "What the devil are you doing in the office at four o'clock on Saturday?"

"Overtime, as usual. What's it worth to you if I've got the Shoreline fire solved?" She heard Tom suck in his breath in surprise. "I won't tell you about it on the radio telephone. How soon can you get here?"

Farley knew Charlene did not joke around about things like that. She took the work almost as seriously as he did. So did Tom's father, Pat, who was the third pillar of the office.

He could not conceive what Charlene might have unearthed, but he was quick to reply. "Fix some coffee. I'll be right in."

Tom ran up the mainsail, brought the boat hard about, and locked in the tiller. The number-one Genoa went up, billowed out, and the cruiser gave way to the racer. He glanced up at the thousand seventy-two square feet of sheet that instantly bit into the breeze and thanked the day that he had had the fore-sight to pick up a bargain just when all the Sunday sailors were flocking to plastic hulls and dreary uniformity. He rushed back to the tiller and, tacking to catch every whiff of wind, headed for the marina in Oakland.

"Come on, *Sapphire*," he pleaded. "Get it up."

The boat responded. Up front, where the bow parted the water, the hiss changed to a higher pitch and added an upwind, slurping beat. He almost flew under the Golden Gate Bridge on an incoming tide.

Wasting no time, he motored toward the slip and sounded the air horn. The dockmaster, Pickles, trundled up as fast as he could. Everything about the old man was vintage sea salt: cap, striped mariner's shirt, Levi's, deck shoes, and a face that looked as though it had been held under water too long. Everything showed hard use. So many years before that even Pickles didn't remember when, someone had said he had more vinegar than a barrel of pickles. The lifelong merchant mariner couldn't recall why he had not been called Vinegar—he would have preferred it to Pickles.

"Ah," he'd say when recounting the story, "other folks are responsible for most of what drops anchor in your life. And I had the hard luck to get harpooned with Pickles."

No matter how weather worn Pickles was, he still had plenty of spring in his stringy muscles. Not only was he always ready to help, he knew everything worth knowing about anything that would float.

"Hey, Pickles!" Tom called. "Would you grab the line and tie her up?"

"Course. I'll wash her down, too. You don't ever quit working, do you?"

Tom hopped to the dock. "You know what they say—work or *schtimm*." He ran, smiling, for the parking lot, leaving a baffled Pickles behind to figure out what *schtimm* meant.

* * *

Charlene tapped her watch as the door to Suite 1812 flew open. "What did you do, row?" she asked, feigning impatience.

"I forgot to mention that I was off Seal Rock."

"I should have known." She stood up. "We're out of coffee. The tea got cold. I'll make some more if you'd like."

Sexy was not an adjective one would immediately associate with Charlene. She was not built like a movie star—her shoulders were too wide, her hips as slender as her waist, and she had an impertinent, masculine backside. Her face was as angular as her body. The high cheekbones, angled chin, and full but straight lips gave her a tomboy look. However, Charlene's eyes sparkled like a pair of deep-blue sapphires. They contrasted boldly with her fair complexion and the long cascade of dark brown hair.

Charlene gave a first impression of being the plain, pleasant, and superefficient young secretary, but everything changed when she smiled—which she did quite often. Her smile wrought one of those marvelous transformations that say, "Underneath I'm warm and friendly—just give me a chance." The smile was involuntarily coordinated with a crinkle of the crow's-feet at the corners of her eyes and a wrinkle of her nose. For a moment she would suddenly be very appealing, surprisingly sensual.

"All right, what's your mysterious message?" Tom inquired anxiously.

"I was sitting at the Laundromat waiting for a load of delicates to dry when I thought of Ronnie Fender."

"Ronnie Fender!" Tom exploded. "Ronnie Fender's in jail!"

Charlene gave Tom one of her melting smiles and ignored the outburst. "So I came down here and went through both of his files. The first one has a note that you suspected a magnesium plant but couldn't prove it and suspected Fender but couldn't prove that either. The second one, you got the magnesium and Ronnie and he was sent up." She handed him the tea and two sugars.

"So? He's up."

Her eyes danced and she continued. "I called somebody in the prosecutor's office, got the sentence and the prison. Called the prison, got the warden on the line, and guess what? Fender was paroled two months ago! Time off for good behavior. Went right back home to his wife in Alameda. I talked to his parole officer, who said Ronnie has a job and seems to be keeping out of mischief. The parole officer did recall that Ronnie is dressing well. Remember? He was a bit of a clothes horse."

"How the holy hell did you get all of that on a Saturday afternoon?" Tom asked, stupefied.

"Good training . . . and the will of a woman," Charlene said lightly. "Think it's worth a raise?"

"No," Tom retorted good-humoredly. "But I *am* impressed. Settle for a dinner at the Top of the Mark?"

"Sold! I guess you'll have the hardest part. Proving that he did it isn't going to be a snap."

Tom picked up the two closed files and the fresh one on Shoreline. "He certainly has had time to think about how to improve his methods. Come on—let's talk about it with food and a sunset."

One good meal and three hours later, Farley pulled the white-and-black Pontiac into his space at the marina. He walked to Dock D, where he collected his gear and files from the *Sapphire*. Sniffing the smell of fresh salt air, he padded the short distance to his house at the end of Dock A.

Sapphire II was an old river barge. For the four years since Farley's divorce the spacious boat had been home. Long before he had acquired *Sapphire II*—back in the forties, when such things didn't cost the eyes of the earth—someone had converted the barge into fifty feet of elegant houseboat. It had been fitted with a wooden superstructure, rounded at the corners, trimmed in teak. The portholes were brass, as were all the fittings. Aft was an ample sundeck. Inside was a salon large enough to have separate dining and office areas, a spacious galley, a bath, and two bedrooms.

When Tom spotted it, the houseboat had been headed for total ruin and had been abandoned at the far end of a repair dock. It had taken Tom ten minutes to decide he loved it, ten months to fix it up. It had been worth it. The interior was all walnut-paneled, nautical and roomy but with the warm intimate feeling so special to boats.

Tom walked up the gangplank. He stood on the deck for a minute in the pale dock lights, watching the intricate play of long masts dancing with the movement of the waves. The burble and slap of water against hulls and pilings had a soft, friendly sound.

"Son-of-a-bitch!" he muttered, still amazed. "Ronnie Fender." He felt good inside. He knew that he often took Charlene's intelligence and initiative for granted, but this afternoon's performance approached some sort of summit. In fact, the evening had, too. It was the first time in five years of serious-minded, intense collaboration that Tom had asked his secretary out to dinner. They had often worked late nights or weekends, even aboard *Sapphire II* and a couple of times while sailing on the *Sapphire*. But for all of their quick lunches and makeshift dinners, tonight was the first time they had simply relaxed. They did discuss Fender and various files, but in short order the panoramic spectacle of San Francisco below them changed the mood. The conversation had shifted to a couple of the men in her life and the lack of women in his. It was comfortable talk. Tom had truly enjoyed it.

He wagged his head and mumbled, "Damn!" He remembered the afternoon aboard the *Sapphire* when Charlene had brought her swimming suit. "You can't work in a bikini," he had protested.

"You watch me," she had replied in her usual independent manner.

At the time he had merely noticed that she was compact and slender. Now the same image seemed unexpectedly attractive. Tom shook his head and dismissed the thought. He had an inviolate rule: never look *that* way at an employee. He recalled his very first secretary and the mess that had created—he had not hired a smashy, well-proportioned secretary since. The memory alone sufficed to make Farley turn firmly on his heel and head for the door.

Inside *Sapphire II* he switched on the lights, tossed the files on the desk, and went to wash up. Everything was in immaculate shipshape order—except the jumble covering the desk. The walls had several prints of nautical scenes, one oil painting by Bob Anderson, a painter who lived on a boat in the marina, a startling blowup of a fire he had investigated, and photographs of his son and daughter.

The barometer was rising; the forecast was "fair"; the temperature stood at 68 degrees; and the clock inside the ship's wheel on the wall said almost twenty-three hundred when Tom put a fresh cup of coffee on the edge of the desk and sat down to see if he could bait a trap for Ronnie Fender.

8

Across the bay from *Sapphire II*, eleven o'clock found Stretch pacing nervously in his bedroom at the Modern Hotel—if three steps in either direction can be called pacing. The Modern—built in the euphoria of post-World War I—was now a rather miserable, run-down remnant of faded hopes, but it had the advantage of being cheap. Not flophouse rates—Stretch Jackson was not yet reduced to that—but fourteen dollars a day, sixty-two fifty a week, or two hundred, and a quarter a month. Miscalculating the length of his stay, he had opted for the weekly rate.

In Room 512, Stretch was busy reviewing the various things that were supposed to have occurred during the last few days. His case of nerves was created by the fact that everything was being set up by someone else. The preparations were out of his control, but his neck and fifteen hundred dollars depended on this job. His predicament bugged him, but he knew it was necessary that part of the amazingly intricate web of a professional torch job was neither seen nor arranged by the torch himself.

Larry Eden of Eden's Garden Women's Wear had made a lot of money on miniskirts. When the fashion waned and he was down to selling two a week, he was still long by several hundred skirts. He moved them from the stockroom to dead storage in the basement.

Larry made a handsome profit during the ankle-length coat period, but in time a lot of them got stacked next to the miniskirts. That's the name of the game in ladies' ready-to-wear. Over the years, the basement became a showcase of the outmoded: clothes, gloves, hats, cape-style coats. One of the stock boys kidded about seeing a pair of high-button shoes. Last year had not been a good year. This year was no better, as the full racks upstairs plainly showed. The neighborhood was running down. And Eden wasn't in tune with the times.

Moe was about to help his beleaguered friend. A description, floor plan, and key were all Stretch wanted. He did not want to meet the owner. Pretending to be seeking a dress for his girl friend he had learned all he needed to know about the interior of the store. Moe had given Larry Eden a precise list of instructions.

Three steps, pivot, three steps. The mistake at Bert's weighed heavily on Stretch's mind. This job seemed dead easy, but—about to be a professional—he could not afford to slip up. He reviewed the steps again. Yesterday, Friday morning, a painter had started to refurbish the shelves with a new coat of varnish. At quitting time for the weekend, he had, per Larry's instructions, stored his materials—rags, paints, brushes, and a tarp—in a corner of the cement basement, away from everything but the new tire, which was supposedly for the store's delivery truck. A cardboard box was on hand for him to put the tarp and rags in. Larry had told him where to store the things and had even arranged the box. The painter wasn't about to question a client who insisted on being helpful—most of them were a pain in the neck.

Saturday morning, Moe had gotten a call at the salvage store that everything was ready. The information had been passed to Room 512 at the Modern.

When he closed the store at five on Saturday, the usually stingy Larry Eden had left the air conditioner going "to get rid of the stink of the varnish."

"Good God," Stretch said to his walls. "How could you screw this one up?"

For sentimental reasons he chose 3:00 A.M. as the time to light up. It would make amends for Bert's disaster.

It was 2:20 A.M. when Stretch switched off the light and headed for his target. The creaky elevator descended laboriously and spewed forth its passenger next to the desk where the night clerk and a long-term guest named Shorty were talking. Shorty was not only an insomniac, he was determined to lock everyone into interminable conversations.

"Where you going at this time of night?" Shorty asked.

"Coffee." Stretch was torn between hurrying past the two men and appearing nonchalant. Two witnesses to his exit were not high on his wish list for the moment.

"Great." Shorty sounded delighted. "I'll come along."

Stretch had the terrible feeling that everything was about to go wrong, that Eden was going to become another fiasco like Bert's. "Well," he stammered, "I was . . . actually, I was going to see one of the girls over on Geary Street."

"Hey, Jackson, why don't you bring her back here?" the scruffy night clerk suggested hungrily.

"I ain't gonna drag no hookers with you, Jackson," Shorty objected.

"Well, maybe I'll bring her back, maybe we'll go to her place." Stretch took advantage of Shorty's reticence to mumble a fast good-bye and rush toward the street.

Before he got to the door, Shorty called after him. "Oh, hell, maybe I'll come as far as the Pompon Café."

Without making a scene, there seemed to be no diplomatic escape. Stretch did not see any alternative to setting a fast pace in the direction of the café.

"Boy, you sure are in a hurry," Shorty laughed.

Far too disturbed to make small talk, Stretch let the little man launch into a monologue of epic vulgarity about the local prostitutes. He practically shoved Shorty into the café, then rushed around the corner to double back to his car. The incident had not helped calm his already nervous frame of mind. All I need now, Stretch thought, is to have trouble with the car.

He turned the ignition key, convinced that something would go wrong, but it started smoothly. Shorty had cost him ten minutes of precious time, although he realized he had chosen three o'clock arbitrarily. Stretch pushed his speed to the delicate limit of being noticeably illegal. I don't need a traffic ticket, either, he said to himself.

At 2:50 he quietly slipped through the alley door to Eden's Garden and went down the basement stairs. At least one thing's perfect, he sighed, surveying Eden's arrangements. The brushes, the can in which they were cleaned, and the box with the rags were all there—right up against the tire. The lid on the can of turpentine came off easily. Stretch dipped in a brush, smeared an ample supply on the tire, then on the cardboard box, and carefully replaced the brush and lid. He closed the top flaps of the box and spread a copious trail of lighter fluid from the turpentine-impregnated tire to the closed box.

There was a moment when he stood back and listened. Yes, he could hear the air conditioning running. Eddie Barker had told him, "Get it ventilated. Spread the smoke, because soft goods don't want to burn and you don't want a lot of water stains. Just smoke 'em out. The insurance pays the owner and your man picks up the salvage cheap—if he's made his arrangements right."

Stretch stood still, breathing in the hard-knotted rhythm of fear. This wasn't Bert's; it was a calculated, professional act. He knew it would change what he had been, but he couldn't fathom what it would mean from here on. Confidence waxed and waned in quick surges. "Okay, Tom Farley, or whoever you are. Just try and catch me now." For a moment, he had no doubts. The race was on. The dare was transformed into a little flash of Zippo sparks. A threshold was crossed, and nothing would be the same.

There was a puff of flame. From the stairs Stretch watched until he was certain that the fire was well under way and that the tire would burn. Who was to say it wasn't spontaneous combustion, what with those oily rags closed up in the box like that for a day and a half! The fire would reduce the evidence to ashes.

Stretch left cautiously and drove away. Because he wanted Eden's to smoke, but not burn up, he personally had to be the one to turn in the fire alarm—and at just the right moment. He had carefully located the alarm box. At 3:12, wishing he had a less conspicuous car, he cruised past the store. Excitement rose in his throat when he saw black smoke at the top vent. Then he got a sudden cold chill. It came crashing down on him that he did not know exactly when to sound the alarm. How much smoke was necessary to total the contents? If the floor joists caught fire, the job was blown, but insufficient smoke would be equally disastrous. "Sweet Jesus," he said, trembling.

He stopped the car around the corner. His hands felt clammy; acid filled his stomach. "Don't panic," he muttered inaudibly. He sat in the parked car for several minutes, then cruised past the shop again. Now smoke was coming out in serious quantities. He drove to the fire alarm box, broke the glass, and pulled the handle. He was petrified when the bell started jangling at him from the box—he had thought it would only ring in some distant fire station. Sprinting around the Camaro, he jumped in and sped off. There suddenly seemed to be hundreds of cars on the street. Had his glaring yellow car been seen? Had anyone noticed his Illinois license number?

Ten blocks away the West Alton flash felt like public enemy number one with the F.B.I. hot on his tail. He wheeled to the Pompon Café, with its usual clientele of pimps, prostitutes, and prowlers of the night's wee hours. The instant he walked inside he remembered Shorty and was stabbed by another shot of panic. It was too late to walk out. He glanced around and went limp with relief. Shorty was gone. Stretch headed quickly to the farthest corner of the restaurant and sat down.

Once the coffee stopped making concentric circles in the cup from the tremor of his hands, he managed to get his thoughts in order. He was being stupid. *Some* passerby had to turn in an alarm at a fire. It wasn't necessarily the torch; it could be an honest citizen doing his duty. If he happened to be driving a yellow Camaro, so what? No one would know the record of an anonymous driver of a not uncommon car. No one could guess that the driver had slipped out of the back door of the burning store minutes before.

Stretch regained control and started to chuckle to himself. Christ Almighty! If it's as easy as that—! Fifteen hundred bucks, no overhead, no tax, no social security. A few of those and he could start thinking of racing again. He pulled himself up short. Whoa, Jackson! A couple of those and you quit. How about sticking around this city?

On Sunday morning his first move after coffee was a quick drive past Eden's. The conspicuous yellow Camaro made him distinctly apprehensive as he approached the store, but the street was Sunday-morning empty. He quickly verified that the windows were smoked. Everything looked physically intact. No trash or burning merchandise had been hauled out to the sidewalk. That took some of the pressure off.

When Stretch went to pick up his cash on Monday, Moe's bags were all smiling. "Good job, Jackson," he said.

Stretch Jackson felt very pleased with himself as Moe explained the next project.

* * *

Stretch slipped five hundreds from the manila envelope into his billfold. The grand would go into the safe at the Modern.

Stretch wanted out of this fleabag—badly. He had purchased a Sunday newspaper, and with the room's only window open spent Sunday afternoon going through APARTMENTS FOR RENT—DOWNTOWN AREA. He plotted the possibilities on a city map. Stretch liked downtown. It was without pretensions and allowed him the comfort of anonymity. The grungy part he wanted to escape, but a clean, older building, not too far away from the heart of the city, appealed to him. He had been amazed by the intimacy of San Francisco. In a few minutes he could drive from the bustling seediness of the Tenderloin to the jabber-wocky circus of Union Square; to Chinatown; to the arty, freaky Polk Street and North Beach areas; or to Fisherman's Wharf, the middle-class tourist's dream. The contrasts of races and places made everything he had ever seen look monochrome by comparison. He felt comfortably inconspicuous in this city, as well as intrigued by its cosmopolitan mix. Stretch had yet to discover that San Francisco itself constituted only fifteen percent of the megalopolis which blanketed two hundred miles of shoreline with some five million people. For the moment, the cozy heart of old San Francisco seemed to approach perfection. He had checked off four ads with a right price, right location, and a description that sounded reasonable.

On Monday, with Eden's cash in hand, he chose the one on Powell and made a deposit—it reminded him of home. The living room could have been a little larger but would do. The owner had installed a newish brown couch that contrasted nicely with the cream-colored walls. A few splashes of color, like the orange shades on the big end-table lamps brightened it up a bit. Everything else was nondescript, but clean and not too badly worn.

The kitchen had little hexagonal white ceramic tiles over the porcelain counter and sink. The refrigerator was old and gave off a cross between a wheeze and a death rattle every time the motor stopped.

"Sounds like a terminal case to me."

"Oh, no," the landlord assured him, devoid of all humor. "It'll run good for years. Freezes things right up."

The clincher was a tiny spare bedroom next to the main one. Stretch intended to ask Eddie to stay over if he ever came back on a trip.

By the end of the afternoon, he was out of the Modern and into the admittedly ancient and had stocked the kitchen with the basics of living. Stretch dozed off during the six o'clock news and woke with a start after nine. Once his blood and brain waves were working normally, the sensation of euphoria returned.

A celebration needs people. The Buddha was not open yet, so he decided to kill some time at Delaney's Bar on Union Square. It was the second time he had entered the place. On

Monday night at ten thirty Delaney's was doing less than a booming business, but it was a good halfway point between the solitude of the apartment and the late crowd at Ho's.

Stretch had an aversion to bar stools. He picked a booth along the wall.

A pert and pretty little waitress bounced up to take his order. Her brown skin and freckles announced that she spent her days at the beach, just as her low-cut red silk uniform announced that the freckles continued right down her abundant, squeezed-tight breasts. Everything was mini-dress and maxigirl. Blond ringlets, snub nose, a full but firm form, good legs. Stretch watched her arrive and remembered what was missing from his life.

Four blue eyes locked grips. Stretch didn't know if she meant it or if that was part of her job.

"Hi, I'm Beryl. What'll you have?"

"What kind of a name is that?"

"Corny, isn't it? That's what I got stuck with. We have great whiskey-sodas tonight."

Stretch cocked his head. "What's so different about your whiskey-sodas on Monday?"

"Nothing special. I'm just supposed to push whiskey tonight. You look whiskey-soda-ish."

Beryl put her hand over her mouth, but nothing could hide the size of her grin. They both broke into giggles.

"Whew, I don't believe it. What you got on tap?" His eyes added a sentence when they dropped to her well-creased bosom.

The waitress flushed and stood a little straighter. "Bud," she said, trying to muster a bit of propriety.

"Then Bud it is."

Watching her departure was almost as fascinating as her arrival had been. Stretch suddenly recognized that beyond fulfilling his neglected sexual needs, a girl would make exploring San Francisco far more exciting. For the first time, he wished he had a girl friend—not just a hop in the sack, but a woman who really meant something to him.

"There you are."

Beryl leaned over slightly to put the beer down. The intention of the uniform's design was to convince the customer that everything was about to be revealed. Sooner or later, if she bent over enough, the truth would pop out. A man had to keep ordering to discover if sooner was later. The trick dated back into the antiquity of sales and trade.

Beryl straightened up and glanced at Stretch Jackson's face. She liked it. "Where you from?" she asked.

"Near St. Louis." He'd learned that saying "West Alton" always required a lot of explanation.

"Really! You got to be kidding!" Her voice rose to a squeak. "*I'm* from St. Louis! Kirkwood. You're the first person I've met from St. Louis since I've been here. Wow!"

"You sound homesick."

"Oh, my God, no!" To Stretch's amazement, she plunked down in the booth across from him and rattled on like a machine gun.

"I mean, I got out of art school and got this flunky job back home doing layouts until I couldn't *stand* it anymore, till I had it up to here—or higher. I stuck it out and I stuck it out . . . I'm good, if I do say so myself. I mean I got a diploma in commercial art, after all. I wanted to come here, but my folks wouldn't have it, so I stuck—just wasting away. Finally, I said, 'Listen, Ma, I'm twenty-eight, and everything and everyone around here gives me the willies and I've just had it up to here. I need some fresh air and some sea breeze and no more goddamn cornfields!' And I split! Just bam, wham! And I took my eight hundred dollars out of the bank and got on the train. Ever been on a train? Nobody uses trains anymore. God, they're great! They just *chugga, chugga, chugga*. I love that sound. We got stuck for hours in a blizzard in Green River, Wyoming. It was *so* good! And everything fell just right for me out here. Zappo! I got this cute room and I found all the good little Chinese and Mexican restaurants. Cheap. Boy, you can eat good for cheap here. I just love this city. And I got this job with a big advertising agency and great pay and then I got a really super apartment. Boy, life was a piece of cake!"

As fast as the torrent had come, it left. Beryl stared at the Formica table. In the silence Stretch managed to close his mouth and recover his senses. Maybe the girl's father was an auctioneer.

He asked softly, "Then what?"

"I hate men with thin mustaches! Thank God, you haven't got a thin mustache."

"Well, yeah," he said, thrown completely off guard. "And here I was just thinking I should grow one."

Beryl got back on the tracks. "Well, my boss was a real jerk. Head of graphics. I mean, that thin-mustached slob had forty-seven fingers—all index and all for me! I could have come to work in an armored suit and he'd still have found a crack. One day I decided to have it out with him and I started off, 'Look, I think . . .' and I look down and he's unbuttoning my blouse. I went upstairs and *his* boss says, 'If you make me choose between you and him . . .' So, I quit! I mean, I'm no yard goods store. So, I pound pavement and run plumb outta money and I'm getting desperate. I know Chuckie over there, the piano player. He says, 'Listen, Delaney's isn't much, but it pays!' Not much! Jesus, help me! Look at this place!"

Stretch gritted his teeth to avoid laughing. "How long you been here?"

"This is the second week." She looked down at her breasts. "Look at my poor boobs! It'll take me a month to get the squeeze marks off me. Good grief, am I getting *out* of here! There are two kinds of girls work in bars: the hard-ups just passing through and those who are stuck with it for good. Man, I'm not *that* hard up. You should hear all the crap I have to take. I'm just supposed to smile and listen and see to it they buy lots of drinks. Sounds okay, huh? Well, let me tell you . . . I thought my boss had lots of fingers! At least he was sober. Everybody comes in here's got the hots. They must think it's a whorehouse. Well, man, I got a job starts Wednesday at Bard and Belding Advertising and *whooee*—am I quitting this joint." She caught her breath, regained her composure, and stood right up. "Listen, I've got to fill these glasses or I'll get fired before the night's over—and I need the money. Want another Bud?"

Stretch was too surprised for anything but an affirmative nod. He watched Beryl hurry off, then scootched into the corner of the booth. He somehow felt lumped in with all those patrons with the fingers and the hots.

"Here you go." She bent over, putting the beer and the breasts immediately in front of him again. Stretch had the urge to ask her out, but there was no indication she was interested in more than his geographic origins. She hadn't even asked his name.

"Oh," she said, still leaning forward. "What's your name?"

"Stretch." He felt the sap race from his groin right up to the roots of his hair. "Stretch Jackson."

She held out her hand, "Glad to meet you. Your name's as corny as mine."

The sap retreated. He'd been called lots of things, but . . . corny? Jesus!

"I love people with corny names," she added, "because I've lived with the worst of them all."

"Come on," he said, encouraged again. "Beryl isn't so bad. No worse than Burl Ives and he did all right."

"Sure, except at home they say Beryl like 'barrel' . . . and you wouldn't believe my last name."

"How bad can it be?"

"B-I-E-H-R, pronounced 'beer.' At roll call it was always, 'Biehr, Beryl? Here!' Isn't that the pits?"

"Well, how'd you like to roll it out with me?" He bit his tongue as he said it, but he couldn't resist.

"Couldn't resist it, could you?" She laughed. "That's all right. Nobody can. Anyway, I can't. Can't go out, that is. Don't take it personal. I go home nights with Chuckie, the piano player. Anyway, my fiancé is coming from St. Louis this week. I already don't know what I'm going to do with them both."

"You've got a problem."

"Or they've got a problem. Beryl of fun." She wrinkled her nose at him, laughed, and went to another booth. She didn't come back, even when she wasn't busy. Beryl Biehr. Bard and Belding. Stretch tucked it away in his memory. Someday she might ditch Chuckie *and* her fiancé. He chugged down his beer. She would have been nice, he thought, but that was no reason to spoil his celebration.

He called her over, tipped too generously, and said good-bye.

It was just as Monday-nightish at the Buddha as it had been at Delaney's, and still too early for the entertainment crowd. Stretch felt a little let down as he walked in. He cheered up when he spotted Benny the fence sitting alone at a low table. The chubby man waved him over.

"How you doing?" Benny asked.

"I'm fine. Maybe even better than that."

"You're getting to be as regular here as Eddie was." Benny was one of the social poles of the restaurant. He always had a glad hand, a good joke, and a broad smile—one of those people who made others feel good. His dress was informal, tweedy, a cross between a tout and a gentleman at the races. He could have been the Buddha's social chronicler. That was a fence's nature as well as his job—to know everyone and everything that was going on. Mister go-between.

"If you ever need anything, you know, cheaper than wholesale, Stretch, you let me know."

That made a new regular feel good. It meant he had just been accepted. As he started to sit down, Benny's face clouded over.

"Hey, come here a minute."

Benny got up and led the way to an empty booth. They sat down and the diamonds flashed as the fat hand whipped the curtains closed.

"You came in with Eddie a lot before he left." The tone was confidential. "You guys just buddies or are you in the same business? A guy wants to know who he's talking to, you understand. I mean, I don't go blabbing it around. It's just between you and me. But over the years, I threw Eddie some nice jobs."

"You got it." Given the events of the weekend, it couldn't hurt to toot his own horn a little, even if he turned down the work. "I came in to take Eddie's place. He was number one, you know."

"I know. He was pretty picky about what he took. I didn't give him the little ones or the shitty ones once I caught on."

"Well, he and I are in the same league," Stretch said, playing along with the game. Curiosity got the better of him. "What do you do with the junk fires?"

The corners of Benny's mouth went up. "Oh, I keep my ear to the ground and find them a home. Do what I do and you get all kinds of connections. On the other hand, when you play the middle of the street, you learn not to give out any secrets. Like they said in World War Two, 'The walls have ears.' You never know when some jerk is going to get in a bind and turn into a squeaker at the cop shop. Guys trust me because they know I know what I can say to who. That's why I get more info than anyone, including the chief of police. I'm the central clearinghouse around here."

Stretch had hoped for some details. He wondered if Benny, with all of his connections, could help arrange some kind of verifiable—but phantom—work as his cover for torching. It did not seem to be the moment to ask, but he moved his need for a convincing alibi to the front of his priorities.

"Listen," Benny continued. "I always say what we do is just like doctors. There's guys who are in general practice and guys who specialize. There's doc's like the one fixed up my girl friend—all he does is shrink noses and blow up tits. He wouldn't take a night call for a million bucks. Then there's others." He chortled. "Like—well, my weight, you know—I sit a bit heavy. I had to go to see a guy spends his life looking up assholes." The double chin jiggled. "You imagine that? There's a million ways to make a buck. Some guys care, some guys don't. A job's a job."

"Right on." Stretch felt obliged to say something, though he was not sure he liked the comparison.

"I think of myself as an S.P.C.A. for lost objects, matching the wayward with the needy. You know how many insurance people would go on the dole if people stopped stealing things?" Benny's paunch joined his chins in the chuckle. "Either it's the insurance rates go up or the unemployment tax." He slapped his ringed fingers on the table. "Comes to the same thing! C'mon, let's get where the action is." Benny stopped short, half standing. "I take you for a straight-up guy, Stretch. You ever need any information, right from the P.D., inside, you tell me. I'll get it." He stood and flipped open the curtains.

Instantly they were spotted by Caruso, who rushed in the direction of the booth. Handsome Caruso looked as tough as a wrestler, but actually he wouldn't hurt a flea. His father had been too young for the first wave of Italian immigrants, but he had made it out of joblessness in Otranto by sailing off to the New World. Young, single, and eager, he had feasted his eyes on the beacon of Liberty, which welcomed him to the Land of Opportunity. His liner hooted up to the Manhattan dock at nine in the morning. It was October 29, 1929. It was also terrible timing. By nightfall, umpteen brokers and investors had jumped out of Wall Street windows and the Great Depression was on.

Raised in the squalid back of a South Chicago bakery shop, Tony Bertolucci learned to sing. His father always said, "You'll die in this country if you can't sing." By his teens, the boy's voice had been fashioned into a brilliant tenor. Everyone called him Caruso.

Mama Bertolucci dreamed that her son would be a famous singer. For better or worse, young Caruso had an uncle, Mario, who lived on the other side of Cicero. Mario was a bookie, and his were the footsteps Caruso followed. He became so adept at picking winners that he finally just followed the horses and became a professional turfside gambler. In a way, it was a shame. He had the looks, the physique, *and* the voice to make a great tenor.

Caruso stopped two steps away from Stretch and Benny and startled everybody in the Buddha by breaking into an aria from *The Barber of Seville*. The words were slightly changed: "Stradella in the first race, Little Jimbo in the third. Sherwood Forest in the fifth. And I've a-wonna the quinella, the quinella—the quinella I've a-won!" He grabbed Benny and gave him a fat kiss on each cheek. Mirth and applause resounded throughout the restaurant.

"Come on," the elated singer said, "let's do the town. Drinks on me."

"That's just what I was looking for!" Stretch said eagerly. He'd come for a celebration, after all.

Three hours and three bars later, the world looked ninety proof. Caruso had sung arias from operas ranging from *Lucia di Lammermoor* to *II Trovatore* via *Don Giovanni* and *The Marriage of Figaro*. Benny told jokes till their sides were sore. Stretch was the joyful spectator, although he concluded opera was not something he would ever pay to see. Maybe, he thought, you had to be Italian.

Finally, it became mellow chitchat, and eventually Benny left Stretch and Caruso at a table in the Five Aces.

A bit groggily, Caruso asked, "What do you do, Stretch?"

In a like condition Stretch answered, "Torch."

"Hmm. That's a good business."

"Yep. Maybe not as fat as winning quinellas. Good business. Yep." He got his eyes focused on Caruso, then wondered foggily if he should have said it.

9

When Benny pulled him aside one night and said he knew someone who needed a job done, Stretch had doubts.

"What do you know about it?" he asked warily.

"Why, I don't know anything about it." Benny looked slightly offended. "I just put people together. I'm not into their business deals."

"Well, yeah, but you have to know enough to filter out the junk."

"I thought you'd just trust me." Benny's face softened and he said sheepishly, "You're just like Eddie. He didn't trust nobody either."

"It's not personal."

"I know. Okay. It's some kind of small factory or something. It's unoccupied. Guy can't rent it. He wants it disposed of. That's all I know, except that the owner's straight." He held out a piece of paper. "Here's the guy's name and number. The rest is up to you." He cocked one of his oversize eyebrows. "By the way, I guess you understand—I get ten percent. Whatever your fee is—I trust you."

It was Stretch's turn to feel defensive. He slapped Benny's pudgy shoulder. "Get off it. Could I cheat you out of a nickel?"

The sparrowlike owner of the building assured Stretch that he had never done such a thing before. The building had stood empty for eighteen months and he was afraid it was too old to rent again without more fixing up than he could afford.

In its present state he would have to give it away. A friend of a friend of a friend had suggested . . .

Too naive to know if the story were a lie or not, Stretch decided it didn't really make a difference. He was stuck in this city until he made some money—and this man's cash was as bankable as anyone else's.

The building was a one-story former factory that barely filled one quarter of the block. It was protected by a six-foot chain-link fence that had been broken through in one corner—no doubt by neighborhood boys who played ball in the large parking lot. Some of the windows were knocked out, which gave the place a forlorn look.

Burning a building wasn't the same as making salvage. It wouldn't be as easy. Then Stretch looked at the building again and suddenly laughed. A crowbar! A crowbar, five gallons of gas, and the cover of night were all any idiot needed. For once it wasn't necessary to hide the fact that it was arson. The more it looked like a crude arson job, the better. The owner could lean on his righteous indignation and scream about vandals, crime in the city, the breakdown of juvenile morals.

He decided to demand twenty-five hundred dollars and give five to Benny. He had forgotten to ask Eddie the price structure on one-shot work like this, but he decided his fencey friend would hardly disapprove of the generosity!

The night of the light he parked his Camaro and walked two blocks to the building. In his right hand was a five-gallon can of gas; in his left a crowbar and a plastic sack. He let himself in with the key the owner had provided. With the crowbar he marked the door so it would clearly look as though it had been jimmied open. With professional foresight Stretch had already half-filled the small plastic sack with gasoline and sealed it before he left his apartment. He coolly spread the gas from the can all over the place, casually leaving the container in the middle of a puddle and the bag a few feet away from the puddle's edge. He took a birthday candle from his shirt pocket and skillfully softened its bottom with the Zippo flame, then stuck the candle upright on the bag of gas and—at 2:55 A.M.

92

sharp—lit it. Stretch walked out knowing that in about five minutes the candle flame would be reduced to a burning wick in a puddle of hot wax, melt a hole in the plastic bag, release the gasoline, and the whole place would go up in a devastating blaze. The night breeze through the open door and broken windows would provide enough venting to avoid the premature ignition of the gas fumes.

As he twisted through the opening in the fence he looked back and remembered Bert's words: "Foolproof and tax-free."

For the first time, Stretch felt confident about a bum. He sat in his car on a side street thinking. Whether this was temporary work or not, he had decided to follow his father's motto: Do it right, be the best. He should take Eddie's advice about learning the trade. The first step was to know his adversary. He waited to see how long firemen would take to respond. They arrived at three fifteen, sirens howling in the night.

At three thirty, Stretch drove the yellow car innocently toward the fire scene. The number of spectators surprised him. The same force that held Tom Farley, that pulled this crowd of curious onlookers together, also began to tighten its grip on Stretch. Watching the fire, he found both his guilt and contentment were drowned in a flood of excitement. His blood skyrocketed through his system. Just as Eddie Barker had told him—torching had all the thrills of racing cars.

Given the size and condition of the building, it was beyond repair shortly after the fire started. For the firemen, there was not much strategy involved, other than sitting back and dousing the flames with high-volume water.

Until now Stretch had always thought there were just two kinds of fire engines—those with ladders and those without. As he surveyed the equipment closely, it dawned on him that almost every vehicle was different. He did his best to fade into the onlookers as he tried to figure out the multitude of different features. The machines fell into three categories. Those that seemed primarily to be for pumping water had a minimum of hoses and gadgets and supported only small, hand-carried hoses. One of these, way up the street, clearly served as a simple booster from a distant hydrant to front-line vehicles.

Ladder trucks were the second kind of unit. Their ability to elevate was designed for sending a stream of water up to a multistoried building or over a roof, as well as for rescue work above the ground floor. Using ladder trucks seemed to be a case of overkill on a one-story building, but Stretch assumed that if that was the equipment the Fire Department owned, that was what they had to use.

The third type of truck was the sort from which most of the fire hoses were pulled. Here the dazzle and diversity were the greatest. These trucks had more lights, dials, knobs, levers, and chromed gimmicks than all of the others combined.

The firemen had settled comfortably into fighting the blaze. There was no panic; no lives were at stake. They had their positions and were holding steady. Stretch realized that other people were ogling the equipment, some from very close. Why not me, he thought, and moved in. He sidled up to a complicated-looking control panel, trying to read the mass of gauges. A fireman was standing there, observing the flames, with his back to the pair of blue eyes that squinted at the instruments.

Tank to Pump, Stretch read, *Discharge One*. Suddenly, the fireman turned toward him. A warning shot through Stretch's body. It was unnecessary. The man gave him a nod and a friendly grin of greeting.

"Uh, complicated truck you've got here."

The fireman laughed. "It's not a truck. The ones with ladders are called trucks. This is called—well, it has three names really. Sometimes you'll say the 'engine,' sometimes the 'pumper,' or else the 'rig.' All the same thing. But never the 'truck.' That's only ladders."

Guilty from every angle, Stretch mustered a smile. "But your engine still looks damn complicated to me."

Pushing his hat back a bit, the man looked the intruder over questioningly. All right, he concluded, here's a member of the public to educate till the fire cranks down. He checked the control panel to make certain that everything was as it should be. "I'm the engineer. Driver of an engine is called the engineer, because he's responsible for all the controls and maintenance on the fireground. Not really complicated, a rig like this. It's just a pump on wheels. This model costs eighty-nine grand."

"Jesus Christ!"

The engineer appreciated Stretch's surprise. He got that response every time. "Yes, and without a pump it's not worth two bits. All the rest of this is just supporting gadgets for the pump. It's like a heart hidden in there. The unit is so big because it has to transport the men, the equipment to support the men, and hoses to carry the pump's water."

He started explaining the maze of dials, knobs, and levers on the control panel. Stretch looked and listened with greater interest than the average citizen.

"We got a five-hundred-gallon tank on board, so the minute we hit a fire we can start pumping, even before we're hooked to a hydrant. Also, that's all it takes for little fires—trash, kitchens, things like that. Saves hooking up. These are all pump controls: preheating, priming, cooling. This big five-inch suction line comes in from the hydrant and this vacuum gauge tells me how much is coming through it. The lever here diverts water from the tank to the pump. Those lights tell me what the level in the tank is. Now, this particular baby will pump out a total of twelve hundred fifty gallons a minute. That's five tons of water every sixty seconds. It's driven by a two-hundred-fifty-horse motor. All the rest of these dials and things tell me what I can do with the water. I can run it out of five different lines, from one-inch to two-and-a-half-inch-diameter hose. It tells me how much pressure I've got in each discharge outlet in pounds per square inch. These levers control each line's water."

"So it really tells you how much is coming in and available, then how much is going out and where, plus the condition of the pump and engine." Stretch's mechanical mind cut through to the essential simplicity of what had seemed so complex.

"You got it. Of course, this is just a standard piece of equipment. Hell, they got a huge baby in New York City called the Super Pumper. Now, I'd like to see that mother operate. It tosses out eighty-eight hundred gallons a minute. That's thirty-seven tons. It'll throw water the length of two football fields." The fireman's eyes gleamed just thinking about it.

"That would make some shower!" Stretch remarked, convinced that such a monster would be able to snuff out his little fire in a few seconds. He was glad the Super Pumper was three thousand miles away—and wondered if Eddie had run up against it yet.

"The rest of the rig here just hauls around hose, oxygen tanks and masks, nozzles, couplings, and the small stuff you need inside like pickaxes, cellar pipes, shovels—all that stuff. Of course, there are lots of special rigs. That one over there has a heavy duty nozzle built right onto the truck. It's called a deck gun and really large capacity nozzles like that we call a water cannon. Any nozzle permanently mounted on the equipment's referred to as a monitor. There are several engines in town known as deluge wagons. They'll shoot up to three thousand gallons a minute as far as twelve hundred feet—that's damn near a quarter mile.

"I guess there's a lot of different-looking pieces of equipment, all right, but mostly they're variations on the same thing: a bunch of men trying to get enough water in the right place to drown a fire. Some fires are high up, some could explode, so you got to keep a distance. There's lots of different situations. Using different trucks or even different nozzles, you get different results. There are hand-held lines and mounted monitors. Monitors shoot what's called a master stream, because they're more powerful than what you can hand hold—"

"Jim . . ." The radio crackled.

The engineer stepped over to the two-way radio on the control panel.

The torch who had set all of this red and chrome into action decided he had better end the lesson before the engineer began to ask *him* questions. The functions and strategies of all the firemen still remained mysterious to him, but perhaps, he thought, the technique of firefighting is no more complicated than the trucks themselves. He looked at everything battling the blaze. The array of equipment that had responded to his fire left him very impressed. He had obviously stirred up millions of dollars' worth of material.

Stretch tapped the fireman on the shoulder, mouthed a "Thanks," and, with a wave, moved back into the crowd.

The novice was beginning to get an idea of what he was up against. It was not easy to burn a building to the ground, and his opposition were not beginners. The flames still leaped skyward, but the smoke had turned from black to gray to white as water got to the fire's source.

At the height of the roaring and crackling, Stretch, exhilarated, tore his eyes away from the battle and started watching watchers. Some were neighbors, sleepy-eyed, hastily dressed. Stretch guessed there were others who just followed fires. That one over there, for example.

Circumspectly, Stretch edged closer to study the man. Something about the way he looked rang a bell. In his thirties, blond, with a pretty-boy face and a weight lifter's build, he stood back from the others, under a tree, as though he were hiding. If Stretch hadn't known that he had lit the fire himself, he would have suspected this man was the torch. His face was transformed by the blaze he was watching. The man wore the rapturous expression of a true believer at a midnight mass.

Stepping closer, he saw that the young blond was so hypnotized by the leaping flames that he was momentarily blinded to everything else. For a minute Stretch wondered if he were praying, lost in some sublime state of grace. Then the "look" snapped into place. Sergeant Hager, that was it, Walter Hager. Walt Hager had had that look of glazed ecstasy after he machine-gunned a whole family. He had it every time he killed, soldiers or civilians, and he had killed them every time he could. Hager had been unhinged—sadistic gone completely psycho. Everyone had hated him. The captain had finally shipped him out.

Stretch closed in, then stopped when he realized the hand in the blond man's pocket was pumping an erection. Fury raced through every fiber of Stretch Jackson. The man under the tree was jerking off at *his* fire!

A couple of steps and he closed the gap. "You fucking creep!" Stretch spat. "Get the hell out of here!" His voice slammed like a door.

The blond was jolted out of his dream. As he lurched backwards in surprise, a silver fireman's badge on a long chain swung out of his open shirt front. His angelic look twisted into a mask of hate. For once, it was not a moment when he had expected to be noticed. "You son-of-a-bitch," he snarled, "I'll get you—" He stopped short, realizing that several people had turned to see what the commotion was.

Stretch instantly recognized Marty Martin. His personal rage turned to professional disgust. "A third-rate torch and a freak to boot," he said, ice cold. "It's because you keep your mind on your cock instead of your business, Martin. I said haul ass! Unless you want it between your teeth!" Stretch was instinctively certain Marty was a coward, and that the weightlifter muscles were a facade to cover up his weakness.

"I don't know who you are," Marty hissed, "but I'll remember you, asshole." He backed off and, as Stretch had expected, Martin spun and stamped off.

Glaring at the retreating figure, it dawned on Stretch that he had just experienced a touch of professional pride as a torch. He vowed not to let that attitude settle into his thinking. For just a moment he had doubts about the wisdom of making an enemy out of Marty, but then he figured it would not matter—he had no intention of staying in the business long enough to cross tracks with Marty Martin again.

* * *

The months quickly turned into money—$1,500, $3,000, $4,500. Stretch managed to salt away a good part of it. He had set his goal: At $10,000, he would quit. That was enough to buy a few cars, fix them up, sell them, and build his way back into owning a car lot. Some spot around San Francisco's sparkling bay would suit him perfectly. His flirtation with the city was turning into a love affair.

Moe's fifth fire was lit at three in the morning, as usual. Stretch went back to his apartment, sipped a cup of coffee, and headed for bed. He had noticed that caffeine affected night people less than those who kept the usual hours. He also found that there was more night owl in him than he had ever suspected. Going to bed at four or five in the morning had become a comfortable routine.

At nine o'clock that morning, he was rudely awakened by the phone.

"This is Moe. Get your ass down here—right now!"

"Wha—"

"Never mind—just get it here!"

The phone was slammed down on the other end. Bleary-eyed, Stretch shaved, brushed his teeth, and left.

When he walked into the office, Moe barked, "Shut the door."

Stretch complied.

"You dumb bastard! You burned the whole place down! Now Meyer's got no business and I got no salvage."

"Well, Jesus . . ."

"'Well, Jesus'? That all you can say? You got a brass brain! I thought you were Eddie quality. Now you listen to me, buster—if you don't know your business, get your ass outta here. I ain't gonna lose my reputation—or go to jail—for some half-ass torch."

"It's an art, not a science, Moe. I don't run the fire department. They fuck up and let one go crazy—I can't control that. I mean, the others were okay and the rest will be. I can't give you a written guarantee any more than Eddie could have."

"I don't want a guarantee, I want salvage. You can't handle it, say so."

"Well, I sure won't charge you for Meyer's."

"Do me a favor! You'd get blood out of a stone easier!" Moe said it so hard all of his bags went rigid. He fished a new cigar out of his box, then relaxed. "Here, for God's sake. Have one."

"Thanks. I mean, I hate losing one just as much as you do. I set them up so they shouldn't get out of control. But if those fire guys blow it completely . . . Shit, I'm really sorry. Was he insured?"

"Was he insured? What do you think, you . . ."

"I mean to cover the whole thing?"

"Yeah, I guess so. Maybe Meyer should take an early retirement. His ticker's lousy anyway." Moe had lost his anger and couldn't work it back up. "Look," he said in his standard rasp, "what you say makes sense. But I want you to watch your ass from now on because mine depends on it. Now get it outta here. I got work. I'll call you."

As Stretch left Moe's office, doubts popped circuits all over his brain. Should he quit now? There was more money under the mattress than he had had when he'd left West Alton in such a hurry. And do what? Bum around? Can't send any money home at this rate. Meyer lost his whole business because . . . because he may have had something in the attic above the ceiling joists that burned faster than usual. How long *did* the firemen take? Really, he was an amateur. The only arrival he had timed was on the night he had seen Marty Martin.

What Stretch wished most was to have Eddie Barker in town. For all the people he met at the Buddha, there was not one who fell into the category of a friend—not one he wanted to see in the daytime, and certainly no one who could give him lessons in lighting fires.

On the way to the apartment he drove past a game parlor, stopped, went in, and beat the bejesus out of half the games in sight. It was not up to Broadway Game's standards, but he hardly noticed.

In the living room the TV flipped on, a beer bottle top flipped off, and a tormented soul flopped down on the couch. Mercifully, indecision cannot go on forever.

Stretch picked up the phone and dialed New York. He didn't like telephones and never knew what to say after the first thirty seconds. It just wasn't like talking face-to-face. He and Eddie had talked often by phone but never about business—they shared the standard law breakers' paranoia about tapped phone lines. But at least Eddie could reassure him.

There was no answer. Eddie didn't work in New York alone; that was his base for the whole East Coast. Big time.

Stretch's dejection lasted only briefly. By midnight he had turned in his first false alarm.

His arm resting on the Camaro's steering wheel, Stretch popped his chewing gum and squinted at his radium watch dial. The siren went quiet when the truck reached the box. Four and a half minutes. Fast!

The firemen looked in vain for the fire, but then they wasted a couple of hours a day on idiots who turned in false alarms.

In the next few nights irritated firemen across the city ran for over thirty false alarms. By then Stretch had a fix on timing.

Meanwhile, he decided an investment was necessary. Even if his career in arson was to be short, it had to be taken seriously. He drove to an auto radio shop and left with the capability of tuning in to the Fire Departments' wavelengths. That set up Stretch's next step into the fire world. He followed trucks to the sites of real fires and paid careful attention to the procedures. He needed to know what firefighters did once they hit the fireground.

One fire chief seemed to arrive for each three vehicles. The chief took command, and the first chief in continued to command in the case of small fires. In a more important blaze the second chief commanded the rear, the next two the flanks. If it was a real conflagration, a battalion chief arrived and formulated the overall strategy. The prime responsibility of the ladder crew seemed to be forcible entry, rescue, and ventilating the building. Men from the pumpers protected steps and stairwell accesses so that the engine firemen could do their job and get the lines in.

Why they were always chopping holes in roofs and breaking windows puzzled Stretch for a while. Perhaps, he thought, they got a kick out of it, like a driver does in a demolition derby. Since the men would make a hole in a roof and not even bother to stick a nozzle in, it was clearly for some purpose other than access to the interior.

One afternoon Stretch was lounging at home, doodling houses with smoke curling out of them. Country music from WSAN filled the living room. Suddenly, the secret of fire and the firemen's obsession with chopping holes in roofs came clear. Stretch stared at the boxlike house he had drawn. "Idiot!" He swore at himself. "Of course!"

A building is like a box. Heat rises. Hot air and gas move upward and collect at the top of the structure. When the temperature rises to a certain point it could get hot enough to start a second fire in the things above the primary flames, because given a certain heat, anything that is combustible will ignite. It's temperature that causes a flame to start.

Stretch slapped the arm of the sofa in delight. He went to the kitchen to celebrate with a beer. Perhaps, he reasoned, he'd finally figured out why Meyer's second floor had caught fire. Maybe there had been things up there with a low combustion point, and as the heat had risen, a second fire had started spontaneously, with nothing ever being directly touched by the flames from below. Trapped heat builds up at the top and backs down from the ceiling. Once it finds something with a low ignition point you have a new fire. The firemen were making holes just to let the heat rise out so the upper areas didn't catch.

Stretch gloated over having discovered this essential principle. It would be very useful either in controlling a salvage fire or making a whole building go down.

That day Stretch tried to reconstruct everything Eddie had told him over two months ago. Bit by bit, he winnowed out most of it and wrote it in a notebook. In the margins he jotted down new ideas, techniques, and materials. He charted fire-houses on maps. The last time he had shown such enthusiasm was when he had started racing. But in his zealous quest to master arson, Stretch failed to notice the inexorable deepening of his commitment to the torch's trade.

* * *

Stretch was sitting in a booth at the Buddha with Caruso and Sweet Pea, the forger, when Benny came over and whispered, "Get in touch with my lawyer. He's got a gift for you. Here's his address."

The attorney explained that on behalf of a client he needed to eliminate an empty three-story frame house. He also mentioned, in passing, that such burdens befell him from time to time. It seemed like a good connection.

Within the week, Stretch left the lawyer's office counting hundreds. Eddie was right, he concluded, stuffing the money into a pocket. All sorts of things pop up. He bounded down the stairs and into the street feeling confident and light of heart. The ten thousand dollars seemed to be just around the corner.

10

Stretch walked into Moe's and the University of Illinois gym flashed through his mind. Moe's glass offices on the mezzanine reminded him of the news and broadcast booths hung behind the bleachers. Stretch had played there once in the state basketball tournament. West Alton had lost, first round, but it had still been a thrill.

The first step into the junk pile of Moe's private office invariably destroyed the illusion. No self-respecting reporter would set foot in the place. A little earlier Moe had phoned and asked Stretch to come by. Now Moe was standing up, stuffing cigars in his pocket.

"Okay, what's the burning issue of the day?" Stretch inquired.

"You got enough corn to sell surplus to the Russians! Want a cigar?"

"Sure. You going someplace?"

"Suddenly I got to go make a bid on some fire salvage. Come along. I can tell you in the car why I called."

Driving through light traffic, Moe exposed their next fire plan—a burn on a warehouse with television and stereo goods.

From the street it wasn't hard to determine that The Fashion Center was what had brought them to the area. The window of the front door was boarded up, the others were smoked. It was the first time Stretch had been on a fire site *after* the fact. It gave him a pleasant, lightheaded feeling even though it was not his fire.

Two steps inside the blackened door, Moe stopped and looked around. "Somebody really wanted to burn this place down. The firemen must have got here too fast, otherwise there wouldn't be any salvage."

Stretch whispered, "See? What'd I tell you? You can't control them all."

Moe looked reproachful. "Who knows, maybe the fire was accidental. Happens, you know." Suddenly he stopped in his tracks, turned to Stretch, and said in a low voice, "Goddamn! How'd you like to meet the enemy?"

"Huh?"

"Tom Farley. That's Tom Farley back there. Best arson specialist in the world. Regular one-man F.B.I. If you're gonna be the best, kid, that's who you'll run up against. Come on. He's an old friend of mine."

"Hey, Moe, wait!" Stretch's blood ran cold, then hot at the idea of meeting Farley face-to-face. But Moe was already huffing down the aisle, letting off cigar smoke like a steam engine. There was nothing for Stretch to do but muster up his courage and follow in Moe's wake. He half expected to see a man who breathed fire like a dragon.

"Heya, Tom," said Moe from a distance. Up close, he stuck out one hand to shake, the other held out a cigar. "Have a cigar. How they treatin' ya?"

"Thanks, Moe. It's rocking along. You bidding?"

"Yeah," Moe grunted. "If there's anything in this mound of junk worthwhile."

The back of the store was not badly damaged. Farley was surrounded by small mountains of stock; stacks of clothes, shoes, and boxes were lying neatly everywhere.

"Hey, I want you to meet my new assistant, Stretch Jackson."

Tom rose. "About time you admitted you need help. Hi, Stretch, glad to meet you. Welcome to the world of scorch."

Nodding a little stiffly, Stretch looked around. "Bit of a mess! When did it happen?" He fought to breathe evenly.

"Ten days ago."

"Moe says you investigate fires."

"He's the best there is," Moe interrupted.

"Aw, I plug at it."

"Well, it looks like you landed a corker here."

Tom scratched under his hat. "This one? No, this one's easy. Real amateur job."

That assessment interested a budding burner. "You mean you know how it started?" Intrigue began to replace anxiety.

Moe smiled. He had suspected they would hit it off. "Listen, kid. You gonna be in the business, you need to know something about his end of it. I'll let you listen to the master a while. Me, I heard him already. I'll get started on this stuff."

Stretch caught the double-edged "be in the business" Moe had thrown at him. He said, mockingly, "Gee willikers, Moe, you're a great boss. On-the-job training *and* free cigars."

"Watch him, Tom—he's smart at both ends." Moe wrinkled his bags into a smile and walked off.

Turning back to Tom, Stretch repeated his question. His curiosity was piqued. "You mean you know who started it?"

"I don't know *who* started it. Not yet anyway. But it's dead easy to figure how it was done. Here, look." He walked to the center of the store.

Stretch followed, already spellbound.

"See there? That's where it started." Tom scraped the burned wood floor with his foot.

"All looks the same to me."

"No. Started here. Used a paraffin-based fluid. Then it went up here. He lit another over here . . ."

"Jesus, how can you tell all that?"

Bending down, Tom dug his pocketknife into the wood. "See how that wood's all crackled there? Called alligatoring. Over here, just a foot away, the wood's burned but flat, even. That means something not ordinary made this alligatored place get hotter, burn deeper. See? You can even follow the alligator trail on the floor."

"But how can you tell it's paraffin?"

"Burn rate . . . depth . . . smell . . . pattern. You get used to it. Some things you can tell right off. Others you poke and probe for, or use the spectrograph. No, this one's easy. I'm not here for that. It'd insult my intelligence."

Mystified, Stretch asked, "What are you here for, then?"

"That!" Tom pointed to the piles of clothing he'd been sorting. "The list's loaded. It's probably all stolen goods. Remind me to mention that to Moe. This stuff's liable to get held up for evidence. It doesn't tally with the inventory so the damn insurance adjuster's got to be in on the deal. He sent in an okay of the sheet and figured no one would check."

"A crooked insurance man?" Stretch said, surprised. "But he hired . . . Who hires you? I thought company guys call you in. Man's not going to blow the whistle on himself is he?"

"Home office." Tom sat, ready to continue inventorying while he talked. "I got wind of this six months ago on a big loss. Told the fire claims manager to keep his eyes open. Figured one of his adjusters wasn't straight."

"Can you nail the guy on this?"

"Can't jail him," Tom said, with evident regret, "but the companies will bust their butts where the police won't—the company has money involved. Big money. It's just a job to the cops. No, the laws are bad. Arson is the toughest crime on the books for getting a conviction. But we can blackball an inside adjuster, run him out of the business, at least. Then the company won't pay the insured. If the owner's not clean, he'll usually drop it before he'll go to trial. Make a lot of noise, maybe, but if he knows we've got the goods, he'll back off." Tom looked up and caught Stretch in the eye. "And then sometimes . . . we get one."

Stretch felt a chill run up his spine. He wondered if Tom would ever get *him*. The hair bristled on the back of his neck. He found the P.I. smart and likable, but the situation gave him a distinctly unpleasant sense of foreboding. It was like staring down a rattlesnake, not knowing if it would strike or crawl away.

"You know anything at all about fire?" Tom inquired.

"Well"—Stretch swallowed his pride—"I've watched logs burn in a fireplace a lot."

"No, you haven't. Wood doesn't burn." Tom smiled at Stretch's surprise. "Nothing solid burns. It decomposes with heat and gives off gases. What looks like burning wood or paper or anything else solid is really the gases burning. They surface, find oxygen, and catch fire. It's a chemical process called pyrolysis."

"Come again?"

"Okay. Start from scratch. Take the fire triangle. It takes three things to make a fire: fuel, oxygen, and heat. That's what we call the fire triangle in the trade. It could rain gasoline, but you wouldn't have a fire without heat. Pine will ignite at four hundred forty-six degrees, Douglas fir at five hundred, redwood at five seventy-two. But you can heat them to twice that and not get fire in a vacuum tank without oxygen. But when the triangle is completed by some event—accidental or intentional—then you get combustion. Slow combustion gives you decomposition of the material, and as either the time or heat increases, you'll get ignition and flaming combustion of the gas that's given off. If one of the legs of the triangle is short—not enough oxygen, say—you'll never get a fire no matter how much fuel there is."

Stretch had already learned that lesson at Bert's.

"Now, if the triangle is completed intentionally—like when we light a cigarette or the furnace or the trash pile—that's fine. If it's closed by an honest accident, that's still okay. But if it is done with willful and malicious intent, that is arson. My job is to find out what or who closed the triangle. Then if I have reason to think it's a case of arson, so far as I'm concerned, there's a kind of personal second triangle: the arsonist, the firemen—and me."

"How do you ever find out who closed the triangle in a mess like this? I mean, to arrest somebody?"

Still working the inventory, Tom talked on. "It's not as easy to burn a building as you might think. Especially without leaving tracks. The law assumes that a fire was accidental unless I can prove it was not. That means every possibility of an accident has to be ruled out *and* a nonaccidental fire ruled in. So I have to show where it started and how it started and also exclude every other possibility. This one's easy. But say the roof had come down. Somewhere under it that same pattern of alligatoring would be present. I'd have to take it all apart, layer by layer, to find the point of origin. Sometimes a witness or the firemen can tell you where it began, but if not you have to dig for it. An intentional fire almost always involves something we call an accelerant—like gasoline, alcohol, charcoal starter—something that will raise the temperature fast and keep it there long enough for the building to give off its heat. A candle flame burns at twelve to seventeen hundred degrees. Hold it to a big splinter of wood and the wood *absorbs* heat. At about four hundred degrees the wood begins decomposing and darkening—that's an endothermic reaction. Depends on the kind of wood, but somewhere between six and nine hundred degrees it's producing enough burning gas that it begins giving off more heat than it absorbs. Then it's in the exothermic stage."

"But if you hold a candle to this wood floor it'll never catch, will it?"

"Right. That's why you need an accelerant. There are whole books on the subject, but, in a nutshell, an arsonist has to start his fire with something that is highly combustible. The area where he places it is going to show—in a special kind of alligatoring, or a V-pattern on the walls, or a color indication on anything metal that the accelerant touches. The damage is usually greatest where the fire started. Light bulbs may point to where it started . . ."

"What?"

"Sure. The glass on the side of the bulb nearest to where the first strong heat came from will sometimes start melting and will bulge out and point like a finger in the direction of the fire's original source. Glass talks. Lots of times you can tell if a fire built up slowly or fast and how hot it got simply by checking the different glass reactions around a building.

Floors normally have different damage from ceilings, since heat goes up. I look for multiple points of origin, because that either means the fire was set or that the temperature got high enough to cause a flashover."

"What's that?"

"The temperature gets so high that something will just flash into flames, even if it's not in direct contact with the rest of the fire."

So that *was* why Meyer lost the whole building, Stretch thought, glad to have the confirmation. He listened eagerly as Farley sketched in the nature of their mutual specialty.

"Finally," Tom said, leaning back to rest a moment, "we have a bit of technology on our side. Since heat decomposes things and makes them give off their gases, I can scrape samples into a can. At the lab they superheat the cans, stick in a big syringe needle, draw off some gas, put it into a gas chromatograph, and get an analysis of the contents. If I did that with a bit of that alligatored wood over there, they could tell from the gaseous traces left in the ash exactly what kind of fluid the torch used to get this bonfire going. I know it all looks like a charred wreck to you, but usually there's enough left to figure out the hows and whys.

"If I prove it was accidental, that's as satisfying as proving it wasn't. But if I can prove it was arson, that's only the beginning. It's nice to show motive, but I'm *obliged* to show intent to burn, and *who* intended to burn the place, as well as *how* they did it. One loophole and I'm out of the game. There are a lot of links along the line where the chain can break. There aren't many really good arsonists, but nailing even the bad ones is complicated by the nature of the crime and the complexity of the law." He heaved a sigh. "Now, when you find a first-rate torch, one who knows electricity and surface-to-volume and temperature/materials tables, things like the nature of fire flow and spread rates—that is a challenge. Rare, but fascinating—from my point of view, anyway."

"So you have to know how everything burns."

"And at what temperatures. For instance, a wire that's pitted, fused, or balled at the end of a break had electrical damage. It was done by something like a short circuit. Then I have to find the source and see if the short was an accident or arranged. On the other hand, if the break in the wire has pointed ends, an exterior fire burned it through, so I'm not looking at an electrical source. These things head me in directions. They are clues, but I have to find them, put them together, and build up a provable case. Take a fire that allegedly started from spontaneous combustion. Everybody knows oily rags will auto-ignite. I had a guy who carefully set up a torch job and used a stack of rags to start it with. After the fire, he was pointing to them. 'Spontaneous combustion,' he said. That was perfectly possible. I took the ashes to the lab. The traces were all hydrocarbon. Oily, okay. Motor oil. Gasoline. All petroleum oils. Oily rags don't auto-ignite if it's petroleum oils. Has to be an unsaturated vegetable oil. The guy's fire burned the house just like he'd planned. The alibi looked good on the surface. Trouble was, he went to jail."

"Jesus!" It was an exclamation due partly to surprise and partly to relief that he had used linseed oil on the rags at Eden's.

"Hey," Moe called out from the other side of the store. "You guys ready to put the feed bag on?"

Stretch tore his attention away from Tom and yelled, "Starved! You buying?"

Tom added, "I can't, Moe. I've got to get through this. Why don't you pick up something?"

"Great," Moe said. "Sandwiches. At that price, I'm buying."

Stretch went out and ordered burgers. They had big buns, little meat, and few onions. The shakes, at least, looked good. While he waited, he pondered his encounter with "the enemy," as Moe had put it. Tom did breathe fire. He probably eats and drinks it, Stretch fancied, but he's not a dragon.

Nothing impressed Stretch Jackson more than success. Money was not the standard—the absolute mastery of an undertaking was. And Tom was simply awesome. He turned over the delicious question of what it would be like to go up against a man like Farley. Just the challenge gave him a chill of pleasure.

Jesus, Jackson, he admitted to himself, you're just a tinhorn beginner. But he could not dismiss the thought of competing against Farley. Even if he *had* drifted into arson like a jellyfish washing onto a beach, there was no reason not to make the best of it. He could do it as well as Eddie if he just knuckled down and learned. That's how Farley had gotten to the top. Learn to think like Farley does—a cool head and attention to details. And a bit of danger.

A smile flicked across his dry lips. What if I'd found Eddie selling insurance or running a restaurant? The waitress looked oddly at Stretch as he suddenly broke out laughing. Awkwardly, he mumbled an excuse, paid the bill, and, still chuckling, stepped into the sunny city street.

He liked Tom, *really* liked him. It would be nice to know him as a friend. Both his personality and expertise were quite special. But if Stretch were ever to succeed in being number one, he was aware that one terrible difference would remain between them. Tom Farley was a man who was proud of his accomplishments—that was why he had so happily fed out all that information. He was also on the right side of the law. Men such as the investigator and the engineer at the fire site had nothing to hide about their professions. If they displayed their knowledge to willing listeners, it was normal. Stretch would have to eat his pride for breakfast, lock his knowledge behind sealed lips, and accept money alone as the reward for being the champion on the dark side of the fence. He was pricked by the fear of winning a hollow victory.

Stretch was riddled with doubts, but pulled like a moth to a candle flame, he headed back toward the dragon's den.

He gave Tom his food first, then walked to the other side of the store, winked at Moe, and gave him his lunch.

"What do you think of him?" Moe asked. "You must be the only torch that ever discussed the fine points with Tom Farley."

"He's good." Stretch tried his best to be blasé.

"You betcha. But if you're good as Eddie, or anywhere close, so are you." Moe bit into the hamburger and looked at Stretch out of the corner of his eye. "You know," he confessed, "I kid you—and for a minute I was really mad about Meyer—but I know you're good. You may not be in Farley's league—you're too young—but you've got what it takes."

Stretch was too embarrassed by the unexpected flattery to answer. He nudged Moe lightly with his elbow and murmured, "Think I'll go back for another round."

Halfway across the store, he stopped to watch Tom Farley work. He found himself admiring the way the investigator handled the merchandise: meticulously, checking the fine details. Not humdrum, this man, but careful and wise. The investigator didn't even stop working while he ate. Stretch walked over, determined to pick Tom's brain a bit more if he could.

"Oh, there you are. Moe let you loose?"

"He said I ought to round out my education—if I don't bug you . . ."

"No, sit down."

"You were saying arson's tough to get a conviction on."

"Oh, yeah. Well, the latest statistics show that out of a hundred fires *officially* called arson—and that's probably not even half of those that are really arson—there is an average of nine arrests, two convictions, and only seven-tenths of one percent ever go to jail. Put that up against the combined average for all other major crimes and it looks pretty puny: twenty-one arrests out of a hundred crimes reported, six convictions, and three jail sentences. In other words, arrest for arrest, only half as many arsonists go to jail. And forty percent of all fires get their causes listed as 'unknown.' A lot of that is because it was a reasonably decent torch job. You can't sweep a holdup or a murder under the rug." Tom stood up, stretched, and sat again to continue inventorying. "Arson's no nickel-and-dime matter; it's up twelve to fifteen times what it was in the late sixties. Fastest growing crime in America. I even hear it's getting common in big cities in Europe, but hell, just New York will probably have as much arson loss this year as the entire country reported twenty years ago."

"You talking a lot of money?"

"Well, everybody keeps statistics, but no two organizations use the same standards. It's garbage in, garbage out, as they say in computers. Put everybody's figures in a paper bag, add salt and a dose of experience, and I'd say there's five to six billion dollars of buildings burned nationwide—"

"Billion?"

"Yes, billion. But that's only direct arson. You have to multiply by four to include secondary costs such as wages, loss of business, and all that. You'll be looking at a total cost of about twenty billion in set fires this year. Arson for profit, my bailiwick, accounts for fifteen percent of arson fires, but at least sixty percent of the dollars. People who set up fires for money are more efficient—they cost the public somewhere around twelve billion bucks a year. Everybody who buys an insurance policy or pays taxes picks up a piece of it. The media gives a lot of play to the poor and the crazies burning a place like the South Bronx. It's good copy, but that's not the story. The real stuff is the guys who do it for business. There's a whole new American industry, spread from Maine to San Diego. The L.A.F.D. is good on statistics. Just in Greater Los Angeles, you're looking at close to a half-billion dollars, primary and secondary arson fraud loss."

"And here?" Stretch inquired gingerly.

"San Francisco only reports what the fire marshals investigate, so things look good on the books, but actually, the whole Bay Area is booming. Inconsistent record keeping like that is why nobody on the national level really knows what's going on in the field. Want to give me those blouses?"

Stretch handed him the bundle and put the question quickly. "You catch many of those guys?"

"It's a drop in the bucket. Find a man in the act and you've got him. Even if I can prove arson and show a suspect has motives, he can wiggle out. I've got to prove he had intent and 'exclusive opportunity.'"

"What's that?" Stretch probed.

"Proof that nobody else had access to the fireground at the time the place caught on fire. That's what sinks us."

"Guy could always say somebody else was there, broke in . . ."

"Sure. A rival, a mob trying to shake him down, vengeance, whatever. They come up with all kinds of stories and alibis. You wouldn't believe it."

It was good to hear Eddie's information confirmed by someone on the other side. Stretch asked cautiously, "But you're talking about a man who owns a store like this. What if he didn't set the fire himself?"

Tom took a gulp of coffee. "Oh, you mean a torch. God, how can a place that makes such good shakes make coffee that bad?" A tone of disdain crept into his voice. "Those bastards are even tougher. At least the owner you've got in your hands. He comes around with his palms up for money. The torch you've got to find to begin with. If you find him, there are bums like the guy who set this one, and there are good ones, somebody to match wits with. I had a guy who used radio waves—"

"Radio waves?" Stretch exclaimed.

Tom gave Stretch a look of reproach. "You don't know anything about this, do you?"

Smarting, insulted, Stretch stammered, "Well . . . I just started." That made his face go red. "I mean . . ."

"Hey, don't take it wrong." The old hand looked at the greenhorn and laughed. "We all begin somewhere. Relax. Can't be embarrassed about starting a new job."

Farley couldn't resist anybody who was as fascinated by his specialty as Moe's new assistant. For the first time he turned his attention away from inventorying and studied Stretch's face. He found it open, intense, and honest. If the fellow was all that eager, then he deserved attention. Tom was always glad to help a newcomer in the business—and to talk shop. He gave Stretch a reassuring smile.

"Sure, you get a tough pro and he's got a real bag of tricks. They can set off a building from half a mile away with radio waves. I had a series of fires where a torch tripped off an incendiary device with telephone rings."

"No shit!" Stretch had relaxed, but *that* awed him. "Did you catch him?"

"No, but he had such a tight pattern that I got very close to it. I think he knew it and left town. Those fires just stopped. He's probably burning up somewhere else. The good torches have connections. They never run out of work. But in the end, the dumb old standby methods are the toughest to pick up on. Depends on the situation. Sometimes a torch just throws gas on the floor and puts a match to it. In the right location, I can tell it's arson, but it could be tramps or vandals, a revenge seeker—anything, including a pro torch getting paid for it."

A drop of ketchup from the last bite of cold hamburger just missed the pant leg of Tom's blue suit. He washed the burger down with the final dregs of bad coffee, loosened his already loose tie, and picked up his inventory pad to get serious again.

"I just keep after them, though. Want to hand me those boxes? I had this crazy case—best torch I ever pegged . . ."

Across the room, Moe paused and watched the two men talk. They could have been a couple of buddies intently dissecting a football game. The unlikeliness of the situation tickled his fancy. The ace arson investigator giving tips to a torch. He shook his head, watched for a moment, and went back to work.

An hour later, Stretch got up just to move his muscles. "Christ," he said, "fire sounds more interesting than salvage." He looked at Farley and the granite soldier came to mind. He felt the same kind of admiration for the man who could become his enemy. Some sort of bond had grown between them.

"How'd you get into investigating fires, anyway?" Stretch asked.

"My father was a fire chief when a burning roof collapsed. A roof is the most dangerous place to be in firefighting. You can never tell when it might go—*boom,* and it just collapses under your feet. Hurt him. Hurt him bad. I was working in the D.A.'s office. Trying the torch on that fire was my first courtroom trial out of law school. The D.A. thought it would be dramatic justice—except I lost the case."

"Jesus!" Stretch was genuinely moved.

"I just couldn't nail down the 'exclusive access' aspect because the original investigation was full of holes. Sloppy workmanship. So I decided to get into investigations myself."

"And plug the holes."

"As best I can, yeah. I don't have much patience with sloppy work."

Moe walked up. "Hey, what are you doing to me, stealing my assistant?"

"Wish to hell he was mine."

They all laughed—differently.

11

San Francisco's Main Public Library is built of such perfectly fog-colored dismal-gray stone that it practically disappears when the real thing rolls in from the sea. Today, however, bright midmorning light harshly emphasized the uninspired murals on the interior walls.

In the Main Reading Room Stretch quietly slipped out box 645 from the card catalog and fingered through *Finland* and *Fiords* before reaching *Fire*. That subject continued to box 646, where his fingers stopped at: *Fire. Investigation—French, H. M.—The Anatomy of Arson, 364.12F.*

At the back table, back corner—the most discreet spot in the large room—he had already accumulated a small stack of books next to a pile of copies of *The Fire Journal*.

This was the third day in a row that Stretch had stuck his long legs under that table and hunched over, avidly devouring texts. A serious three-ring notebook was slowly filling with tight scribbles on fires, building materials, electricity, even chemistry. He had found nothing useful on radio waves, but did have some jottings on architectural engineering and explosives.

He would have checked the books out, but he didn't want his name on all those library slips. That same night, in the Buddha, Sweet Pea was scheduled to give him a driver's license in the name of Mark MacDonald. Sweet Pea could provide anything forged, from a passport to an irreproachable I.D. identifying the bearer as a bona fide agent of the Federal Bureau of

Investigation. To accentuate his seriousness, Sweet Pea added, "Naturally, it's signed by the current director of the Bureau. You know how often they've changed since J. Edgar died."

A driver's license was *almost* beneath his dignity, but since it was for Stretch, he agreed. Tomorrow the studious torch could begin taking books home for closer study.

* * *

Toward the end of the week, Stretch stopped by Moe's office with a new fishing rod.

"Yep, going fishing! Back in two weeks."

Moe tongued his cigar into the corner of his mouth. "Fishing!" he exploded. "What about the job next week?"

"It'll wait. You were the one who said it's not urgent. Right?"

That stumped him. "Yeah, but . . . I didn't mean for you to go futzing around the countryside for a month."

"Two weeks."

"Well, two weeks." He dropped the butt into the already filled ashtray. "What are you doing going fishing all of a sudden, anyway?" he inquired, curious as to whether he might be missing a trick.

"Thought you'd never ask. Even the best of us take a little refresher course from time to time."

Moe's mouth sagged open. "You guys got a school?"

"T.U.—Torch University. Yep, complete with diplomas and honor rolls. We have courses on combustion, chemical accelerants, radio waves . . ."

"No shit!" Moe gripped the arms of the chair, astounded.

"Even a lesson on making bail. Eddie Barker is Dean of the Lighting Department—" He couldn't keep a straight face any longer at tough old Moe's gullibility and doubled over laughing. "I'm just going off to try working up an idea I got. May come in handy for both of us. Hope I get a fish that bites that hard!"

"You putz! And I was about to believe you."

"I'll do the job soon as I get back."

"Here, take a box of cigars." Moe fished a fresh box out of the bottom drawer, obviously chagrined.

"Got so I don't smoke anything except your cigars anymore. Thanks, Moe."

"You get back on time or you'll never get another. G'wan, get out a here."

Stretch gave Moe a wink and left.

He tossed the fishing rod atop a pile of camping gear and supplies on the rear seat of the car. Stretch pulled into the morning traffic and headed for the place Benny had promised was "so remote God has to think twice to remember where he put it."

* * *

A pair of raucous Steller's jays—males, no doubt—were screaming at each other, chasing through the pine trees. The noisy argument went on for hours. In the moments when their chatter did die down, the soft, steady pecking of a red-breasted sapsucker could be heard as it drilled a neat row of holes.

A stream gurgled over a rocky patch, formed a pool, and gurgled on. Stretch's fishing rod was perched hopefully over the pool, its butt end wedged solidly between a rock and a hard place. A fish idly considered the bait.

The clearing beyond the bank was suddenly shaken by a violent explosion. A shower of wood chips flew skyward, then fell back with pattering sounds. The jays were stilled, the pecking stopped, the fish shot to the far side of the pool. The forest went dead silent.

Stretch approached from the far end of the clearing and studied what had been a two-foot section of six-by-eight lumber.

"About half that maybe."

He put the hand detonator on the ground and walked to the yellow Camaro, where he had stored his supply of puttylike plastic explosive gel. Also in the trunk was an odd assortment of quarter-inch and one-inch plywood sections, lumber, boxes, bottles, cans, wires, and carpenter's tools. There was a blow-torch, solder, plaster, and even a small sack of cement.

Fifteen minutes later, Stretch had another section of beam suspended. The hole he drilled in the board was packed with explosive. The wires were in place. Both jays were involved again in their dispute for dominance. The sapsucker was trying his luck in another tree.

By the time Stretch had walked back to the far end of the clearing an olive-sided flycatcher had missed an insect and fluttered to a landing on the edge of the beam.

When this beam exploded, Stretch could tell he had the quantity right. It would drop a rafter without blowing the ceiling completely off. He had closely measured the charge and recorded the results in the fat notebook.

The flycatcher had spotted another bug and flown off in time, but the explosion came too late for the fish, which was now trying to get the hook out of its mouth. The wagging movement of the pole caught Stretch's attention and he raced to the stream's edge. He would fry up the fish for dinner.

Before they had been drafted, camping had been a favorite activity of the Jackson boys, but Vietnam had taken care of the urge for the great outdoors. Hot nights, freezing nights, pouring-down nights, under-enemy-fire nights—that and the death of his brother, Wayne, had killed every atom of pleasure in sleeping under the stars. Only a solid roof had appeal—until now. All of a sudden camping was magic again. Waking at sunrise, the smell of boiling coffee—real coffee—in crisp morning air, washing in the stream—it was all exhilarating. It made him feel fresh and self-sufficient. The years since Stretch was nineteen were gone, *poof!*—reduced to nothingness. The bad times, the dull and boring ones, even the excitement of racing, which had papered them over—all of it was powdered and blown away like the dust of time.

However unwittingly, Tom Farley had thrown down a gauntlet, and Stretch Jackson was here to pick it up. He still refused to say yes to the mirror—yes, I am a torch, I am going to take Eddie's place. But, unexpectedly, there was this new dimension—the challenge of Tom Farley, the challenge to play Farley's game, at Farley's level, to keep it clean, and win. If it was not socially acceptable, as his sporting ambitions to reach perfection had been, Stretch put aside his qualms. For better or worse, for the moment at least, it was the only dream he had. For as long as he would light fires, one or ten or a thousand, one decision was made: he would be the best. He would be as good as Eddie Barker and Tom Farley put together.

In the forest days that followed he memorized his notes, studied books, and experimented, experimented.

He braced three panels of plywood upright at a distance from each other and doused each one with a measured amount of liquid. One got kerosene, one gasoline, one charcoal starter. A "trail" was made to light them simultaneously. Stretch timed each one's consumption with a stopwatch. It brought back memories of lap timing at the track.

Charcoal starter burned the fastest. He inspected the burned remains minutely. Charcoal starter left the least ash. Stretch felt and sniffed the ashes. Charcoal starter seemed to leave no trace. Times and comments were recorded.

Simulating a dividing wall, Stretch built three boxlike forms of quarter-inch plywood. One was stuffed with rock wool insulation, one with fiberglass bats, the third with loose fiberglass resembling the blown-in kind. A steady, dull roar frightened the forest creatures to quiet. Only man plays with such sound and fury.

The continuous thunder of fire issued from a blowtorch. In turn Stretch aimed the flames at each panel and recorded ignition time—front panel; effect on insulation; ignition time—back panel; rate of bum; time of completion; nature of bum; nature of remains; comments. Only rock wool seriously retarded the fire.

He lit various sizes of candles and timed their burning speed. He fashioned different ignition devices and tested them, then experimented with delayed-timing techniques. Each test was run and rerun.

At the end of two weeks the clearing looked like a battle-field. Stretch carefully cleaned it up. As he left, he surveyed the space, breathed in the forest air and was flooded with a sense of feeling brilliantly alive. He gave a parting salute of thanks to the field, the trees, and stream, turned on the motor, and drove off.

The trail not only led away from the clearing, but, in a sense, from all of Stretch Jackson's past.

* * *

The only missing element in the forest was electricity, but that shortcoming was remedied in an anonymous, concrete structure that stood alone in the city's industrial area. Had Eddie Barker still been in San Francisco, the trainee would have received a tight course in the standard techniques of reducing buildings to ashes. Instead, Stretch culled his information from perfectly public books and journals found in any major library. It was a slower, zigzag manner in which to learn, but digging things out in bits and pieces also provided room for imagination.

In the forest and the empty concrete room, Stretch's fertile mind invented variations on the classic methods. Necessity forced him to use the ideas he found at hand. That spirit, plus his determination, quickly forged a unique and fearsome talent.

Fall turned into winter. There were Moe's jobs to be done. Benny's lawyer called him back, and Benny himself provided two more clients. The stakes went up—and so did the fees.

Back in the snows of Illinois, Mrs. Jackson received her share of the bonanza. She would have sent the money right back if she had known its source. A straight, Midwestern boy couldn't lie to his mother, so Stretch simply wrote of being off to a good start in the salvage business.

* * *

"I want you to pull something real special out of your bag of tricks," Moe told Stretch over coffee one afternoon. He took the toothpick out of his mouth and pierced the end of his cigar with it. "We're gonna do a different number—just this once." He jabbed the cigar into his mouth.

"What you got in mind?" Stretch moved his pie plate to one side and leaned forward conspiratorily.

"Competition. I got a guy that's on my back all the time. A real ball-buster. Years he's been a pain in the ass. Okay, some of my competitors probably think I'm a pain, too. That's biz. Then—bingo—this guy's picking them *all* out from under me. Last two months he's topped every single one of my bids, even one you lit. I got connections. I find out he's coming in twenty-five dollars, thirty-five, fifty tops—right over my figures. Some of it's big bucks, too. You win a few, lose a few. Sometimes it's a two-bit difference, okay? But not all the time—every time! Not by twenty-five, fifty lousy smackers each shot."

Stretch shifted uneasily. "What the hell's going on, Moe?"

"I'll tell you what's going on!" Moe checked the people in the next booth and lowered his tone. "I got five people work in the office, four sales clerks on the floor, and the stock boys. When I tell the secretary, 'Type a bid,' it doesn't get locked in a safe with a C.I.A. Top Secret seal on it. It goes in the file drawer under 'Bids.' I never thought of sneaking around in my own office."

"You mean somebody's stealing them?" Stretch asked, shocked.

"I mean that son-of-a-bitch is paying somebody off to tell him the numbers. It makes me sick!"

"Two months with no bids—"

"It's not that," Moe protested bitterly. "It's not just the money. It means there's somebody I can't trust in my office. And I don't know who. I can't look at everybody that works for me like a thief."

"And you can't fire everyone."

"Right." Moe put an angry flame to the end of his cigar. "I've turned it every way from Sunday. All I can think of is to put the bastard out of business. He's insured for over three hundred grand, so it won't kill him to take a vacation. I'll see if any of my people get nervous. It'll give me time to poke around. But in any case he'll be off my back for a while. Who knows? Maybe he'll get the message."

For a moment, Stretch studied Moe. This wasn't just any client. The man was definitely not lovable, but they did have a special relationship. There was more than fury in that creased face—there was a personal hurt that someone he trusted had betrayed the trust. If Moe was not sweet, he *was* straight.

"Thirty-two years in the salvage business and I never had an employee steal a nickel from me. Goddamn, it makes me want to cry."

Stretch didn't think that was a real possibility, but he wouldn't want to see if it was. "Anything you want, Moe," Stretch said. "There won't be any salvage. Just don't tell me there are apartments above his store."

"No. He's got a shop and warehouse combined. Old building, two story, and it's all his, lock, stock, and title." He took a deep, uneasy breath. "Let me swap an honest question for an honest answer. Every store you lit, the owner knew about it. This is a different ball of wax. It's got to be neat and total and not leave a clue. It'll sure get investigated and we've got no cooperating owner. He'll be crazy, suspicious and out for revenge." Moe took his cigar out of his mouth and studied it. "Can you handle that?"

"Jesus, Moe, you trying to hurt my feelings? I'm not some amateur who gets off lighting fires." The image of Marty Martin popped up from his subconscious. "I'll find a way that's so right for the building it'll make everyone scratch their heads and ask what hit it."

Stretch decided that after months of experimenting to perfect an idea, this was the time to put the new technique to the test. If it worked as spectacularly in a real building as it had in his concrete laboratory, Acme Salvage would make history in the annals of arson. Stretch looked up at Moe. "You're talking to number one," he said with absolute conviction.

"Okay, kid, I believe you," Moe replied. And he did, too.

* * *

A few days after Acme Salvage was reduced to cinders a large black Cadillac was parked conspicuously, illegally, by the curb near the main entrance to a shopping center grocery store. Two very burly men sat in the car—one in front, one in back. The main difference between them was that the one in the rear dressed with a certain elegance.

"There he is," the driver said. "The one with the blue shirt who's just coming out. You said you just wanted to lay eyes on him in the flesh, Frank. Well, you got it."

A voice suddenly came from the two-way radio on the dash. "You got him, Henry? That's Jackson in the blue."

"Got him, Ben. Good job," the driver said.

"I figured he'd be in there long enough for you to get here. See you." The radio clicked off.

"He'll be going to that yellow Camaro, Frank," the driver said. "Want to follow him to his house?"

The man in the back gave a negative grunt.

"Well, you're not missing much. The building's a nothing, and when we did the night entry into his apartment last week—shit, is he a sloppy housekeeper? Like I already told you, the place is all full of fire junk." He looked into the rearview mirror at his passenger. "Think you want him, Frank?"

There was another grunt—this time noncommittal.

The two men watched Stretch load his groceries, pull the Camaro out of its space, and leave.

The man in the back was serious and thoughtful. Whatever it concerned, he had clearly not yet made his decision. After a moment he said gruffly, "Come on, Henry, let's get the fuck out of here."

12

Having taken a deep snort of crisply salted morning breeze—what Pickles called the "salt air fix"—Tom was bubbling with goodwill and high energy. On the way to his office he made a quick detour to Oakland Headquarters and Station House I to see Jonah West. Tom doubted that Arson Liaison would be much help with his present problem—the Acme Salvage fire—but it was worth a try. It had already proved useful on several occasions.

For several years Tom had coddled an idea, looking for a place to plant it. He found it wasteful, unjustifiable, and downright dangerous that adjacent fire departments did not share their information on criminally suspect fires—and that was the situation in almost every urban complex throughout the nation.

Raised in a firehouse family, Tom knew from firsthand experience that fire departments were all teamwork at the bottom but all too often riddled with rivalry at the top. They were clannish, historically, from the days when the control of city employees and control of the political machine went hand in hand. The divisions had resulted from the fights of the Irish and the Italians, the cities and the suburbs, and finally the inner power struggles that mark all bureaucracies. Efficiency at the scene of a fire rarely suffered, but Tom couldn't overlook the detrimental effect the bickering had on other activities such as his own field of arson and he developed a plan to counteract the interdepartmental rifts. It would be a coordinated arson program under the control of a liaison officer who would link everything that happened anywhere around San Francisco Bay that gave off even the slightest hint of arson. At least he might get *his* region to rise above political rivalries.

The first part of Farley's scheme was to have a gathering point for short summaries of all Bay Area fires of suspected or known incendiary origin. In the same way that a doctor reads a cardiogram or a meteorologist watches a weather graph, a careful observer could study incoming arson data and spot recurring patterns in method, accelerants, names, or places. It would not only be an early-warning system of repeating, suspicious fires, it would also be an invaluable asset for building a case against any multiple-fire arsonist, professional or not. The fire investigators would finally have a tool that police departments take for granted.

In addition to being an interdepartmental channel, arson-related professionals—the P.I.'s, attorneys, and insurance claims men—would have somewhere to focus their information when it merited feeding back to the fire department investigators, as it often did.

Tom had zeroed in on a dynamic department—Oakland—and some months previously he had dropped the suggestion into an ear that led to endless energy.

Although Jonah West was a union leader, he had been strictly a front-line firefighter until now and had no "front office" political taint.

"Great idea!" Jonah had exclaimed, and promptly started working Tom's proposal up through the ranks. It had gone just as Farley had hoped it would.

So Jonah was no longer just Jonah West, fireman. Tom had subtly snookered him partway down the rungs of Ladder I and a bit farther up the ladder of the Oakland Fire Department hierarchy. After several months with Jonah at the head of the new Arson Liaison Department, everyone was wondering how they had lived without it. Tom was convinced that Jonah would learn arson inside out and never get trapped in the internecine sniping that separated men who should be working in unison.

While Jonah studied the report Tom had handed him, Tom picked up the freshly arrived issue of *Firehouse,* the largest circulation trade journal for firefighters. The latest annual fire statistics were out: 6,600 dead in fires, over 1,200 of them victims of suspected or proven arson, plus 128,000 injuries. Tom whistled and shook his head. He wondered if this new Arson Liaison scheme with Jonah, or anything for that matter, could slow the explosion of those statistics. If murder, rape, or robbery were expanding as rapidly as arson, gun laws would finally be passed and police forces tripled. Suddenly, out of the corner of his eye, Tom saw the sheet of paper he'd handed Jonah flutter down to Jonah's desk top. He looked up expectantly.

Jonah puzzled a second, then slapped his big hand on top of the paper. "Nope," he declared, "I've never heard of anything like it!"

"That's what they said across the bridge."

"Of course, I'm just getting this office cranked up. Some of the departments aren't very fast on their feet yet. But nothing like that has crossed my desk. You know, a fire salvage man might have collected some strange ways to burn a building."

"But Global Insurance has insured Acme Fire Salvage since nineteen seventy and they trust the owner completely."

"If they gave you the case, it wasn't as completely as all that."

"You know, salvage men are salvage men—odd breed of ducks. But this one's got nothing doubtful in his past. At first, I think, they just wanted a routine check. Vic Whitlock, Global's loss manager, is a tough nut. He's usually pretty thorough. When I got into it and saw the report, I thought I'd take a shot and ask you."

"Maybe it's just a freak."

"Could be, but you read that part." He picked up the report. "'When the first-due trucks arrived it was burning in every single corner of the building and on both floors.' Like it broke out everywhere at once. By the time they got their hoses hooked it was too late for anything but making toast. I've been over there once, poking around. Nothing's special.

But I never heard of anything like it—a building that size engulfed eight minutes after the first alarm!"

"Think it was torched?"

Tom stood up. "If it was, we're up against someone very special. Five gallons of gas in the right place will involve all of a two-story in ten minutes, but not that completely and not without leaving tracks. I can't even find a point of origin! If it is arson, it isn't the work of some ordinary street torch."

"Maybe we got a new guy in town."

"Really sophisticated jobs usually get done by some joker who flies in from New York or someplace like that. The odd thing, though, is that Acme isn't that big a deal moneywise—unless there's something we don't know about." Tom shrugged his shoulders. "I smell arson, but I can't find a thing to hang my hat on." He walked over to the window, looked out, and continued talking, half to Jonah, half to himself. "Sure, all sorts of crazy things occur when a building starts to burn. Worst thing that can happen to an arson investigator is to start seeing a torch under every piece of ash he can't explain. A guy could go bats if he couldn't live with the ones with no answers." He turned back toward Jonah. "The problem is to know when you're seeing things that aren't there. Most investigators stop before they've plugged all the possibilities in a case. Some of them can't even imagine all the possibilities. Acme could have been a fluke. Or it could have burned for half an hour before anybody saw it to turn in the alarm. Without going off the deep end, I'm just not ready to buy one answer over another yet—or write this off as a mystery, either." Farley pushed his hat back and wrinkled his brow. "But maybe someone knows a trick we don't." He added, only half in jest, "And that would *really* tick me off."

* * *

It only took a few minutes of pristine bay air to melt Tom's pensive mood. It was one of those mornings when the other side of the bay looked binocular close without the binoculars.

For a moment, it became unimportant to know whether Acme Salvage was a freak or a new wrinkle. High energy returned.

Tom parked the Pontiac and headed for his office. It was in one of those downtown buildings that were the pride of the era when the Modern Hotel was still modern. Some architect with an artistic bent had put up twenty-two stories of Art Deco's finest. Striking, geometric carving over the door announced THE FRED WEIK BUILDING. Tom would glance at that from time to time and hope Weik had fared better than the building.

The sculpted elevator doors slid open haltingly at the eighteenth floor as if uncertain that they could stand another trip. Suite 1812 was marked in plain letters: TOM FARLEY—FIRE INVESTIGATIONS. Inside the office everything was Art Deco geometric, all right—cubes. All of the art had gone into the facade and the lobby; the tenants got a series of boring boxes whose only merit was the low rent.

When Tom rushed in Charlene looked up, startled.

"There you are! The phone has been ringing off the hook this morning. Gordy Ingebritson's been trying to get you all morning on the Waller file. Jack Baer wants—"

"Hey, whoa, bright eyes. I'll get all that in a minute. Is Pat in?"

The answer floated out from his father's cubbyhole office in the corner. "Yeah, I'm here."

"Baer," Charlene insisted, "has got to have the report on Walt Millar. Millar's about to get out of hand again."

Tom walked toward the cubbyhole. "I'll be right back, Charlene. First let me get a couple of things started on Acme Salvage."

Like everything else, Pat Farley's little office was painted in the safe pale green used by timid decorators short on imagination. On the wall to the right of the desk was a pair of crossed fire axes that set off a framed—and faded—newspaper story. The photo above the headline showed a man of about fifty propped in a hospital bed, surrounded by fire chiefs, and an official who was obviously presenting a plaque. The headline read: INJURED FIRE CHIEF FARLEY HONORED.

The rest of the room was undistinguished—except for the presence of the honored Fire Chief. Pat Farley was now gray, lean, and knocking on the door of seventy. It is always surprising to see a man of that age whose face gives the impression that he's about to do something mischievous. It came from something in the elder Farley's eyes, combined with a frequent I-just-ate-the-canary grin.

"What you got, Tom?" Pat pushed his wheelchair back and spun to face the door. His right brown pant leg lay flat and empty below his knee. Out of sight in the corner was an artificial leg, which he swore made his stump itch. He unabashedly took it off whenever he sat for more than an hour or so.

"Hi, Pat. I've got some records that need checking in a hurry on that Acme fire. Here's the list. Get these two items at the courthouse, would you? And run a survey on those three names for police or fire records. Oh, a full credit on them, too."

"Want a C.B.I. fraud report?"

"Sure, why not? Check all three."

Pat Farley swung his wheelchair back around to the desk. "Wish I could do more than just come in and do all your idiot work."

"You're indispensable, Pop. Keeps me from going crazy—and you from chasing skirts!"

Over his shoulder, Pat gave his son a reproachful look—but his eyes and grin acknowledged the veracity of Tom's statements. Both of them.

Tom went straight into his own office, knowing Charlene would be right on his heels. His personal cube was hardly grandiose. As Moe's office was jammed with junk, Tom's was crammed with char. Resident for varying periods—ranging from weeks to years—were charred beams, charred detonating devices, a charred TV set, and even a charred telephone, one of the ones that ignited on preset rings. Each item had been neatly tagged, then unceremoniously shoved on shelves or in one of three corners. The fourth corner, by the door, had once been filled, but Charlene threatened to quit if she couldn't enter without smudging her dress every time.

As Tom had expected, she whizzed right in behind him. "Here's the list of hounds baying at your door." She placed the call sheet on Tom's desk before he even had his hat off. "Monroe and Crimmons will wait. Baer and Ingebritson won't." She cocked her head and smiled her smile, which would melt rocks. "Hey, Mr. Farley, how are you today?"

Tom had already plunged into the list of callers. Charlene's informal, friendly tone brought his head up sharply. He answered her smile with one of his own. "Actually, I'm great. I'd be even better if I didn't have to go digging through Acme's ashes this morning, but the day's beautiful, the fire department finally got off its duff, and Jonah West is going to change our lives." Then it slipped out, fresh as seabreeze. "And it's good to see you radiate in here in the mornings."

That was more than Charlene had bargained for. Her boss was not given to offhand personal compliments. She knew she was appreciated, but hearing it said was as rare as romance. Somewhere inside her, his comment set off a pleasant sensation.

The two quiet, normally undemonstrative people looked at each other for a moment. Each of them was surprised—and awkwardly enjoyed it.

"Well . . ." He broke the lengthening pause, but did not know where to take it.

"Thanks."

"Yes. Well. Could you pull that old file on R–B Salvage? I want to compare some notes with Acme."

"Sure I can." She walked out with a twinkle in her eye. It's going to be an interesting day, she thought.

Pulling himself together, Tom turned his attention again to the phone list. After making the urgent calls he leafed through the R–B Salvage file. He found what he was looking for, but it didn't fit with the Acme fire. Before the hatband had even cooled off, Tom's hat was back on his head and he was out the door.

* * *

Farley parked the Pontiac in the rubble-strewn lot and eyed the ruins through which he had to comb. It was the dirtiest, most exasperating part of an investigation. Unfortunately, it was also vital. Steeling himself, he got out, opened the trunk, and prepared for the chore. As usual, his suit looked a bit unpressed. He took off his jacket and pulled on coveralls, which would keep his pants clean, but add a further bit of rumpling. He traded shoes for boots and armed himself with a shovel, a rake, his camera and flash, a Safari light, and a cardboard box. Then he walked through the doorless doorway into the grime that had been Acme Salvage.

Methodically, Tom began at the front and worked back, shoveling, turning, poking, kicking through ashes. Occasionally there was something worth putting into the box. When he was through, he took his finds into the daylight of the parking lot. One by one he checked each object. At the end, disgusted, he threw the whole batch into a pile of junk the firemen had hauled out. Nothing from Acme would grace the shelves of gritty evidence in his office. His good mood of early morning had been deflated.

* * *

Tom banged open the office door and then banged it closed again.

"Hey, what's eating you?"

Tom stopped at Charlene's desk, irritated. "Damn. I spent four hours up to my ass in ash and I don't know one thing more than I did before I left."

"Well, they can't all fall in your lap."

"You're a help," he said testily.

Charlene pushed her chair back. "Cuppa tea help cool you down."

"We out of coffee?" he grumbled.

"No."

"Make it coffee."

"Grouch."

Tom looked at her blankly, then took his hat off. "I'm sorry," he said in an eat-humble-pie tone. "I always take it out on you, don't I?"

"That's what God gave me these broad shoulders for. It was written in the heavens that I would find a job working for an arson investigator. That's why I prayed for help a lot in Sunday school and why I got my degree in abnormal psychology."

"Okay, okay. God's not always kind. I guess I'm not either." He unfurrowed his brow. It was neither tea nor coffee that usually cooled him down—it was Charlene.

As she got up to get the coffee supplies out of the file drawer, he gave her one of those solid love pats—where the cup of the hand perfectly fits the curve of a bottom.

Charlene stopped dead, then turned and looked at him with amazement. "What was that?" she demanded.

"I don't know," he said, totally flustered. He really didn't and he charged into his office to hide his confusion.

Charlene smiled to herself. It wasn't very often that she had seen Tom Farley stammering and awkward, and he'd certainly never touched any part of her that could be called private. Whatever it meant, she could only take it as amusing.

"If you don't phone Ingebritson, we're going to lose that account," she called from the file drawers with what seemed to be her usual unflappable efficiency. However, she did pull out tea, quite forgetting he had switched his request to coffee.

* * *

The day wore on as office days do—one file opened, one file closed. Tom was engrossed in dictation when he realized Charlene was standing in the doorway with a peculiar, indecipherable look on her face. "What's wrong?" he asked, pushing back from the desk.

"Remember when we pulled into the Shell station and you said, 'Stay here, I'm going to see if I can convince the owner—'?"

"And you said I should talk to that good-looking mechanic instead? Sure I do."

He remembered, all right. He remembered more about the incident than Charlene realized. They had been driving back from a session of depositions at the San Leandro District Attorney's office. Tom had had another stop to make.

Ronnie Fender had been Charlene's brainstorm on the Shoreline Office Supply fire and she had taken a personal interest in the case ever since then. Through Fender's parole officer, she had traced the ex-torch to his new job—working at a Shell station near his house in Alameda. Although the dye traces pulled from the ash samples at Shoreline had proved to be from Shell fuel, no link had turned up to nail Fender to the fire. It was circumstantial evidence, at best. But now things were different. Tom had a trap to bait. If Fender was in the fire game again, sooner or later he would be taking home some gas. Farley would like to have someone keep an eye on Fender. It had been Fender's day off and Tom had stopped at the station with the intention of having a brief, private talk with the owner. As the car door closed, Charlene had made her abrupt suggestion about the good-looking mechanic.

"Charlene," Tom had said, "this is not a beauty contest. If you pick a watchdog that bites the postman and licks the hand of the burglar, you blow the whole case!" He leaned back in through the window of the car, trying to sound authoritative and bosslike. "A fellow employee is more likely to tip off Fender than his employer is." His voice was low but emphatic. He did not want to make a scene in front of the station.

Charlene's Irish eyes had flashed. "The employer just hired Fender! He's got a vested interest—his ego! If the guy he just hired turns out to be a torch, then the boss looks like a real jerk."

Tom flushed. What sort of bullshit female intuitional logic was that! If Ronnie Fender, slipped through his fingers and killed someone with a magnesium charge, it wouldn't be Charlene's fault, it would be his. A case was *his* responsibility. She knew that. Leaning in through the window cost him his dignity and he was not certain why he was bothering to explain.

He had looked at the determination that hard-edged her angular face and at the set line of her mouth when he had a sudden, irrational, inappropriate, and urgent desire to lean in farther and kiss her, from her blue eyes to her full lips. The sensation was so strong and yet so strange that he had recoiled from it like a spring. He slammed the back of his head against the top of the window. In angry, mute confusion he had walked like a robot to the mechanic's stall, convinced that his secretary was sitting in the car laughing at him.

The mechanic had agreed to alert them to any unusual activity on Fender's part and Tom's odd urge had left, but the drive back to the office had been decidedly strained.

Now Tom studied Charlene's face in the office doorway, praying she was not about to announce that talking to the mechanic had been a mistake.

For years Charlene had simply been The Superb Secretary to Tom. She had first crossed his mind as a desirable woman at the Top of the Mark dinner. Then he had had the Shell station experience, and now, this morning's involuntary hand-to-bottom event. Whatever caused these incomprehensible oddities was in *him*—and he neither understood nor liked it. Tom wanted to stuff Charlene back in the box as Woman and bring her out permanently as Secretary once more. This was all very troubling and he had no time for such distractions. Tom would have fired Eve before he would let her bring an apple into the office!

"What's wrong?" he asked again, fearfully.

"Ronnie Fender just slipped a five-gallon can of regular in the back seat of his car." There was a faint overtone of righteous pride. "He goes off duty at six."

The surge of relief Tom felt was promptly displaced by embarrassment at having so automatically rejected Charlene's suggestion. "Sorry about that," he apologized. "I treated you like a category instead of a person. You were right." He was not about to mention his flash of wanting her as a person rather than a category. "You were *perfectly* right." Her very rightness made his resolve to ban the apple wane.

Charlene was also relieved. She had been unable to guess why Tom had done the startling turnaround at the station. She had experienced a vague feeling that his reaction was stronger than her logic justified. Immediately after he had bashed his head she had begun to have waves of doubt. Had she pushed too hard? What if she were wrong? Was he testing her? Could the strange look on his face have been anger? Not a day had passed when she did not fear that the mechanic had been the wrong choice—and that the result would be losing some measure of Tom Farley's respect. Not for a second was she worried about her job; she felt perfectly secure there. Nor was it related to man/woman—she was not certain Tom had ever so much as noticed that her breasts were larger than his. No, it had to do with the awe in which she held his professionalism, his drive, his striving for perfection. Although Charlene was not the kind of woman who would blind herself to everything but her job—there was too much love of life in her for that—she was forever respectful of Tom simply because he was so good at what he did. She idealized him perhaps, but she wanted to be equally outstanding at what she did. Charlene was more a partner than a secretary, and she knew their respect for each other was mutual, if different. She savored the *perfectly* in Tom's "You were *perfectly* right."

"Let's go to it. I'll call Cliff. Do you want to plant a Jitterbug?" Tom had noticed long ago that a little excitement made Charlene's earlobes quickly flush with pink. His question gave rise to instant rose and he almost laughed as she nodded her head. "Good. It's best that *you* do it, because Fender knows me and I don't want him to spot Cliff. We have"—he checked his watch—"one hour and fifty minutes before he leaves work, and there's a lot to do. Do you have gas in your tank?"

"Somehow you make that sound like a personal question." She spun to go to her phone. "But yes."

"Sometimes I don't know what I'm going to do with you."
Tom's intent was jocular, but in the back of his mind he realized there was a second question that had to do with apples and Eve.

He put it aside. For the moment it was disturbing enough that Charlene might soon find herself in danger.

13

At six o'clock a nondescript blue-gray van was parked where it had a clear view of the Shell station. On its front and sides were signs that read: J. & L. ENTWISTLE, PAINTERS.

Behind the van Charlene was waiting in her car for the first sign of movement. According to the plan, if Ronnie stopped before going home, she would make the plant at his first stop. If he went straight home—as Tom guessed he would—she was to follow the van. If she lost it, her destination was to be the little house the Fenders rented.

Cliff Lawrence sat in the driver's seat of his van. His shirt matched the plaid baseball cap, which, in turn, matched the seat covers and the identical plaid panel behind the seat, which seemed to seal off the rear of the truck. From fifty feet away the van looked empty.

Cliff was a lean, taciturn young man whose only known pleasures were collecting and repairing antique fountain pens—a patient man's hobby and one he could do in the van. He was also one of the best drivers in San Francisco, known for his ability to glue the van discreetly to the tail of anything from a Ferrari to a bicycle. His specialty was vehicle follows and film. It was an odd little field, but often invaluable to the P.I.'s who employed him. Someone making drop-offs of things they should not be leaving, or meeting people they did not want to be seen with, could often spot or shake off an ordinary P.I., but they rarely ditched Cliff Lawrence.

Tom, one of Lawrence's original clients, had personally conceived a few of the van's refinements such as the changeable signs on the sides and front. A quick pull on three strings replaced ENTWISTLE with MODERNE CLEANERS or DALE ARVIDSON, PLUMBING CONTRACTORS—or no signs at all. The changes could be crucial if Cliff suspected he was being recognized on a long surveillance.

Hidden behind the plaid panel was a swivel seat from which a second person could have a clear view in all directions—also a Farley concept. While they waited for Ronnie Fender's move, Tom was occupying the swivel seat back in the van's sophisticated film department. He was filling Lawrence in on the details of their target.

In the ten minutes since they had arrived Cliff had already shot film of the Shell station, Fender's car, a close-up of Ronnie working, and the starting location dead ahead. Once the van started up, a frame would be exposed automatically as often as Cliff wanted or at a minimum of every thirty seconds. Auxiliary remote camera controls were at his fingertips. The lens was locked to shoot straight ahead of the van and give a running account of everything Cliff followed.

"There he goes!" Cliff exclaimed, pumping his brakes three times in a signal to Charlene. "I just hope he doesn't sit on that can of gas for a week and then use it in his lawn mower."

Tom laughed. "Hell, I'd be tickled pink if Ronnie has gone straight. But I'd lay two to one he bags that gas and heads off to light it between now and midnight." He squinted ahead. "Damn! He's heading north. He's not going directly home."

Swiveling around, Tom checked to see if Charlene was right behind them. She was.

"Okay, Tom," Cliff said. "We don't know where this character is going to light his fire. Run through the plan for me. We're not going to make a citizen's arrest when he's got a match in his hand, are we?"

"Not if we can help it. It's the same old story. If the State Fire Marshal's office were less hostile to P.I.'s, we could alert one of their marshals—since state marshals don't have any problems with jurisdiction—and get him to join us wherever Fender sets up. But those guys won't give a P.I. the time of day if they can help it."

"Be nice. They've never gotten over the embarrassment of having their headquarters and all of the records torched in Sacramento—and then never getting close to nailing a suspect."

"Watch the light." Tom went to the back window and verified that Charlene had squeezed through. He made a sign and she waved a tight-lipped acknowledgment.

"If you call the police on short notice," Tom continued, "they take you for a dodo. Usually cops don't know anything about arson. So our best bet will be to phone a local fire marshal. Just pray Ronnie heads for a city where we know someone. If Fender's inside setting up and I have to explain the whole case to some marshal I've never heard of in a South Bay town, we may end up with a citizen's—" Tom broke off. "Well, Jesus. Pull it over. We sure can't follow him there."

Up ahead, Ronnie Fender had just pulled into the drive-in teller's window of a bank. Cliff swung quickly to the curbside. Tom hopped out of the back and rushed to Charlene's window.

"What's happening?" she asked.

"You okay?"

"It's the best part of the job."

"At least we know where he keeps his money. Let's hope he's depositing a partial payoff. Now listen: From here he's probably going home. Stick with us, but if anything goes wrong, head for his house. You know where it is. If the car's in the drive, you know what to do. If not, wait for it, or us, until twelve. Pat will be parked nearby. Let him know where you are. Take care." He winked, got one of those marvelous smiles in return, and jumped back into the van.

Cliff had changed the signs, just in case Fender had noticed the van while it was parked across from Shell. ENTWISTLE bit the dust. They were now DALE ARVIDSON, PLUMBING CONTRACTORS.

In a few minutes the chase was on again.

"He's a lousy driver," Tom complained.

"Nope. You're in my territory, Thomas. The guy's good. Enters the lights on orange, corners quick. Lousy for an average citizen, but it leaves anyone who's tailing running all the red lights and looking conspicuous."

"I guess you're right. He's headed home now though, for sure."

"Tell me when we're two blocks away."

Cliff let Fender string a block ahead.

"Now," Tom said. "He lives on the next street on the right parallel to this street and two blocks up."

"Safe to cut over?"

"Try it."

Cliff signaled and snapped into a right turn. Charlene sailed straight on without turning.

"Boy, you've got a fast-thinking woman there," Cliff said, impressed. "Just *if* he was looking back, she's disassociated us, takes a right in the next block, parks on the street, and does her number. Neat lady!" He hung a left. Fender appeared one block ahead of them.

"You're a block away."

Cliff stopped curbside in a hurry and leaped to the camera. When Fender pulled into his driveway behind his wife's car, Cliff was already focused and waiting.

Ronnie got out and looked at his neighbors' houses. He was a skinny, mean-looking man in his early forties with a bombed-out face the color and consistency of shaving cream. He ducked back into the car, hurriedly retrieved a blue plastic jerrican, and hustled houseward.

Cliff switched off the camera for the first wait. As they waited he boggled Tom with an explanation of his latest invention. With the touch of a button he could switch from black-and-white to color film or vice versa. The Shell shots had been in color; tailing Fender had been in inexpensive black-and-white; and now the house—and especially the blue jerrican—in color again. "It'll go great on the witness stand . . . if we get to that."

"Here she comes," Tom said.

Cliff flipped a switch on the dashboard. An odd intermittent hum immediately filled the van's interior.

Swinging a briefcase in one hand, carrying a clipboard in the other, a businesslike Charlene walked briskly up the street toward the Fenders'. She marched firmly up their drive but suddenly tripped on a child's toy next to Fender's parked car. The clipboard clattered to the ground, the briefcase dropped, and Charlene barely managed to save herself from ending up nose down on the gravel driveway. With all of the grace she could muster under the circumstances she dusted off her hands, picked up her briefcase, and continued more carefully to the front door. Then she knocked purposefully.

Mrs. Fender was short, like her husband, but stocky. The look of her eye peeking out as she cracked the door ajar gave Charlene a chill.

"What do you want?" Mrs. Fender demanded in a loud nasal whine.

"Good evening, ma'am," Charlene said politely. "I'm doing a new product marketing survey, picking one in a block and—"

"You drop something out there?"

"Why, no. I tripped on the duck."

"What's she want, Ma?" Ronnie's voice came from some adjacent room. He sounded edgy.

"What do you want?" the missus repeated.

"It's for a survey. Just a dozen questions. About how you clean your kitchen and what—"

"Don't you let nobody in here!" Ronnie called out.

"Well, that's interesting. Sure. Come on in."

"Now company rules don't let me enter houses, but . . ." Charlene got the clipboard up in position to write.

"No, you come on in. I'll give you answers, but you just come in and sit." It sounded friendly, but it was unquestionably an order.

Charlene decided compliance was better than resistance and crossed the threshold. The door closed loudly behind her.

In the van, Tom lowered the 8 by 40 binoculars. "Now what the hell did she go in for? She doesn't usually go in."

"Well, she made the plant. This end of the Jitterbug stopped humming." It was true. The van was quiet now.

"Yeah, but I don't like her going in, that's all. She's got twelve questions. Give her six minutes."

The two men waited for six minutes. After eight minutes, Cliff turned and said, "You got an alternative emergency plan?"

"No." Farley's brow knit with concern. "I can't go in because Fender knows me. Here." He reached for his brief-case. "You take this. You're from the Sample Service. You were working the other side of the street when you saw your colleague, et cetera. Take it from there."

"You got it." Cliff shoved his hand under the dash and grasped his steely blue .38, which he slipped into an ankle holster.

Eleven minutes after Charlene had entered the house Cliff Lawrence pushed the van door open and jumped out.

"Hold it." Tom stopped him. "Get in, quick."

The Fenders' front door had just opened. After an agonizing pause Charlene stepped out of the house, turned back, and clearly looked up the street toward the van.

The binoculars were trained on Charlene as she apparently tried her best to break away from a talkative Mrs. Fender. At last, Charlene waved, walked down the driveway and continued up the street in the direction of the parked vehicle.

"She's going to have to explain that," Tom said, flushed with relief.

Only Tom and Cliff saw her throw a kiss at the van, then do a right face to circle the Fenders' block and return to her car. Her assignment was completed.

"A *kiss*?" asked Cliff, his curiosity thickly iced with disbelief. "You got a thing going with Charlene?"

"Oh, come off it. She's just glad it's done. Now all we have to do is wait for the bug to go off."

While pretending to trip over the duck, Charlene had slapped an invention of Tom's under the rear bumper of

Fender's car. Tom had thought up the Jitterbug, tinkered it into perfection, and had then had them made for himself and close friends. Chromed to match a bumper and held in place by a powerful magnet, the transmitter—the size of a quarter—only sent a signal when it was jiggled—hence it was dubbed, Jitterbug.

One of the most wearing aspects of surveillance is watching a car. It may remain empty during a suspect's long lunch, three-hour meeting, or night-long sleep, and then in ten seconds someone can jump into the vehicle and be off. Merely slamming the door or starting the motor, however, was vibration enough for the Jitterbug to hum its alert to an open transmitter. It was transmitting as Charlene moved and it stopped when it was affixed to Fender's bumper. They knew it was working and now they could relax. The next move was Ronnie's.

Cliff relaxed, disappeared into the seat cover camouflage and changed the subject. "Hey, I hear Oakland has some kind of a coordinating program for you guys."

"True. The Oakland chief and one of his captains are trying to make a breakthrough. What's the use of bothering to keep records if nobody has access to them? The trick was to get the fire departments to cooperate between themselves. Now we just have one guy to talk to. Most fire marshals treat private investigators like we were some kind of rivals. Too many people in public service forget the point is to serve the public. Listen, from chiefs to marshals to recruits, firemen are probably the most dedicated group of civil servants there are. They're a tough, proud bunch. The front-line firemen are united because they have to be—there's just too damn much at stake on the fireground to quibble around, but when a man stops pushing water and starts pushing paper, that's when Kafka works his way into the system. Then there's time to get into politics and jealousies and seniorities even though there's an army out there every night with matches in one hand and the other hand in the public's pocket. They may have more security and I may make more money or they may have better hours and I may have more freedom, but that's all petty kid stuff. What counts, for God's sake, is getting a job done. And I think we've all got the same job."

The two men eased into comfortable professional banter and waited for Fender's move. They were halfway through a coffee break at 7:30 when Ronnie Fender came out of his house. Cliff jumped to his camera and immortalized on film Ronnie's careful placement of two large brown paper bags where the jerrican of gasoline had been. Ronnie went back into his house and stayed there. They finished their cold coffee and speculated about Ronnie's next move.

"I'll bet he doesn't budge until after dark," Tom insisted.

He was right. Cliff proudly showed off his recent fountain pen acquisitions, some stunning Parkers and Water-mans from the 1920s—all shiny reds and blues, silver and gold. Then, as deep evening shades began to darken the residential street, Cliff decided to shift the van's position. The van's pale blue-gray was the hardest color to spot, but Cliff knew his headlights would give him away if they were on the same street as Ronnie when he turned them on, but for some reason headlights turned on from a cross street were rarely noticed.

"I'll go round the block and pull up to that corner on the cross street. We can still eyeball his driveway," Cliff said.

"Just don't get out of the Jitterbug's range," Tom cautioned.

"Don't be such a worry wart."

They were exactly halfway around the block—as far from Fender as they could get—when the Jitterbug's receiver suddenly hummed. Ronnie Fender was on the move.

"Holy shit!" Cliff floored it.

When Fender decided to take off, he took off! The only tail lights on Fender's street were rounding a corner a block away. Cliff gave chase and got a glimpse of a vehicle at a stop sign almost a hundred yards away. It turned out to be a camper, not Fender's car. Cliff slammed to a stop.

The hum was still going. The transmitter only had a five-hundred-yard range and to a trained ear the signal strength was a distance indicator. Its sound put it three or four blocks away and moving off fast.

"Take a shot at the tunnel on Sixth!" Tom barked. "If he's not headed north, we've lost him."

Cliff left a trail of smoking rubber.

All three fires where Fender had been a suspect were in San Francisco itself. Farley gambled on that being where the torch had his connection. The fastest way there was via Sixth. If Tom's hunch was wrong, Ronnie Fender would be loose in the city with five gallons of gasoline, matches—and probably a charge of magnesium.

The van pulled onto the busy street that led to the tunnel. The hum steadied and grew louder. Cliff worked through the traffic with kid gloves and a lead foot.

"If we don't get a visual on him soon, there are three different directions he can take after he gets out of the tunnel," Tom said desperately.

"And if he gets away," Lawrence added through clenched teeth, "I'll shoot myself."

"It was just a bad break. You did what we always—"

"There he is! Hung at the light!"

The almost tangible tension blew away. Tom pulled the signs and the van became anonymous. If Fender had by chance noticed the plumber's truck, he would no longer recognize it. They settled in and followed. Night's charcoal replaced twilight and a torch was crossing Oakland Bay Bridge from east to west. There was enough traffic to cover their presence but not enough to get in the way except for one tight moment coming off the bridge. Fender weaved through the busy center of San Francisco and onto Mission Street.

"He could be heading for Daly City," Tom said.

"That good or bad?"

"They're a little more cooperative with P.I.'s than the San Francisco crowd. But there's no problem unless he goes another fifty miles south."

"There's your answer."

At the stoplight ahead Fender made a right turn into the worn-out heart of the Mission District. Eight blocks farther on he pulled into a space that Tom noted would allow a fast departure. It was directly in front of a grimy, ramshackle group of stores. Above them were two floors of apartments. Of the four stores, only one appeared to be occupied. At first glance, the apartments seemed to be abandoned.

Cliff turned off the lights and slipped into an illegal space.

"Classic," Tom muttered. He let Lawrence get to the camera while he moved to the van phone and dialed San Francisco Headquarters.

"He's taking both bags into a store."

Tom identified himself to the dutyman who answered. "This is urgent. What fire marshal is on duty?"

"There's Haferkamp, sir."

Tom's heart sank. He remembered the scene in Shoreline Office Supply's debris. Haferkamp was not only uncooperative with P.I.'s in general, he was the least efficient arson investigator on the force and capable of bringing the whole effort down in ruins.

"I think Captain Edison just came in, too," the dutyman added.

"Edison!" Tom blurted out shamelessly. Bob Edison was not only an outstanding arson investigator, he was Tom's best contact on the San Francisco arson staff.

When Edison came on the line, Tom sketched in the background, described the situation, and suggested a plan for the Marshal to follow. Edison instantly got the picture and even added some refinements to Tom's suggestions.

Cliff had filmed both bags being taken in, then stepped out of the van and into the street for a surreptitious look. He popped his head in the door and whispered urgently. "There are lights in a top-floor apartment—like someone's living in it!"

Tom broke off with Edison. "Okay," he said to Cliff. "Sink the son-of-a-bitch and wait for me." He turned back to the

Marshal and advised him of the possible occupancy. "Make it sure, Bob—and make it fast!" Tom knew he could count on the Marshal to quickly, efficiently convert their ideas into action.

He hung up and moved out of the van. Ahead he could see Lawrence's crouched form by Ronnie Fender's car. There would be no fast getaway. Fender had just been "sunk"—Cliff had just removed the inside of his left front tire's valve stem.

Cliff returned. "Because of the angle, I couldn't tell which door he went in, but it's not the corner one. Any way to warn those people on the top floor?"

"Not yet there's not. He has to set up. The way this building is laid out, he only needs one ignition point if he does his usual magnesium plug."

"What's that?"

"Plugs a joist with a chemical powder and it explodes on contact with water. To set up all of that he'll be in there for fifteen, maybe twenty minutes. Edison will have the task force here before then, police and all. Still, the bagful of gasoline has to ignite in order to get the little bastard on an arson charge. If we put the fire out too soon, it's just *conspiracy to commit,* and that's useless. Get to the far end of the building, just in case it's you and me and a citizen's arrest."

They waited in quiet shadows on the street at opposite ends of the building. An occasional car passed. A young couple giggled by, not noticing the two men.

The first vehicles to arrive—a pumper and a ladder—were moving slowly forward, lights low. Surprisingly, they were even more ominous without sirens and flashing lights. It seemed eerie and unnatural.

Tom stopped them a good distance away and huddled with the captains. They spoke in urgent whispers, calculating the risk. They would allow a gasoline bag to go. They would have to use hand-held foam extinguishers. They must be ready to enter on the run. A one-and-a-half-inch hose must be brought to the door, but under no circumstance could it be used because of the magnesium hydroxide.

Two unmarked detectives' cars scurried up with a third car clearly lettered FIRE MARSHAL on their heels. Again the men huddled, speaking in hurried undertones. Cover the back, just in case. Ready the ladder for rescue, just in case. Cover the front door with no possible lines of crossfire, just in case. There will be no more than one hundred twenty seconds before ignition. Clockwork. The huddle broke.

The weasel scuttled out of the center left door and turned to close it quickly but quietly.

"Don't move, Fender! Police! Raise your arms slowly. Turn around." The detective had his gun leveled at Fender's chest.

Bug-eyed, Ronnie Fender complied and was instantly surrounded. His voice was a thin squeal of outrage. "Motherfuckers!! Mother . . . fuckers! Mother—"

"Handcuffs!" They snapped on.

"Where's the gas, Ronnie?" Tom demanded. He yelled "Firemen!" and the hose team appeared.

Captain Edison shoved the door open. "Get your ass back in there, Fender! Show us where the goddamn gas is!"

The three firefighters with the hose pushed forward. Fender was shoved ahead of them. He turned, terrified, looking at the hose.

"Where's the bag, Ronnie?" Tom repeated.

"Not water!" Fender yelled. "Don't turn on—" He stopped, not knowing which fear was greater. "Back here! I'll show you. At the stairs. Run! Oh, Jesus."

Why doesn't the damn bag go, Tom fumed as the whole group rushed through the empty store to the back room.

"Extinguishers!" the fire captain called. "Everybody keep your distance."

The bag, still swinging slightly, was almost, but not quite, motionless over the candle. Two firemen crouched in the door and released their extinguishers at the bag.

Oh, God, Tom groaned to himself, all this work and we're just going to get a conspiracy charge.

The foam was running down the hanging plastic bag when the bottom gave way, caught the last spark of the candle, and flashed into a fireball.

"No! No water!" Ronnie yelled in terror as he leaped backwards, away from the flames.

Tom jumped in front of the cringing man. "We must be standing right over the magnesium, right, Ronnie?"

"Farley! You motherfucker!!"

"Magnesium?"

"I don't know anything."

Tom grabbed the hose from the fireman. "Here, Ronnie?" He started to open the nozzle.

"No! No! . . . Yes!" Fender whined, defeated.

Edison looked at the detective. "I'd say you'll have to book him on attempted murder as well as arson, Lieutenant."

* * *

It was after midnight before the formalities were accomplished. Numberless coffees had slipped from paper cups to throats. Ronnie Fender was waiting for his lawyer, Cliff was waiting to take Farley to his car, and Edison was saying good-bye.

Tom excused himself, went to the phone, and dialed. "Wake you up? Sorry about that. . . . That was a perfect fall. . . . What'd you do, go in for tea . . . ? I thought you'd want to know, it helped put your man in a cell."

"Really? I'm glad you called, late or not. I was . . ." Charlene did not want to admit she had been worrying. "I was wondering how it went."

After a few minutes they said their goodnights. It left a question in Tom's mind. Had he honestly thought she would want to know—or did he just want to share it with her? Was Charlene becoming more than a part of the office?

14

A large black suitcase bumped open the door to Stretch's apartment. Stretch entered and put the suitcase down. "Welcome to my house," he said with pleasure and a certain pride. He had looked forward to having Eddie pay a visit, however brief.

Eddie came in and looked around. "Well, pardner, you should be able to rent something better than this dump pretty soon."

Shocked, Stretch surveyed the living room as if he'd never seen it before. It had looked all right when he had rented it—simple, but satisfactory. However, an accretion of materials from his experiments had gathered so slowly he had not realized how cluttered his drab little living room was now.

"I guess you're right—it's worse than Moe's. It really is a mess."

They took the five steps to the spare bedroom. With the sting of Eddie's comment, the apartment now seemed incredibly small. "Want one of your Texas Tranquilizers?" Stretch asked.

"Nope. Don't touch hard stuff the day of a job."

"I sure wish you'd stay longer. Hell, that's why I got a two-bedroom place."

The two had talked nonstop for over an hour since the 747 had landed. When they were settled with a pair of beers in the living room, Stretch picked up where they had left off.

"I still can't believe you're the telephone torch Tom Farley was talking about!"

"It was a great gimmick, but that bugger was getting on to it, so I quit. One clever son-of-a-bitch. It was me and Farley—best in the West! But I sure got tired of looking over my shoulder to see if he was there. Funny you meeting him, but like I said, Stretch, you watch out. He's mean as electric fence."

"Not to worry. I already figured he's as tough as they come, but I'll tell you, he sure is a likable guy. Have you run into any P.I.'s in New York?"

"Not so I know it. Like I said, I've been at mostly big stuff myself, but scattered. Shreveport. Scranton. Been to Sarasota, Florida, and Cincinnati twice. Half my stuff has been out of New York. Working in one place is different. Here you'll have to keep changing your accelerant, like I did when I quit using the telephone setup. You get feedback from your clients. But what I'm into now is big, impersonal, like being a heavyweight slugger. Go in, *paw!,* and get out. You, cowboy, you have to learn to live with yourself, welterweight style, dancing, ducking, fancy footwork, use your head, in-out." Eddie gave a melancholy sigh. I'm making goddamn sensational bucks, but, honestly, I miss working in Frisco."

Stretch drained his beer. "I could always give you part interest in my territory." He went to the kitchen for a refill.

"Yeah, well, my disillusionment with megabucks is not yet total," Eddie chuckled. "But I'll keep it in the back of my head."

Stretch recounted his fires, his experiments in the forest, the lights he'd done for Moe. The one fire he did not discuss technically was the Acme Fire Salvage job, though he did point out the irony of burning merchandise that had once before been snatched from the jaws of fire. Acme was like returning the phoenix to its ashes. Stretch was not ready to reveal his extraordinary method of sending Acme up in smoke. He had only tried the approach that once. Before he mentioned it to the master he wanted to know for certain that his invention was foolproof. Even without Acme, he knew Eddie was impressed.

"Hey, I forgot to tell you about crossing that creepy ex-fireman, Martin!" Stretch exclaimed.

After listening to Stretch's story, Eddie hunched up his shoulders and said, "Remember when I told you you'd do okay because you're smart and honest? I wasn't just making small talk. You're in a business full of creeps, bona fide ding-bats, crooks, and incompetents. You know, I learned a lot tending bar. People think the barman just smiles a lot, yacks a lot, and washes lots of glasses. Maybe most of them do, but you can also learn a lot. One of the things I learned from listening is that some whole fields of business are full up with guys who've got the I.Q. of a range steer. Talk to the clerk and it's 'duh,' talk to the salesman and it's 'duh,' talk to the foreman or even the manager and it's, 'yeah, duh.' Pardner, a dude who's straight and uses his head can skim the cream in a field like that—be on top in no time flat. Torching's like any business—that's why you and me are going to get rich. Arson's no place to make the society columns or get put on the Board of Education, but, Jesus, you can haul in a bunch of money if you're better than the herd. Now a guy like Marty, he's going to go to the jailhouse or the nuthouse, and in the meantime just make ends meet. That's not our style, is it soldier?"

"Guess not. Hope not anyway." Stretch was momentarily uncertain. He still had plenty of doubting periods in private. He had wanted to put up a more solid front for Eddie Barker, but suddenly his real problem spilled out. "It's not Farley that bugs me. It's being so damn solitary. It really gets to me sometimes. I mean, seriously. Sometimes I'm talking to myself. Sometimes I just get in the dumps for days for no reason."

"I told you that up front. It drives you kinda nutty, but that's part of the business. You never know who'll spill the beans. I knew right off you'd be like me. You don't feel blood brothers with the kind of people you could tell you're a torch, and the kind of people you want for friends, you don't dare hang around with for fear you'll say the wrong thing in a bar one night."

"I've thought of asking Benny if he could set me up with some kind of a cover, something respectable I could tell people about—where they could even call and check if they wanted."

"Yeah, I thought about that for a while, too," Eddie said. "Problem is, there are only two kinds of covers—the job you do and the one you don't. A job or business that you really check into regularly—well, since you don't need the money, it has to be something that really turns you on. Otherwise it makes no sense to put up with the time it takes out of your life. Say you bought a little business selling racing accessories. That would give you an excuse to race, too. But by the time you keep the shop in business nine to five and do your racing, sooner or later you're into conflicts with your real work. If you take a fake job or set up a fake business, you're sure as hell going to run into someone who has an office down the hall or next door to the address you give or someone who wants to buy what you're selling or sell what you're buying. Then you're really in trouble. Nope. I tell you, you're better off suffering a bit and keeping your freedom of action than you are if you hem yourself in by any kind of phony cover. At least, that's how I figure it—and I spent a lot of time thinking it over."

Stretch grunted in reluctant agreement with Eddie's reasoning, then said without much conviction, "Maybe I'll get used to it."

"Nope, you never get used to it. Just learn to live with it, that's all. Kinda like you were a cripple or something. But the money talks. That's what you get used to." Eddie scootched his cowboy pants around on the Naugahyde. "I'll tell you," he said, "you're off to a start like a jackrabbit, but you're still hustling. Once you're going good, you'll do fewer jobs and make more loot. Then you can hightail it off to Acapulco or Vegas and live high off the hog. That's when making it pays off. That makes me forget the lonesomes every time."

They talked until late afternoon, when Eddie had to leave.

"I'm off on the turkey vulture at eleven thirty, so I won't see you till next trip." He hefted the ominous black suitcase. "This weighs as heavy as a pack of rattlesnakes and I didn't even bring a change of socks." He clapped Stretch on the shoulder. "You need help, you can count on me. And . . . get a better place, boy. A coyote wouldn't live in this hole."

After Eddie Barker had gone, Stretch decided that he really would get a less conspicuous car and a respectable place to live—just as soon as he was a little more ahead.

* * *

The idea recurred to Tom every time he walked into the fourteenth floor, which housed the claims department of Global Insurance Co.—the big-city offices of an insurance company resemble its policies: cramped and endless. People who worked at one end of the floor-through, football-field-sized room couldn't possibly know everyone at the other side. The desks were jammed together, separated only by hedge-rows of green filing cabinets. Below the senior executive level the men invariably wore shirts and ties, but left their jackets off. The women seemed to go to the beauty shop a lot.

The wall that separated the fire claims section from the other departments was, appropriately, glass. There was nowhere to hide. You couldn't even pick your nose in private at Global Insurance unless you were high enough in rank to be rewarded with a solid wood door.

As he walked into the fire loss department, Tom Farley automatically raised his hat, ran his hand over his hair, and checked his tie. He walked toward the far corner, past another warren of desks and files.

Dee Hatford noticed her favorite private investigator imme-diately. Unconsciously, she pushed up her already uplifted bosom and fluffed her hairdo—which had to be one of the few surviving beehives west of Louisiana.

"Hi, Tom—what've you got that's hot today?" The double meaning was accented by her Southern lilt.

Tom wished she would get transferred to somewhere like the wet marine loss division, but Dee *was* the fire loss manager's personal secretary, so he made his standard reply to her standard question.

"Everything I've got's burning, Dee."

"Tom Farley, you're so *for*ward."

He gave her a wink and plunged on fearlessly, "I can't be backward and look at you."

She giggled and leaned back, accentuating her cleavage.

Tom glanced at the solid wood door behind her. The sign read: V. WHITLOCK, FIRE LOSS MANAGER. "He in?"

"Sure is—and waiting for you. Go on in."

Tom knocked, opened the door, then closed it behind him.

"Hello, Tom—sit down."

Tom tossed the Acme Fire Salvage file on the desk and watched Whitlock's poker face. The claims manager had the solid door—and he kept his jacket on. Vic was the president of the Bay Area Fire Insurors Association and rumor had it that he was in line for V.P. in charge of Global's Western region fire loss department. Tall and crew cut with heavy gold rims, he was known as tight and tough. He had a deep, commanding voice that reverberated as if he were talking in a rain barrel. His face didn't flinch at Tom's news—it rarely did.

"No dice, huh?"

"No. We checked it three ways from Sunday. Outside of the crazy way it started it's all dead ends. Nothing to do but pay it."

"That kills me! Three hundred and forty-seven thousand dollars down the drain."

"That's why people pay their premiums."

"I guess so," Whitlock said grudgingly. "Wish we could have nailed him, though."

"Next time. Who knows? Maybe it was legitimate. All I had to go on was that strange start and a hunch."

"We tried."

"Yeah. Incidentally, would you get out the Greenwood file. Remember? Nineteen seventy-seven—Robert Greenwood

Drugstore. I think I have his uncle on a burn. I'd just like to have a flip through it to see if any bells ring."

"You've got a memory like . . ." Vic Whitlock shook his head in awe. "Why, you didn't even handle that case!"

Tom just smiled and pointed at the intercom.

Dee came in with her habitual bounce, doing her best to look efficient and sexy at the same time. Tom knew from several years of dealing with her that despite the overkill exterior Dee was a perfectly competent secretary. Otherwise, she would not have been Whitlock's right arm for the last five years. All Tom knew about her was that she came from Baton Rouge, *loved* country music, swore Randy Newman was a redneck, and lived in Oakland. He guessed Dee was about thirty-two. Tom found that everything Dee did made her seem sad, lonely, and a bit desperate. But San Francisco is known for its excess of lonesome single women who harvest frustration's bitter fruit. It is hard enough to be numerically superior, as women are in Washington, D.C., but to be in the "gay capital" of the country adds a heavy psychological handicap to the statistical injury.

To sidestep the intolerable awkwardness of a strongly one-way attraction, Tom had turned their chitchat into a ritual exchange of catchy phrases. Familiarity may breed contempt, but it may also breed other things—and whatever they might have been, Tom gave them no chance to hatch.

"Dee," Vic said, "Tom wants to check the Greenwood Drugs file from seventy-seven. Would you pull it for him?"

Dee hesitated, blushed, and looked very uncomfortable. "Vic, that's one of the ones that got destroyed." Dee knew that Vic knew the file was gone—and she knew what was coming and hated it.

"Damn. I forgot, Tom, but Dee threw out a group of files some months ago and, by mistake, some of the old arson-related files hit the trash can." He looked apologetic.

Tom was stunned. It was the first breach he knew of in Vic Whitlock's reputation for perfection—even via a secretary. "I can barely believe it! You two are normally so efficient! Well, it was just for a routine check—I'll live without it." Tom smiled politely. "At least I know you're human."

"I'm sorry." Dee looked at the floor. Vic had asked her to destroy a group of fire files almost a year ago. And once before, when someone had requested one of the files, Whitlock had accused her of being responsible for their "accidental" disappearance. She assumed it was important to Vic so she had loyally submitted to the lie. After the person had left, she demanded an explanation from Vic—but got a polite flurry of excuses and the brush-off. Dee had secretly studied the list of destroyed files, but could not find any connection between them. There were some arson files, some where nothing suspicious had occurred, new files, old files—twenty-eight in all. The only thing they seemed to have in common was that rather large sums of money were involved—and Vic Whitlock's interest in their disappearance.

For months Dee had conjured up intrigues concerning those files, but she remained the picture of total discretion. After all, Vic had given her an unscheduled raise right after he had embarrassed her the first time. He was hiding something. That Vic would do this to her in front of Tom Farley was excruciating. One of her great assets was her infallible efficiency—and now it was blown in the eyes of the man she wanted most to convince of her qualities. She didn't care what kind of hanky-panky her boss was pulling with those files, he was going to have to give her another raise or an explanation if, in the future, he expected her to relieve him of the blame for destroying those files. Loyalty be damned.

15

A lot of months had been ripped off the calendar since Stretch Jackson had headed west out of West Alton. Fear had given way to frustration and frustration to the excitement and challenge of the Fire God. In the same way that racing and the car lot had consumed his life before, Prometheus consumed it now—and yet he had never had so much free time and so few friends.

Beryl Biehr was the first girl he'd met up close in the city throngs with whom he felt any personal contact, and she was taken—twice. Stretch had been properly seduced and laid by a nighclub singer he'd met in the Buddha. In a matter of days a doctor had told him the welts in his pubic area were merely a well-fed colony of *Phthirus pubis*, commonly known as "the crabs."

"Listen," the doctor had said. "You screw around with strangers in San Francisco nowadays and come up with something as minor as that—consider yourself a lucky man."

Stretch felt the need to see something woman, but he hated the phony singles bar hustle. At least at a strip joint he did not have to get "involved"—better some vicarious sex than none at all. So he walked into the Silver Doll on a Wednesday night.

The three-man band was playing the intro for the ten o'clock show with an uneven roll of the drums and a loud fanfare of trumpet. The cymbals crashed and onstage swept "Fabulous Kitty from New York City." Kitty seemed to have Scotch-taped the corners of her mouth up to maintain a permanent smile. Her stretch marks told tales of several births and advancing age; disinterest did the rest. It was a dull, sad performance. Stretch turned his attention to his bourbon and water and watched the few other clients. He found it strangely repulsive when a man at a front table waggled his tongue as the bare-bottomed stripper bumped her crotch within a foot of his nose.

Stella Starlight was younger and passable, although she didn't have enough breast to honestly twirl the tassles and her wig looked as if it had been bought in a hurry at a super-market. Stretch was bored. A guy could get more excited at a sheep auction. Stella finally got it down to her G-string and walked off.

Fanfare. Drumroll. "From the sweet heart of America! From southern Illinois and the home of Fairmont Track, where the purebreds run, the purest bred of them all—Karen from Collinsville!"

From Collinsville? Stretch couldn't believe it. The band broke into Arabian Nightsy, vaguely Middle Eastern belly-dance rhythms. Stretch did a double take when the dancer appeared. In contrast to the previous jaded, overly made-up strippers, she was a fresh, innocent-looking girl who couldn't be a day over twenty. Not a trace of makeup or lipstick blem-ished her face. Long brown hair matched deep brown eyes set in a full, high-cheekboned face. The nose was aquiline, the nostrils flared. The look was outdoors-healthy. Perhaps the contrast with the other dancers helped, but this Karen definitely did not have that hard, used look. To top it off, she could dance. She danced like a vixen. A virgin vixen. As she peeled off the layers of veils she revealed full, tight, girl-breasts, a carved, flat stomach, and squarish, muscled thighs.

From Collinsville! The thought echoed in his mind—and elsewhere. Halfway through her act, Stretch had to scootch his Levi's down.

He remembered what a biology graduate in his company had said in a Saigon strip joint. "It's called the *mons veneris*, the mountain of Venus, just in front of the pubic bone. Girls who tuck their *mons veneris* in and stick out their bottom have sexual guilt problems and are trying to hide their vagina. They're full of rigidities and complexes. Find one that keeps her mountain forward and still has a good rear end—now *that's* a woman." The language wasn't graceful but the meaning was clear—and Karen was a woman on both counts.

Ever since the explanation, Stretch had understood why he loved to watch the way a girl was shaped below the stomach and the way she held herself. The sexiest single thing he found about a girl was her mound of Venus and the way it folded under to her ultimate treasure.

Karen left him breathless. She was pure and sensual and Stretch Jackson fell in love with her right then and there. She didn't bump, she didn't grind, and she didn't drop it on any front-row table as Kitty had. She wafted like a reed in a gentle breeze, finished, and left every man in the place agasp.

When she was called back for bows, the bald man in front stood up and waggled his tongue again. Stretch wanted to punch him, but decided he'd better not make a scene. She must be used to it, working in this place.

In a few minutes the strippers started circulating among the sparse group of customers. Kitty from New York City headed for the appreciative bald man with the wagging tongue and another heavy breather who sat with him.

Stella came right up and sat in the chair next to Stretch. She put her hand on his thigh and said, "Hi, I'm Stella. Want to buy me a drink? What's your name, honey?"

Stretch's eyes were glued on the backstage door. Karen did not appear. "Where's the one named Karen?" he asked bluntly.

"Oh, she doesn't come out with the customers." Her hand moved up his thigh. "I do, though. Come on," she coaxed gently, "I'm dying of thirst. Girl needs a drink after a workout like that. Did you like it?"

Too distracted to pussyfoot around, Stretch asked, "What do you mean she doesn't come out? Why not?"

Stella's hand slid right up to his crotch. "Oooh. Hey, I think we both need a drink, honey."

Stretch got out a twenty. "Look, *I'm* from Collinsville, too. I really want to talk to Karen. Why don't you just keep this and tell her there's a guy here from her hometown who would seriously like to say hello. If she thinks I'm putting her on, tell her I used to work at Swanson Cadillac."

Stella hesitated.

"Come on, Stella. Take the twenty. I'm not going to bite the girl."

"I don't think she will. Honest, she doesn't come out."

"Try it." He laid on all the blue-eyed charm and sincerity that were in him.

Five interminable minutes later Karen stood in the door. Stella pointed to the good-looking young man at the table. Karen hesitated, Stella prodded, and finally the girl came in Stretch's direction.

In fact, he hardly knew Collinsville. He had occasionally been there to buy cars, but he didn't like the town and had never stayed long enough for lunch. No matter, he thought, I'll come up with something.

As Karen approached the table, Stretch's heart began pounding, a tight knot formed in his stomach, and his mouth went chalk dry. Stretch felt an intense desire to run his fingertips across her full lips, very gently, very slowly.

"Hi," Karen said suspiciously. "You really from Collinsville?"

"No." He gulped at the chance he was taking. "No, I'm really from West Alton, but it seemed close enough."

She tilted her head, looking doubtful.

"But with all those phony names, Kitty from New York City and that last one, Blossom Buttercup, and all, I thought maybe Karen wasn't from Collinsville either." He couldn't tear his gaze from hers. "At least I'm honest."

She sized him up, moved her finger along her lips. "Okay— I'm not from Collinsville either."

"Ah-ha!"

A smile rippled across her mouth. "Everyone who plays horses has heard of Collinsville. I'm really from Litchfield.

Only you and I know where that is. But West Alton! That's even worse!"

Stretch laughed with joy and relief. "Litchfield!" He half rose. "Jesus, Litchfield! Sit down." He felt an aura of warmth and faint woman smell approach and occupy a space which somehow overlapped with his. "And is it really Karen?"

"Karen Canfield . . . the real McCoy."

"Litchfield! Can you beat that!" He studied her peaches-and-cream face, not daring to drop his eyes lower. "I'm Stretch Jackson. Played on the only team that ever drubbed you guys two years in a row. But you must be just out of high school—wouldn't remember that. How'd you get to this place, anyway?"

"High school! Am I ever sick of that. I've got a B.A. and two years of teaching at Litchfield High and I'm twenty-five going on twenty-six."

Stretch sucked in his breath. He wasn't robbing the cradle after all. "A bachelor's?"

"Yes, I stayed close to home and went to Cranston. Did a major in French and phys. ed., then came back and taught. Dad was head designer at the International Shoe factory. Just when I settled in to teaching French and women's phys. ed. he got promoted to St. Louis. I hate St. Louis, so I rented a cute little house and stayed."

"And here?" Stretch inquired. Karen shifted in her chair and accidentally brushed his leg with hers. Hot pokers emanated from the touch.

She bit her lip. "About six months ago, I'd had enough. Needed some sea, sun, and distance between me and it."

"Just like me." He was not about to tell her why he had really left home.

"Stella Starlight," she laughed, "is really Marie Jerzinski. We were friends right up through high school. My mom disapproved. You know, coal miner's daughter from the wrong side of the tracks, all that junk. But Marie was always fun and generous. Well, she was home on vacation just when I decided to leave. She kind of mothered me to here."

A waitress came up and squeaked, "Want a drink, honey?"

"I didn't even think to ask you," Stretch apologized. "Do you want one, Karen?" It broke the intensity of his feelings. Turning to look at the waitress was the first time he had glanced away from Karen's eyes and lips since she had sat down.

"Ginger, Marlene."

"Don't you want something real?"

"I never drink here."

Stretch ordered a bourbon and water. Questions flooded his head. He wanted to know everything about her, to hold her, to take her to a beach, to make love to her. Whoa, Jackson, he said to himself. Don't scare her off. College grad! Christ!

She gave him a smile that melted what little was left of his heart. "And you?" Her eyes smiled like her mouth.

"Damn, it's good to talk to somebody from home. Got to come clear across the country to meet someone from thirty miles away."

Laughing, she put her hand on his arm, naturally and for just an instant. That instant changed something for both of them.

It was only after the light touch on Stretch's arm that Karen realized what she'd done. Over a year had passed since she had touched a man, except for relatives and handshakes. She had not even thought about touching Stretch. It had just happened, casually, comfortably—as though her pain had gone away. A luxurious tingle went through her body.

Karen watched the masculine face carefully. It was strong. The eyes were honest. No threat or danger came from anything he did or said. She felt the presence of someone she could trust, completely. Stretch Jackson moved and spoke cleanly, quickly—and she knew instinctively he wasn't playing games with her. If ever her eyes had gazed upon a man more smitten, it escaped her recollection. The way his thoughts and feelings read openly, like a book—or like a boy—extended a charming invitation for her to be as guileless as he was.

"I really don't understand how you made the switch from teaching French in Litchfield to being a stripper here. I really don't."

"Sometimes I don't either. I hadn't the foggiest idea of doing it when I came. I was just Marie's guest, and at first I had the same reaction toward Marie. You know—how could she do this? It's everything nice middle-class mothers keep their daughters away from. Dirty. Low class. But eventually everybody here befriended me. After a month or so I had to get a job and find a place of my own. Couldn't camp at Marie's forever and hang around here waiting for her to finish every night. Kitty—sweet, over-the-hill Kitty—was the one who talked me into it, backstage one night. I'd been trying to give her some new ideas about body movements—imagine *me* telling *her* how to shake it—but I'd studied modern dance a lot. She called in a couple of girls and got me to demonstrate, sly like she is. Before I knew it, everybody was talking me into it. Marie had her reservations, knowing me, but they got the manager to agree to my not coming out afterward, which means pushing drinks and getting felt up all the time.

"Easy—he's the big bouncer over there by the door—he takes care of me like I was a baby or something. Any guy gets out of hand and Easy's all over him. Hours are good, pay's good, and I couldn't be safer in a nunnery. They watch me like a hawk. Every one of them mothers me—even Easy." She leaned close in and whispered confidentially. "I think that big galoot's more scared of women than anything in the world. Fact, I think he mothers over me because he's gay."

"No shit!" Stretch looked at the huge bouncer and couldn't believe it.

"Oh, come on—don't be so southern Illinois. He's sweet and easy—like his name."

"I just . . ."

"You don't have to be antigay to be virile, you know. Anyway, he's been super. They've all been super."

"But . . . don't you care about showing off all you've got? I think it's fabulous, but—I mean . . ."

Laughing, she put her hand on his sleeve and left it there. "Yeah. I was just as hick as you get. I'd danced in tights in public at school recitals. They climb up your crotch a bit, but

167

the idea of showing all of it to a bunch of drunks in a strip joint seemed—ick! The folks here kept saying, 'But listen, movie stars do it and theater actresses do it and it doesn't mean *anything* anymore.' After . . ." Karen abruptly changed her course. "One evening, Kitty conned me into stripping to my panties to show her some movements in the dressing room. She said, 'See, that's all there is to it.' When I looked up, a couple of the girls and the manager had been watching from the door and they started clapping. It was like Kitty told me—you don't even have to be aware of the audience."

"So you said yes."

"Pretty much. They would get me to strip in the dressing room and pretend they were the customers, staring and making noises so I'd get used to the rowdy part. When I went on for real about four months ago, I was pretty ready for it. Except the first few nights I got goose bumps and my . . . well, my nipples stayed so hard it hurt." She put her fist over her mouth to cover a half-embarrassed giggle.

They talked intensely. She painted in the numbers of her life. Stretch, the "salvage man," did too—with a few changes and omissions about the recent past. Strong, mutual vibrations wove them together. Stretch yearned desperately to do things he couldn't do in the Silver Doll.

"Oh, my God," she gasped. "I'm on next!"

As she jumped up, Stretch said, "You'll come back?" worried that she might disappear.

"Yes—I'll come back." She said it sincerely, but a wrinkle— like fear—flicked across her forehead.

Lighthearted as a robin on a worm farm, Stretch could not get over the fact that this girl had come all the way from Litchfield to meet her fate. Nor could he believe that he was falling for a stripper. His mother would have chewed his ear off. She's a French teacher, Mom, is what he'd say. As Karen said, strippers are people, too, and so are bartenders, waitresses, and queer bouncers. Must be multimillions of them in America. And torches, he added, smiling to himself. He wondered what

Karen would say to that and instantly concluded that he was not ready to find out.

The Silver Doll had filled up. The Wednesday night meeting of some Kiwanis Club had adjourned and regrouped for a little fun away from the wives. By the time the midnight show began they were well enough oiled to even get rudely excited by New York City Kitty, who rose to the occasion and let ones and fives and tens get tucked roughly in her G-string. The bald lech at the front-row table threw the Kiwanians into a rage of laughter when he put out his tongue, slapped a new twenty-dollar bill on it, and did his idiotic best to get it slobbered into the center spot.

Uneasiness about what this loud bunch might do when Karen came on advanced across Stretch's epidermis. He felt possessive, though he knew he had no right to feel that way. During Stella/Marie's act, tension turned him crisp. He thought it might be better if he left rather than watch Karen debase herself in front of this ugly crowd of slobs, but he stayed, because more than anything else he wanted to see her perform again.

When Karen did come out, Stretch was so absorbed by her sensual beauty as she danced that he saw nothing else. He had no doubt that it was all for him—and it was even more hypnotizing than the first time. Karen looked right at him once or twice, which turned his mind to butter. He catalogued everything, from the fact that her bare feet were smooth and round and perfectly formed to the small mole slightly below her lower left rib.

She danced longer and more slowly than the others, dropping the veils at a leisured pace even as the tempo quickened. She was the only girl who didn't tease the customers openly. She didn't have to, for there was something in her very nature that made her wildly desirable and, at the same time, ephemeral as smoke.

Karen's nipples were welded into tight brown knots. When the dance attained blood heat and her body was almost nude,

Stretch sat, paralyzed, transfixed by the Moving Mound. Karen seemed to be reaching for a climax. She arched her back, dropped her hands behind her to the floor, and yoked her lithe body to the throbbing rhythm. Below the G-string, the muscles on the insides of her thighs tightened and were sculptured into narrow hollows that led the way right to that sacred inner sanctum. Stretch's mind made love to every inch of Karen Canfield on the spot.

It ended without warning. Karen sprang to her feet, bowed quickly, and ran offstage. Jolted conscious, Stretch realized that the bedlam rivaled the decibel level in Broadway Game. There was every kind of whoop and whistle known to man. Bills were raining on an empty stage. Karen came out, bowed, smiled, waved, and left. An assistant quickly rounded up the bills.

So it *was* true. She did her act as neat as you please, and because it was erotic instead of porn, she was not only the star but stayed untouched.

Christ, he thought, I hope she's not a virgin! In a place like Litchfield it could happen—even in this aphrodisiac era.

When a waitress came by Stretch ordered another drink and started counting time. After ten minutes, mild panic set in.

He was ready to get up and head for the dressing rooms when Karen stepped through the door and made a beeline for him, avoiding all eyes and invitations to sit elsewhere.

"I didn't come sooner because I wanted this mob to settle first."

"You are fan-tastic."

"Thanks. But that's just my body out there."

"No, I mean all of you. All of it put together."

"You sure know what to say to a girl."

"I don't 'know what to say'—it's what I really mean." He allowed himself to put his hand on her bare forearm. "I think you're very special."

Karen immediately broke the contact by lifting her arm to run her fingers through her hair. The words coupled with the touch were more direct than she was prepared to cope with at the moment. "God, it gets hot out there under those spots."

"You think it gets hot out *there*!" He laughed to take the hard edge off his words. "Don't you ever get attacked by any of these lulus?"

"Oh," she snorted, "once in a while. One guy took it right out of his pants and came charging at me like he was Saint George and I was the dragon. I didn't even see him till he was about a foot away and Easy had him by the neck. I don't think his feet touched ground till he hit the pavement outside."

They were off on a story-trading trip. About twenty minutes later, Stretch was working his way up to inviting her home when a big, sodden Kiwanian weaved his way to the table.

"Hey, buddy, this little shtripper," he said, "is the prettiest girl in the place. You got her cornered long enough. How'd you like to buzz off and give me a shot at it?"

Standing up, furious, Stretch said, "I'll give you a shot, fella—right in the mouth! You always talk like that to ladies?"

"Ladies? All these broads put out, stupid. Come on, move over."

He gave Stretch a push and got one back. He stumbled into a chair and, yelling an obscenity, got up, and charged forward.

Karen jumped out of the way. "Stretch, leave him alone!" she said, clearly meaning "He's not worth it." She tugged at Stretch's arm.

Suddenly, Easy's ham hand dropped a painfully tight grip on Stretch's shoulder. The bouncer didn't know what was going on, but he *had* heard Karen tell this guy to leave the man alone. "Hey, buddy," he said to Stretch, "why don't you cool it!"

The Kiwanian yelled at Easy, "Yeah, get that cocksucker out of here!"

Insulted from the front, attacked from behind, and feeling humiliated before Karen, Stretch saw red. He wrenched his head around and snarled, "Get your hands off me, you queer—"

"Stretch!" Karen screamed, horrified.

The next distinguishable sentence was Easy's as he dumped Stretch outside. "You come back in here and you'll carry it home in a paper bag—asshole!" The bouncer spat the words at Stretch and slammed the door of the Silver Doll.

When Stretch sat upright at the curb, a sharp pain stabbed his neck muscles. "Shit!" he said, pounding his ineloquent rage and frustration into the sidewalk with his fist. "Shit! Shit! Shit!"

A moment later, the drunk who had started it all was shoved out the door. Stretch stood and made a move to bloody the bastard's nose but checked himself. The mess was his own fault. *He'd* lost his head. The way Karen felt about Easy, it was unlikely that she was going to come out and hold Stretch Jackson's hand.

"Shit!" he hurled in the drunk's direction, and, feeling defeated, turned to get into the Camaro.

* * *

It was after three when the lights went out at the Silver Doll. Karen stepped into the darkening street with her home-town friend, Marie. Stretch had been the first man to touch sweet chords inside her since she had fled from Litchfield. It was the first time she had felt herself begin to open up once more, which made the abrupt ending doubly agonizing. Depression's pit began to suck her in again.

Marie looked at her, recognized the symptoms, and said, "Come on, baby, leave your car. You stay over with me. I'll cheer you up." She put her arm around her friend's waist and gave her a hug.

Karen nodded.

Marie had always had that pragmatic resilience to hard knocks, but Karen got steamrollered by life and then required slow, gentle nursing to return to normal. Streetwise Marie enjoyed the role of nurse. She'd come a long way from Litchfield in six city years.

En route to her cozy, if disorderly, apartment, Marie kept up a kindly stream of chatter. Little of it registered on Karen's unhappy mind. The harsh memories of Litchfield strode too painfully through her head. It was the first time in several months that they had come back to bully her. Each time they came she rummaged about in the little terrors of recollection, just as one continues to scratch helplessly at an already painful mosquito bite.

Southern Illinois lay in the heart of the Bible Belt, and Cranston College, in the heart of the heart, was one of those fine, small institutions built first around the Good Book—then the others. The school was strict in its religion (antidrinking, antigambling, antismoking, antidancing, antimovies, and so antifornication that the subject was the central topic of conversation.)

Although the Canfields were not of the school's evangelical religion, they had chosen Cranston for Karen because it was near Litchfield and had high scholastic standards. Karen avoided most of the hellfire-and-brimstone prayer meetings, and despite constant prodding from both her professors and peers, she did not "repent for her sins." The guilt and repentance cycle offended her sensitivity. She simply was not disposed to public confessions of sins, jumping over pews, or writhing in the aisles, possessed by Christ. In fact, Karen thought the flailing, screaming confessions, the anguished repentance, and the inevitable, ultimate writhing part looked suspiciously like having an orgasm. She knew perfectly well what many of those pious souls did when no one was looking, and neither hypocrisy nor marring life's pleasures with a cross of guilt seemed to her a reasonable way to live. Four years of exposure to that strident morality did leave a mark which would, no doubt, follow her for life. The emotional extravagances of fundamentalism failed to mar Karen's delicious loss of virginity or the tender, if infrequent, loves that followed.

Karen majored in French, because of the grace of the language and the profound bittersweet philosophy of the literature. She dreamed that after college she would travel to Paris, walk in the gardens of Montsouris, haunt the Left Bank bistros, and fall in love to the music of Charles Aznavour.

The postgraduation reality turned out to be a position back at Litchfield's Craig Memorial High School.

Ralph Sweeney—married, bald, and a bastard—had been the principal when Karen was still in high school. One of those men whose lipless mouths turn down in a permanent crescent, he had been feared as a strict and merciless disciplinarian for fifteen years. One of the reasons Karen won the teaching job was because Sweeney was a zealous Cranston graduate with a soft spot for his fellow alumni. What the students didn't know, and few of the teachers suspected, was that one of their iron-fisted principal's few pleasures was luring young teachers to bed. Despite his flabby, aging body, his mind was sharp and so was his drive for sex and power. He was shrewd, he was a bully, and he wanted Karen Canfield.

A new teacher has so many events and ideas to juggle that subtleties can be overlooked. Originally, Karen thought Sweeney must be kidding. Her real problem was how to maintain student discipline when her puppy-love face gave her the deceptive appearance of being eighteen, like her pupils.

But it was that very childlike innocence, coupled with her completely womanly body, that spurred Sweeney on. Karen had a purity that needed to be broken.

Her first year was trying, but eventually she earned the respect she needed to get the students' cooperation. Ralph Sweeney, however, refused to cooperate and frequently cornered her with increasingly insistent suggestions. She tried laughing it off, avoiding him whenever she could, but once she realized how determined Sweeney was, Karen became truly frightened. Sweeney knew very well how to play on her guilelessness and beginner's lack of confidence.

Just the effect of surviving the first year made Karen begin the second one in better spirits. Phillip Griggs, a friend of her younger sister, had been Karen's brightest French student right from the beginning. Phil would graduate in January and go away to Cornell. During his last semester, they spent many hours after class together, talking French, polishing his accent, and sipping coffee. Sometimes she even invited him to the little house she rented. To the surprise and profound delight of both of them, Phil's joking "Voulez-vous coucher avec moi?" turned into reality one early autumn evening.

Mutual admiration of teacher and student is hardly rare, nor is it unknown for esteem to blossom into another dimension. Yet, God knows, a teacher/student affair is a truly forbidden liaison, especially in a small town. But the couple was very discreet and a delicate relationship blossomed, lovely and guiltless. It ended, with only a twinge of pain, when Phil headed east to college.

Glad to be through at the end of a hard Friday, Karen had stopped by the principal's office. He had asked her to see him after his last appointment to discuss a problem student's grades. He assured her it would just take a minute.

They had had a low-key discussion of grades until Sweeney looked up and said without warning, "I hear you spent a lot of last semester in bed with Phillip Griggs."

"I . . ." Karen's blood turned icy. She went deathly white and groped for words.

But Sweeney had just begun. He jumped up, red-faced, and shouted at her about corrupting student morals. Criminal charges had nothing to do with it— this was a graver offense. "You knew that, too, didn't you, when you lured the boy into your bed like a whore! How did it feel, teaching an eighteen-year-old to do it?"

Karen sat riveted, grasping the chair, too stunned to move. Even seated, her knees shook with a tremble she could not control.

"You're a disgrace to the school and the community! You're a shame to your family and your profession! You just thought about what went on between your goddamn legs—didn't you?"

Her chin quivered. "I . . ."

"I'm going to have to fire you and put it on your records. You may never teach again!" He put his face close to hers.

Stammering, Karen tried to explain, to protest, but he screamed her to silence. Clever Sweeney knew his art. He hurled threats and accusations like God's lightning bolts and pierced every atom of her conscience with them. What would her father say? How could she live in this town as a slut? He turned the tender love affair into a sordid melodrama and her into a cheap whore.

He stopped behind her chair, put his hand on her shoulder, and said in a quieter tone, "I hate to say all of this to you, Karen. Coming from Cranston, I thought you were a woman of high morals and a good upbringing."

"I'm sorry, Mr. Sweeney," she said weakly.

"And me—you didn't think what you were doing to me! Casting doubts on all of our morals, on the kind of school I run!"

Tears coursed uncontrolled down her cheeks. "No. I didn't think. It just . . . happened . . . I'm sorry."

He gripped the nape of her neck. "You're sorry?" he bellowed. "You're guilty, you slut! You have sinned!" He lashed her with shame, his own and hers. She must accept her guilt. She must repent. She must learn contrition. He didn't want to take this to the school board.

Now he softened, now he changed. Karen saw her life coming down in ugly ruins: the years of study, the sacrifice of her family, her reputation, the future. Her thoughts were jammed in crazy disorder. Neither her mind nor her body were able to function. Yes. It was her fault. She felt Sweeney's hand. She knew what he wanted. Contrition. Repentance. Oh, God. She was guilty, but she didn't want him.

She floundered. She looked up at Sweeney to ask his forgiveness. Her mouth moved. Inaudibly hoarse, she repeated "I'm sorry" again—and again. She put her hand on his. If this is repentance, she thought, please, God, make it quick.

In that early winter darkness, Sweeney hustled her, full of fear and confusion, straight from his office to the bed of her shame, to her own room, where she had committed the sins. He took off his belt and whipped her like a naughty child. Salt-bitter tears clogged in her throat. Her skin burned. Her thoughts raced wildly, out of control. I repent. I deserve it. I am guilty. I will. I hate you. Do it fast.

She felt him come into her roughly, then slide in and out with an increasing ease. Karen's mind went one way, her body another. Slowly, her muscles grew tight, then, defying all but Cranston logic, they gradually gripped into rhythmic contractions that grew urgent and rapid. She resisted, yet found herself rushing to repentance, blinked her eyes open, and then closed them hard to the shame of a climax. I submit to contrition. Sweet God, I'm coming. I'm sorry! I'm sorry. One by one Sweeney forced repentance into every intimate corner of Karen's young body. There were cries of "I'm guilty. I accept it. I'm sorry." And spasms of pain, of pleasure, of hate, of I'm coming, Christ, I'm coming!

Two hours later, Karen lay dazed in a numb, naked heap. Sweeney tucked his shirttail in his pants, bent over, smiling, and brushed his hand across her face and said, "You were marvelous. Now that you've learned, we will do it again, for not only is penitence a continuing experience, it is far more profound and rewarding than sin." Sweeney no longer harbored any intention of going to the school board—of course, he never had.

Marie pulled the car to a stop in front of her apartment. The two women got out and went upstairs. They showered, made a final cup of coffee, and sat at the kitchen table.

"He looked different," Karen said wistfully. "There was something straight and kind about Stretch."

"Straight? Honey, that's the understatement of the year! I admit, he *looked* nice, but lots of them *look* that way. It's when you start eating the pudding that you find the lumps. They don't float on the surface, you know. And it works both ways. Sometimes the best ones look rough as a cob."

Karen looked at Marie. "Why do men always have to play so tough?"

Marie gave her a warm and reassuring hug. "You weren't made for this world, honey. You'll find a good man one day. They're just few and far between. Meanwhile, you got a choice between being as tough as they are—or being lonely as hell. It's a lousy choice. Come on, baby. Time for bed."

"I don't know what I'd do without you. You got so wise since we graduated, and I've stayed so dumb."

"Hush." Marie pulled Karen to her feet, turned off the light, and headed for the bedroom.

They lay close and comforting in bed. Marie cradled Karen in her arms like a child.

Karen said quietly, "Somewhere there's a soft man. Not mushy, just sensitive—and gentle."

"Yes—somewhere. Don't be so impatient. Gentleness isn't a common commodity with men these days."

"I don't want to get gray waiting."

"He's just around the corner, baby."

Sighing deeply, Karen said, "You mother me so." She moved closer to Marie. "I keep falling down and you keep picking me up." She paused and sighed again. "Oh, God, Marie. Why can't men be like women—but still be men?" Marie didn't answer. Her tongue slowly rippled its soft buds across Karen's tight-bundled nipple, felt the rising of the silk-smooth breast. Her hand moved tenderly over the fine girl-hairs of Karen's thigh. Athletic dancer's muscles firmed and trembled very slightly. Just below the downy V, tension sculptured a narrow hollow along the inside of the parted legs. Marie caressed that concave space and with infinite care, and caring, followed it to the moist mouth of Venus, followed the tunnel into the mountain.

"Sweet Jesus, Marie," Karen moaned like a pine wind, "You are always so gentle."

* * *

From the Silver Doll Stretch had gone to the Buddha. Waldo sat with a new, pretty playmate who was, no doubt, dazzled by his diamonds. He sat in gentlemanly aloofness under the statue, paying Old World court to a girl who wasn't half his age.

Stretch joined Benny and his blonde with the Styrofoam superstructure. Sweet Pea came in and made it a foursome.

178

But it wasn't any of these people who Stretch really wanted to see. He was waiting for the musician-stripper crowd to come in after the clubs closed. He planned to ask around, to see what he could find out about the Silver Doll people—especially one named Karen.

He had decided to give tonight's wound some time to heal. Then he would find a way to start all over. Every pure detail of the child-faced woman was branded in his head—every detail of her body, every movement, every single word she'd said. Something profound was stirred in Stretch Jackson that had never been touched before.

Karen Canfield was not going to be just one more meteor flashing through his life. Not as easily as that. Not if Stretch could help it.

16

Hunger doesn't usually look in the fridge before it strikes. With a lunchtime stomach twitch and not even a leftover in the larder, Stretch made a quick trip to the grocery store. When he returned, a colossus who resembled an escapee from Central Casting's selection of thug/bodyguards was leaning ominously against the apartment door.

"Hey! You Stretch Jackson?"

"Why?"

"I got a message for you." He held out a business card.

Stretch read it: AMALGAMATED BUILDING TRADES UNION. FRANK SIEVERS, PRESIDENT. The address and telephone number followed.

"Mr. Sievers would like to see you at three thirty tomorrow, in his office."

"What for?"

"Most people get a message from Frank know what it's about. He don't tell me." He gave Stretch a bullet-biting look. "When the boss asks somebody to come, they usually don't ask questions. And they're usually right on time." He turned and swung down the hallway like a gorilla in shoes.

"Hey!" Stretch called. "What if I can't make it?"

The man stopped and looked back. "Them's *your* apples, Jackson." And he started down the stairs.

Stretch was putting mayonnaise on a ham sandwich when it hit him. Other than Eddie and his mother, no one, strictly no one, had his address! Eddie would never have given it out without telling him. His mother certainly didn't send this Sievers around, and his phone had been unlisted ever since he'd been in San Francisco.

Amalgamated was no major union—if it were he felt certain he would have heard of it. He opened the Yellow Pages. They were big with Ma Bell, which only deepened the mystery.

So far, he'd followed Eddie's advice to the letter and had been a model of discretion. Only Benny, Caruso—if he remembered—and Stretch's handful of clients knew what he did. All they had was a telephone number, and they would have phoned first if they were introducing someone new.

Whoever this Frank Sievers was, he had somehow found out about Stretch—and evidently had had him tailed. Stretch didn't like the whole situation, but it seemed wiser to go, if only to find out what the devil was going on.

* * *

"Have a seat. It won't be a minute." The raven-haired receptionist looked like she might have a bit of gypsy in her blood. Her smile suggested that people did what she asked.

Stretch sat. He smiled back, although he didn't honestly feel like smiling. The receptionist returned to her desk, leaned another smile on him, and went back to typing. Her smile had made him flash on Karen. It didn't mean anything in particular. Since the Silver Doll encounter, every attractive woman he saw reminded him of Karen. It was becoming an involuntary reflex, like heartbeats. In the surrounding of Amalgamated Karen's dancing image did not last for long.

Something about the setup made him nervous. He studied the room, which was paneled in honest-to-God wood paneling, carpeted in wall-to-wall thick blue pile, and plushly furnished. It looked legitimate enough. Too legitimate, in fact.

The intercom beeped. The gypsy receptionist talked into it, then ushered Stretch through the door marked PRESIDENT.

The president's office decor was slightly reminiscent of San Francisco Whorehouse 1900's style. Posh, all right, but *too*

181

much leather and red velvet. On the wall behind the oversized desk, flanked by flags, was a large, carved logo, obviously the union's: a muscular arm, bent 90 degrees at the elbow, with bulging biceps and a clenched fist.

Sievers stood behind his desk, studying some enlargements. A man in his mid-fifties, he had gone slightly jowly, slightly puffy-eyed, slightly overweight—yet the shape of what had once been a pile-driver body remained very much in evidence. He could probably still drive his fist through a wall—even with someone between the fist and the wall.

He looked up as Stretch approached the desk. His manner exuded authority before he said a word. The president was clearly used to giving orders that were not to be contradicted—unless one liked pain. Like his office, though, Sievers missed the smooth urbanity he so clearly sought. His gray suit, for example, although obviously expensive, was not quite well tailored enough to hide the beef-and-brawn essence of a roughneck construction boss.

"I'm Frank Sievers, Jackson."

"I've got that impression." Stretch wasn't feeling like small talk. "What is it you want?"

"Come 'round here and look at this."

Stretch moved around the desk. The blowups were of a large, heavy-equipment storage garage.

"Now, I don't care what it costs. I want you to burn that son-of-a-bitch to the ground!"

Fear whipped across Stretch's face for a split second before he exploded. "Who the hell do you think you're talking to?"

"You're the torch, aren't you?"

"Somebody put fucking looney bugs in your Cream of Wheat, Sievers?" Stretch stormed toward the door.

"Hey, Jackson—"

Stretch whirled and barked, "I don't know who you are or what your game is, but you got the wrong approach and the wrong guy!"

Frank watched the door slam, pushed the intercom button, and said, "Tell Henry it's okay."

Stretch got no farther than the door to the receptionist's office. Henry—the brute who had originally delivered Siever's card—blocked the door.

"Mr. Sievers would like to have another word with you, Jackson," Henry rasped.

There was not a sliver of room for argument. Stretch angrily allowed himself to be shown back into the presidential office. The gypsy smiled as he passed her again.

"Okay, Jackson. You passed the first hurdle. If you'd reacted any differently I'd have kicked you out. If you'd come on talking business, Henry'd have shown you right to the elevator." He flashed a grin. Even when Frank Sievers's mouth smiled, his eyes didn't. "Now we know who we are, let's start again. I have a very special proposition for a man who's first class *and* very discreet."

"You talk, I'm listening." It wasn't as if there was much choice.

"Sit down. Call me Frank." He motioned Stretch to a corner sofa that had red leather cushions and a contrasting burgundy crushed-velvet back. "Let me start from the beginning. We're an independent local union—big, but local. We cover the San Francisco area and the East Bay. San Jose and the South Bay is someone else's, at least for the moment. I built this union from scratch by amalgamating three weak little outfits in the building trades back in the late fifties. Contracting's a tough business. I didn't get here by pussyfooting around. Did everything I had to do to build a top-notch organization, and I had only one thing in mind—my workers. I got one slogan: Full Employment, Full Pay. Used to be easy for builders to hire scab labor, pay cheap, and get away with it. Goddamn, we've made that tough to do anymore. My men stick with me because I deliver. They don't ask *how*, they just want jobs and top money.

"Well, times change, we change, methods change. There are still builders, especially in Oakland—including some big ones—who won't cooperate, don't have a closed shop, or won't buy our terms. The days are long gone when you could get away with making physical threats. I can't go breaking arms or dropping builders in the bay . . . and I think I've developed a plan more effective than just muscle."

Stretch moved uneasily on the couch. It was designed so that one sat lower in it than Sievers did in the facing chair. One could neither perch on the soft and formless cushion's edge nor stand up in a hurry. "I still want to know what you know," he said.

The union boss walked over to his desk, pulled a legal pad from a drawer, and tore off two pages that were covered with fine writing. He put them in the big ashtray on the glass-topped coffee table in front of the couch. With the table lighter he set fire to one end. Frank sat down again, looking at Stretch across the flames.

"Everything, Jackson. I've seen you before, my men have checked you out from A to Z, I know all about you—and you're clean." He caught Stretch's startled look across the table. "Don't worry. You're not on anyone's record, not even the police's—and mine just went up in smoke. You only got in here because you're spotless—because I am, too. An upstanding member of the community. Right? My specialty is knowing what goes on in the cracks and corners. I get where even the police can't. In certain circles—extremely closed circles, I might add—you're considered to be very good in your profession.

"Now, I want you to understand, I'm not going around putting guys out of business. This is for the union. It's to earn workingmen better pay and pensions and to avoid long strikes that cost us—and our members—a fortune. It'll save millions in strike pay, which comes out of union funds and the worker's pocket. I want these sons-of-bitches to get the message before it comes to that. Besides, their insurance company'll put them back on their feet in no time flat. It'll save us, it'll save them on strikes—and so what if their premiums go up a few cents a thousand? Everybody's money ahead and grief saved. No, I got pull in this city—and I also got clout." He leaned forward to emphasize his statement. "In the old roughhouse days they called me S.S.—Strong-arm Sievers. Well, it's not S.S.

anymore. We got a good union. I'm a respectable business-man. We got classy lawyers and control more money than lots of banks. This here's my own private project. There's some tough work involved and I don't want no scumbag for the job. I want a guy to be my new strong arm, somebody who reports to me and me only, who can make a fire without even a sniff of arson in the smoke—because I will break the news to the builder personally. I'll provide all the inside info needed on a job. It's the old days brought up to date—quiet, with class. What I hear, Jackson, you could fill the bill."

The information, the logic, and the compliment restored Stretch's confidence. "Sure. I could fill the bill, but what about the specifics?"

"It's full time. You work exclusively for me. Seventy-five hundred a light and more or less a burn a month."

"Nope. What you're asking is ten cash—and up front," Stretch said boldly.

"All right. If you're good enough. Not in advance on the first one. But you pull it off, it's up front on the rest."

"As long as it's clean. I won't touch anything lived in."

"It's strictly clean, industrial."

"You ask for anything else and I'll burn you out."

"You'll do *what?*" Frank's eyes registered twenty below zero.

"I didn't mean that literally," Stretch said, realizing he'd gone too far. "I just like things nice and clear."

"Sure . . . okay, that's fair. That's your reputation. You're smart, Stretch. I like a guy who comes on strong—if he can back it up. That's the next step. Come over here."

Frank and Stretch studied the blowups on the desk. The big one-story brick building was filled with trucks and earth-moving equipment.

"Nothing's impossible, but that's a real bitch," Stretch admitted.

"Trial by fire. You pull it off and you've got the job."

* * *

185

Stretch gingerly edged a long broom handle upwards. At the far end the handle was fitted into a metal holder, which in turn he had soldered to a three-pronged grappling hook. Attached to the hook's eye end was a rope. Standing on the ground, Stretch cautiously raised the tool through the cool night air. Ten feet above him a large, steel-casement window was open. He deftly maneuvered the hook around the window's steel central divider and pulled the rope tight. Stretch lowered the broom handle, glanced up and down the long dark wall of the building, hefted a heavy knapsack onto his shoulders, and climbed up the rope to the window. It was two thirty. By the time the first-in rig arrived he planned to be out of Oakland.

Stretch had stopped by the garage three weeks before, milled in among the workmen, and inconspicuously inspected the structure. He had also clocked the night watchman's outside rounds and had pored over Sievers's detailed photos. If the union president wanted to know the extent of his prospect's talents, he could not have chosen a tougher site for the test.

The building seemed to be an ordinary big brick rectangle, but to the specialist it was an oddity because its high semicircular roof was supported by wood instead of steel. The "barrel" roof indeed resembled a giant barrel sawed in half lengthwise, then placed on brick walls. In the era when the garage had been constructed, laminated wood beams were unknown and steel was expensive, so the builder had supported the rounded roof with trussed wooden girders. Above the unobstructed garage area, parallel half-moons of timber formed a lacework maze that held up the planks of the roofs decking. From the concrete floor one could see through the beams and girders right up to the underside of the roof's deck boards.

The old wood girders and the many layers of felt-and-tar roofing were an arsonist's dream. Once ignited, they would burn like matchsticks. However, Stretch's target was not the roof but the dump trucks, Caterpillar tractors, backhoes, and bulldozers stored under it. The problem was to get the fire down from the tinder of the roof structure to the vehicles before the firefighters could confine the damage to the roof alone.

The challenge of the building had sent Stretch back to the library and even on another fast trip to the forest. Now he was satisfied that he had the answer.

The two night lights left the garage in gloomy semi-darkness. Stretch peered across the dim-lit scene, running his eyes across the routes he would have to follow to do his job. Fortunately, the "tie beams" that ran across the building and the two "crossties" that ran the building's length were all made of twelve-by-twelve lumber, giving him one-foot-wide pathways around the roof supports and difficult, but usable, access to the entire girder structure. With a grunt of satisfaction he turned and hauled up the rest of his materials, swung them onto one of the tie beams, and got under way.

With great delicacy Stretch took three canisters out of his knapsack and strapped them to three key girder joints. The cannisters appeared to be identical to the small hand-held fire extinguishers found on each of the trucks and caterpillars below. If they were discovered in the debris later, no one would suspect their role in spreading the fire. In reality they were quite the opposite of fire extinguishers—each cannister was a portable container of the acetylene gas used for welding. When the fire raised their temperature to the right degree they would explode. Stretch placed the cannisters strategically so that the explosions would cause one side of the rafters to fall, dropping the flames down to the floor where they would ignite the gas tanks of the earth-moving equipment. Stretch timed the detonation so that it would occur after the fire was well under way—too soon and the collapse of the roof would simply snuff out his work. The gas tanks, in turn, would blow up and drop the rest of the stressed and blazing roof, burying everything in flaming havoc.

At least, that was Stretch's plan. He had calculated that the detonations of the acetylene cylinders would be the night watchman's first clue to the fire's existence.

The containers would have to explode within ten minutes of the fire's inception so that no fireman would already be in the building or on the roof when it all came down in a fiery mass. Stretch had not forgotten Tom Farley's story about his father losing a leg in a roof collapse—nor would he ever forget the burning body in Vietnam.

The job would require perfect timing. When his work was finished, Stretch would leave by the window through which he had come without ever having touched the garage floor. It was a delicate and ingenious scheme that left little margin for error.

If all went according to plan, the owner of B.B. Builders would come running to Sievers to sign a closed-shop contract almost as fast as he would run to his insurance company. And Stretch would have moved in a hurry from selling cars in cornfield country to clearing one hundred twenty thousand dollars a year. He stepped across empty space and swung onto the girders to begin the operation—not wanting to think of the consequences if all did *not* go according to plan.

* * *

Ray Barnett, the night watchman, was sitting in the front reception area, separated by a long corridor from the garage where Stretch was working. Barnett, officially retired, was held spellbound by a detective novel. His job was easy—helped round out his pension and allowed him plenty of reading time. At home, the missus always had the TV on and his age seemed to prevent him from concentrating on two things at once. For eleven months the night watchman had faithfully stood guard and his reading pleasure had not been marred by even one call to duty. Of course, he preferred it that way. He was a peaceable man—not at all eager to use the pistol in his holster. Barnett liked to read about trouble, not live it.

Back in the gloom of the garage area, Stretch was braced against a girder, quietly boring one-inch holes in the roof with a stubby hand drill. The holes were just above the outside wall and spaced about twelve feet apart. With a rubber syringe, he squeezed accelerant through each hole onto the tar roofing and then ran the fluid to join other flammable lines that now neatly laced one side of the wood trusses. Once the tar caught, it would burn like wildfire. He had been careful to bring in the starter fluid in jerricans that matched those found in the Caterpillar cabs. If they were later found in the ruins they would be given no more attention than the acetylene cylinders.

Stretch tightened the adjustment on his knapsack, which was now nearly empty. He stood in the silent, almost sinister shadows above the mechanical mammoths, reviewing every step before he set the timer. Once that was done, there would be no turning back. Without moving, he ran his eyes through each step, checking the acetylene cannisters, roof plugs, the trailways of accelerant, each of their vital connecting points, and then, finally, the window two girders away through which he was about to exit.

Stretch gave a grunt of satisfaction and picked up the timer. In five minutes it would turn his plan into blazing reality. The delay would give him time to slide down the rope, disconnect the grappling hook, and disappear. Exactly ten minutes after the timer had lit the fire, the bottles would blow and the inferno would be well under way. Stretch checked his watch. He would wait a few minutes in order to set the timer for two fifty-five. That would light the blaze at three o'clock sharp and collapse the roof at three ten.

* * *

The stunning, beautiful blonde arched her back in the California sunshine. Her bikini revealed why Lew Archer, ace detective, had trouble resisting the invitation. Ray Barnett, ace night watchman, had trouble putting the paperback down. He did, however, because at his age the call of the stomach was greater than the call of vicarious sex. It was midshift and time to get a quick snack from the lunch box his missus had packed. Barnett rose to go down the hall to his locker. The row of lockers stood just inside the hushed garage. As he reached the end of the darkened corridor, he switched on his long flashlight. The locker door was sticky, so Ray tucked the flashlight backwards under his arm in order to give the locker's handle a two-handed jerk.

At 2:55, as Stretch started the timer and bent over, placing it on the crosstie, the beam from the watchman's flashlight struck him right in the face. The locker opened with a bang like a gunshot. Cat quick, Stretch flattened onto the beam. In one smooth motion he grabbed the beam, slipped his body downward, hung for a fraction of a second, and then dropped the remaining distance to the floor. His right ankle twisted slightly as he absorbed the fall. He ignored the pain that shot through his foot and ducked behind the huge tire of a grader. What the hell was the guard doing? How had he been spotted?

Barnett's back was to the interior of the garage. He had not seen Stretch, nor had his diminished hearing picked up the muffled sound of Stretch landing on the concrete. Unsuspecting, he fished in his lunch box, deciding what to take back to the front desk.

Stretch now knew the bang had not in fact been a gunshot, but he could not tell where the watchman was. He assumed he had been spotted and was being tracked. He was agonizingly aware of the timer that was ticking away far above his head. Hidden behind the tire, Stretch tried to decipher the odd scuffing sounds coming from the guard's direction. It dawned on him that there was no way to get back up into the girders and that his only escape route was past that guard. He tried to determine where the man could be.

Barnett stood before the locker angrily. He'd told his wife he didn't like the olive-studded lunch meat, but here it was again. He was going to take the whole damn sandwich back to her and let *her* eat it. She bought it because it was *her* favorite. He rewrapped the sandwich, took the chocolate chip cookies, and slammed the door shut violently.

Stretch ducked. The light flashed through the trucks and Cats, then vanished as suddenly as it had appeared. Barnett's crepe soles made no sound as he moved up the hallway. Stretch had no way of knowing for certan that he had gone. Slowly, Stretch sought a vantage point from which he could see his pursuer. He eased under a dump truck and past a grader. He could neither see nor hear any sign of life.

Without warning, the flames flashed above his head and raced through the timbers along their predetermined trails. The torch glanced at his watch—3:00 A.M. on the button.

If the night guard were still in the garage, he would have made a sound, run for an alarm, a phone, fire extinguisher—something, for God's sake! Stretch paused for a moment. Fear crept into his veins and hunkered down between the corpuscles. He was sweating, judging the trouble he was in, weighing the possibilities. He was trapped—that was clear. If the gaurd were still in the room, he was really in trouble. If the man had gone back up the hall to the reception area where Stretch knew he usually passed his night shift, then there was no way out—other than right past him.

Fire *whooshed* up the sheathing and out the plugs to the roofing's tar. Red tongues of flame licked the girders' bone-dry wood. The fire would be well under way before the acetylene cannisters blew.

At 3:01, the interior of the garage was well illuminated by flames. There was no longer any possibility that the guard was still there. It's you or me, pal, Stretch thought, picking up a steel crowbar. A sick feeling crawled into his gut.

In the office Barnett had wolfed down the cookies and wanted a cigarette to go with his coffee. He fished in his pocket for a cigarette and realized none were left. He read a few more lines of the poolside seduction scene before heading back down the corridor to the cigarette machine.

The thought of bludgeoning the guard frightened Stretch more than facing the man's pistol—but less than being in the garage when the blazing roof exploded downward. He cursed himself for getting into this position. He felt ashamed. Physical violence had been strictly off limits and here he was with a lethal crowbar in his hand. He worked his way toward the office.

At 3:02 the watchman rose, checked his change, and headed down the hall. He saw the reflection of flames before he got to the end of the corridor and, without even checking to see the extent of the fire, spun in his tracks and raced to the phone.

Stretch Jackson suddenly thought of one desperate, but conceivable alternative to smashing in the watchman's head. The big, electric garage door could be another way out—*if* he could find the switch. On his swelling ankle, he sprinted through the heat and glare to the far end of the garage, where the big overhead door was. If he could spot the button instantly, he didn't give a damn whether the guard heard the door opening or not. Escaping was preferable to crushing the watchman's skull. If he couldn't spot the switch fast, however, then too bad for the night watchman! Under no circumstances was Stretch going to be in that room at 3:10.

* * *

Mannie Rojas was in the officers' quarters of Station House 1, contemplating marriage. During these wee hours of the morning several men were having their emotions wrenched by a TV rerun of *The Conversation* and a threesome was making coffee and sandwiches in the kitchen.

Seconds after 3:03, the long bell stabbed through the night.

"Okay, Engine Thirty-two and Ladder One! Go!" the intercom barked.

Bud Pyle chugged his coffee and jumped to go. "Maybe it'll be a real one!"

"Shit!" Owen Pavitt complained. "It's like rain and a car wash. Every time I start a peanut butter sandwich, it guarantees a fire!" He dropped the bread, gobbled the blob of peanut butter off the end of the knife, and started running.

The men shot out of every corner, sliding down the bright brass pole. The shouts and instructions, hastily grabbed equipment, and flying feet were all part of the station's carefully structured chaos.

On the apparatus floor Pavitt jumped into the rear seat of Ladder 1, next to Bud Pyle. "Think I should stop making peanut butter sandwiches?" he shouted.

"Christ, no," Pyle replied. "We need the business!" The engines and sirens roared to life, a promise of violence in their sound.

Station 1 was near the contractor's garage, but they were only a part of the task force that would converge on the burning building. By 3:05 A.M. they were racing to B.B. Builders, only a two- to three-minute run on the deserted streets.

The front driver, Dan Branch—skinny but steel-strong—muscled Ladder Company 1 down the avenue. High up, behind the ladder, Les Black rode tillerman at the separate steering wheel, assisting the one-hundred-foot ladder rig around the corners.

At 3:07 they could see flames licking the sky ahead of them.

Mannie—who often captained Ladder 1 now that Jonah West was involved with Arson Liaison—picked up the mike. "First-due has a good loom-up showing."

"Ten-four, Captain."

Jack Runyon leaned forward from the backseat. "Look at that, Mannie," Runyon said excitedly. "We got a working fire. Hot damn!"

Rojas was already calculating, coolly. He'd have something to tell his fiancée about tomorrow.

* * *

After Ray Barnett called the Fire Department, it struck him that he had not taken the time to see what was actually burning. So he grabbed an extinguisher, checked the instructions, and raced toward the flames. Halfway down the corridor, he heard the hungry roar of fire eating oxygen and felt the heat. The realization that the fire was out of control shot him through with fear. He knew how much gasoline was in the cavern of the garage.

"Holy God!" Barnett yelled, suddenly terrorized. He dropped the extinguisher and rushed back to the telephone without ever having actually seen a flame.

Stretch heard Barnett's exclamation and the metallic crash as the extinguisher hit the hallway floor and rolled. He knew the guard was armed and that in this room, ablaze with dancing light, the night watchman would instantly spot him. Stretch flattened himself in his tracks, hugging the oily cement floor as if he could disappear into it. He waited precious seconds for the man's appearance. No one came.

At 3:07, when Mannie Rojas had radioed in, Barnett was frantically dialing the owner to tell him his garage was on fire.

Bullets, no bullets, Stretch knew he could no longer just lie still. He had to act. He was only ten feet from the right-hand side of the big door and could tell the switch was not there. He glanced at his watch: 3:07. He tightened his grip on the crowbar and decided to run for it. Suddenly he heard distant sirens above the snapping of the fire—the alarm had been given sooner than he had planned. The firemen would be there at 3:10 when it blew.

The watchman must be in the front, waiting for the fire-fighters. Stretch looked up at what seemed to be acres of blazing timber above him. The heat was becoming intolerable. He took a desperate chance, leaped up, and streaked the forty feet to the other side of the door.

Stretch gave an audible groan of relief. He had finally found the switch. He slapped the top button. Nothing happened. A finger of fear poked at his chest. He jabbed the bottom button. No reaction. In a frenzy, he stabbed at the top one again and worked it around in its socket. UP had a loose contact, but once the connection was made, the door began to rise. When it had risen three feet, Stretch hit DOWN so that the door would be shut when the firemen arrived. He shuddered at the possibility of their driving right in. Rolling, Stretch threw himself under the door's descending sheet of iron. He picked himself up and bolted around the corner of the garage just as the headlights of Ladder 1 turned onto the building. Stretch cut up the long, dark side wall and leaped over the fence, shaken but unseen.

Barnett hesitated between waiting for his boss to answer the telephone and opening the gates for the approaching engines. He chose the latter, dropping the receiver. The gate slid open as the first trucks arrived. Mannie ordered Dan Branch to pull up parallel to the burning side of the garage.

"Stay fifty feet out!" he yelled. "There's plenty of gas in that garage."

They were part of a clockwork army. Before the truck was at a dead stop, Les Black had vaulted out of the tillerman's seat to pull the levers that lowered the hydraulic outrigger jacks and blocked the vehicle.

Runyon leaped to the controls of the hundred-foot "big stick" and in seconds raised it, turned it toward the roof, and ran it up thirty-five feet, moving the five hundred GPM jet/ fog nozzle into place to throw a heavy master stream on the roof.

The little roll of leader hose, called the doughnut, was already in Pavitt's hands, automatically unfolding the main intake line behind him as he ran for the nearest water plug. Branch and Black prepared the truck end of the hose hookups. Mannie bounded up the ladder to hand-lock it and prepare for connecting the monitor nozzle as well as to survey what they were fighting.

Before 3:10, pumpers were plugging in to hydrants, engines were pulling up, men were unreeling hoses on the run. They would pump water directly from each unit's self-contained water tanks until the pumpers could connect their hoses into the supply waiting to pound out of city hydrants.

After opening the gate, watchman Barnett had conquered his fears and decided to see if he could get through the corridor to open the garage door from the inside. He thought that letting them in would *really* help the firemen.

Mannie paused for an instant at the top of the ladder. The near side of the roof was burning. The fire had to be very involved on the underside, probably 1,800 to 2,000 degrees.

He had to find a way to vent it. That was as far as his plans had gone when the acetylene bottles exploded in rapid succession. One side of the roof, only fifty feet away, went down in a roaring cascade of sparks and flame, dropping an avalanche of fire onto the trucks, bulldozers, and graders inside. Mannie slid down the handrail as if it were the brass pole at the station. Runyon hit the lever to drop the ladder. Everyone ducked for cover until the rain of burning ashes stopped.

"Unblock this son-of-a-bitch and back off another fifty in case that wall goes!" Mannie screamed. They did—fast.

Ray Barnett had just started down the corridor toward the garage when the roof collapsed. A blast of air filled with heat and burning sparks blew through the hallway and knocked him off his feet. He scrambled upright and ran outside, singed and scared dead white. He assumed—as did everyone else—that the equipment was blowing up.

Then the equipment did, in fact, start blowing. The wall Mannie had backed away from blew outwards, forever burying a grappling hook and the ashes of a rope.

The Chief was already on his radio. ". . . a Squirt. If available, two more tasks, the Darley attack unit, and four towers." He knew the value of what was in the building. If he could, he wanted to save some of it as well as the office area.

Explosions rocked B.B. Builders.

". . . Up to me," Mannie was telling Bud Pyle, "I'd soak hell out of that far side and keep it goddamn away from the two-story section with the offices."

The fireground was now alive with pumpers, trucks, and rigs. As it turned out, Rojas wasn't second-guessing his superior officer—their ideas were identical. The Chief was yelling into his walkie-talkie. "Two more relays. We go a deluge gun or—" The buggy radio started cackling. The Chief tried hearing the radio and the walkie-talkie at the same time, lost it. "Skipper," he thundered, "you're coming in broken up. A deluge gun and . . . Bafalis! You hear me?" He held the walkie-talkie to his ear. Another gas tank blew with a muffled roar. He shifted the box back to his lips, "Yeah, dammit, and get two relay pumpers in line on that Siamese . . ."

At that moment the red lights of a resplendent red buggy flashed up next to the Chief. Battalion Chief Jack Plunkett stepped out of the shiny splendor and came around to the Chief, who slipped into a relaxed, seen-one-seen-'em-all tone. "Heya, Jack," he said. "It's just business as usual. I think we'll keep the two story out of the fire all right."

After an hour had passed the office section did seem spared. Bud Pyle was off the ladder, getting relief. He leaned up against the rig, talking to Owen Pavitt.

"How you coming on the fire marshal exams?" Pyle asked.

Pavitt was due for active fire duty retirement in three years and had been studying hard for months to get a head start into white-collar work away from the fireground.

"I dropped it."

"What! What do you mean you dropped it? You were working your ass off!"

"Bud, nine years of this . . ." Pavitt looked across the fireground. "I got three years more at most. Maybe it's adrenaline addiction. Beats hell outta me, but I can't get away from front-line duty. I'll go white collar three years from now, but till I have to, I can't give this up—Christ knows why." He shook his head at the mystery of it. "Christ knows why."

* * *

At noon the ringing of the telephone roused Stretch out of bed. When he jumped up to answer it, his first step sent a dull pain shooting through his ankle. If he needed any reminder of the night before, that was sufficient.

"Stretch Jackson?"

He recognized the gypsy smile in that voice.

"Mr. Sievers would like to see you at three."

"Okay. See you then." He wasn't feeling up to eloquence and left it at that.

At five minutes before three he entered the reception room of Amalgamated Building Trades Union feeling cock-sure and buoyant. He'd pulled it off *and* he hadn't been obliged to use the crowbar. According to the *Morning Chronicle*, no one had even been hurt.

The gypsy held out her hand.

"We may be seeing each other often. I'm Hazel. Glad to meet you." The smile was all for him.

Hazel? The image of hot gypsy blood came away with a rip.

The door with the presidential lettering opened. Hazel looked up, smiling, and said "Good-bye, Mr. Bradshaw," to the heavyset man who exited.

Stretch stared hard at the man called Bradshaw.

"You can go in now, Mr. Jackson."

Frank Sievers rose and came quickly around the desk when Stretch came in. "Well done," he said, his beefy hand out for a shake.

"Thanks."

"Got a limp? Hurt yourself?"

"No. Would you believe I slipped on the stairs coming in this morning?"

"Any problem last night?"

"Nothing unusual. Had to drop the roof to get it down to those gas tanks."

Frank laughed. "You brought the fire to old Barney Bradshaw, all right. That was him just walked out. B.B. Builders. Him and his attorney. He stopped in to sign this." He hefted a sheaf of legal papers. "New closed-shop contract. He's been telling me to drop dead for six months. By coincidence, our attorney called him only this morning. Imagine that." Siever's voice went flat and grim. "That's all I wanted. It's for his workers' good and his own. That's what counts. This union's only strong if those thick-headed bastards knuckle under."

"We'll make them say 'uncle,'" Stretch said seriously, taken with his new status. "I'll make anyone you want knuckle down and sign. You just tell me who."

"Well, welcome to the Amalgamated Building Trades Union." He clapped Stretch on the shoulder. "The good fight for the workingman."

"I guess I get Blue Cross and a pension plan," Stretch said lightheartedly.

"Well, now . . ."

"You mean you're using scab labor?"

"We'll have to call you part of the management team. Come over here and sit down. We've got to get some things good and clear." The tone turned confidential and serious. "I knew the score by nine thirty this morning. I knew Bradshaw was going to sign because you did a first-class job. I like a comer—and you're one of them. I'm going to pay you a helluva lot of money, because you're going to do what I want and *do it right*."

Hearing his father's words come from Sievers made Stretch feel proud of himself. His decision to be the best was paying off.

"Frank Sievers is going to take you under his wing. Now, officially you've got no connection to Amalgamated. You're an independent organizing consultant. We work hand in glove—you and me, not the union. You never drop the union's name. I'll introduce you to those I trust—and it stops there. Got it?"

"Okay by me," said Stretch, remembering his vow to be his own man. "I really am an *independent* contractor—even if you've got an exclusive lease."

"I owe you ten grand. C'mon, I want to introduce you to a guy I got in my pocket."

The president of Amalgamated knew he was putting Stretch Jackson in a new league. He had lots of plans for the still-unsophisticated newcomer, and he wanted to get the bit in right, before the young stallion could buck. Frank Sievers had spent his life sizing men up and handling them. He wasn't used to making mistakes in judgment—and he was quite sure he had this one figured out.

The two men glided down in the elevator and stepped around the corner to California Street in the heart of the financial district.

"It's just in the next block," Frank said. "And that shop over there, Wolff's, is where all the smart dressers get decked out." He raised an eyebrow at Stretch and continued, "If you go in, ask for young Wolff and say I sent you. His old man picks my clothes, but the kid's got snappier taste for a guy your age."

"All right, I might just do that." Stretch not only took the hint but was flattered that Frank Sievers should send him to his personal shop.

Frank turned and entered Western United Bank's marble, Neo-Georgian palace of finance. The guard at the door tipped his hat to Sievers. The secretary didn't even ask him to have a seat and wait but showed him right into the private office of George Calhoun, senior vice-president. Stretch was very impressed.

Fifty-five, temple gray, smartly dressed, and distinguished-looking, George Calhoun had the obvious class that Frank would have liked to possess.

"George, I'd like you to meet Mr. Jackson. He's an independent consultant on membership organizing and he's going to be working with us."

"Delighted, Mr. Jackson. If there is ever any way at all in which Western can be of service, let us know."

"Actually," Frank added, "I was suggesting to him that he might wish to open an account here. . . ."

Stretch got into the swing of Sievers's game. "Yes. The bank is handy to the union offices. I'll stop by in a few days and do that."

"You just come straight to me," Calhoun said with a smile.

I'll be goddamned, Stretch thought. It's magic time.

George Calhoun controlled the union's mass of money, and in the conversation that followed Stretch noticed the deference the banker paid to Sievers. What he lacked the savvy to catch was the subtle hint of condescension in the banker's choice of words. Even Sievers could not put his finger on it after all these years, but he somehow knew that outside the realm of business he was not quite in Calhoun's class. In fact, that made his power over Calhoun all the sweeter—over him and over the union's fancy attorney, too.

The secretary stepped in just before the parting amenities and gave a manila envelope to Calhoun, which he in turn handed to Frank. Calhoun then walked them to the lobby.

"All right, then, Frank," he said, "we're set for lunch at the club."

Frank turned to Stretch. "How would you like to join us—if you're free, that is?"

"I'd sure be pleased—" Stretch caught himself, and, pretending to think for a moment, added, "Yes, I believe I can clear things away for that." Get your goddamn act together, he said to himself. Buddy, you're going places!

"Delighted. See you then." The banker gave a gracious nod and left.

Striding across the lobby, Stretch Jackson, former hick, felt he could match the grandeur of the setting. Before they reached the bowing doorman, Frank pulled out the fat manila envelope and handed it wordlessly to his new protégé. Tom between rising to his new standard of decorum and yelling "*Whooee!*" Stretch took it as though he got a clear hundred hundreds every day and put it in his pocket.

Stretch's first stop after leaving Frank was at a pay phone. With a pocketful of change, happy fingers dialed New York.

"That you, cowboy?"

"Hey, pardner!"

"I did it, you old son-of-a-bitch, and it's all your fault!"

"You sound like you just cut a fat calf."

"I hit the jackpot, Eddie—the big time! Remember the figure you bowled at me in the Buddha?"

"Yeah."

"I got me a sure-fire, guaranteed, long-as-I'd-like-it contract for just about that—with a really high-class outfit. Whooee!"

"Well, I'm a sidewinding son-of-a-bitch! What'd I tell you, pardner? I knew you could get that stowed in your saddlebags.

Next step's New York City. How'd you like them apples, peckerwood?"

"Bet your sweet A. I'm coming up the tree after you, Texas. Save me a branch at the top!"

"Stretch, I'm near happy as you. I mean it. You've come a long way since that dirt-farm kid came into basic training. I guess we both have. It's been a long road. I'm proud of you, Jackson. You could almost be from Texas."

Everybody was making Stretch feel good that day.

> Dear Karen,
>
> You can tell from the address that I know where you live. I like your little red Fiat. I know your phone number. If I wanted to bug you I could, but I don't want to bug you.
>
> I just want to apologize for being a real idiot at the Silver Doll. The only thing I want is to be nice to you. I wasn't kidding when I said you were special. I have never, never, ever met any other girl who left me feeling weak in the knees, to say nothing of the head and the heart.
>
> I guess I just saw red because Easy stopped me from throwing out the slob who insulted you. I'm really nice and gentle, not rowdy. I lost my head and it was because of you. I'm sorry, really sorry. I'd walk clear back to Litchfield to find you if I had to.
>
> We were fine until I said that dumb thing. I wish I hadn't. Please forgive me and we'll be fine again, I promise. I'd rather see you than win the Daytona 500.
>
> In this sea of strangers, I'd like to be—
> Your friend,
> Stretch (Jackson)

Before putting the envelope in the mailbox, Stretch hesitated. That wasn't exactly the letter he wanted to write. He had wanted it to soar with poetry, to overpower Karen with strength and romance, but he didn't know how to quite get that out. He had looked up a few words in French, but decided that would sound pretentious. One of the scrapped versions said, "I think I've fallen in love with you," but that seemed too forward and might have frightened her permanently. In fact, it had jolted *him* to see it written down by his own hand, because love was a word of dramatic proportions in Stretch's vocabulary. He had never said it to any girl.

He sighed. Irretrievably, the letter slipped into the box. He would just have to take his chances with it as it was.

17

The paths of three people crossed, by coincidence, and with no earthshaking significance. It was Oakland, a pretty day—without exaggeration—Saturday and midmorning.

Dee Hatford, distracted by thoughts of romance, was in an absolute dither. Failing to look, or even slow down, she pulled right out of the parking lot behind the Normandy Apartments onto Lakeside and straight into the path of an oncoming car.

Charlene, en route to Tom's houseboat, was suddenly confronted by a ton of powder-blue steel. She slammed her brakes on violently, wrenched the wheel, and skidded crabwise toward a large black Cadillac that was parked by the lake. A collision seemed inevitable.

Seeing Charlene's car hurtling sideways toward him, the man in the back seat of the Caddy instinctively pressed himself into the far rear corner of the limousine. When Charlene's car ground to a stop about a foot away, Frank Sievers straightened up and said loudly out of the open window, "Fucking women drivers!"

Dee screeched to a halt, jumped out and ran to see if anyone was hurt. She and Charlene had spoken to each other a thousand times by telephone but had never met. "Oh, my God, I'm so sorry! You okay? I'm insured. Oh, my God!"

Henry, trapped in the front seat of the Cadillac, growled out of the driver's window, "If you're not goddamn careful, lady, you'll kill somebody! You ought to haul it back to driving school."

Charlene had a short-lived shot of adrenaline fury. "Learn to drive it or park it, for God's sake," she snapped at Dee. She shoved her car into first and angrily shot off down Lakeside toward the *Sapphire II.*

Dee slinked back to her car in wordless embarrassment. She'd been thinking about last night, when she'd met a man with gray eyes, sandy hair, and a face full of freckles who had recently moved west from Boise, Idaho—and who not only locked her tightly in conversation all evening, but had also asked if she was free for Saturday dinner. Dee was, perhaps, easy sweepings, but she was thoroughly swept off her feet. After thirty minutes of the conversation, she had completely forgotten to bat her eyelashes at him and look sexy, which had allowed her to become unaffected and simply, naturally sexy. She had said yes a lot, including to the dinner invitation for this evening.

Frank had been parked by Lake Merritt casting an avaricious eye at the Normandy Apartments. Henry usually had a shadow, Ben, with whom he worked in tandem, driving, escorting, and guarding Sievers or doing odd jobs—like when they tailed Stretch and did the B&E on his apartment. But, unlike Ben, Henry had worked with Frank since "the old days." They had seen a lot together, been in some tight places and done some dirty things. Frank Sievers did not give Henry credit for having any brains, but since he knew Henry could be trusted to the death, he sometimes talked to Henry alone, letting him in on secrets. For Frank, it was almost like talking to himself, but with the advantage of hearing the yeses from another person—and once in a while Henry came out with a brilliant, intuitive suggestion or warning.

Frank had already told Henry that the Normandy Apartments belonged to Jim Vada, probably the most important East Bay building contractor who remained stubbornly nonunion.

After a few remarks about women and drivers and women drivers, Frank returned to feasting his eyes on the apartments. "Wouldn't you just like to get your hands on that?" he said, almost to himself.

"Bet your sweet ass. Gonna give it to me, Frank?" Henry looked in the rearview mirror and smiled a broad, dumb smile. He was not without a certain sense of humor.

"That's what the new boy's for, Henry."

"Jackson?"

"Yeah. He's going to make Jim Vada a solid supporter of closed-shop unionism and a champion of Amalgamated. Why, that holdout son-of-a-bitch is liable to be so sorry he held out on us all this time that he might just propose giving me a peace offering."

"Like the Normandy Apartments?"

"Well, Henry, the Normandy Apartments—now, that's a big bite. But I've got this plan. I think Jim Vada may just let me *use* his apartment building."

Henry's beetle brows knitted together. Frank could only see the back of Henry's head, yet he could read the expression.

"No, Henry," Sievers said, "I'm not going to move into an apartment with a view of the lake. I've got a very special plan for the Normandy that is much better than owning it. Once I get Stretch Jackson's wings clipped, Vada is only going to have to loan me the building for a month." He paused with a sigh, anticipating pleasure. Suddenly he didn't give a damn if Henry understood or not. "Come on, Henry," he ordered. "Let's get out of here."

* * *

Little wavelets slapped soft rhythms on the side of *Sapphire II*. Undulating gleams of light ran down the hull, reflecting sunshine. Inside, the dining table was covered neatly with stacks of files. The neatness was Charlene's, not Tom's.

"You know, I think we're almost up to date." Tom leaned back and let out a long, deep breath.

Charlene gave him a long-suffering look of secretarial tolerance. "It will last until about Tuesday."

"Better than nothing. Want another cup?"

She stuck her pen in her purse. "No, I've got to go:"

"Thanks for coming out to get this done—and on a Saturday as glorious as this." He added teasingly, "Why don't we just get hitched?"

Charlene picked up the purse and stood up, watching his eyes. Suddenly she leaned forward across the table. "Okay, let's!" She looked serious.

Touching a live wire would have given Tom Farley the same electrified expression.

Charlene pealed out lady laughter. "You should see the look on your face! Scared you, didn't I? Wouldn't you just love to get me working day *and* night!" she said good-naturedly. "I don't know if you were born to work or born to be a loner, but either way, marriageable you're not. The only thing a workhorse hitches up to is a plow, Tom Farley."

"Sometimes, when you hitch up to a plow you become a workhorse. Sounds like you've been talking to my ex."

"I'd be talking to myself if I lived with you." Charlene didn't want to make that sound too hard, so she added, "Anyway, you're too old for me." That made it even worse. She gave him one of those try-me-I'm-really-warm-underneath smiles and touched his shoulder. "You know I don't mean all that. I think we've worked too long together."

Melted, he patted her hand. "Know me like a book, huh?"

"Well"—she smiled again—"a good book's got surprises right to the end."

Charlene turned to go, basking in a glow of internal amazement. She felt as if she had just stepped out of an invigorating sauna. Something certainly was changing radically and rapidly, for it was the first time she had found her emotions being tugged by Tom, towed into waters that left her wondering what he would be like on a more personal, intimate level. The thought created warm spots at unexpected places in her body. It was not until she climbed into her car that she realized she had walked off the *Sapphire II* and up the dock without saying so much as good-bye.

Aboard the *Sapphire II*. Tom had already dismissed the incident. Banned might be a better word. No sooner had

Charlene stepped out than he firmly decided that this dallying around with his secretary had to stop immediately. It was clearly disturbing their routine. Becoming too personal would get in the way of work—and Tom Farley would have none of that.

18

Karen was the wettest, sweetest bundle Stretch had ever picked up. She laughed and protested and dripped all over his chest. His strong right arm circled under her knees, his left behind her back. His tightly clenched knuckles closed the circle around her.

"I'm going to dump you in if you don't say yes!" He fixed her with his blue eyes, his emotions feeding on the warmth she radiated.

"Yes, yes, yes!"

He carried her a few feet through the surf. Like any devilish high school boy, he started to toss her in anyway. As she began to fall, the man in him won the upper hand. He decided he'd rather feel her in his arms than play a schoolboy prank, so he scooped her back up.

"Oh, Stretch, you're impossible!" She hung on more tightly than ever.

The water was cool and the breeze even cooler. The bright sun convinced the Chamber of Commerce that the swimming was great, but not those on the beach. Only fools, lovers, and snowbird tourists would be beaching on a day like this. Karen and Stretch—with blue lips and more bumps on their skin than a plucked chicken—fell into all three categories simultaneously.

"Put me down, you fool, you, I'm freezing," Karen said through clenched, chattering teeth.

Grabbing a towel, Stretch dried her off, timidly, then draped the towel around her shoulders. What he really wanted to do was kiss her. He was not used to feeling shy, but all of his experience had been in getting laid, not in courting a woman from whom he wanted more than that. Karen made him feel more like an awkward teenager than a man in his thirties. That was why he had suggested the beach for their first date—it seemed private, yet had the neutrality of a public place.

"The sun'll warm you, soon as you're dry." He dropped onto his towel beside her, watching her dry her long brown hair. "You know what? I think you're even prettier in the broad daylight than you were in the Silver Doll."

She glanced at him. "Well, I hope so, because I don't think you'll get to see me in there again. God, did you put your foot in it." Her eyes creased as she smiled. "I spent a week wishing I'd never told you. Then it wouldn't have happened."

"You mean you spent a week thinking about me?"

"Uh . . ." She had not meant to admit it. "Yes, I guess I did."

"Guess?"

She put her hand on the sand and twisted to face him. "Okay, I did—every time I saw poor Easy."

"Oh," he said, crestfallen.

"Hey, let's go for a jog." Karen jumped up, grabbing his hand to pull him to his feet.

They trotted wordlessly along the wet sand for a bit. Out of the corner of his eye Stretch watched her trim form.

"You mean you never just thought about me . . . for me?"

Karen leaped into a half-twist and landed in front of him so unexpectedly that he had to grab her in his arms to keep from knocking her down. "Yes, I did. Does that make you feel better?"

Stretch held her and this time it wasn't playfully. His eyes caressed her face. He kissed her lightly on the freckles where her soft cheek met her nose. From breasts to thighs they touched each other's length, hands clasped behind their backs. They closed their eyes and pressed their lips in a hungry, needed kiss.

"Hey," she murmured a minute later.

"Hmm?"

She leaned her head back. "I thought you weren't dangerous."

"I'm not—just friendly."

"Whew! With a friend like you, who needs danger?"

She pecked him quickly on the lips, wrinkled her freckles at him, broke away, and bolted back toward their towels.

Running along behind her, Stretch admired the view. He smiled the smile of a wicked thought: Fat Bert Morton wouldn't have liked her at all. No pear rested on those limbs—not even one ounce of fat.

"Hey, Stretch!" Karen pulled on her sandals. "You like crabs?"

He stopped dead in his tracks.

"There's a great place up the beach to get them."

*　*　*

At the Crab Shack, he started to order shrimp. He didn't really know how to handle a crab.

Karen read his hesitation. "Not really a West Alton specialty, huh?" Diplomatically, she introduced him to the process.

"Messy, but they're good, all right," he admitted.

"Have you ever been to a modern dance concert?" Karen peeked up at him, anticipating a negative. When she got it, she asked, "Want to go to one tomorrow night? It's my night off and there's one I want to see."

Stretch put his hand on hers and smiled. "If you'll let me take you to the stock car races one day."

She glittered. "It's a deal. Kind of different worlds, but I like that."

When he drove her home, he followed her awkwardly into her apartment, pretending that he was merely helping her

211

carry her things. Just as awkwardly, she allowed him to follow her in and to find her lips again.

The atmosphere changed from warm to ardent, from standing to sitting on the couch, from restless touching to the burning of two people trying to melt their bodies into one space. Stretch slipped off the top of Karen's bathing suit and grazed the velvet hardness of her breast. All of a sudden, she moved away, took his head in her hands, and buried her face in the back of his neck.

"I can't, Stretch. Don't. Please. I'm sorry."

"Wha . . . what did I do?" he asked, shocked and confused.

"Honest to God, Stretch, it's not you." She held him tightly. "It's not you. It's me. It's . . . I can't."

"Never?"

"I can't," she whispered despairingly. "It's . . ."

He flushed with the anger of frustration, but compassion gained the upper hand. Stretch pulled her to him. "What is it, Karen?"

"Hold me, first hold me," she pleaded.

The Litchfield possibility of virginity flashed to his mind. "Haven't you ever made love before?"

The question made her feel faint. She forced a weak smile. "Of course I have. And I want to make love with you. I can't even talk about it now. Will you trust me?"

"You know I will." Stretch felt dazed. "Whatever it is, we'll work it out." He held her away and dipped into her soul. "You know I want to be more than a friend. You're not just a hop in the sack."

She whispered, "I know."

"And tomorrow? Am I still invited?"

Karen stroked his cheek with her hand and brushed his lips with hers. "Sure, tomorrow. I was the one who asked you." She studied his pale eyes, his rough, handsome face. "I'm sorry. I take a lot of patience and I can't promise you I'm worth it."

* * *

Stretch Jackson was willing to consider modern dancing on Sunday evening if only to give pleasure to Karen. The bogus, bulbous padded crotches of the men dancers struck him as a bit ridiculous, but that was balanced by the lithesome movements of female forms. At the intermission she began to explain some of the finer points and was pleasantly surprised at his receptivity.

"Jesus, I wish I could ask you to my place," he said when the concert was over. "But it's a tiny, awful apartment. I'm looking for a house." He didn't mention the nature of what cluttered the living room.

"Well, come on back to mine. I even remembered you drink bourbon."

"No sh . . . no kidding?"

Certainly enough people had said *shit* in her presence—she could hardly care less—yet Stretch's restraint pleased her. It seemed a sign of effort, of respect. She took his hand and felt it full and strong in hers. Karen ran her thumb along his. If he's a diamond in the rough, she thought, he *is* a diamond. They both had new horizons to explore.

* * *

"You put Coke in your bourbon? That kills the taste!" he said, appalled.

"That's exactly why I do it." She snickered.

Stretch Jackson sat in the corner of the couch and cradled Karen in his arms. They fitted well together. Conversation about the concert and modern dance, plus another round of bourbons, led them into a close and mellow mood. Finally, Karen scooted around, her back warm against his chest. One advantage of that position was that Karen could feel safe and snuggled, yet not be staring into Stretch's eyes if she wished to open up. Hard though it would be, she wanted desperately to share her wounds with Stretch, to see if he could take the truth—and if he could, to lean on him. That, to Karen, was a man—someone strong she could count on, whose judgment would be based on her, not her circumstance. Could she trust Stretch? She bit her lip. First, she would have to have faith in her own estimation of him. So the question really was whether or not she could trust herself.

Wavering at first, she slowly began to bare the tale she had told no one but Marie. Stretch held her, encouraged her, hugged her, stroked her hair, gave her the courage and confidence to tell him of Phil and then, with far greater pain, haltingly unburden her soul about Ralph Sweeney.

When she finished, Stretch cupped her face in his hand and held her head close to his breast.

"I'm sorry." He sighed quietly. "I'm really sorry. But you mustn't take one sick bastard out on everyone who's male." That was all there was. Stretch didn't make a mountain out of it.

A tender, compassionate man kissed Karen's eyes, her cheeks, her lips, and slowly, gently, firmly caused her to remember the soul-shaking joy of truly making love.

When she awakened on Monday morning, Karen watched the sleeping Stretch. She realized she hardly knew him, but time wasn't always a matter of the clock. Somehow he had stolen into her confidence and had made her whole again—in a way that Marie could not. Perhaps because the damage had been done by a man, only a man could repair it. He was more than the gentle refuge of Marie. Stretch could restore her heart as well as her mind. She smiled and was pleased that she had found his strength, that she could once more trust her own instincts.

After eggs and bacon, toast and coffee, Stretch scratched off his stubble with the razor she used for her legs. "Jesus, doesn't this thing kill you?" he asked.

"If I had iron whiskers on my legs like you have on your face, I guess it would. Didn't you notice the difference?"

He gave her a lathery kiss.

Stretch had a rendezvous with Frank scheduled for that afternoon and was obliged to dress at his apartment, then go to the Amalgamated office. He told Karen it was for his union advisory business—but lying to her didn't feel right, especially after the things they had shared the night before.

Frank Sievers was in a particularly good humor.

"Well, if it isn't the best union organizer in the city—next to me, of course. I'm the guy who organizes organizers." He opened his desk drawer and extended a fat manila envelope. "Ten, in advance. Want to count it? Even a banker can make a mistake."

He outlined the new job, gave Stretch the details, and noticed that his protégé looked both bleary-eyed *and* bushy-tailed—a condition often brought on by a good night with a good broad.

Frank clapped his torch on the shoulder. "Don't forget—we got lunch with George Calhoun on Thursday at the Mayfair Country Club. Fanciest one in town. You're gonna see a new piece of the world, Stretch Jackson."

Stretch headed straight to Calhoun's office at the bank. He confidently reeled off a false social security number and Calhoun arranged for his rental of a safety-deposit box. In the vault, Stretch stuffed the money in a box, the key into his pocket and bid farewell to his new banker, who also reminded him of Thursday's lunch. As if Stretch could forget it! The senior vice-president of one of the city's fanciest banks escorted him to the lobby, and the doorman, who had noticed, smiled and said good-bye.

Stretch fairly sailed off to see Miss Karen Canfield. Money, status, and love—what more could there be to life? In no time flat Stretch Jackson seemed to have acquired them all.

*　*　*

The week following the B.B. fire left Stretch as giddy as a moonwalker. When Calhoun was obliged to postpone lunch for a week, Stretch had no objections. His days were passed in a heaven named Canfield, his nights in planning the next fire.

Karen and Stretch visited Wolff's, laughing through the excitement of purchasing a new wardrobe for Stretch like a pair of newlyweds. Actually, the young Mr. Wolff subtly set the style of the new Stretch Jackson, but he let his customers debate the little details.

They tried out some of San Francisco's fascinations, but more than anything else they explored and plumbed the topography of love. Lips, fingers, tongues flicked across both hard and tender spots. Heat and desire fused in delicately soft, warm, moist places, consuming only the surface bits of passion's apparently endless energy.

With delicious amazement Karen perceived the difference the spirit makes. She discovered that an orgasm could be unbelievably more than *just* coming. She felt closer and closer to Stretch as he built her a bridge to wholeness.

It was a time of gentleness, of lying in bed, touching, reminiscing about growing up Midwestern, laughing at the way it had been—not daring to believe that this was the way their lives would continue to be.

* * *

Every major city has its haven for the superrich: Westchester County, Shaker Heights, Grosse Pointe, Lake Forest, Ladue—and every haven has its haven. The Mayfair Country Club, a bit south of San Francisco, was one of them.

George Calhoun knew that it did not bring admiring glances from the other members when he brought someone like Frank Sievers to lunch, but once or twice a year it was a business necessity—and he knew he was not the only member with such burdensome obligations. Calhoun's social position was unshakable, not so much due to his personal wealth, but more because of the family heritage on his mother's side. He was, therefore, above reproach, yet it had been a bit of a shock when Frank had asked his new organizing consultant to join them. *Noblesse oblige* prevailed, so Calhoun had smiled politely and seconded the invitation.

Tact was not Frank's strong suit, but he had used all he could muster to suggest to Stretch in advance that he learn by listening and watching. As soon as they entered the club-house, however, Stretch was too awed by the atmosphere to talk. The wood-paneled dining room had large windows overlooking the rolling greens and San Francisco Bay beyond. He eyed the pink linen tableclothes and napkins, engraved sil-verware, white-gloved waiters. It was a long way from West Alton.

The young man intrigued Calhoun. He had undergone a radical change since Frank had first brought him to the bank only a few weeks earlier. Jackson was now wearing a dark choc-olate turtleneck sweater under a brown tweed jacket. Leather elbow patches were not the last word this year, but the ensem-ble looked chic—and expensive. The touch of class also seemed to have brought a change of personality. The banker noticed that Stretch seemed more subdued, spoke only when spoken to, and had better manners than he would have expected. For all that, there remained a streak that did not sit right. George had surmised that Frank Sievers was paying off the kid with those envelopes of cash, and that the money was obviously going into the safety-deposit box. Calhoun looked briefly at Sievers, then at Jackson again. The very thought that Jackson could even be a hit man left him rattled.

The meal passed quietly and coffee was served. George turned to Stretch and asked, "Play golf?"

"No. Never learned."

"Too bad. Frank here never got around to it either."

Missing the subtle disparagement in Calhoun's voice, Frank replied, "I always figured if I ever got my weight behind a club, I'd flatten the ball out like a potato chip." He turned to Stretch. "Listen, George and I have some business to discuss that'll take twenty, thirty minutes."

"You could stroll around and see the grounds if you like," George suggested. "The setting is really very striking."

Stretch got the point and excused himself. He checked his watch and headed for an inspection tour.

Outside, everything was trim and well kept. The fair-ways were slightly less green than they might have been. Even the rich can't grow grass on rocks, he mused. But it was evident that they did not have to stand in long lines to tee off.

The tennis courts were full. Some of the players seemed very shapely, so he ambled over to watch. In the near court, a strawberry blonde—about twenty-five, he guessed—drove a hard forehand deep into her partner's court. It touched, inches inside the back line, and sailed against the wire fence.

The dark-haired girl threw up her arms in defeat. "You did it, Dori!"

Stretch would have been delighted to play a different game with either one. Under Stretch's appreciative gaze, the girls walked to the benches to gather their things. As Stretch moved closer, the blackboard with the court hours came into view: 1:00/2:30—Dori Calhoun. Son-of-a-bitch! Good-looking like her father, except that George Calhoun had brown hair—they had the same long face and appealing, sad-dog eyes. Dori looked up at the stranger.

"Hi," Stretch ventured. "You George's daughter?"

Straightening, the blonde replied, "Yes. Why?"

"It just figures. You look like him. The good parts, that is. He and I were having lunch. He's going over some details with my associate, so I decided to wander a bit." He played it to the hilt, stepped into the courts. "I'm Stretch Jackson. Glad to meet you."

Dori grasped the extended hand. "I didn't know Dad was here." She turned. "This is my friend Shane Jenkins. We play every Wednesday."

The Jackson-Jenkins eyes clinked together like two glasses of champagne. Hers were as emerald as the Irish Sea. She had that lean look of an aristocratic Irish/English hybrid: long, straight, dark brown hair, fair skin, fine features, and natural reserve. No sooner had she said hello than he knew he had ruffled the normal Jenkins calm.

"Is Dad at the bar?" Dori inquired.

Tearing away from the emerald glance he replied, "No, I think they're still in the restaurant." Careful, he reminded himself. It's Calhoun's daughter you want to pay attention to.

The threesome headed up the path toward the clubhouse. Shane walked a step behind, boldly admiring the masculine figure. San Francisco's male shortage did not know any social boundaries.

Stretch asked Dori what she did, knowing the question was a bit forward.

"I work part-time as a fund raiser for the symphony and some for the opera company, too. And you?"

"It's a bit related," Stretch answered mischievously. "At least, it has to do with organizing funds. I'm a special consultant on union organization."

Dori looked at him with a twinkle in her eye. "Coming to the Mayfair is a bit like stepping into the lion's den for a union man, isn't it?"

"A bit, but then I like living dangerously." Stretch cocked one eyebrow at her. "You don't look dangerous to me." He flashed a grin, which took the hard edge off the remark.

"She is," Shane chimed in from the rear.

"Thanks, Shane, dear."

Stretch looked back at the lithe girl behind him. "And you, Miss Jenkins?"

"Harmless as a pussycat."

A peal of laughter swelled from Dori's throat.

Once inside, Shane stopped before turning down the corridor to the locker room. She held out her hand and gave Stretch a look with a crystal clear message.

Dori and Stretch entered the dining room. George was leaning back in his chair, unhurriedly smoking a slim cigar. "Well, look who's here," he said.

"And look who I found," Dori replied lightly.

With an air of stiff respectability, the banker rose. He knew his daughter very well—and her occasional offbeat flings. He had caught the gleam in her eye. Stretch and Sievers's eyes were riveted on his daughter. Calhoun caught Dori's gaze and almost imperceptibly shook his head in a negative warning. "Frank, I don't think you've met my daughter. Dori, Frank Sievers."

After a quick round of polite exchanges, Dori excused herself to hurry off to the showers, where she and Shane bantered on about Stretch like a couple of randy football players over a new cheerleader.

* * *

In the parking lot the three men said their good-byes. Calhoun climbed behind the wheel of his silver Mercedes. Henry, as usual, held open the back door of Frank's black Caddy. It irked Henry to have to continue holding it for the pushy new upstart, Stretch. Today Ben was at the wheel. He and Henry made eloquent cornerstones for any argument regarding the dominance of muscle over mind.

Settled into the mushy comfort of the backseat, Sievers studied his new man a moment, then gave one of his iceberg smiles. "The thing I like about you, Jackson, is that you're really on the make."

Assuming Frank was referring to Dori Calhoun, Stretch admitted, "Well, she really is something . . ."

"No, no, not the girl," Frank interrupted. "The setup. You make the setup, you can get any girl."

Relaxing into a corner, Stretch gave one of his most winning smiles. "Yeah, you read me, Frank."

Ben pulled the car out onto Highway 101 to head back downtown.

"Sure I do. All that back there—people who blab on about save gas and soak the rich—they don't understand anything. The rich have the soft life *and* the power. They're not about to give up any of it—and those who haven't had a shot at it aren't about to kill their chances of getting there. Even if we barrel over a cliff, we'll barrel on. That's the whole world's dream—making it. What I say to my people and what I know in my heart isn't always the same. That's the role of a leader. It's not always easy to lie convincingly, but if you can't do it, then you're a follower. A good leader knows the difference; a bad one believes his own bullshit."

He paused thoughtfully, then continued. "And there's sure as hell no shortage of lousy leaders. It's a thin line, knowing whether you're doing things for yourself or for your people. Once you're into it, the followers are easy to forget. You start living in the nice, comfortable world at the top and start to forget what it was like before—what it's still like for your people." He shook his head. "It's easy to lose touch. You remember that, Stretch, because you're going up the ladder."

The younger man smiled.

Sievers half turned to his new disciple. "And you keep in mind something I learned a long time ago. God created the four elements: air, fire, earth and water—then we made two of our own: power and money! That's what he gave us a brain for. If you get power, you get money. If you get money, you've got power. Don't you forget it."

"You can count on me, Frank," Stretch said, surprised with the philosophy the boss had shared with him and the confidence he seemed to have in Stretch. What Frank had just said surely wasn't what he propounded at speeches and rallies. Stretch was convinced he had been given a rare insight into what really made Frank Sievers tick.

He glanced sideways at the burly figure. So that *was* the thinking at the top. Maybe Bob Schmollinger was right back in West Alton, he thought. Maybe he'd been wrong.

Still, something bothered him profoundly. He liked the money and the power, but the "any means to an end" philosophy ran against his very grain. He wondered how he would feel about introducing Karen to Sievers. Perhaps that was now his ultimate standard. Hell, he reasoned, even the President of the United States has shaken Sievers's hand. Why shouldn't Karen be just as proud to do the same? As Frank had said the first day at Amalgamated, the roughhouse days are a thing of the past. Whatever things Sievers may have done to get to the top were over and buried. That was no concern of Stretch Jackson's. It was dawning on him that everyone who makes it to those upper reaches has a dungeon of hidden skeletons.

But for himself Stretch hung on to his idealism like a bull-dog to a postman's pants. There had to be a way to "do it right" and still get to the top. After all, it was his decision to be the best that had brought him to the Mayfair Country Club and into the backseat of the Cadillac of one of California's most prominent union leaders.

It crossed the torch's mind that Frank might be setting him up for something bigger than burning garages. Perhaps he had decided to groom him to play a major role in the union. Stretch Jackson settled back and toyed with the idea that a lit-tle arson was merely a prelude to becoming a major, legitimate figure in the Amalgamated hierarchy.

19

Almost a month had eloped with the past and for Stretch and Karen the result was an intoxicating mixture of peace and passion. However, Stretch's double life was becoming more difficult with each day of their increasing closeness.

"Can you get by on a snack and a bit of loving?" he asked one afternoon. "I want to take you to a special place for a late dinner." It was one of Karen's days off and they had spent an idyllic twenty-four hours together.

Snacked and loved, Karen held out until midnight. Even on a quiet Monday all of the regulars were at the Buddha, and very intrigued by Stretch's first appearance with a girl. Ho treated the couple with deference. Before the curtains closed, Benny came over for an introduction and Caruso arrived to sing a love song. Sweet Pea, Gene, and Elwood all trooped up. To Stretch's surprise, even Waldo left his latest lady to come and say hello—as well as to inspect the new arrival.

Showing off, Stretch ordered sashimi. Sushi was still a bit more brutal than he could face. He suggested teriyaki to Karen, who neatly one-upped him by asking Ho for sushi.

As soon as the curtains were closed, Karen put her hand on his and asked, "Who in the world are all your friends?"

"I knew you'd like them."

"Well, I don't know if I *like* them or not, but they're an impressively odd collection. I thought I'd walked into a weird group at the club when I first got to town, but not by these standards."

"Well, I'll tell you." Stretch started with Ho. The food came, the waitress left.

"The distinguished guy who came up last is Waldo, ex-great diamond thief, now reduced to the minors."

"What?"

"Yeah! Sure. He steals diamonds. Sweet Pea forges documents. Any documents—passports, I.D. cards. He specializes in police, F.B.I., even C.I.A.—that kind of thing. He even did me a beautiful driver's license." He looked at Karen and asked seriously, "Need anything in the way of rearranged documents? He can start you off on a whole new life."

"No, I do not, thank you very much. I'm getting along with the life I've got."

"Well, Gene there forges bonds. Or stocks—I can never remember which. And his buddy, Elwood, manufactures fives—no, I think he's into twenties now."

"What is this place, Ali Baba's den of thieves?"

Stretch was so engrossed in his explanations that he failed to notice the crisp quality of Karen's question.

"Naw," he went on, "just a bunch of fringy guys who've got independent ideas about how to make a living."

"And the one who sings?"

"Caruso? He's into full-time gambling. Benny's my best buddy of the lot. He's a fence."

"A fence?"

"Yep. You lift it, he sells it. The original man in the middle." Stretch laughed. "The middleman all right—Benny's got to have the biggest middle in the house, next to the Buddha's!"

"And how do you fit into all this, Stretch?"

He looked at Karen carefully. He had just intended to introduce her to the Buddha. He loved her and she loved him—at least he hoped she did. He wanted to share his secret with her. Ever since she had confided in him he had felt a desperate need to tell her. Stretch wasn't certain that this was the perfect time and place, but faced with such a direct question he felt it was now or never. Feigning lightheartedness, he began, "Okay. You told me everything—it's only fair I do the same. I really don't want to start off with you telling me your secrets and me lying to you." He took a breath. "I'm a torch. That's *my* secret. Only my best friend, Eddie—who's a torch, too—and Benny, and my clients know." He was pleased that he could get it out. He looked to Karen for her approval. "Now you know, too."

"A torch?"

"Yep. I make my living setting fire to buildings."

"Are you kidding me, Stretch?" She prayed he would say yes.

"No. And I'm the best in San Francisco. I just got a new contract with a very reputable union that'll net me over a hundred and twenty thousand dollars a year, foolproof and tax-free."

"Burning other people's property." The tone of reproach was now unmistakable.

"Yes. Oh, come on, Karen. It's all right. It isn't dangerous. And if you look at it right, it's not nearly as bad as what a lot of perfectly respectable people do. In fact, I don't work with a bunch of thugs. They're a very prominent, upright group—"

"But you're a *criminal*. Right? It *is* a crime. The police . . ." She felt the sick, fainting feeling again, as if the world were being stamped out around her. Tears welled up in her eyes.

"Karen, the police don't really investigate arson. It's not like robbing people or using guns. I'm no killer, for God's sake! I don't hurt anybody!" The first pinprick of panic jabbed Stretch's stomach.

"*I* . . . *can* . . . *not* . . . *handle* . . . *that* . . . Stretch." Each word struck like a hammer pounding on velvet. She fought to keep the drops running down her cheeks from becoming a hysterical flood.

"But I love you, Karen." He tried to recapture her hand.

"Don't. I don't want to get involved. I told you what I've been through for a year and a half. I can't deal with the idea of being with someone who the police might come after, who could disappear on me one day into jail. You want me to come visiting you in prison? Is that what you want from a girl?

Enough love to come to your jail?" She had let herself be vulnerable again. Never, never, never more! Steel gates slammed shut inside her.

"Karen, there's no risk, it's absolutely safe. I make a lot of money. It's with respectable people. Karen—I *love* you. That's why I wanted to be honest with you."

"I understand that. Honesty pays, unless the truth is that you're dishonest. I appreciate your telling me, but I thank God we didn't get any further!"

Stretch no longer knew where to turn or what to say.

"If you love me, call me a cab. Do not phone me, see me, bug me—or think of me. Please. I mean, I *beg* you, please! I can't. I can't, I really can't." It was more a cry for help than a command.

"For God's sake, Karen," Stretch pleaded, "if I can't tell you, who can I tell? Don't desert me."

"Tell these people in here—or a woman who can't get hurt, if there is such a thing. I'm . . . sorry. Stretch." It was clear that she really was saying, "Call me a cab before I fall apart—please!" She wanted to curl up again, disappear, cease to exist. That way she would feel no more pain.

"I'll take you . . ."

She bit her lip and shook her head violently. Stretch felt helpless to do anything but what she asked. Shaken and shamefaced, he grimly pretended not to see the friendly nods as he made his way to Ho's telephone.

* * *

The fire at B.B. Builders never came across Tom Farley's desk—nor that of any other arson investigator. Even when the roof comes down, the walls blow out and half the contents explode, it is still sometimes possible to unravel a fire's cause, but the undertaking becomes very complex and, worse, extremely expensive. Since even the night watchman saw nothing suspicious, and since there was no overt reason to suspect the good citizen Bradshaw of being involved in arson, the Fire Department report listed the cause as unknown.

Given the amount of money involved, the insurance company might have turned to a P.I., but the report of "Cause unknown" plus the total absence of any apparent reason for a prosperous contractor to send part of his livelihood up in flames led them to pay. They also had a business-interruption policy on B.B. Builders, so the longer Mr. Bradshaw was shut down, the greater the payment would ultimately be. Bradshaw had his check in a fortnight.

At first, the contractor was livid about the closed union shop. However, as he began to contemplate acquiring new, more efficient equipment and calculated the tax write-offs and a handsome profit he'd make for rebuilding his own garage, he concluded that the cloud of smoke had a silver lining.

Truck salesmen, heavy equipment salesmen, builder's supply house reps, even an architect trooped happily through Barney Bradshaw's office—and checkbook. As Frank Sievers had predicted, the fire had made almost everyone better off. An enormous insurance company and the American citizenry— via the Internal Revenue Service—had just pumped over eight hundred thousand dollars into Oakland's economy.

Once Sievers had explained this last statistic to him, Stretch wondered briefly if he should not be given the keys to the city—but after Karen's withdrawal, he was too plunged into gloom to care.

* * *

"Good morning, Stretch," said the velvet tone over the telephone.

"Morning, Hazel," he said testily. Velvet was not enough to soften his hangover.

"Frank asked me to tell you that he is ready for you to deal with Richmond."

"Sure."

227

"Uh . . ." She hesitated. "Maybe I shouldn't pass this on, but he sure thinks you're great." Hazel looked up at Frank Sievers for approval and smiled as Frank nodded his head.

"Well . . ." It was the wrong morning for quick repartee. "He's a great guy to work for." That seemed insufficient. "Actually, it's a great organization. I think everybody up there's just great." He was beginning to hate himself. "I'm sure glad he likes me. How are you this morning, Hazel?"

"Just fine."

"That's great!"

There was a brief pause until Hazel said, "Well, I've got to run—the other phone's ringing. Take care. See you next week, Stretch."

"Yeah. Thanks. 'Bye, Hazel."

He sat on the couch, mulling it over. Then his brain started functioning. He felt certain that there was a second level to what Hazel had said, but he could not quite fathom what it might be. She must know everything—absolutely everything, he reasoned. That's what a perfect secretary is for. Someone to handle all those little details like getting across to Stretch that Frank *really* liked him. That explained Hazel's call. It pleased him.

He eyed the apartment again. Goddamn, he thought. Over twenty-five grand stashed in Calhoun's vault and more on its way. It seemed time to take Eddie's advice and get out of the "coyote hole." He'd send some money home and ditch the Camaro, too. He felt better just thinking of it. If there could be no Karen, at least there was plenty of work to be done.

Every time Karen's name crossed his mind, so did the visuals. He saw her smiling, or at the beach, or at the Silver Doll, or, most vividly of all, in bed—warm, happy, and gloriously naked. It seemed impossible that love had flicked from full to empty with no intervening stages. He covered his eyes, trying to block her out. Waves of tight fury consumed him. Stretch kept repeating: Who the hell needs a screwed-up, prissy schoolteacher from Litchfield? Bible Belt and hypocritical! Doesn't she work in a strip joint? Besides, he added piously, I'm just a temporary torch—and a damn good one at that.

After breakfast, he hit Van Ness Avenue, San Francisco's main automobile row.

In a short time he was bidding a fond farewell to the yellow Camaro that had served him so well. Then he walked up the street to a different car lot and—using his alias from Sweet Pea—Stretch bought an inconspicuous tan Pinto wagon. In the huge underground parking lot below Union Square he rented two adjacent spaces on a monthly basis. It was early afternoon when he drove out of the somber garage in quest of his next objective.

F. JANDA—HIGH-CLASS PROPERTIES: SALES—RENTALS. "High-Class" struck the right chord. Stretch headed straight to the proprietor. "It's got to have a view of the bay. And none of those wood houses with all the doodads—I don't want the work involved."

Janda looked at his assistant. This was a switch. Everybody was always clamoring for the hard-to-find Victorian jewels, for which San Francisco was famous. People who sought modern usually headed across the bridge to Marin County, which was one of the three sources of all modern American residential architecture.

The real estate man got a gleam in his eye. "I may have just what you're looking for—complete with a swimming pool."

Only a newcomer would be impressed by the pool. Anyone local knew that the city of San Francisco itself had a micro climate that averaged fifteen degrees cooler than either the East Bay or Marin County. Except on rare occasions, the pool was a folly that only an Eskimo would use.

"Sounds fantastic!" Stretch bit hard. They made an appointment to see the house several days later.

Stretch devoted the rest of the week to Amalgamated's second target. When Sievers gave him the assignment he had said that a burn for the union in Richmond would be a rarity. "That place expanded like a mushroom during World War Two. Hasn't done much since. Not like the rest of the East Bay, which is just taking off. We've always been pretty well

organized in Richmond, but I've got one new guy up there—
Kirk Dowell—who's stealing lots of business at nonunion
prices."

Stretch drove out to Richmond to survey his next site,
another garage. Richmond turned out to be quite industrial.
Stretch found it plain and poor compared to most of what he
had seen around the bay. The torch job would be a snap—he
knew within minutes how the garage should be handled.

If the East Bay was going to be his bailiwick for a while, as
Sievers had implied, it seemed reasonable to explore it. Oakland was the key. Berkeley, welded onto its northern bound-
ary, was the brain. Stretch had long known of those cities, but
had never heard of Richmond, Concord, or San Leandro. The
Bay Area Rapid Transit system had suddenly put all of these
towns within quick commuting distance of downtown San
Francisco—closer than Oak Park to the Loop or Yonkers to
Manhattan. They were booming with residential growth—and
building contracts. Trapped between forested hills and brilliant waters, a million people had already nested on the narrow
strip of East Bay land.

When Stretch spotted the fire-red, white-top convertible
Mustang in Alameda, he skidded to a stop and backed up.
Stretch had never heard of Alameda, either. The city of one
hundred thousand people snuggled on an island between a
mile of beach, the harbor, and the naval air station. As he pulled
into the car lot, looked the Mustang over, and made a down
payment he was glad he had decided to cruise through it.

* * *

Frank Janda, a flunked-out architecture student, could
quote the Mexican architectural genius who said, "A square
corner is like a knife in the heart." By the Mexican's standards, the international-style house he was showing Stretch
was a veritable pit full of daggers. Janda decided it was more
appropriate to sell the fine genealogy of square-and-bare, from
Gropius and Mies van der Rohe through southern California's

masters of the angular, such as Richard Neutra and Craig Ellwood.

The realtor failed to mention that sooner or later the house's cold, sterile corners overwhelm the eloquent theory. The harsh reality of living within all-white square spaces usually proved far more powerful than the abstract beauty of the structure—which was the reason everyone else wanted the old Victorian. However, Janda's masterly dissertation hit its mark. What could be more enticing than to be "in step with both the times and California"? With one eye on the swimming pool, Stretch pulled a large roll of bills from his pocket to nail down his new abode.

"I don't generally get paid in cash," Janda said, eyeing the wad of green, "but since this is one of my personal rental properties . . . well, if you wanted to make all your payments that way, I'd certainly be willing to give you a discount. Say fifteen percent?"

Stretch hesitated.

"Save me all that bookkeeping." It did not occur to Janda that anyone with that kind of money might also be naive. He gave his new tenant a wink. "Don't run it through the books—don't pay the Uncle."

* * *

At 3:17 A.M. on a Wednesday morning the long bell rang in two Richmond fire stations, summoning the task force that responded to first alarms in the commercial, nonexplosive, nonchemical category. Before his truck had hit the driveway at the Dowell Construction fire the captain of the first-in unit had already called for a second alarm. The entire building was in flames. By dawn, the fire was out, the garage was rubble, and the clouds over Wildcat Canyon Park to the east were going glory pink.

Karen, no Karen, it seemed that Stretch's life was moving on.

* * *

Jonah West picked up the phone in his office at the Grove Street Station and dialed Tom Farley. Charlene answered the phone and talked for a minute while Tom finished another call. Jonah was curious about what Charlene looked like. Her voice had something relaxed and comforting in it. She "sounded" pretty. Jonah had often wondered if Tom had chosen his secretary simply because the first half of her name spelled "char."

"What's up, Jonah?" Tom asked, getting on the line.

"I'm not sure. I've been going over East Bay records for a quarterly report. I'm only supposed to check fires on the 'suspected arson' list, but it popped out at me that we've had three fires at contractors' garages and one at a construction site. That's pretty unlikely as a coincidence, but I can't figure it out. Mean anything to you?"

Tom's voice betrayed an avid interest. "How many were actually on the suspected arson list?"

"Only the construction site. The rest were listed 'cause unknown.' That's not the end of it, though. Two of the three garages—Dowell up in Richmond and Vada Construction Company here in Oakland—had the same MO as that salvage company you were asking about three or four months back. Remember? First-due equipment arrives and the whole building's going up from one end to the other."

"Remember!" Tom sat up so fast he hit his knee on the desk leg. "Acme Salvage—that's the only case I've had all year where everything I touched in the investigation left me dissatisfied. Wouldn't say it haunts me, but I certainly dredge it up a lot. Did an arson man investigate either of those two garages?"

"Not that I know of. There wasn't any reason to. Only the construction site had a serious inspection by a fire marshal. He just punched out blanks and gave up."

"Both contractors and both instant, total involvement. We'll put that in the pot and stir it. It sounds to me like you may have fingered something major, Jonah. It may justify the whole Arson Liaison program before we're through . . . *and* salve my conscience about having left a loose end on the Acme file."

"I'll stick these reports in the mail to you."

"Oh, no you won't! I'll pick them up on my way home."

Jonah chuckled. "That's what I thought you'd say."

Hanging up, Tom spun his chair around and looked out over the bay. He bit lightly on his thumbnail and furrowed his brow. "What the *hell* is going on out there?" he asked aloud.

"Tom?"

He whirled around in his chair.

"You starting to talk to yourself?" Charlene inquired, smiling.

"Uh . . . maybe I was," he admitted. "Jonah's come up with something that may be a new lead on the mystery of Acme Fire Salvage."

Charlene took the dictation from his file basket, looked at Tom intensely, and started nodding her head in an exaggerated up-and-down motion. "Uh-huh," she said, beginning to back out of the office. "I read it, master. 'Get me the Acme Salvage file.'" She laughed and turned to leave.

"I hope you don't ESP all my thoughts," Tom said, amused.

She stopped at the threshold. "Don't tell me you have indecent thoughts you have to hide," she teased.

How did their exchange take this turn? The thoughts were not indecent, he said to himself. They're just about making love to you.

"Don't ask embarrassing questions," he said.

As Charlene left, he became aware of a fragrance she left behind. He had never noticed it before and could not decide if it was perfume or woman. He wondered seriously, for the first time, if he should stop fighting his desires. Simply allowing himself to pose the question in a lucid moment was a shock. He visualized making love to Charlene and promptly stamped a NO! across the picture. Yes, it's no, he sighed, but it *is* a pretty picture.

With difficulty he channeled his thinking back to business and toyed with the idea of calling Vic Whitlock at Global. Tom decided against it, since Acme Salvage was paid and resting in peace. He would call Whitlock if—and when—he managed to come up with something more concrete. Tom gritted his teeth. Call Whitlock—like hell! There's some high-class torch out there setting fires so cleverly that I can't even find the end of the string to start unraveling. Wouldn't that make Vic smile? "Damn!" Tom said aloud in frustration. "Someday I'll put this bastard's head on a platter and walk it right into Vic Whitlock's office!"

20

Stretch was crouched behind a pile of lumber and building materials in a dark corner on the second floor of a half-finished structure. At precisely 2:45 A.M. the shadows were suddenly illuminated by the flame of his Zippo.

Outside in the portable construction shack, the steadfast guard, Josh, sat engrossed in a comic book. A large sign nearby announced:

ON THIS SITE WILL RISE
THE OAKLAND AGENCY BUILDING
GENERAL CONTRACTOR: VADA
CONSTRUCTION COMPANY

The three-story structure had, in fact, already risen: the concrete had been poured, the roof sheathing was on, barnwood siding already covered much of the exterior, and the interior had been rough-framed in, the hundreds of two-by-fours resembling a maze of matchsticks.

Josh finished a chapter in his comic and jumped up to get some fresh air. Outside he stretched. "Jumping Jesus," he announced to the empty lot. "That's a great story!"

Less than thirty feet away Stretch instantly dropped to his stomach behind a pile of lumber. The memory of the last time a guard had surprised him raced through his mind. He considered making a break for it.

Josh breathed in the cool night air, drawing it deeply, refreshingly into his lungs. He gave the full moon a passing glance, then turned, and sauntered back into his shack.

Peering around the edge of the pile, Stretch—badly rattled—watched the figure in the yellow light of the shack's interior. He waited for the guard to settle in to read some more, then got the hell out. Behind him a candle attached to a plastic bag of clear liquid was slowly melting down.

Despite the kindling-wood aspect of the site, finding the best way to burn it had taxed Stretch's ingenuity. Frank's orders were to throw the project into the maximum period of shutdown possible. Stretch wanted the wood to burn down completely and the concrete to become so hot that it would lose sufficient tensile strength to require its removal and replacement.

Stretch sat in his car a block away. Remembering when he had sat in the yellow Camaro in a dead sweat after his first job for Moe—Eden's Garden Women's Wear—Stretch could hardly help but laugh at himself. Eden's had been just a dumb little job. Now he had lit what would be a major conflagration and he was perfectly calm. He eyed his watch: 2:54 A.M.

This was the second time Stretch had hit the Vada Construction Company. Apparently after the garage fire Jim Vada had told Frank where he could stuff his contracts, so Sievers had given him just enough time to get back into business before striking again—biting him right through his trousers and deep into the uninsured part of Vada's wallet—his business interruption policy would not pay for lost time and expense on a job under construction.

Three o'clock! The candle was burned down to a flaming wick that lay in a little pool of wax. Stretch could visualize it perfectly. The plastic bag would melt and collapse, shooting out accelerant, which would bloom into flame. Fire would race down the network of lines of flammable gel that Stretch had carefully trailed to other, smaller quantities of accelerant. He had spread the special water-resistant, jellylike substance only on wood surfaces, which would burn away, taking with them all evidence of the gel's existence. Within two minutes tons of wood would be ablaze. By now the guard would hear the roar of the fire, if he hadn't already seen its reflections.

By 3:07 A.M. Stretch could see the red glow. At 3:12 he heard the first sirens. He started the Pinto and glided away, knowing that he had done a perfect job.

Deep in the menacing underground caverns of Union Square's parking garage, Stretch eased the tan Pinto wagon around a pillar. He checked to verify that he was alone, then pulled into his space, jumped into the adjacent red Mustang convertible, and slipped into the night.

* * *

Before Stretch had reached Union Square, the Oakland Agency Building site had turned into one angry shaft of flame crowned by a plume of nasty black fumes that boiled upwards, even blacker than the night heavens. The scene was less than fifty yards from the Berkeley city limits and the Berkeley Fire Department had dispatched a special unit at Oakland's request: a "blitz pumper," which carries an on-board tank of seventy-five hundred gallons, arrives with preconnected hoses, and by the time it stops is heaving a veritable river of water on a blaze.

Ladder 1 had responded, captained by Mannie Rojas and crewed by the regulars: Pyle, Branch, Runyon, Black, and Pavitt. They also carried two new recruits who were spending their first day observing real fire conditions. The recruits were instructed to watch, listen, and "keep the hell out of the way." The ladder was now positioned between the guard shack and the building.

"You can see where the phrase 'barn burner' comes from," Engineer Branch said to one of the recruits. "Barn wood bums like it wants to get it over with lickety-split!"

One end of the building had started to collapse into a heap of burning wood. "Dan," Mannie called down from the ladder, "give me light water! Fast!"

"You got it!"

Light water, the recruits knew, has an additive of foam detergent that eliminates much of the water's surface tension, helping it to soak deep down into burning materials.

"If I move the lever to the other tank of additive, what do I get?" the engineer asked one of the recruits.

"You'll go off the tank with the detergent and . . ." The recruit was so caught in the excitement of the fire that he lost his thought.

"Frictionless," the second recruit blurted. "Breaks down hose lining and nozzle friction, stream goes two and a half times farther than standard hydrant water." He seemed to be reciting from a textbook.

The blaze was what Mannie Rojas called a "no-fun fire": no strategy or tactics, no drama, no risk of spreading to calculate, no potential insufficiencies in the water supply/nozzle capacity ratio.

In contrast to Jonah West's squareness Mannie Rojas was all fine, thin angles. His deep-set eyes danced against their olive-skinned background. Mannie seemed like a bird—always perched for flight. He came down the ladder after a short while. "Nothing to do but dump water on one like this. Bor-ring!"

He noticed the quizzical look on the face of one of the recruits. "Listen," he said. "You ever see a professional soldier who wasn't a little itchy in peacetime?" He patted the brilliant red paint of the truck. "If you just like to polish these things, you get a job in a car wash. Face it—it's the fire that turns us on."

"We're adrenaline addicts," Dan Branch added. "Get hyped and get paid for it! You don't get into firefighting for thrills, but once you're hooked, it makes every other job look dull as stale buns."

As if to emphasize the remark, the closest end of the roof's decking collapsed and the blast of sparks would have pleased a Fourth of July crowd. It made them all duck for cover, the startled new recruits diving into the cab head first.

When the shower was over, Mannie continued. "There's one basic truth you got to get clear—or it'll cost you your life." He pointed his finger, and the sparks in his eyes underscored each sentence. "The only thing this fancy equipment does better than the old fire brigades with a horse-drawn pump is pump more water. Except for a couple of tricks, all we've learned in a century is how to get more water on a fire faster."

"Captain," asked the recruit who had the textbook memorized, "isn't that important?"

"It's only part of the story," Mannie continued. "We've learned to build bigger structures faster than we've added new firefighting technology. So it's great if it's a small house burning—not worth a damn if it's a fifty-story high-rise or a chemical factory. For all of these mechanical marvels, the backbone of firefighting is you." He looked hard at the new recruits. "It's the men, the teamwork, determination, and quick wits on the fireground. Sometimes it's plain brute strength. If you get hurt like I did in that Gloria Pump fire or collapse from fumes inside a building, you want to *know* that your mate can pick you up and haul you out. Or, if it's your partner who's hurt, your lungs may burn, your nose may pump snot all down your front, the wall is going, and you think of one thing and only one thing: your duty! That's teamwork! It may sound corny to you now, but, I promise, I've been there—and that really is the way it is. You've started a career where you can count on getting hurt a lot. But you can also count on giving help a lot."

Mannie waved his hand toward the smoldering rubble that was to have been the Oakland Agency Building. "I promise you guys—they're not all that easy."

* * *

The following morning at ten thirty sharp. Bill Hopkins, fire claimsmanager for the Union and National Insurance companies, received an unexpected visitor.

"Look, I know this is unusual," Tom Farley explained. "I'm not looking for work, and I know you guys rarely call in independent investigators, but I'll make you a deal. If I can't nail your insured, there's no charge. I'm not really interested in

Vada or this file. I'm trying to pin down something bigger and—well, I don't even know what it is."

Hopkins was a round-faced young executive with a brisk manner. The unusual was his business, but this seemed down-right bizarre. Although he knew Farley by reputation, this was an exceptionally odd way to actually meet the man. Sticking his fingers in his vest pocket, he met the question head on. "I've got the authority, Tom, but you realize that, in the first place, the insured hasn't even called us yet." He had some reservations about it all. What if someone upstairs—

The thought was interrupted by Farley. "Call the agent. He'll tell you if Vada's checked in. If he hasn't, that's *really* strange."

"With all the agents we've got, how should I even know—"

"You had a fire loss on his garage a couple of months ago. The agent will be on that file."

How the hell does he know that? the claims man thought. He was puzzled and slightly annoyed that a stranger could drop in and remind him of one of his own files. No wonder he's a goddamned legend. "Okay." He buzzed his secretary and asked for the file. "You know, the problem is that it's on a builder's risk so the policy starts at zero and only increases as the builder adds value to the structure. There's not enough money in it yet to justify a P.I. investigation from what I under-stand. I mean, if it's arson, our staff men could check it out." He humphed a bit and finally figured. What the hell. "Okay, Tom, just keep the bill down."

"Tell you what," Tom said, feeling victorious, "even if I can prove it's Vada who ordered the fire, I'll just bill you expenses—unless you end up feeling you want to pay a fee, also. What I really want isn't money, but your authorization to dig into the case. I think there's a whole can of worms out there."

The decision made, Hopkins relaxed. "Glowworms, I suppose."

* * *

Sapphire II cast white reflections of moonlight on the water. The lopsided globe was rising late and waxing. From the aft portholes, rings of a more yellow light glistened. For three days Tom had put everything else on ice and had concentrated on Vada. Unfortunately, the fire at Vada's garage had occurred four months ago and not a trace of the building remained. The clock hands had left midnight slightly behind when he heaved a sigh and looked at the Oakland Agency fire's checklist on his yellow legal pad: Josh Marshall; Jim Vada; the job foreman; three workmen; the mortgage holder; the insurance agent; the owner and his general manager; the first-in firemen. In all, there were notes or statements from fourteen people. An interview with the fifteenth—Barry Krulick, chief accountant, the last one on the list—was scheduled for the morning.

Several scattered pieces of the puzzle were in place, yet ninety percent remained unfinished. The fire marshal who had investigated the first of the two construction site fires several months earlier had found the origin suspicious, but finally had to settle for a "cause unknown" case. In an hour Tom had found enough tracks—even though they were now stale—to know that whoever lit that first building site did a very amateurish torch job—surely unrelated to the sophisticated arsonist who set the other construction-related fires. That left a lot of questions. He shifted uneasily in the chair. Tom could prove the Oakland Agency fire was arson, but that merely made deeper mysteries appear. Why was Vada the only contractor hit twice? Why did two garages have that immediate, total involvement and why did one of the three garages and Vada's new construction job get torched differently? Was there one torch or several, one motive or several, and were they all connected by some conspiracy—or not?

He pushed his chair away from the desk. If he was going to keep his appointment with Krulick at ten, it was time to close up and go to bed.

* * *

A big man with a permanent scowl on his face, Krulick was outwardly very helpful. Because an accounting department is often privy to an employer's dirty work, Tom had saved Krulick for last. Tom studied the job log, the order sheets, the ledgers, and asked a lot of apparently innocent questions. Bill Hopkins had provided him with copies of the entire file on Vada's garage, which had burned earlier. Now was Tom's chance to compare the paid loss with the real costs of building and resupplying the new garage, which was already under construction. Had Vada had it torched for profit? One thing was beyond doubt: Jim Vada ran a very large operation, and the job that had just been burned was only of middling size compared to all of the company's work in progress.

Krulick's big-boned face, which matched his body, spoke of someone tough, quick, calculating—nothing unusual for the man who ran the financial side of an organization the size of Vada's. He was not the squeaky, stereotyped little accountant.

"Could you get Jim Vada on the line and ask him to come in for a minute?"

"Sure. Everything okay?"

Tom did not answer, so Krulick dialed the number and made the request.

Vada seemed less rough and tumble than most contractors, downright fragile compared to his accountant. Forty-three, prematurely balding, of medium build, he had somehow found the formula for success. Tom looked at the gray-flannel suit, the rimless glasses, and the over-worked, nervous toothpick. Judging by their outward appearances, the two men should have changed roles.

Tom decided on a frontal attack. "Look," he said, firmly taking command, "I've analyzed company accounts with some of the finest crooked CPA's in the business, and you're not going to pull the wool over my eyes about what goes into a construction job."

Vada's toothpick stopped. Krulick's scowl deepened and went mean.

"What are you talking about, Farley?" the contractor demanded.

"Mr. Vada, these books are cleverly set up to fool *some-one*." He watched the two faces carefully. "There's no way that *that* many board feet of lumber or *that* many yards of poured concrete were on site when the building burned. Without getting down to the penny, I'd say there's an eight- to ten-thousand-dollar overage—but what's strange is that I don't believe for a minute you redid those sheets in the last three days just to shaft Union and National out of a few thousand bucks. If you did it for the owners or the IRS, that's your business, but you can hardly expect your insurance company to pick up the tab." He suddenly realized the shock on Vada's face was genuine. "Unless . . ." He looked at Krulick. "Unless, Mr. Vada, the figures are designed to fool you."

It was thirty minutes before Jim Vada and Tom seated themselves in the owner's private office.

"I'm sorry to have stirred up the hornet's nest," said Tom, pushing the hat back on his head.

"Sorry! I'll have to have a whole audit to find out how much Krulick's skimmed off me in the last year." Vada was genuinely outraged, but decided he might kill two birds with the same proverbial stone. "Tell you what," he added. "You just saved me a lot of money. Seriously. I'd be happy to give you a reward of five thousand. After all, you're a working guy, too."

"You trying to buy me off?"

"Why, not at all!" This time Vada's surprise was manufactured. "I don't have anything to buy you off *of*. Listen, I get hit up by electrical inspectors, plumbing inspectors, building inspectors. I got to kick back to architects, prime contractors, suppliers. You know what part of building cost goes to payoffs under the table? Has to be fifteen percent. It's a way of life. And all that's just to stay in business. And for nothing. You, you did something, saved something. It's like I'd offer a burglary reward." He fingered the little round dispenser on his desk before selecting a new toothpick.

"Well, forget it," said Tom. "Everybody else's morals can go to hell, that's their business. I sleep well nights."

"So do they," Vada interjected. "That's the bitch of it."

Tom took his hat off, balanced it on the corner of the desk, and sighed. That was the kind of truth that always sent the fatigue of depression through his bones. "Yeah, I guess they do. Look, Jim, I'm going to level with you. I can go to court and prove this was a torch job. Your last fire—the garage—had already been bulldozed off the site when I got called in, but this one I've got dead cold. It was a damn good job, but provable arson."

"How can you prove that?"

"Spalling, Jim, spalling. Poured concrete takes twenty-eight days to cure to its normal maximum of three thousand pounds per square inch tensile strength—and even longer to dry out the very last of its original water. After five, six days you pull the shoring, your guys can walk on it, and since you're an efficient outfit, that's exactly what you did. You poured the second floor exactly twenty-two days before the fire."

"Yeah, but what's 'spalling'?" Vada asked suspiciously.

"Put a sudden high temperature on concrete and you get steam. Even bone-dry concrete usually has five percent moisture content. That's its permanent condition. A three-week-old floor like you had has an even higher percentage of water still in it. Sudden heat vaporizes the moisture that is trapped inside the cement. The water content expands violently and the surface of the cement—or little areas of it—pop off. That's called spalling. Sometimes whole slabs will just explode into thin layers if enough combustible is poured on it. Josh, your night man, told me where he first saw fire. I didn't have any trouble finding where the spalling was. I've got some chips at the lab with candle wax content. It was a good pro job because there's no evidence of what kind of accelerant he used, but by simple elimination that means it had to be alcohol. I've still got enough to nail an arson label on it. The alligatoring, spread rate—all that will leave no doubt in a jury's mind."

Vada looked frankly worried. "Now, I can't find any reason to believe you personally had anything to do with it, but I have a great deal of difficulty believing that a man with your savvy doesn't have some serious ideas about who might have set both your garage and your construction job on fire." Tom fiddled with his hat brim. "You want to level with me?"

* * *

A few blocks away, firemen groped through a smoke-filled room. "Here he is!" a muffled voice called out. The fireman bent over, picked up the limp body, hustled to the sunlit stairs, and down to the blacktop where Jonah was waiting.

"Well done, Ramey. Four thirty-two." Jonah entered the time on a pad.

The "victim" stood up and removed his mask. "Okay," Jack Runyon said, "I'd have lived, but it's the fireman's carry, remember, not the farmer's. I'm not a sack of beans. The person you carry out of a burning building won't demand comfort, but they're not supposed to be injured by the firemen."

"It's all right, Ramey." Jonah eyed Runyon, who was pushing the department's weight limit. "He's not the local lightweight, either."

The sweating trainee looked at his "victim." "If he got any fatter, he'd leave grease in his tracks." Ramey knew he should not have said it, but he couldn't resist.

Fortunately, Jonah West laughed and slapped Runyon on the shoulder. "He got your number, Jack. I'll have to remember that line."

"Mark him down five minutes for insubordination," said Runyon, but even he had to smile.

Jonah started to comment, but spotted Tom Farley approaching the training tower. "Well, look who's here! Hey, Tom! Come to see how the real thing works?"

Tom pushed his hat back with his thumb. "You kidding? I took that simulated fire training so many times the battalion chief was going to give me an iron lung."

"Men," Jonah announced, "this here arson ace is Tom Farley. He finds out after you've risked your ass why you risked it," He and Tom headed for Jonah's office.

"I just left Vada," Tom said as they sat down. "He's got to know something, but whatever it is isn't going to be public knowledge. He's clammed right up tight."

"Well, I ran the whole bunch through the agencies you don't have access to from the state fire marshal's office to the F.B.I. Haven't heard from the F.B.I. yet. Checked Barney Bradshaw, Vada, Dowell, every one of our contractor fires—owners and employees. Dowell in Richmond is the only one with a prior 'suspect' and the investigating marshal thought it was probably a workman he had fired."

"Damn." Tom felt a twitch of frustration. "Let me know as soon as you get the F.B.I. reports." He checked his watch. "Chow time. Want to come have lunch at Jack London's?"

Jonah looked undecided. "You know how it is at the station: forty-eight hours on, forty-eight off and don't leave except for a fire. This liaison job is only half-time you know—I'm still working firefighter's rules. Les Black is the lunch cook today and he promised Southern fried, biscuits, and gravy. Best cook in the house. They're stuck with me for dinner. Still . . ." Jonah considered his weakness for shrimp. "Let me go tell the Chief."

* * *

To the west, beyond the concrete umbilical cord that connects Oakland and San Francisco, Stretch was relaxed in Amalgamated's vulgar red leather and velvet couch.

"It's been going beautifully," Frank admitted. "The new Vada job brought him around. I've got him set up just perfectly. I don't mind telling you I've been planning a little something for myself." His icy eyes took on an extra luster. "What the hell, we're in the business. I might as well take advantage of it."

"What you got in mind, Frank?"

"A little trick. Just concerns you, me, and Vada. It's part of the reason I had to come down on him so hard. Not that his rejecting a closed-shop contract wasn't enough, but this is special because it's personal. I'll tell you when it's ripe."

Stretch's interest was piqued, but after six months of working for Frank he had learned not to push. The man in charge rose. Their conversation was over. It was lunchtime and both men had appointments.

"Incidentally," Frank Sievers added, "the grapevine has it that you're moving in interesting social circles." The tone was half-jealous, half-venomous. "You parlayed one lunch at the country club into a whole affair. Listen, even I don't play that fancy league!" Not only did Sievers viscerally resent the social upper class, but he would not tolerate such aspirations in a subordinate.

The remark struck Stretch's stomach like a fist; it meant that beyond a doubt he was still being tailed. How *dare* Frank Sievers spy on his private life! Anyway, he seethed to himself, a few rolls in the hay with Shane Jenkins hardly constituted a social scene. He forced an amiable tone. "You don't miss a trick do you, Frank?" Like it or not, Sievers was where all the gravy came from.

"I didn't get behind this desk missing tricks. How the hell do you think I found you in the first place? Newspaper ads? You'd better start being careful." It was a firm warning. "I mean it, Stretch. We're going to make a ton of money together. Don't screw it up socializing. What gets you in trouble gets me in trouble." The atmosphere seemed unfriendly all of a sudden. "And I won't have it!"

"Don't worry, Frank." The old blues flashed sincerity. "I'll keep it cool."

As soon as Stretch had left, Sievers sent for Henry. When the bodyguard came in, Frank was pacing, worked into a proper steam. "Goddamn it, Henry, I won't have it!"

"Won't have what, boss?"

"He's been fucking phenomenal up to now, and all of a sudden, what's he doing? Screwing around with the daughter of Avery Jenkins! All I need is for him to knock her up."

"Jesus, Frank, you're getting all worked up over nothing."

Sievers wheeled on Henry. "*Nothing?* You work for me and you'd better goddamn well remember, you get rich WASPs on your side to *use* them, to make your image legit, to pick their brains, to push them out front in a fight. Because otherwise they're the bastards who sit on the other side of the negotiating table telling you to eat shit while they clean their nails with silver pocketknives. You can bend their daughters over in the dark if you want, but you don't get seen dancing with them in public—not and keep your self-respect, you don't."

"Hey, Frank, I'm not doing it. Stretch is. Don't take it out on me."

Sievers stopped. "You're right, Henry. I'm sorry. Look, I want you or Ben on his ass every night. I'm not setting up the Vada apartment number for nothing. If he doesn't come to his senses so I can trust him . . . how can you trust a guy who'd do a thing like that? If he keeps seeing that rich bitch, we'll make him a goddamn castrato. That'll get his mind on his work full time!"

* * *

The incident put a serious damper on Stretch's appetite for lunch. In twenty minutes he was to pick up Shane for their first daytime rendezvous. After the long tortured loneliness that had followed Karen's sudden departure, Stretch had phoned Dori. Going to places of the Mayfair's standing seemed an exciting new frontier. Stretch had a moment's letdown when Dori had lied about being out of circulation for a while, but his spirits soared when Dori gave him Shane Jenkins's phone number. He vividly remembered Shane's inviting emerald eyes, the aristocratic look, and the pert figure in tennis shorts.

The first evening with Shane had not gone quite the way he had expected. He had given a low whistle when he had checked Shane's address for the third time. Jesus, he reckoned, she's got to be living in a million dollars' worth of real estate. He rang the bell with a hat-in-hand, intimidated manner.

Shane had apologized for not being quite ready. In fact, she had just come out of the shower and had on a bathrobe that revealed more than was modest. "Just to make the waiting bearable," she fixed him a drink. She also fixed herself one. Provocatively, she leaned against the bar talking, then gave him a tour of the imposing house. All the while, she flashed and revealed, led the conversation to suggestive corners in the bedrooms, brushed against him in the hall. She made him another drink and turned the music lower. The glimpses of her breasts and thighs flashed firmness and bronze. With increasing frequency Shane's tongue moistened her lips; her eyes dropped to the growing form of his crotch. Stretch found it more and more difficult to make small talk, and yet, dazzled by Shane's evident wealth and social distinction, he hardly dared follow his urges so precipitously.

Next to Stretch on a living room couch, thirty minutes after he had walked in the front door, the lady of the house turned to him in midsentence, got a firm-handed grip on what was now an iron muscle and bent over to kiss it, then quickly turned her head, sighting up his stomach to lock into his startled eyes. "Going to Banbury Cross?" she asked hoarsely. In response to Stretch's baffled look she recited the nursery rhyme phrase: "Ride a cockhorse to Banbury Cross," and she pulled down his pants, opened her robe, filled herself with willing horse, and, right on the flowered silk sofa, rode until both the steed and the rider were roiled in sweat and too fatigued to move another muscle.

To suggest that Stretch disenjoyed the performance would be inaccurate. He had, after all, repeated it a dozen times in the last few months, but at some point, every time, his thoughts turned to Karen. Karen would have been less aggressive, more gentle, less brassy; she would have had more to say to him. With Shane it was body work, with Karen it had been love. When Shane laughed and said, "Christ, I love to jump your frame," Stretch felt he was only there at her pleasure, for her pleasure. It was the old macho shoe put on the other foot. He decided it fit no better on women than on men—maybe worse.

His visits were mostly bumping bones, though he and Shane did venture out from time to time. He was introduced to a few choice restaurants, a chic disco, and they went again to the country club. Shane seemed to be permanently starved for sex, and Stretch finally wondered if there was anything more to their relationship than the drive between their thighs. He had invited her to lunch to draw her into the daylight to find out if the attraction exceeded four-letter activities.

The quiet waterside terrace at Jack London Square seemed the perfect way to impress Shane with a spot she surely didn't know. At least, it had seemed right until Frank had delivered his unpleasant warning.

Shane had been surprised all right. No one had ever suggested Oakland to her for lunch. Nonetheless, she had mustered her spirit of adventure and said yes. Although Stretch was as good as she and Dori had anticipated in their steamy locker room discussion, she could not find anything to say to him. Neither the Vietnam experience, nor some dumb small town in the Midwest, nor, for God's sake, racing stock cars was worth discussing. Still, as they drove toward the mall and the terrace by the water's edge came into view, she had to concede that the place had an unexpected charm.

However, if Jack London, author of *Call of the Wild*, *The Sea Wolf*, and *Martin Eden*, could come back to see the modern barn-wood shopping mall that was named in his honor, he would be horrified. For a man who, despite his birthright of poverty and hunger, had risen to become one of America's most famous exponents of socialism, a sophisticated shopping center monument would have collided head-on with London's idea of how his beloved city should remember him. Visitors to Oakland, however, are delighted by the maze of boutiques along the estuary where shops abound with chic, with antiques, with taste and class. Not socialist, but it was a pleasant, capitalist place to leave money—as Tom and Jonah were leaving theirs.

Their luncheon conversation had been restricted to arson, except for a brief excursion into the Oakland A's American

League prospects. Both of them had happily put away the large cocktail of local shrimp. Midday reflections played off the estuary waters. The sun was warm, the bay air fresh.

"Someone's found a new kind of 'match,'" Tom was saying. "It buffaloes me. If it was an inflammable it might start in three, four spots at most. Even the best torch, that's all it would take. You're the liaison man—how'd you like to talk to the marshals and put out a bulletin to every station in the Bay Area to keep an eye out for an MO like that? We've got to widen out, check everywhere. He'll trip up on one of them and I want to be there."

"Okay, Tom, I'll get on it. That gives me a reason to try lighting a fire under the crowd across the Bay. They're not uncooperative—they just don't go out of their way." He turned to follow Tom's gaze to the parking lot. "Who are you staring at?"

"I know that guy from somewhere. Can't place him."

"The one next to the Mustang?"

"Yeah."

"With a woman like that, you could forget the guy in a hurry."

When the waiter led them to the only table by the water and held her chair out, Shane sat down, feeling encouraged. Maybe Stretch did have some taste.

Stretch was halfway seated when he saw who was at the next table. A sensation akin to rolling his red Chevy over at the Highland racetrack shot through him. There was no way to hide, nothing to do. *Roll with it*, he thought. But what about Shane? Moe's sentence was propelled forth by some magic button: "How'd ya like to meet the enemy?"

Stretch sat down and averted the steady gaze that he knew was coming his way like an arc welder touching the fine steel of a bank vault, seeking secrets, treasures, hidden information. Six feet separated them. It was impossible to avoid contact for long. *Roll with it, damn it.*

With all the cool he could muster, he turned to Shane. "Like a drink?" She nodded. Casually, but with a heavy thumping in his chest, he risked eyeing the panorama and engaged the glance of his potential pursuer. He gave half a nod of recognition.

Nodding in return, Tom looked away, still unable to quite place the man. He stared at the red-and-white Mustang, studying it as if it would yield the clue he sought. Nothing. Neither the girl, the car, nor continued study seemed able to unlock the identity of the new arrival in the well-cut jacket.

Leaning over discreetly, Shane asked, "Who's that?"

"Tell you later," Stretch whispered back. Maybe it would be all right. If Tom did not engage them in conversation he could tell Shane any story he wanted.

The waiter arrived and left to bring back the drinks. Feigning starvation despite a total loss of appetite, Stretch hid behind the huge menu. The ploy was only good for a short time. The service was prompt. The cocktails arrived. The waiter noted two orders for lobster and retrieved the menus before heading to the kitchen.

"You work as Moe's assistant in fire salvage, don't you?" Tom said suddenly, leaning toward the couple, confident he had found the answer.

Machine-gun fire would have been equally welcome. "Yes." Stretch looked up, friendly-like. "Well, I did. You're Tom"— he hesitated—"Tom Farley."

"Stretch . . . Jackson, right?"

"Right on."

"How are you? How's Moe? This is Captain West, Jonah West, Oakland Fire Department."

Glad-to-meet-you's went around. Tom continued, "Sure. Long time since we met. Saw you pull up in that slick machine. Moving up. You and Moe must be partners now."

To Stretch the sentences did not sound innocent. He heard questions implied in each comment.

"Well, no . . . actually . . . gone into business for myself."

"Still fire salvage goods? Guess we're all into fire. Once you get in it, it's hard to get out."

Stretch gulped and decided to duck the question and accept Tom's assumptions. Not missing a beat he rushed on, "Hey, what's been burning up lately?" He turned to Shane. "Tom here's the best there is in arson." Moe's words came back. "A regular one-man F.B.I.—a P.I., private investigator."

"Oh, how exciting. Like a policeman?" She could not quite get up enough enthusiasm. There seemed to be something else going on that she failed to grasp but didn't like.

Tom said modestly, "I'm just doing the usual."

"Moe always said your usual was great."

"Well, he's got a tough nut this time," Jonah chimed in.

"Yeah," Tom allowed ruefully. "Bugger bums everything. We were just talking about it. Doesn't even leave anything for you salvage guys."

Stretch asked with genuine curiosity, "How's that?"

"Some nut's burning his way through the construction business over here. I hate to say it, but he's brilliant. Damn brilliant. Hey—" Tom shot Stretch a curious, piercing look, "You wouldn't be dealing in burned earth-moving equipment, would you?"

The directness of the question skewered Stretch's stomach on a hot acid needle. "I wouldn't even know where to start with something like that," he parried. But the question implied that Tom had other questions. Did he also have other answers?

"Might just be," Jonah said to Tom, "that we're dealing with a heavy equipment dealer. No kidding! Given the dollar values involved, someone has to have sold a million bucks' worth of earth movers."

"Hey, maybe that's your answer." Stretch tried to say it half-seriously, half-joking—anything to lead this unwanted conversation elsewhere!

Tom looked from Jonah to Stretch. "I wouldn't believe that for a minute." As soon as the words were out, he decided that he *should* check the heavy equipment angle. He glanced at Shane. She smells of money, real money, he thought. He was about to ask Stretch for his business card, but the lobster arrived.

Jonah needed to get back to the station, so the two men rose to leave. Tom said, "Good to see you again, Stretch. Glad to have met you, Shane."

She smiled demurely. "Hope you get your man, Mr. Farley."

"He will!" Jonah added with conviction.

"See you both," was all the torch could think to say, praying he would not.

For all of the sunlit brilliance outside, Stretch's mood descended into dark shadows. He relished the compliment, but the exposure and the implications of Farley's knowledge about the garages left a hollow feeling in his stomach. The awkwardness with Shane was now unbearable. Their conversation resembled damp crackers.

Shane concluded that Oakland really was the wrong side of the Bay. Here she was meeting a fireman and some offbeat species of detective who spills the information that her escort is in a mysterious sort of trash business and not a union organizer, which was already a dubious vocation. Shane decided to take the bull by the horns. Some things were even more important than getting laid. "Stretch," she lied sweetly, "I've got a confession to make."

The last bite of pie had to slip by his vocal cords before he could ask, "What?"

"I've been going with someone for a long time. He proposed to me a couple of days ago, and I've decided that if I'm going to even think about it seriously, I should stop seeing anyone else, give it a chance. I hate to break that on such a beautiful day, but . . ."

It was obvious that she was lying, but Stretch relaxed in relief. "Jesus, Shane, I guess I can't get in the way of anything as serious as marriage." The hell with climbing the social ladder. Frank would be happy. And with Farley eyeball to eyeball at last, life would have to be restricted to business. Do it right, be the best—or Tom Farley will get you.

21

Soaring skyward, the mountains in mid-San Francisco bump right up to nine hundred feet—not quite alpine, but offering an abundance of quiet opportunities to build homes on winding streets surrounded by calm, green, and fresh air. The red Mustang turned into the drive of a large, comfortable house. Fresh and frisky, Stretch hopped out and up the steps. The door knocker was a replica of the Amalgamated logo, and as Stretch raised it to strike the brass plate a soft voice called out to him. He turned to the figure coming around the corner of the house.

"Hello, Stretch. Isn't it just delightful today?" Mrs. Sievers always had a good word. The arm and the fist were Frank's public image, but she was his private life. A wee bit overweight, but spry and good-natured, she seemed to be Mrs. Housekeeper personified.

"How are you?" she continued. "I've just been cutting flowers for the table. I don't think Frank ever notices them, but . . ."

"I bet he would if they weren't there."

"Maybe. Rhubarb pie, he'd miss. You know, I've made him rhubarb pie once every week since we've been married. I guess that's a little crazy."

"Or a lot of rhubarb."

She laughed. "Come on in. He's in the office."

The house was simple, homey—except for Frank's study, which was a garish miniature of the one downtown. He lost no time telling his protégé the latest news.

Stretch jerked back in his chair in astonishment. "No shit! George Calhoun."

"I told you I specialize in cracks and corners. They weren't looking for new partners, but like it or not, I've dealt us in. They've built the scheme around businesses that are in the process of going under. That's how George got into it. He knows who's in trouble through the bank and offers them just enough to bail them out. Bill Taylor, a lawyer, buys the business in the name of some phony client. Joel Cargill, an insurance agent, overinsures it. They've got some torch who plans and lights each job. Cargill writes it all through Global Insurance—he's got a guy named Vic Whitlock, their fire loss manager, and also their top adjuster in his pocket. They do the paperwork, pay it, take their cut." Frank leaned back contentedly.

"Slick as a whistle. George Calhoun! With all his fancy shit! Sounds like half the town's in on it."

"Seven at one time or another." Frank gave his best tight-lipped grin. "Now nine. George decided he could see fit to cut us in on every other deal. I let him get away with that . . . for starters. You'll light the ones we're in on."

"They into big money?"

"Ready for this? Six and a half million in the last three years—net. And to think I got into arson just for the good of the union. The crazy thing is, something for a little personal profit has been crossing my mind for the last few months. Since we've got Vada kneeling in our corner, I've been lining up a job for myself. You're going to be very busy." He drove the point home. "How'd you like it if I negotiated twenty thou a light for you with George?"

"I'd hate it . . . all the way to George's vault." He gave Frank a gleeful wink.

* * *

The distinguished banker and his burly former-client-now-partner sat in the opulent inner sanctum of Western United, one of the country's major banks. They were sealed into the quiet privacy of the senior vice-president's office. The vice-president himself was a bit flush in the face, an uncommon event. "Twenty thousand! You must be joking, Frank! We pay our ex-fireman twenty-five hundred. He's done all right so far and he doesn't hang around my country club! No wonder Jackson acts so nouveau riche! Twenty thousand—"

"He's my man, George." There was a deadly finality to the words.

"Okay . . . so he's your man. I can't imagine why you run the risk of being seen with him in public."

"Thank God you understand figures, at least. He's going to make me very rich, George. He depends on me. You see, I've addicted him to money. Money's the most habit-forming narcotic known and it's not only legal . . . it *is* the law." Reassuringly, he added, "And don't worry—I've kept my fingerprints off the gun." He gave Calhoun a rock-hard look. "It's not the first one I've handled, George."

Several days later George Calhoun personally accompanied Stretch to his safety-deposit box in the vault. Calhoun inserted the bank's key in the box, verified that no one could overhear him, and said in a low, snide voice, "I thought there was something peculiar about your 'business' story, Jackson."

Cheerfully, Stretch replied, "Puts us in the same boat doesn't it . . . George?"

The senior vice-president didn't like that, Stretch could tell clearly, but they did have a future together, whether Calhoun liked it or not. The new associate jabbed his key in and opened the drawer, which was packed full of hundred-dollar bills. He smiled. "I think I'm going to need a bigger box." Suddenly he snapped off the smile. "I want one thing absolutely clear, starting now. Don't you *ever* give me an occupied building to torch. I'd burn this bank down around your ears first! You guys sit in your cushy offices and I take all the risks. Okay . . . but keep the risks you give me clean!"

* * *

Tom Farley stepped right up to the desk and stood there wavering between doubt and shock. The woman's back was to him. Had Vic Whitlock gotten a new secretary, was this a substitute, or had something dramatic happened to Dee Hatford?

"Oh!" The long black hair swung around. "I didn't see you come in."

It was Dee, all right. "Well, I'll be damned, Dee!" Without the beehive hairdo, Dee looked softer, prettier, and years younger.

"Startling, isn't it?" she said proudly.

"First time I ever came into Fire Loss and you didn't see me five desks away. Don't love me anymore?"

"Oh, Tom, I was just—"

"I get it." So she *was* a different Dee Hatford. "You look like a woman in love! Someone sneak up when my back was turned?"

Blushing scarlet, Dee nodded her head. "Changed everything."

"I'm told it does. How long's this been going on?"

"Three weeks. Not much, but it's a start."

"Well, hang in there. Vic in?" Dee nodded, and Tom moved past her desk toward the door. He stopped. "Jesus!" he exclaimed "What's that?"

She followed his glance to the set of glossy color blowups sitting on her desk. The top one was of two carbonized bodies huddled in the corner of a burned room. Dee lifted the photograph by a corner, handling it with the same fear and disgust she reserved for picking up spiders. "I know y'all have to snap pictures, but does one like that have to be close up *and* in color? Honest to Pete, I've seen so many of these since I started working for Vic I don't have alligator nightmares anymore. They're all about fires. I go absolutely batty thinking about being in a fire."

"Well," Tom reassured her, "it's about a one in thirty thousand shot. Those are pretty gory, though."

"Aren't you sweet, Tom Farley, trying to make me feel good. But remember—we get all the fire trade journals here.

One in thirty thousand is my statistical chance of *dying* in a fire *this* year, not of *being in* one sooner or later."

"You are touchy about it, aren't you?"

Dee couldn't control a shudder. "Gives me the willies. Especially living alone."

Tom smiled. "Okay—I'll remember to hand my nine-by-twelves directly to Vic . . . and maybe you won't be living alone for long." He walked on to Whitlock's office.

Whitlock, in his usual dour mood, waved him to a chair.

"Jesus, Vic, she let her hair down and everything changed."

"Yeah, and she gets twice as much work done. I got about three other secretaries I'd like to get a boyfriend for if that's the standard result. What can I do you for?"

"Remember Acme Salvage?"

"Sure."

"Remember B.B. Builders over in Oakland?"

"Yes."

"And Kirk Dowell in Richmond?"

"Okay, what's up your sleeve? Ah-ha! I didn't call you on two of them, but you know I don't unless something rings a bell."

"How's this for a bell, Vic? Same guy lit all three."

"You got to be fucking kidding me!" He pulled his glasses off and wiped them hurriedly as if that would help him see what was happening.

Tom carefully laid out the situation, confessing that he could not yet prove one thing. "You know," Tom said, "I get intuitions like some people get rheumatism in wet weather. Because of high-priced business interruption payments, losses with 'cause unknown' reports have mostly been bulldozed and reconstruction started in no time flat. There's a ton of money going down in the East Bay, and I've just been assigned a couple of those cases. I need them all, because whatever's going on is so damn clever I need every clue I can get. You know I don't need more files." Tom pushed his hat back and smiled wryly. "But I just can't stand frustrations. I need to see some of these cases *before* the evidence is bulldozed away. And you— you've got a million bucks extra on your loss ratio so far."

"Well, I'll sure as hell call you on every case in the building business. I'm as interested as you, especially since we insure such a stack of builders and buildings under construction."

After Tom left, Whitlock worked for a few minutes—he wanted the feeling that Farley was completely out of the building—then he picked up the phone and dialed George Calhoun at the bank. They wasted no words. "George," Vic said, "I'd like to see you after work tonight. The usual? At five? Good." He hung up.

Running his hand over his crew cut, Vic leaned back and grimly pondered the new arrangements. He was mean about the company's money, but his personal dollars were practically laminated to his wallet. Whitlock had been less than thrilled about cutting in Frank Sievers and outraged at some torch who allegedly was worth a twenty-thousand-dollar fee. He was going to set up such an impossible burn that Sievers's man would look like an idiot. Then maybe they could wrestle his fees down to reason.

* * *

Tom got the word around for major insurers of contractors to be on the lookout for the signs of arson. Jim Vada's agent was worth a personal visit, so Tom dropped by the Aughenbaugh Agency.

"You're the biggest agency in the East Bay for contractors, Gene. What's going on in building over here?"

Skinny, permanently nervous, charged with a salesman's drive, Aughenbaugh looked like a bird wearing horn-rimmed glasses. "So far as I know, nothing special. Why? Vada? He's only had two losses."

"True, but I don't want him to have a third. That's only part of the problem, though. We've had a whole series of contractors with odd losses."

"It can't be because business is bad—not with the East Bay boom."

"Any other problems you've heard of?"

"No."

"Just do me a favor, since you're so involved in builders. Keep an eye out, Check around, quiet-like—and most important, call me if there are any signs among your own insureds. You know, the usual: a sudden request to cover a substandard building, any big increase in the limits on old buildings or remodeling jobs."

"All I need is more holes in my loss ratio. I'm getting gray fast enough without more arson to worry about." He ran his hand through his thinning red hair. "But I'll keep an eye on our own policyholders. You can count on me."

Tom left satisfied, knowing he had recruited a major ally.

* * *

Vic Whitlock lost no love on Frank Sievers, but if he had known that his newly acquired partner was behind the East Bay burnings, he certainly would have refrained from calling Tom Farley. But he did not know that Frank, on his own, had been keeping Stretch busy lighting fires for Amalgamated—so he lifted the receiver and dialed. Charlene took the new assignment: a relatively small builder who housed his trucks in and around an unguarded Quonset-style garage in Berkeley had just had a fire.

Tom pounced on the case immediately. He hopped into his car and went straight to the site, but the building had collapsed so completely that the first inspection showed nothing unusual. He had workmen peel back one entire eight-foot section of corrugated steel. Nothing. Legwork time. Interviews and statements began.

The next day the black-and-white Pontiac cruised up Adeline Street in Berkeley, followed the bend of Shattuck Avenue, and hooked a left on Bancroft. Pat Farley sat sharply upright in the passenger's seat next to Tom. His artificial leg was unstrapped, but resting lightly in place, ready to quickly become a part of him again.

"There she is." Tom pointed to the Quonset. "And she won't tell me a thing. You sniff them as good as I do." He pulled up alongside and parked. "Say anything to you?"

"Any explosion?"

"Nope."

"Got to have wood beams to come down like that, then."

"Yes."

They got out, not to actually stand in the ashes, but merely to be close enough to get the feel of the charred hulk.

Pat surveyed the remains. "Must have been put up right after the war. My war, that is. They haven't used wood trusses for years. Got to watch the electrical on those. They didn't use much flexible cable in those days. Ran the wires through pipes. Insulation wasn't plastic—it was rubber—and that wartime stuff tended to crack at the bends. Since the codes were different, a lot of those pipes weren't grounded and we'd get electrical fires all over the place. Most of the East Bay didn't tighten their codes till somewhere between 'fifty and 'fifty-three."

Not only did Tom enjoy his father's company, he loved mining Pat's brain, so full of odd fire tidbits. Most of it he had already harvested, but there always seemed to be a little more.

"I checked that," Tom said. "The landlord—it's a rented building—told me that two years ago he renewed the wiring, put in circuit breakers and all. So the problem couldn't have been electrical."

Father and son kicked around the few ideas they had. "I hate to say it, Tom, but it leaves me dead cold. Haven't a clue."

"It's the first one of them I've had intact and it makes no more sense than those I got to after the bulldozer had scraped them away. Why the devil was the whole building involved right off the bat?" Frustration gnawed at him—and it was getting worse. But since he had Pat out of the office, he figured they might as well do something pleasant together. "I'm in a hurry, but we both have to eat. Want to grab some shrimp?"

That brought the expected twinkle back to his father's eyes. They got into the car and headed back toward Oakland.

* * *

Several weeks later, Farley was working into the evening aboard the *Sapphire II*. He was surrounded by floor plans and blowups of each garage suffering from the "instant" syndrome, as he had begun to call it. The diagrams and photos were carefully laid out, pinned to every available wall space, covering the couch, the floor, everything but the ceiling. Agitated, Tom was furiously pacing, trying to work off his frustration.

"What the *hell* is he doing?" he demanded of the mute prints for the hundredth time.

There was a knock on the door. A glance at his watch told him no one should be coming by at this hour. He opened the door cautiously.

"What are you doing here?" he asked, dumbfounded.

In the shadows Charlene gave her best smile. "Stephanie and I went to a movie at the university. I knew you'd be up working on an ulcer. It was just an impulse—thought I'd tell you to get some sleep. You're wearing yourself down to a nub."

"Well . . . come in and have a cup." Just seeing Charlene was relaxing. His hands rubbed his temples. "You're right. I'm letting this get to me."

Stepping in, Charlene looked at the plans and pictures and heaved an exasperated sigh. "I'll bet you've got them pinned in your bedroom so as not to lose a minute."

"No comment. Old tea or fresh coffee?"

"Fresh coffee means if I make it, right?" She slipped off her coat with a smile and moved to the galley.

Tom pushed a floor plan off the divan and sat watching her as she prepared the brew. He wondered if her reason for coming was really to give him moral support, or whether she had begun to share the attraction he kept trying to snuff out. It was not the first time Charlene had been his mainstay during a time of high tension, but . . . he was probably reading *his* feelings into *her* actions. He watched her carefully; boyish or not, she had an interesting figure. He'd seen practically all of it on the occasions when she'd sunned on board the *Sapphire*. He leaned back, relaxed, and pictured Charlene in her bathing suit while she gave a funny synopsis of Charlie Chaplin in *Modern Times*. She finished the story while they sat sipping the hot, aromatic brew.

"I guess the jokes would have been funnier yet if—" She broke off abruptly, got up, and leaned against the edge of his desk. "Would you miss me if I left?"

"Oh, cut it out," he said flippantly. "Who else would hire you?"

"No, I mean . . . if I left the city?"

He sat right up. "Of course. C'mon, what are you up to? You putting me on?"

"Ryan called just before the movies. You think I should marry Ryan, Tom?"

"Sure!"

"Really?" She went white.

"If you want to live with an old-maid accountant in Chicago, sure. He makes good money and he's safe. Did he ask?"

"Yep."

"You want security and all that?"

"Yes."

"That badly?"

Charlene waved her arms in empty, feeble circles. A sigh of exasperation passed her lips. "I . . . guess not really."

"You want me to say it, don't you? You know damn well I count on you."

"For the office?"

"Sure . . ." Suddenly he was stuttering again. "Sure, you know. . . . Did you really come by to ask if I thought you should marry Ryan?" He was suddenly convinced that she was leading him on.

"You know better than that." She mussed his hair quickly, playfully, and grabbed her coat. "I came to make sure you get some shut-eye before your favorite torch wins by a TKO. You can't get them all, you know."

She headed toward the door. Tom jumped up, caught her hand, and said in an unfamiliar voice, "Okay . . . thanks."

He let her hand slip out of his. There was no more to say. He opened the door and watched Charlene's slender figure walk lightly down the dock, get into her car, and drive away.

* * *

The little diamond-edged wheel of a glass cutter inscribed a square around the suction cup. In the inky darkness the crystal sound of *tap* . . . *tap* barely carried twenty feet away. The glass gave way. Stretch gingerly lifted out the piece and inserted his arm through the hole. He unfastened the lock and gently lowered the skylight. He anchored his rope and checked it with a tug, then slid down to the garage floor. The plans were etched in his memory. Stretch threw the circuit breaker to the OFF position, pulled a short wire out of his pocket, and within minutes had finished his work and was climbing up the rope again.

At three o'clock the tan Pinto wagon, California license plate OUX 829, moved into the bowels of Union Square's garage. The receiver below the dash was tuned to the Oakland Fire Department wavelength. As yet there was no report. Stretch switched cars and headed the red Mustang for home. Once inside, he flipped on the radio, popped open a beer, flopped onto the couch, and relaxed.

The house was oddly bare. The large living room was furnished with only a dark brown sofa, two chairs, an end table, and a lamp. The lighting was indirect fluorescent. Yards of bookcases contained exactly five paperbacks. The rubber tile floor went begging for a rug. Stretch kept intending to properly decorate the place, but could not figure out exactly what it needed. The stark white spaces he had coveted were beginning to wear on him. Karen would have known what to do, but there was no Karen—or anyone else. The architect's inherently cold style ended up being accentuated rather than broken up by warm colors as it should have been, and the psychological igloo was beginning to tell on the lonesome tenant. At four o'clock Stretch sighed and headed for bed.

* * *

Stretch put out two eggs, four strips of bacon and three oranges—California had taught him the difference between fresh squeezed and the industrial juice—then decided to shower before he cooked breakfast. First, he opened the door to get the morning *Chronicle*, then he dropped on the sofa and leafed through it. He got as far as a headline on page four:

TWO FIREMEN DIE IN OAKLAND
Capt. Manuel Rojas and Fireman Jack Runyon were killed in an early morning explosion as fire ravaged the garage of Grohs Builders.

Stretch Jackson sat in a state of shock, unable to continue, unable to think. A tremor made the paper wrinkle audibly. He struggled to his feet and slid the terrace door open, then stepped into the chilled morning air and dropped into the pool with his pajamas on. The jolt brought him to his senses. He showered and shaved in record time. On his third reading of the report, the phone rang.

"Yes. I know. I'll be right there."

Hazel gave him a curt good morning. Frank's reception was explosive, but slowly calmed. In fact, he was calmer than Stretch.

"Okay," Sievers said from behind his desk. "You can't know some idiot leaves a case of dynamite caps in his trunk, but I don't like it. Even if it blew all the evidence to hell, they're still going to exert pressure to find out—"

"Pressure!" Stretch interrupted. "You crazy, Frank? I don't give a flying fuck about pressure! They can't prove any-thing. Can't even find a lead. I *do* give a goddamn about two dead guys! They *are* guys. They have *families*. It makes me sick, Frank. You don't race if you don't like the risks either, but that doesn't make you deaf, dumb, and heartless after a crash."

"Firemen get paid to take their chances, just like you. You damn well know that. They're not little kids."

"Sure, I know that. You think it makes me feel any better?"

Frank didn't give a damn about the firemen, but he was getting pretty concerned about the lack of spine in his torch. "Stretch," he said firmly, "get ahold of yourself! You can't crack up every time some little thing goes wrong. The unexpected happens in every business. You roll with it. That's the game, that's what you get paid for."

"I'm still the guy who loaded the gun. And I don't take pay to kill people, Frank—I've told you that. Stop worrying about your hide—it's perfectly safe. Start thinking about your conscience." Stretch was serious, though if he had been less agitated he might have held his tongue.

"Conscience!" Sievers exploded, not knowing whether to laugh or rearrange Stretch's impudent face. "Conscience . . ." He sighed, shrugged his shoulders, and decided to play it safe. Playing nursemaid was a role he hated, but Frank figured Stretch still needed the carrot most—the stick would wait for something more important than a lousy couple of firemen. He reined in his urge to use his fist. "Look, I understand. Knock off a few days. Go to Tahoe or Vegas, whatever. Get it together. You'll be okay." He moved around the desk and put his hand on Stretch's shoulder. "Accidents happen. You did your best. And I'll see to it that the owner of Grohs Builders keeps his mouth shut." He turned on his most paternal manner. "Listen, you just decide where you want to go. I got connections that'll put you up free."

By lunchtime, Stretch had decided on Vegas, bought a ticket to the most vulgar piece of desolation in America, and, without knowing it, checked into the most recently torched of the big hotels. Sievers had made the arrangements and Stretch was received like royalty. He didn't care if he lost a few thousand gambling. He was far from the headlines and it was hot by the poolside. By five o'clock, he had fallen asleep in a lounge chair under a blazing sun.

* * *

The pall in the dining room at Station House 1 that night hung heavier than bay fog. Chief Bennett stepped in to announce that funeral services were set for Thursday afternoon. Tears welled up in the eyes of big, strong men. The chief found Jonah in the locker room hiding his salt-streaked cheeks.

"Come on, Jonah," Bennett said gently. "Knock off for tonight. Pyle can cover. I know how you feel, especially about Mannie. I've been there, too."

Managing a wavering smile of appreciation, the captain replied, "Thanks, Chief, but I think my place is right here." He toughened up, wiped away the tears in embarrassment, and added, "Especially tonight."

* * *

Jonah phoned Tom about the fire and Farley quickly picked up the assignment from Grohs Builders' insurance carrier. He mapped out the battle plan with his father.

"I don't care how you do it, Pat, but here are all of the 'instant' fire dates. I want the passenger lists checked on all nonstop flights for the following mornings to New York, Boston, and Philadelphia. A guy could case a job for two days or two weeks, but anyone that good will be out of town in six hours after it's lit. Any name comes up more than once, we want to know why and who he is."

"That's a long shot and a mass of work."

"I know. It may just add up to ruling out one possibility. But I'm going to catch that son-of-a-bitch and the guys who are paying him if it kills me."

Charlene brought in a stack of files. "Okay—here's everything we have on every one of them."

"Good enough. I'm going to go back through all of them and see if we left any stones unturned."

The atmosphere was almost as funereal in Farley's office as it was at the firehouse—but the firemen could only sit and await the next fire. For Tom Farley the grim part of the chase was just beginning. The torch had made one step too many into Farley's territory. All that had preceded was only the preliminary sparring for a deadly hunt.

"You going to the Oakland D.A.?" Charlene asked.

"If he calls me I will," Tom said grimly. "If not, no. I'm going after this one myself. I'll go to the D.A. when I have a scalp."

22

The days that followed were a frenzy of checks and counterchecks, interviews, and poking through ashes. The Grohs fire had been particularly devastating. In addition to the thoroughness and the exploding gas tanks Tom had come to expect in the construction fires, the dynamite in Grohs's truck had blasted away all traceable evidence of how the blaze might have started. The only things not in doubt were the instant, overall nature of the ignition and the 3:00 A.M. hour. Steve Grohs was impervious to leading questions or even threats. He swore he had no idea who would have set his garage on fire. Suggestions of nonpayment by the insurance company, of a trip to the district attorney's office, or even of being suspected as an accessory to murder failed to shake him from his stubborn and repeated answer, "I don't know." Whatever had been said to Grohs had proved to be *very* effective. Tom couldn't determine whether he was innocent, an accessory, or simply scared to death.

After a whole week, there was not a single break in the case. And then the phone rang.

"It's for you, Tom," Charlene sang out. "Captain West."

"Tom!" Jonah's voice was charged with electricity. "Haul your ass over to Oakland Police Headquarters! They've got our construction torch nailed. Picked him up red-handed early this morning lighting a remodeling job. Ask for Lieutenant Boskowitch. I'll be there in about fifteen minutes, okay?"

"Okay? You bet your life it's okay! I'll be there in twenty minutes."

Tom was beside himself with excitement. He turned squarely in front of Charlene, beaming. "Break out the champagne, beautiful—they've got our man!"

Tom wheeled into the police parking lot as if he were coming in for a pit stop. Jonah came in right behind him.

"What'd they do?" Jonah demanded. "Shorten the bridge?"

The two laughed and slapped each other on the back, overjoyed at the prospect of seeing the killer in a cage. All of a sudden the mood changed. Jonah grabbed Farley's arm and stopped him. "Tom . . . for the sake of Mannie and Jack Runyon, don't let me touch him. Stop me if I start."

Both men instantly sobered.

"Don't worry, Jonah. I understand. I'm just caught in the chase. You lost a best friend. I know the feeling . . . and I know the difference."

They headed briskly into the station. Lieutenant Boskowitch was also in an up mood. It was not every day that they caught a fish this big. "If the address on his license is valid," he explained, "we're getting a search warrant for his house. He knows the ropes. Won't say anything more than that he's Bob Johnston, that that's his address, and he wants to call Melvin Belli for his defense. It's probably all phony—name, address, the lot. But we'll get it out of him."

"Let me at the bastard," Tom demanded. "I'll get the rest of it."

They started down the hall toward the cells.

"You checking it out yet?" Jonah asked Boskowitch.

"You bet we are, Captain. Two officers caught him right in the act, lighting a vacant tenement building where a remodeling job was about to start."

"Who was the contractor?" Tom inquired anxiously.

"Jesus, Mr. Farley, I didn't think to ask that. But here we are. You ask him." He threw open the cell door.

Huddled miserably on the cell cot was a skinny man in his late fifties.

"You son-of-a-bitch!" Tom yelled. "Dino Candelli, you son-of-a-bitch!"

The police officer beamed. "That's our man."

"Hi, Tom," the disheveled prisoner said weakly.

"You keep him, Lieutenant! That mother couldn't light a Roman candle on Nero's birthday!"

The faces of Jonah and Boskowitch went long.

"I've had him twice in ten years on jobs he's muffed. He's not half good enough to be who we're after! Jesus—"

"Tom," Dino said hesitantly, "could you get me in touch with Melvin Belli?"

"Oh, fuck off, Dino!" Tom turned and stomped out, utterly dejected.

* * *

Charlene had taken the boss at his word. In suite 1812 a bottle of champagne, complete with a red ribbon, chilled in a cardboard ice bucket. Pat and Charlene were in animated discussion when Tom walked in.

"Well?" Pat looked up eagerly. "Tell us."

"It's not our man." He eyed the suddenly inappropriate champagne. "I guess we might as well drink it. It looks sad just sitting there—although eleven in the morning's not the usual champagne hour."

Charlene got out the paper cups. The mood was not quite unfettered gaiety. "Everything we've done so far," she said, "is just useless."

"Not really." Tom pulled out the dripping bottle. "We're finding out who it's not. It's narrowing down. It's not somebody out of the East Coast. It's a really top-notch pro, and there's a fifty-fifty chance he's right here. He's agile as a monkey, so he's no antique like Dino Candelli. He doesn't use a standard trigger." Tom ran out of conviction. "And . . . and . . . well, we're getting there." He aimed the bottle out the window. "And I'm going for a sail."

With a pop the cork flew outside and dropped eighteen floors, glancing off the shoulder of a matronly tourist from Scottsdale who looked at the object on the sidewalk in utter astonishment, rubbed her shoulder, and before moving on studied the heavens to see if a champagne bottle would follow.

* * *

If the great prescription writer in the sky had filled out the form for the antidote to what ailed Tom it would have said: one dose of *Sapphire.*

"If I was you," Pickles volunteered, clopping down the dock after Tom, "I'd take that pretty secretary out for a sail, too."

"You old sea goat—you'd take out a mermaid if you could figure out what was below her belly button."

Pickles doubled up. "You're worse'n me given half a chance."

The breeze was stiff, but not so demanding that the skipper could not spend most of his time staring at the photographs that surrounded the cabin hatch. He sailed, worried, relaxed, worried—focusing again and again on the photos. The Quonset hut that Vic Whitlock had assigned him kept coming back to his attention. Why? he kept asking himself. Something's in there. Something's in there. Sure, something's in there— goddamned ashes, that's what! He kept staring, trying to both relax and concentrate simultaneously.

Something *is* in there! He was suddenly convinced he knew where the answer lay and snapped the boat around to head pell-mell for the dock. Still fifty feet out, he started leaning on the air horn. The alarmed dockmaster came racing up.

"Grab her, Pickles! I have to run."

Still wearing his sailing whites, he ran for his car and sped to the Quonset, where the bulldozer operator was preparing to make his first charge at the rubble.

"Stop!" Tom yelled with an intensity bordering on delirium. "Stop!"

273

He rushed past the startled bulldozer operator and started pawing through the charred heap, not even knowing himself what he was looking for. If he had not produced his P.I. card, the workmen would have taken him for an escaped lunatic. In the course of his frantic search Farley tried to move a section of the corrugated-metal roof sheeting but could not budge it, not even with a pickax. He backtracked to the bulldozer, pushed the stammering operator out of the way, and expertly moved the machine forward, crushing across a section of metal to get at his goal. With the lead edge of the bulldozer blade he turned over the other half of the eight-foot roof section. He jumped down into the ruins and began to hack with his pocketknife at a wooden beam he'd exposed. That still was not fast enough. He grabbed the pickax and gouged along the length of the beam to the circuit-breaker box. Triumphantly, he pried it out. He pulled it open and turned it over, trembling with anticipation as he inspected the wires.

"It's not there! Goddamn, it's not there!" he screamed at the box, beside himself with the rage of frustration. He buried the pick up to its head in the metal sheet. Tom was spent with exhaustion and humiliation, but only for a moment.

"Watch that box! And I mean *watch* it!" he ordered one alarmed workman. "You." He pointed to the bulldozer operator. "Come with me."

Charging into the adjacent building—a plumbing supply house—the investigator in filthy whites received the permission of a startled secretary to use the phone. The bulldozer operator dialed his employer and passed the receiver to Tom, expecting his boss to chew this guy up.

"Kelmenson, Tom Farley, investigating the fire on the Quonset garage. I want you to hold up on clearing the site. No, I don't give a damn! If you want to get paid for it that's an order! And if you want it doubled, call Vic Whitlock—it's his money."

He hung up. The stupefied bulldozer operator humbly followed the man in the dirty slacks. Tom stopped and stared at the collapsed Quonset. It's in there, he said to himself. It's in there. And I'll take it apart with my bare hands if I have to.

* * *

Five days in Vegas had confirmed Stretch's worst suspicions. Eddie Barker cured his loneliness with trips to garish watering holes like this—but Stretch Jackson could not. He had always been part of a group: school, army, West Alton, the race crowd. He was not a loner. He never could be. Batting around, picking up women, talking to guys in a bar, being part of the outlaw crowd at the Buddha—none of that was for him.

He knew now that he would be happy to be half of a twosome—Karen had taught him that. And he realized that Karen, by example, had also taught him he would have to make a choice between who he was and what he did. He'd gained enough self-understanding to suspect he wanted a normal life again. The jam of bills in George's vault failed to make up for an increasing emptiness inside him. Bored by the pool, bored by gambling, whether he won or lost, he started thinking about his condition—something he was unaccustomed to doing. What were the alternatives? The blank he came up with also yawned at him emptily.

Stretch would lie by the pool asking questions. What made him obstinately stick with torching? In the beginning it was having ten thousand dollars, free and clear. But once he had the union connection, that sum had become peanuts—he had raised his limit to fifty. Then he had fifty and upped to one hundred. As he closed in on one hundred, Frank had discovered the Calhoun ring. Two fifty was a possibility. Suddenly Stretch got a lump in his throat contemplating two fifty. Two-hundred-and-fifty-thousand-U.S.-dollar-bills! It's legal tender—never mind how you got it—it's one-quarter of a million dollars, neat, net—and mine. He would slump into a chair and plan the construction of a grandiose West Alton home for his mother, then realize she wouldn't want it. That tarnished money's image.

There had been moments when he thought he would quit once he'd had a chance to do a fire that no one else could handle, something that would stump Eddie or any of the high-tone East Coast torches. He looked at every building he passed in terms of "how would I burn it?" He devised methods to light bridges, airplane hangars, buildings of every odd construction or dimension. Once he had pretended that Calhoun had called, proposing the impossible: a shipment was leaving California in a boxcar headed east. The contents had to be burned halfway across the country without the slightest smell of arson. Only a month before he'd come to Vegas Stretch had run around San Francisco frantically for weeks, learning about the railroad's complex cross-country routing procedures, switching techniques at humping bowls, boxcar construction. *If* he could follow the zigzag route a boxcar takes across America, how should he light it, how could he gain access, and with what means could he burn only the target car—for any idiot could destroy the entire train. Once he was totally immersed in his planning, he began to wonder if many of the spectacular train wrecks that grab the headlines are in fact merely cover-ups for the destruction of something contained in but one or two cars.

Eventually he found a perfect, hypothetical solution, which consisted of using complex electronic tracking devices and a braking defect triggered by radio waves—for he had finally mastered radio waves. Ultimately, of course, the pleasure went flat when he realized that he would never get such an assignment.

Yes, he admitted, he did like the money, the chase with Tom Farley, the reaching to be better than any torch in the world. But then why was he bored? He wondered if in the final analysis he was torching for the same reason many good minds stay in wasting places: it is better to ride the devil you know than one you don't—or if not better, easier. And there is always some wise counsel, from a Sievers to a spouse, who is just waiting in the wings to soothingly convince you to not make a move—for greener grass may also hide snakes. So, for the moment, he would simply stay put and wrestle with the lucrative, the excitement of the work.

He went to bed with a bikini-clad poolside rover, and the result left him feeling even more lonesome than before. He packed his bags and left Vegas in the lurch. No sooner had Stretch opened the door to his stark and impersonal house than he realized it was the perfect reflection of his soul—getting hard and short of warmth. He decided not to call Frank for a few days. It seemed a good idea to be alone for a bit and think.

Tube glue welded him to the TV set for a while. The actors sang, danced, walked, talked, loved, fought, cried—everything he didn't. But it was not him, it was the tube—flat, two-dimensional, a substitute for life. He sat propped up by his pool, watching the electronic version of living. Accidentally he touched the set with his foot and it rolled a few inches. The TV was balanced on a table with wheels. He moved it again slightly. A malicious smile crossed his face. He pushed again, a bit harder. The table rolled toward the pool's edge. He jerked the lounge chair he was reclining on closer to the box, pushed the table again—then gave it a good shove and watched the set drop into the pool with a sputter and splash, drowning Hollywood, sinking, turning, electrifying the water instead of the watcher.

Stretch leaned back, content, and soaked up a bit more sunshine. Twenty minutes later, he rose, went into the house, and noticed the number of empty beer cans littering the room. Time to clean up the act. He began to pick up the cans, arrange the disorder. Being clean and lonely somehow seemed more desirable than being a lonely slob.

At four fifteen he phoned. "Hi, Frank. Just got back. . . . Yeah. . . . Fine, great. Sure, I'll come by. . . . Three it is. See you tomorrow."

Thoughtfully, he replaced the receiver. Once you're on the tracks there's nothing to do but move. Somewhere there would be a junction, but others, it seemed, put the junctions there. You can't pull into the pit stop until a pit appears.

Parking the car in the middle of the race and walking away was an option a Stretch Jackson could simply not imagine. If an outsider had mentioned the idea, he would have laughed. No, he would say, there's a pit around the corner—somewhere. The trick is to know in which lap you need to find the pit and make a pit stop. Too soon, too late, you lose the race. Me, he would say, I'm just the driver. Someone else places the pits.

Stretch missed Karen. In some strange way he missed the two firemen, too. They had been part of the new world he had conquered. The fly had conquered the flypaper; something was very wrong. He wondered if he would ever get away and fly free again. He sat down and wrote his mother a note. In the morning he would send it off with a money order. He spent the night sleeping badly.

* * *

"You're not going to believe this one," Frank said to Stretch, handing him a piece of paper. "You meet this man at this time. He's the one with all the details. To quote our friend, Calhoun, he said, 'If that son-of-a-bitch is twenty-grand smart, let him figure this one out!' Fact of the matter is, they wouldn't trust their own guy with it. But, take care, it may not be possible, even for you. It's in your hands and if it can't be done—safely, without a trace—back off, for Christ's sake! There are plenty of others where this one came from."

A short time later, a red Mustang and a Mercury wagon were parked alongside each other at the beach near Golden Gate Park. The drivers of both cars were talking in the Mercury.

The crew-cut executive who was driving the station wagon had introduced himself as Vic Whitlock. When he revealed the job, Stretch had to struggle to keep the disbelief from registering on his face. He took the plans and every detail he could glean, then promised to return the plans later, since Whitlock would need them immediately after the fire to pay the claim.

First, Stretch wanted to study the idea to see if it was too crazy to pull off.

Feeling like a rank amateur again, Eddie Barker's successor headed straight to the library. It was almost a week later before he agreed to commit himself to the job.

* * *

Cars coming across the Oakland bridge slowed to watch the spectacle. Lacy streams of water arched high into the sky and fell earthward toward San Francisco's Pier 19. From a distance there was no sound, only the sight of the delicate flight of water from a fireboat that crisscrossed with streams from several landside fire engines. It was like a huge, fairy tale fountain—or it would have been if great billows of black smoke had not been roiling angrily to the heavens.

Up close, the scene was very different. The massive pumps of the S.F.F.D. fireboat roared, vibrated, sucked water from the sea at a terrifying pace, and poured it out through heavy monitors at the berthed freighter, *Tania T.* Oakland's fireboat was on its way, as was another from the Coast Guard station.

On the dock, the task force commander, Pat Betaudier, was yelling into his buggy's radio. "We just got the bill of lading. It's for Guatemala. That mother has everything on it from general freight to pesticides. . . . I don't give a damn! You've got to get a tug on it and get it out of here, fast! If that thing blows—or even sits there and burns—half the city's dead!"

The fire had been signaled at 6:37 A.M. and pumpers had arrived within minutes. The fireboats were slower. By seven thirty a tug was struggling to get a line on the freighter. It was successfully made fast, but a second tug was needed if they were to get the boat beyond the Golden Gate Bridge quickly enough. It was a major emergency. The second tug had trouble getting its line fixed. It was panic time.

The Chief of the San Francisco Fire Department had struggled out of a deep sleep and run out of his house to take command.

The department chief huddled in desperate conference with a divisional chief, two battalion chiefs, and Chief Betaudier. What if the *Tania T.* exploded under the Golden Gate Bridge? The results were unimaginable—just as they were if the boatload of pesticides blew up right in San Francisco Bay, Civil Defense was alerted.

Tania T. was surrounded by every fireboat available and, finally, four volunteer tugs. Maximum line was paid out. Everyone kept what was hoped to be a safe distance. At full speed the movable fountain and its deadly charge headed for the mouth of the bay—and the city's vital northern lifeline.

Police sealed off the Golden Gate Bridge, creating a monumental traffic jam that wreaked havoc during the morning rush hour. Thousands of cars stretched in an impatient line into Marin County to the north.

The tugboat captains thanked the Lord that they were on a fast outgoing tide. Just before the cluster of boats reached the structure, the flotilla had to break formation to avoid the bridge's great feet. If the ship was to sink now in the channel, it would be equally—but differently—catastrophic, blocking shipping for weeks in one of the country's major ports.

The department chief had given instructions that if the ship blew up the Presidio district was to be evacuated. Backed-up traffic was to be turned around in an "orderly fashion" and held one mile north of the bridge to avoid any possible pesticide fallout. The wind was still, but the light fog would be an unpredictable vehicle for any airborne pesticide. Everyone held his breath—the men on the tugs and fire-boats as well as those in the mobile Emergency Command Center parked at the bridge's edge. According to the bill of lading, there was enough dynamite aboard to blow the whole works to hell—boat, bridge, and all.

The entourage seemed to proceed at a snail's pace as the span was approached. Slowly the burning boat was pulled directly underneath the main span. "Go! Go!" was on a hundred lips. The procession almost seemed to stall right where it should have gone the fastest. But go it did, slipping beyond the bridge, drowning the million tons of metal in dense, deadly smoke.

"Now, get out of the narrows, please God," Chief Betaudier prayed, for all the danger had not passed.

In slow motion, the *Tania T.* finally reached the open sea. The fireboats no longer needed to take risks. The tugs held her steady against the tide but at a great distance. Without warning, there was a muffled explosion. A new blast of black plumed skyward. *Tania T.* tilted sideways, rolled over, and went down in an eruption of steam and bubbles. Calm returned.

The watery lacework of fireboat monitors stopped. A helicopter collected air samples for pesticide traces and raced them to the police lab, but the worst was over. Blessedly, there was no pesticide trace at all.

* * *

A thick-billed parrot screeched in the jungle. It moved its heavyset green body farther out on the limb, its red forehead patch making a bright splash against the dense green foliage.

Below the bird, a tall man moved casually down the path. "Here you go, Stretch—one bourbon and water."

The temperature was tropical, the air warm, with that special, moist odor of equatorial arboretums. This one was grandiose—vast, heavily planted, worthy of the rain forest that rises in the Budongo beyond Masindi. The huge curved-glass oval contained specimens collected from the entire tropical belt. The setting had an otherworldly aura, as if Tarzan might drop down on a vine. A gorilla would not be unexpected—or a shy bongo with its great curved horns. Instead, there was Global's humorless fire claims manager sitting in his private kingdom. Adventure, Whitlock's personal obsession seemed to say, is where you find it—or where you make it.

Whitlock sat in a canvas camp chair in the clearing beyond the branch where the parrot perched. "Goddamn stroke of genius," he said to his guest. "I'd never have thought of adding the phony pesticides and dynamite to the bill of lading."

"That way they had to pull it out of the harbor. It justified blowing it up and sinking the evidence at sea."

"Neat job of timing. You figure it out or was it an accident?"

"I don't leave *anything* to accident—not if I can help it. I even timed it for an outgoing tide."

"I saw it on TV at breakfast. What made all the smoke—and why the hell couldn't the hoses put the fire out?"

"Jesus, Vic, I can't give you all my trade secrets. Let's say some chemicals just love water and leave it at that." Stretch smiled so that Whitlock would not be ruffled. "But I hope the next one's easier."

"Even George tipped his hat to you this afternoon, and that's no minor compliment. You're okay with us. Our guy is good, but I don't think he could have handled that ship."

Basking in Calhoun's benediction, Stretch relaxed. He took in the bizarre surroundings, dripping with orchids. The atmosphere gave him the courage to ask a question he would have resisted otherwise. "How did you get into this arson thing anyway, Vic?"

Artlessly, Whitlock confessed, "Oh, everyone cheats a little, one way or another. Got to, if you want to make out. A little on the expense account—the company not only expects that, but encourages it. A little on the taxes—government expects that, too. Then, one day, something bigger comes along. You figure, why small potatoes all the time? So when one of our good agents came up with this deal—hell, the setup was beautiful. You know, it's insurance money anyway. We're so goddamn big, it's like taking money from the government." He rose and began pacing around the clearing. "Funny, big business money. It's all faceless—like we stole George Washington's picture off it. Doesn't mean anything. If somebody else tries to screw the company you get mad as hell, but when your chance comes to steal some you find yourself sticking it in just like all the others."

Whitlock moved to the bamboo bar. He chugged a quick jolt, then made them each a fresh drink. Though Whitlock kept his stem demeanor, Stretch could see that he was not shy with the booze.

"One thing I envy you guys," Stretch said, "is that you've got a legitimate cover. Real businesses. You keep a secret or two and still have a life. Me—my whole goddamn life's a secret."

Whitlock leaned toward the younger man with a conspiratorial air. "Stretch, I'll make you a deal. I'll give you my tight-assed wife and her golf clubs and her dippy friends. She comes with a full wardrobe and a BMW, two fucked-up teenagers—spoiled silly—three poodles, a gardener, and fourteen hundred thirty-two bucks a month just in house payments. And I'll take your sorry secret life and disappear." Abruptly, he leaned back and belted down the last of his straight-up Scotch. "How's that?" he asked and rose to get another drink.

"You don't make it sound very appetizing."

"It's not. That's the reason for this jungle. Spent a fortune building this. Love it. Come in, lock that door. It's peace and quiet. Somewhere else. Everything out there is death. Guess that's why I started with arson—to buy myself a little life." Vic moved to the bar again and said over his shoulder, "Well, that's my end of the business. Now tell me what you do. You work for Frank often?"

That's a no-no, mister, Stretch thought. He could smell the prying. Flattered by the group's newly won approval or not, Stretch wouldn't trust Vic Whitlock for a minute. He glanced at his watch. "It'll have to wait for next time, Vic. Got a heavy date for dinner." It was not his practice to tell anyone anything—not even a new associate.

"Oh, come on," Whitlock urged. "Let's have one more. Oil your joints for the evening."

If Jackson had stayed and confessed a little about the Oakland jobs, his life would have radically changed—but instead he took his leave politely. Whitlock stayed in the dark about the fires in the East Bay—and whoever was torching over there remained an anonymous screwer of his company with whom he was "mad as hell."

23

Another front door was closed—politely, this time—in Tom Farley's face. He stood on the step and decided he'd had enough for the day. Digging in ashes may be the dirtiest part of arson work, but a door-to-door canvass is by far the most tedious. Doors get slammed—or are not opened. Daytime lovers are the shortest tempered of all. Old ladies may chatter on or complain about being roused from a nap. Everything is theoretically possible—even getting results—but Tom usually turned this bit of drudgery back to the assigning company and had an adjuster grub for the long shot.

This time he did it himself. Painfully, he had worked his way through the neighborhoods of each "instant" fire. It had taken days of questions, knocking on doors, more questions. Nothing—not a single lead. Hot, footsore, and bone weary, he headed back to the office. The best he could muster for Charlene was a mere hint of a smile.

"You're starting to look worn out," she said.

"Not really. Just a bad day. Zip, zilch, zero—a nothing in the universe."

"Good grief. It *is* getting to you."

"How are we fixed for that fine instant black plastic?"

"Now that's what I like. A nice practical question." As Tom turned away from the locker, Charlene stood up. Her crow's-feet crinkled, her eyes twinkled, the corners of her mouth rose—exposing her heart. "We're fixed fine for coffee, sir. The call list is on your desk."

Days like this one had marched lead footed across the calendar until his quest seemed to border on masochism. But that was Farley's way. Every morning he would do a brief stint in the office, then head out for another round of sidewalks and doors.

The following day the legwork began again. On one of the streets was a small wood house that was desperate for a new coat of white paint. The worn porch had a pair of feet silently weighing on the boards. The feet belonged to Tom Farley. He knocked again on the door. The canvassing on "instant" fires had led nowhere, so with his endless patience he had broadened the scope to include the areas of *all* the building contractor blazes. He had begun by knocking on every door within a three-block radius of the fire at Vada's Oakland Agency construction site. There was no answer to his knocking. He lifted his clipboard, noted the house number, and wrote NOH—No One Home.

At the next house he opened the tipsy gate of a limp picket fence and rapped. The neighborhood was substantially less than affluent, and had all of the neighbors come into some money it would have become a painting contractor's heaven. Unfortunately, the area remained run-down and drab. After years of trudging, Tom knew that very rich and very poor areas were the best to work because lots of people were at home. Someone or other was usually in at the large houses. In poor neighborhoods he could count on seeing mothers of large families, oldsters eking it out on pensions, the jobless, and night workers. Middle-class neighborhoods were a nightmare, for the price of achieving middle-class seemed to be that both adults had to work and shove even the toddlers out to nurseries and preschool. The only hope of finding anyone in was before they ran off in the morning or after six in the evening.

This knock brought a quick response. An age-furrowed face peered past the door curtain. Tom was used to that reaction. He held up his P.I. card. The little lady opened the door and listened while Tom patiently explained the nature of his search. He noticed that he had caught her with her false teeth placed somewhere other than in her mouth—probably still in a glass in the bathroom. Farley asked if she had noticed anything unusual the night of Vada's fire.

"Say . . . I sure did, young man," she said, slightly embarrassed by the absent choppers. "Don't sleep good no more and I was out walking Lilly—she's my shepherd, don't you know. Can't be too careful nowadays. Well, at the corner there I started hearing the sirens. Hearing's good, still got my hearing. Thank God for that. Well, then, just in front of me this car starts up and turns its lights on. Now, at three in the morning this here neighborhood's dead quiet, don't you know. That wasn't no car from this street and ever since they caught that killer in New York with his license number—Son of What's-his-name—well, I come right back and wrote it down. Plumb forgot about it ever since. Memory's not so good, don't you know."

The pit of Tom's stomach tightened. "Do you still have it, ma'am? It might be very, very important."

"I wouldn'ta throwed it out." She gave him a toothless grin. "If I can remember where I put it, don't you know."

Tom was ready to go inside and tear up the whole house to find that scrap of paper. An insomniac lady walking a dog at three in the morning! Now *that* was a break. Tom waited at the door, tapping the clipboard nervously, while the old lady went to look for the precious scribbling. It seemed to take her two minutes longer than forever—but when she returned, she held out a scrap of paper. Tom thanked her with a profusion of his sweetest adjectives, then headed straight for Lieutenant Boskowitch.

"Okay, that's it, Tom," the lieutenant finally said, beaming and patting his computer. "OUX 829 is a tan Pinto wagon registered to Mark MacDonald. Here's the address and all."

Tom raced his Pontiac back to San Francisco. As he approached 905 California Street his rising excitement began to mix with a sinking sensation. He realized that either he was dealing with a rich torch with a lot of savvy who flew in for the jobs or else the guy had a nasty sense of humor. For at 905 stood the Stanford Court, where the superrich and superstars seek luxurious anonymity when they stay in the city, "That smart-ass son-of-a-bitch!" Tom said aloud. He consoled himself with the vague hope it might be an employee.

Quiet elegance was not going to stop the investigation. The P.I. card flashed and Tom explained the situation to the condescending manager, but the MacDonald he sought was neither an employee nor a known guest. Politely, the man explained that he could not divulge his guest list short of a police request. At last, faced with an obvious criminal matter and Farley's threat to return with the director of the F.B.I. if necessary, the manager agreed to allow Pat to come back later and verify the register for one week preceding the auto's registration as well as for one day before each fire.

"Pull off your leg and club him if you have to," Tom instructed his father.

It proved to be a dead end.

"Smart bastard," Tom fumed, half in admiration, half in fury.

Pat sat in his office, his artificial leg propped up in the corner. "No phone, listed or unlisted; no police record; no credit record; not a taxpayer or property owner. The salesman who sold the car doesn't remember a thing."

"That's got to be him." Looking out the window, Tom surveyed the city. The torch was out there—somewhere. "Smart bastard," he said again. "I'll see if I can get a general police call out. A tan Pinto wagon, OUX 829. He's too smart to use a phony license plate. That's why he set up the fake registration. That plate is the only part of him that's not invisible. We're going to get him, Pat. I can smell it."

Tom walked back into his office and made some calls. Shortly after, Charlene came in to drop a file on Tom's desk. He was immersed for the hundredth time in the Vada file. For a moment she studied him. "Tom Farley, I think you're falling in love with this guy."

Farley's head shot up from the file. "That's crazy!" he exclaimed, but his eyes dropped back to the file. "Well . . . he *is* pretty special. He's just so good!"

"See?" she teased. "That's what I mean."

"I'd kill the bastard if the law would let me."

She gave a warm try-me smile. "*And* if you could find him."

"Come on, get out of here! You're keeping your boss from working." For a moment, he could actually think of something he'd rather be doing.

* * *

It is difficult to hold a meeting of firemen. When half of the men are living in, the rest are off and at home. While two-thirds are awake and working, the others are on their sleep shift. However, this was a special occasion and the room was jammed full. Jonah and the union negotiating team had just worked out a new contract with City Hall. If the death of Mannie Rojas and Jack Runyon left a legacy to Oakland's firemen, it was in dramatizing their daily risks. All too often, good sense waits for tragedy to wake it up.

"Come on, guys, hold it down," Jonah was saying. "If I'm going to be our union rep, give me a chance to talk, will you . . . ? Okay . . . that's better. It's little enough consolation, but the union leaders had the intelligence and muscle to use the headlines to push through this new contract. You got the details. Now we have to vote on it. Three groups of guys risk their lives defending the public: soldiers, policemen, firemen. And we all get treated like second-class citizens.

"Everybody knows about the risks policemen take, but a cop gets shot or he lives on. In public service it's firemen who have the shortest life expectancy. Inhale all that heat and smoke, nobody notices it whacks ten years off your life down at the far end. One out of every thirty-two hundred career fire-fighters is going to die on the job in the next twelve months, to say nothing of the injured. But it's the dying early that no one sees. It's the dying young that's nasty. At the fireground it's all glory, but no one's interested when you're only sixty and your lungs are all burnt out. Well, goddamn—that's what this contract's all about. That is what our union is for—and that's exactly what it did. Let's hear it for the union, men! Let's hear it for the union!"

* * *

It was not ten minutes after the meeting ended that Jonah, freshly settled at his desk, took Farley's phone call.

At the end of his explanation Tom said, "Come on over and I'll show you how it works." There was not really any need to urge Jonah to jump in his car—wild horses could not have kept him away.

The best arson investigator west of the Mississippi hung up the receiver of the pay phone and leaned against the side of the booth, staring out through the glass. Across the street was the Quonset garage, laid out like an autopsied whale. Each curved corrugated metal sheet had been laid back with its wooden ribs exposed. Tom could not suppress a certain surge of pride—not vanity, but a good, deep sensation of having attacked a brain-cracking job and succeeding against all odds.

While he waited for Jonah he decided to share the satisfaction. He dialed his number, listened to the ring, then, smiling, heard Charlene answer. When Jonah pulled up, he said a quick good-bye and rushed back to the dissected Quonset, eager to explain the anatomy of a fire.

Leading Jonah through the corpse, Tom explained the bizarre cause of the structure's fiery death. "The torch got lucky and unlucky. See the charring on this beam? The alligatoring is deep and uniform. That's where the burning started. He was lucky to have an assignment on a Quonset with wood beams—they're rare. But here's where he was unlucky, because he finally left us some evidence. What does this next beam over say to you?"

"It's alligatored different. Shallower. The heat source was farther away."

"Right! Now, the next beam over is the same. The day I came charging in here like a mad bull, that's all the sheeting I took off. Don't even remember if I saw it or not, but if I had, it wouldn't have struck me as really weird. When I started laying it all belly up, here's what I found. Look at the fourth beam."

"Just like the first."

"And so is every third beam from here to the end. How the hell could every third beam have been subjected to a source of ignition?"

"Christ, I hope that's not a question. *You're* the expert, Tom."

"That's what I was kicking myself about. It scrambled my brain like eggs for a whole afternoon before the light came on. Each bad beam has a wire to the overhead fluorescent fixtures. Everywhere the wire cable touched wood, fire started."

"I'll be go to hell—so it's electrical. But what about the circuit breakers?"

"That's what threw me off the track in the first place. I tore into the breaker unit and it was perfectly in place and operational—just like a breaker should have been after a nonelectrical ignition. So from then on I assumed it wasn't electrical—but I couldn't find anything else."

"What the hell did he do?"

"You scrape away the ashes at the fuse box and you get your answer in a little bit of melted aluminum. The guy comes in—he's got to be a fucking expert—uses gloves and a plastic tool, and bares the wires coming out of the box. He's got to have guts, too. Hooks on one wire, flips the circuit breaker off for a few seconds or minutes and hooks up the other wire, then flips the breaker back on. The wire he uses is aluminum and he's bypassed the whole circuit-breaker system. Then he hooks a hot line to either a grounding or grounded conductor and every wire from the source to the switch heats up. It's exactly the same idea as an electric toaster."

"Holy hell. That's it—absolutely—the toaster principle. You could do that to a house or a high-rise."

"This son-of-a-bitch has got everything figured. All of this garage's wires run in armored cable, so I cut out a cable section. The insulation, instead of being melted onto the wire, like an external heat source would do, is sleeved away from the wire, like it would be if the copper wire itself was burning hot. But even better than that, being enclosed in the flexible, exterior metal casing, the insulation has no oxygen to ignite it and it simply gets hotter and hotter until the steel outer cable glows white hot. But our guy's not finished calculating tricks yet! The wood beam has a smoldering combustion; it builds up some charcoal, decomposes, gives off gas in open air/oxygen. Around six to nine hundred degrees the gas ignites. Every stick of wood that is touching the cable catches on fire simultaneously all over the building, but the cable heat still keeps rising, building up the wood's temperature till it's bonfire time.

"Inside the flexible cable and the insulation, the copper electric wire won't melt until it hits nineteen hundred eighty degrees, but down here, at twelve hundred Fahrenheit, the aluminum wire that short-circuited the system in the first place melts out. The torch couldn't care less. By then, he's got the whole building involved in a roaring blaze. The evidence melts down to a few drops of aluminum buried in a pile of ashes. The aluminum wire goes and the electrical system pops right off at the breakers, since he's got his short circuit somewhere. But that is exactly what should happen in a fire as bad as this—and it thoroughly covers up arson as a possible cause. Then the roof structure weakens. Vehicle tanks blow and the whole damn works comes tumbling down in a heap of burned trash. Our torch friend's a long way off by then. I ran a test. From the time of the hookup until ignition he's got a neat twenty minutes."

"He could be home in San Francisco."

"Or San José, or checking into a hotel somewhere. He's lit a great fire, not left a trace. I'm convinced it's only one man—and he's a master arsonist. Where there was a structural problem like Vada's building site, he used standard, but high-class, fancy footwork. But this—I've never seen anything like it or even heard of it before. He's no Tom, Dick, or Harry. The guy's local, too. Remember, all this started at Acme Salvage, which has to be unrelated to the construction jobs."

"God knows what all else he's burned."

"If he hadn't done this Quonset with that regular beam pattern, we'd still be scratching our heads."

"Or if he hadn't gotten your back up. You're a frigging genius at this. Know how rich you could get if you switched sides?"

"Thanks. I know of a P.I. back in Boston who thought the same thing. Got himself thirty years on a murder rap."

Tom and Jonah tagged, photographed, and identified all of the evidence to be given to the Fire Department so that the evidence chain would remain intact. Contented, they headed back to their cars.

"Now the sticker is," Tom said, "we know how it's done—but why is he doing contractors? Who is it for? Who *is* the smart son-of-a-bitch that owns the Pinto wagon—and how the hell are we going to find him?"

24

A brilliant, fogless morning brightened San Francisco, but it did not do much for the spirits of the city's best arsonist. He had gone back to the Buddha the night before for the first time in many months. Instead of cheering his flagging mood, all the greetings and where-you-beens merely confirmed that his close friends would never be Benny, Caruso, Sweet Pea, and company. There was a moment when he was half tempted to sneak quietly into the Silver Doll. Instead, Stretch went back to dear old Broadway Game and beat on the machines as though Karen might somehow receive the vibrations of his frustration. If she did, she did not materialize in the pinball parlor or at the empty house to which he returned.

Hazel, however, called late the following morning. Even Hazel was beginning to appeal to him. "Hello, Stretch. Wake you up? Listen, Frank wants to know if you can make it around four this afternoon."

"Hazel, I'd come in at four just to see your smile."

"You come, Stretch, I'll smile."

What the devil am I doing, he asked himself when he hung up. As he flopped idly onto the couch, a thought came out of the past. He fished through the phone book and found Bard and Belding Advertising—then Beryl Biehr. Beryl was more than unavailable—she left him with the distinct impression that she had become part of the wacky, doped-out North Beach scene. Not only had her fiancé from St. Louis stayed, but he, she, and Chuckie, the piano player, were living as a *ménage à trois.*

A bit after four he stood over Sievers's desk studying blowups of an apartment building. Frank sat expectantly in his leather desk chair.

"You can't do it, Frank."

"*What do you mean?*" Sievers demanded, amazed.

"You can't burn that building without killing people."

"Oh." Sievers relaxed. "That's what I was afraid you'd say. I want you to figure out a way to minimize the risks."

Stretch looked up at the boss. Had Frank forgotten? A split second of puzzlement creased Jackson's face. "Minimize? I won't do it, Frank."

"Oh, shut up, Stretch. Of course you'll do it! Look, we're in this up to our eyeballs anyway, and this isn't a union case, or Calhoun's—it's mine! *All* mine . . . and for lots of money. Lots and lots of it. It's the one I mentioned already. Vada's building. Since it's so special, I upped your usual ten thousand to thirty-two thousand—a straight ten percent of my three-hundred-twenty-thousand-dollar profit. And, incidentally, George is lining up a beaut too. Tough, but really a beaut."

Stretch Jackson could not believe his ears. "You think I'm just your Zippo, don't you? A walking, talking Zippo!"

A rare laugh shook the beefy man behind the desk, but it wasn't exactly a laugh of amusement. "You're not just a Zippo, Stretch, you're a gold-plated Dunhill." His chuckle over, Frank leaned back, relaxed. "Let me level with you. I started rank and file—with nothing. This is a tough business. I used plenty of strong-arm when I had to. When you play a rough game, you either play a little rougher than the next guy or it's *you* that gets the broken arm or ends up stuffed in a garbage can. Sure, I've done okay, but it's never conflicted with what's good for my union. Full employment, full pay. Listen, I never got rich out of it. Now it's time to think of number one for a while. I've got a family too, you know!"

The confidential tone took the edge off Stretch's incredulity. He could exchange confidence for confidence. "Okay,

Frank, but you remember the first day I came here? I only made one demand: clean bums. Either you forgot, or you got me wrong. I won't do this kind. I wouldn't touch that job with a ten-foot match if my mother asked me."

"*Who the hell do you think you're talking to?*" Frank Sievers exploded. "*I'm not your fucking mother!* You're some goddamned punk I picked up fresh off the street and now you're loaded and feeling smart!"

Sievers jammed a thick finger on a hidden button. Henry and Ben burst into the office.

"See them?" Frank demanded in icy fury. "Either one of them would skin his sister if I said to. And you'll do the same—or they'll turn you into sausage meat! This isn't the goddamned country club! You just remember you're a fucking firebug, not the president of the bank." He slammed the desk with his ham hand. "And I was busting my ass to be generous!" He took dead aim at what he was certain would be a weak spot in Stretch's armor. "And if you don't give a personal damn about getting laced with lead, I'm sure Henry and Ben could manage a trip to that jerkwater town in Illinois to see what your family thinks about it. Now take the pictures and go to work . . . and get the fuck out!" He shoved the photos into a pile, flung them across the desk, and gave Stretch a look that was more foul than his words.

Stretch was ash white, shocked to speechless submission. He took the photos. Seething with a mixture of rage and fear, he stalked to the door, voiceless.

"Goddamned smart-ass punks nowadays!" Frank said aloud. "Calhoun's fucking right!" His target was closing the door. "Jackson!" Frank bellowed.

Like a wild horse, almost but not quite broken, Stretch returned and stood numbly in the doorway, painfully registering the savage blows of a master tamer.

Sievers was used to upstarts and renegades. His voice was level—and deadly. "Every stick bums, you hear? You'd better do it right. We've got two, three weeks . . . and you're the smartest torch in the business. You *find* some way so no one gets killed. No trace! No killing! That's what you get paid so goddamn much for! Now get out."

* * *

Tom pulled his Pontiac into the lot of the Aughenbaugh Insurance Agency, then got out and went to see the owner. "Morning, Gene," he said. "Charlene said you wanted me to stop by. What's up?"

"I don't know." Aughenbaugh was hesitant. "I hope it's nothing, but on the Vada account—well, you asked to be notified if there were any major increases." The slender man was even more nervous than usual. "One of the men in the office put an additional three hundred forty thousand on a thirty-day renewable binder for a remodeling job Vada's doing." He leaned back, fluttering his thin hands, trying to be coy and confident at the same time. "You got to understand, Tom. I don't think it means a thing. Jim Vada's a big client for me. I really—"

"Hey, Gene. I'm not interested in doing you out of business. On the other hand, neither of us wants to see Union and National Insurance get burned out of town, either. I appreciate the tip and so will the company, but I'm not going to go barging in and kick your insured in the ass. I realize he's important to you. Let me have the details."

Aughenbaugh stopped twitching and called in the salesman who had taken the information. Somewhere inside himself, Tom felt one more tumbler of the lock fall in place.

When they were finished, Tom sprang buoyantly across the lot to his car. He had a light-in-the-head, tight-in-the-gut sensation as he sped to his next stop.

Lake Merritt, at the edge of downtown Oakland, is a large irregular body of water that resembles a clenched fist—seen in profile—with the index finger extended. The long, crooked finger heads north, then bends to point accusingly at Berkeley. Ringed all the way around by a green belt, the northeast shore spreads into the city's main park, complete with a small zoo and other public buildings that hide in the lush landscape. The narrowest place, halfway up the thin finger, was Tom's destination. Where Madison Street dead-ended at Lakeside Drive stood a seven-story Tudor-style building—the Normandy Apartments.

Tom Farley sucked in his breath when he saw it. In addition to the swarm of workmen passing in and out of the doors, there also were children and adults. It was immediately obvious that some of the apartments were still occupied despite the remodeling going on.

After a preliminary inspection, Farley returned with Jonah to show him what they were up against. The handsome old building was set well back from the street. Trees dotted the lawn, dating from a period when builders felt that breathing space was natural for apartments. When new, it no doubt had been a prestige residence, with its architectural style of France's Normandy and the luxurious site overlooking the lake. Now it was more than ready for a face-lift.

The two men entered the L-shaped building. "Fix the plaster, paint, add new carpets, new elevators, and new plumbing fixtures, and you've got a high-class, lakeside investment. It's a big job," Tom said. "They're remodeling one floor at a time, relocating all of the families on that floor for a ten-day period. Then they move up to the next floor. As the leases run out, no doubt they'll bump the rent and renew the clientele. It's an intelligent scheme for an honest builder, but something tells me they'll never get past the second floor. As a torch job, it's a crematorium."

"If that's what's in the cards, it wouldn't make sense to do more work than was necessary just to keep up appearances before you lit it. And you say Vada just tripled his insurance?"

"Right. He's owned it for about a year. Contractors as big as he is run into deals like this from time to time. On the surface, it looks perfectly straight. If it was anyone but Vada, at any time but now . . ." Tom stopped and stared down the corridor, which was crowded with scaffolding and workmen. He looked puzzled. It made no sense that Vada would burn his own garage, then a new construction job, and now this. Where was the link? How could this have anything to do with the other contractors' garages? Suddenly he was filled with doubt. "I don't know, Jonah. Maybe I'm just imagining things that don't exist."

The same thoughts had crossed the fireman's mind. Where, he wondered, could the connection be? In silence they worked their way down to the corner where they had a view of both wings of the building. Busy workers were spread to the far end of each corridor. The scene certainly looked normal and efficient. Maybe they both were overexcited, caught up in a game. Still, the situation was too deadly and too sinister to ignore. Jonah no longer knew what to think.

"Jonah," Tom said hesitantly, exploring his own thoughts, "what if it isn't a profit motive? There's no way anyone could be collecting money from all these fires. It can't even be someone knocking off his competition, because some of them weren't competitors in any way." He paused and pushed his hat back. "What if it's a racket?"

"What kind of racket is going to hit one guy in Richmond, one electrical contractor who's not a builder, all the rest, then this?" Jonah asked.

Stumped for a moment, Tom stood still, looking blankly at the captain. "A union?" He turned the idea over. "Yeah, Jonah, a union getting some kind of sweetheart contracts."

"Not sure I follow . . ."

"Sure, a union," Tom broke in. Now he was getting excited again. "All of these fires have shut down the contractor briefly. That's why they were set in garages. You can replace trucks fast and easy. They wanted the builder to get a message he wouldn't forget, without putting him clear out of business."

"Makes sense till you get to the construction job and this, which are both Vada's."

"No. Vada's a scrappy little cookie. He gives the impression of being an easy mark, but he's really tough as old boot. Say they had to burn him *twice* to get what they wanted. After the garage was gone, they had to hit him right in the pocketbook . . . like one of his *new* construction jobs."

"And this? This doesn't figure at all."

"What if Vada got the message and when he did collapsed completely? If somebody's got their hooks in him deep enough they could get him to do anything." Tom paused to hammer it home. "Like overinsure this building, then torch it, and force him to knock back a piece of the profit!"

"Jesus, you make it sound convincing."

They started back toward the entrance when Jonah stopped and turned to ask the obvious. "Why the hell can't they just cancel the policy?"

"The company has already issued the increased coverage. They'd have to give Vada ten days' coverage even after he and his mortgage holder received registered letters of notification that the company was canceling the policy. With okays, paperwork, and mail delivery—hell, that would put them on notice and they'd still barely have to change their plans. The foreman told me they would only take ten days a floor. That thirty-day binder is renewable, but I imagine the renewable part is just for appearance's sake. If they don't invest beyond the second floor—say, the third at the very most—we're looking at a three- to four-week schedule for the burn and conceivably as soon as ten more days from right now. No, they would burn it with hardly a shift in the arrangements. And anyone ready to send this place up, with people and all, isn't going to get stopped by anything."

"No, I guess not." Jonah almost wished Farley didn't sound so right. The prospect was more gruesome than he wanted to contemplate.

"Anyway," Tom continued, "don't forget Vada has a huge, respectable contracting company. I just have a strong hunch. We have no grounds on which to tell a company to cancel a multimillion-dollar policy. It sure isn't Vada himself lighting matches." Tom's eyes narrowed. "I'm going to pay him another visit and see what I can pry out of him."

* * *

Two days later, Jim Vada was leaning over Sievers's desk, agitated. "Frank, I'm telling you, it's too risky! Farley comes in asking all those innocent questions. You should have seen how that son-of-a-bitch nailed my chief accountant before. He's got a mind like a data bank. But I catch between the lines. He knows all about the Normandy remodel. He's got to have been snooping around there."

"Calm down, Jim. I'll take care of him."

"You'll take care of everything—according to you. You know the odds on burning that place without anyone getting hurt? I don't give a damn if you say you've got the best torch in America. A goof and I'll end up spending my life in jail. I didn't put all those years into my business to end up stooping to this kind of crap!"

Frank Sievers exploded like muffled dynamite. "You listen to me, Vada, and listen good! I had to burn you twice to get you to hear me in the first place. You goddamn contractors got a million ways to get rich over our dead bodies and you do it every day. My only shot is muscle. That building's a once-in-a-lifetime break for me. I've got months of planning and twenty-one grand of my own cash invested in setting this up. I said I was going to ask one personal service in return for the trouble you put me to. We made a bargain on the Normandy Apartments and we're both going to stick to it. Nobody backs out of a deal with me. I'm committed, and that son-of-a-bitch is going to burn! I'll take care of the snoop. No creep from an insurance company's going to stop it either." He leaned right up to Vada menacingly. "And if I hear one, *one* more peep out of you, that torch I mentioned will fry you and Shirley and your three kids in bed one night! Now, let me do the worrying. For a quarter of a million free and clear I can worry a lot."

"But—"

"No but's," Frank snarled. "The only butt around here is gonna be yours if anything goes wrong with that bum. I mean it! Get out!"

Picking up the phone, Frank watched Jim Vada storm out. The contractor did not bother him. Frank knew when he had a man by the short hairs—vulnerable; not submissive, but compliant. That's the way he liked them. Vada fell in the

Calhoun category: smart, class, big time. Those were the men Sievers liked to make jump the hoops. They confirmed his power. The docile ones were boring. He pushed an intercom button. "Henry, come in here. Bring Ben." Insurance people, he had found, were all in the dull, docile category. He would have to turn the pipsqueak off—inspector, adjuster, or whatever he was.

* * *

Stretch Jackson was not polar bear enough to jump into his pool. A camelhair sweater picked out by young Mr. Wolff took the edge off the poolside chill. Agitated, nipping nervously at his fingernails, Stretch was locked in a telephone conversation with his mentor in New York.

"They'll burn anything, Eddie. They don't give a good goddamn what. That's not what I signed up for. They've got no standards but money, man, and that's just not me . . . and it's going to get worse."

"I never said it was kid stuff. You deal with guys who play for keeps."

"I know that, but I didn't know they'd change the game in the middle of a hand."

"Pardner, it's their game, their rules, their money. We may get to drag from every pot, but we're still just hired hands."

"When the hell do you say no? Where do you draw the line?"

"It's like life, cowboy. Sometimes you have to do things you wouldn't want to tell your mother."

Stretch jumped up and began to pace almost hysterically. "The hell with Mother, Eddie! I have to do things I can't tell myself!"

"Old buddy," came the calm reply, "*that's* where you draw the line."

Stretch stopped, dead still.

"Other than just moralizing," Eddie continued, "you in trouble?"

"I guess it's nothing I can't handle, Eddie. Look, I'll keep in touch."

Stretch cradled the receiver. He picked up the skimmer and started to absentmindedly clean the surface of the pool.

* * *

For the second time, Tom found that it was he who extended the conversation with Dee Hatford. Love had wrought its wonders on her. She now exchanged bits of news about her boyfriend, a programmer for IBM, and what they did, where they went. The distance Tom had formerly kept was so reduced that even he was surprised when he found himself inviting her to stop in at *Sapphire II* should the two of them ever stroll down his dock.

Dee almost reciprocated by suggesting Tom come by the Normandy Apartments some weekend afternoon, but she halted herself. The building was such a mess at the moment. She would wait before extending an invitation.

Eventually Farley stepped into Vic Whitlock's office, closed the door, and sat down with an expression sufficiently severe to match the insurance man's usual pokerfaced countenance.

"I'm not here on Global business, Vic. It's about your extracurricular activities."

Whitlock looked up sharply. He had everything set up flawlessly. Obviously no arson investigator ever got assigned any of his *personal* cases. But Tom Farley's intuition, his bulldog tenacity, and bloodhound interest in everything that smelled of fire always left Whitlock with a vague sense of unease. He felt absolutely comfortable about his private source of income, save for the remote possibility that the man across the desk from him might someday stumble onto his trail inadvertently. He waited for the next sentence with bated breath.

"I've got an unusual situation and an unusual request. Since you're the President of the Bay Area Fire Insurers Association, I guess you're the man to see."

Vic Whitlock's twitch faded away. He listened attentively as the investigator carefully laid out the case. Once or twice Whitlock posed a question. His third question was, "How much are you talking about? Thirty days of your time isn't cheap, Tom." That seemed a bit undiplomatic, so he hastily added, "But cheap isn't why any of us hire you."

"I've never done anything similar. I'll still have a bit of time to work on the files in the office, which should pay the rent and such, but I'll turn down everything new for a month. I'm not in it for the money. If I was, I wouldn't even make the suggestion, but if you guys can come up with ten thousand dollars, either you'll save a million by breaking this up—or we'll all be out a bit."

"Why don't you hit Union and National? They've got Vada's coverage."

"I thought of that, but you're all in it. Every company in the Fire Insurers Association has a stake in it. You are all getting eaten up by arson."

Whitlock recognized that Tom was out to get "the others out to screw the company." His jaw set firmly. "Okay, Tom, I'll buy that. I can't make the decision, but I'll push like hell for the idea. Luckily, we've got a board meeting Friday. I could call around, but I'd rather wait two days and lay it out all at once. It seems to me that's what the Association's charter talks about: promoting the exchange of information for the good of the industry and the protection of the public."

"Understand, there's no guarantee."

"Understood. I'll call and let you know the result after the lunch meeting Friday."

* * *

Inside the Normandy lobby, a worried-looking man in electrician's clothes studied the building's layout. He shifted the small roll of electrical cable to his left hand so he could pick up the little iron hammer that hung beside the fire alarm. *In the event of emergency, break glass, pull handle.* He gently tapped the hammer on the breakable surface, then realized he should not be seen concentrating on the alarm.

A horde of painters, carpenters, plumbers—the gamut of the building trades—scurried around the ground floor. The man whose intention it was to undo their hard work figured that one more electrician would go unnoticed. If anyone asked, he had prepared an answer. He walked the entire building from the basement up. The more he saw, the more he worried, and the less he liked the whole setup. There were too many tenants, too few exits. The remodeling job was a perfect cover for him, but he understood the work would have moved up to the second or third floor before light-up time. That would even further complicate the tenants' escape. Stretch broke into a nervous sweat. Uncontrollably, images of the two dead firemen and the burning Viet Cong kept racing through his mind.

Stretch walked past the elevator on the fourth floor just as the doors opened. An elderly lady stepped out, one hand holding a grocery bag, the other fishing awkwardly for the key in her purse. Because her eyes were on her problem rather than where she was going, she walked right into Stretch. Surprised, she dropped her purse, the contents spilling up and down the carpeted corridor. Stretch immediately stooped to retrieve the purse and what had been in it.

"Oh, I'm *so* sorry," the woman said. And she surely was, but the fleeting look she gave the stranger who was handling her intimate belongings was fearful. The man could grab it all and run.

Stretch was polite and reassuring. He gathered everything and, at her request, handed her the culprit key separately. Their eyes met and as he took in her pleasant, delicately wrinkled face, clear dark eyes, and their frame of snowy hair, the horrible realization that he was about to endanger her life struck him like a sledgehammer.

She was smiling. "Why, you remind me of my son, Lloyd. Well, I certainly thank you." She turned and went toward her door.

The remark left Stretch thunderstruck, for the thought had just occurred to him that if his mother dressed more smartly the two women would bear a resemblance. A bit dazed, Stretch continued his tour of inspection. He was torn between thinking that despite Frank's threats he could not, would not, do this job and, on the other hand, that he alone could do it and not hurt anyone in the process—although he still had no clue as to how that could be accomplished. He moved upward, tormented by the conflict.

On the seventh floor he pushed the elevator button to go down. While he was waiting, a form that was clearly female came out of a door down the hall. A sweet-faced brunette who could not have exceeded twenty came quickly toward the elevator.

"Hold it!" she called.

"It's not even here yet."

"Oh, okay."

Stretch tried to stop thinking of her running down that hall—on fire! He was aware that she was staring back at him.

"You an electrician?"

"Uh-huh. Sure am."

She was young and pretty. The slow-moving elevator finally arrived and they stepped on.

Just as he pushed the button for the main floor she said, "You're good-looking."

Stretch managed a shadow of a smile.

"You want to come back to my place? Want to fuck?"

He was struck dumb past the sixth and the fifth floors.

"I mean, I've just got the hots today and you look good. That's what I was going down for anyway." She smiled brightly. "Don't worry, I don't have anything catching—except the urge. C'mon, I'm great."

At any other moment he might have been tempted to say yes. Instead he said, "Uh . . . I've got someone waiting for this wire."

"Seven sixteen. Give him the wire and come on up." She moved close.

"I . . . I really can't." It all seemed unreal. Was she stoned? Was he going completely off his nut?

"Jesus," she said, backing off. "Forget it. I hate a reluctant lover."

"Well, you'll sure find one who's not." The elevator bumped to a stop and the doors opened. Stretch glanced out quickly. "God, I forgot—I have to take this to the basement. Another time."

"I doubt it," she said tartly, stepping out. "Too bad."

At the basement, Stretch got out and leaned against the wall to reorganize his mind. Maybe it was his Midwestern upbringing, maybe it was California, maybe it was a generation gap, maybe it was this job. Whatever it was, he didn't feel ready to deal so bluntly with either his sex or his involvement with crime. After a moment, he went to reinspect the circuit-breaker system, but one look at it and all of the pressures overwhelmed him. He decided to take a coffee break to think things through more clearly.

At the lobby, he stood for a second, looking down the scaffold-cluttered hallway. All of a sudden a man making notes on a clipboard came into focus. At the end of the hallway was Tom Farley!

Every fiber of Jackson's body galvanized into action. He slipped out of the investigator's line of vision and quickly headed for his car. Distance, he thought as he pulled the Mustang out of its parking space. Distance. He wanted distance between himself and the whole Normandy nightmare. At the farthest possible point around the lake, he pulled into Merritt's Bakery and Restaurant and chose a booth with a view of any approaching cars.

The fear that Farley might have seen him kept recurring, but, just as important, he wanted to know what in God's name Farley was doing on *his* job when he himself had only gotten the word from Sievers two days before. Was he being framed—or set up? Not possible. Was it pure coincidence? Not probable. Was there something he hadn't been told? Probable. Was Farley catching up to him? Blank. Stretch remembered what Eddie had said about the telephone triggering device: Farley got so close Eddie could hear him breathe every time he dialed. So Eddie had quit using the telephone trigger. But here the son-of-a-bitch was wandering around Stretch's building *before* it was even set it up.

He went back to the possibility that he was being framed. Of the people he had seen around Sievers, he alone was completely vulnerable. He was single and a drifter. The word made him cringe inside, but he had to admit he had drifted into town and into arson. He had no business, no close friends, not even any legal, official existence. And, God knows, he had no connections—none with greater clout than Benny, the fence. Stretch certainly would not want to be in a life-or-death struggle with only Benny to use as leverage. However, no matter how defenseless he might be, Stretch could not imagine why Frank would set him up. Sievers, in fact, now needed him for the Calhoun jobs as well as for his own and the union's. It ran vividly but quickly in and out of his thoughts that Frank might have found a cheaper torch, like whoever serviced the Calhoun/Whitlock group for twenty-five hundred a light. But both Calhoun and Whitlock had conceded that their man was not as competent as Stretch. No, he concluded, a setup is probably out—but what the hell is in?

Stretch could make neither heads nor tails of the questions. In the end he decided to call the source of all of the questions. "Frank? Hi. Frank," he asked from the restaurant's pay phone, "what the hell is going on?"

"What do you mean?"

"I mean there's an arson investigator named Tom Farley who's already casing the place. *How* does he know and *what* does he know?"

"Don't worry, Stretch. He got there because he was assigned one of the Vada cases. I don't know who he is and I don't care. Some insurance jerk. Jim Vada already told me about him and he's being taken care of. He'll be out of your way quick."

"What do you mean, he's being 'taken care of'?"

"What's it to you? It's what I said."

"He's the best there is, Frank."

"You going nutty on me? Jackson?"

It was no use yelling—Jackson was slowly replacing the receiver, horrified by the idea that Tom might "end up stuffed in the garbage can" as Frank had so vividly put it only a few days before.

Stretch paid for the coffee and left. Instead of calling it a day and heading back to San Francisco as he had intended to do, he turned back north on the street that ringed the lake and then into the park on the east side of the narrow finger. He got out of the car and sat on the bank, staring at the Normandy. Only fifty yards of water, plus the little strip of green and Lakeside Drive, separated him from the building on the opposite side, from the man who was after his skin—and from several hundred potential fire victims.

Children's voices came from the playground. Strollers wandered through the maze of trees. Pelicans and ducks glided on the water, waddled on the island, but all of that quite escaped Stretch's notice. His eyes were fixed on the structural features of the L-shaped, seven-story, Tudor-style apartment house across the lake. He estimated that about two hundred residents would be sleeping there at the time of the fire. There was no way out. If the Normandy was going to burn, Stretch couldn't help feeling the burden of responsibility. He needed a miracle: either find a way to stop Sievers or find a way to burn that building without killing anyone!

He flashed on the pretty, California-style horny girl. Wackos have as much right to live as anyone else. Suddenly he felt very protective toward her and for just a second, he wondered who, in fact, was wacko—the girl with the hots, Sievers, Whitlock, Calhoun . . . or Stretch Jackson. Where the hell, he asked himself, has sanity gone?

In the absence of an answer to the unanswerable Stretch returned to the problem at hand. Stop Sievers, he repeated, or burn it without killing anyone. But how?

25

Tom plunged ahead with his investigation. If all went well with Vic Whitlock, the Fire Insurers would pay his fee. If they didn't, he would bump up his bill on the open contractors' files, pick up a few thousand extra that way and eat the remaining loss. He was far too involved to back out over money. For months he had been closing the noose around some unknown neck, and since the firemen's deaths he had been going flat out, with little sleep. He was used to the chase and knew the sensation of becoming glued to the tracks of his prey. True, sometimes his quarry, like the telephone-trigger torch, vanished into thin air. Just as often the ones he caught got off or got out of jail so fast that it hardly seemed worth it. But not this one, his bones said, not this one. Farley was determined to make this torch pay double—and to nail it down, he moved ahead full tilt. Neither Pat nor Charlene were spared the overtime. This was a race against a killer.

Tom had started diagramming the Normandy. He roughed in the circuitry for the "toaster" and spent the night analyzing what countermeasures could be taken. Pat was doing records checks. Charlene wrestled with all of the open files he was neglecting.

Vada's private office had become familiar territory. He had already gotten some sound information about the Normandy project from Vada. Tom was back once again, dredging up bits and pieces, doing his best to seem casual. This time, his goal was different. He and Vada talked for fifteen minutes on everything and nothing. Vada seemed relaxed. Tom decided the time was right.

"I have to do the final report. I've got to admit, it's all dead ends, but when I was going through my notes on your first fire, I noticed you mentioned some union organizer named Mel Ferrone who threatened you." Nothing changed, but he sensed a minor tightening in Vada's body. "Ever hear from Ferrone again?"

"Why, no. You know, that was months ago. I get so many dodos through here, I hardly remember one from the next."

"Remember what union he was with?"

The contractor raised his eyebrows. "Mel Ferrone?" He checked through the Rolodex on his desk. "Nope. Just one more faceless turkey, Tom. I don't remember and I didn't even note it down."

"Are you a closed shop?"

"Sure. All union and no sweat."

"Let me get my pen out. I'd like a list of your men's unions. You wouldn't mind, would you?"

"How could anyone object to that?" It was said lightly, but very dark clouds were forming in Vada's mind. He didn't dare go back to Sievers again about backing out, but the risks were getting out of hand.

Farley headed back to his office, plotting his next step. Interesting, he mused. He had lied to Vada. Mel Ferrone was never in his notes and Vada had never mentioned him. So Vada had just made a slip—he'd admitted that he'd been threatened by the man and then, all of a sudden, had clammed up. Tom would have loved two minutes alone with Vada's telephone index. He was positive Mel Ferrone was listed. Jim Vada was hardly the kind to forget who had menaced his business. Somewhere in the course of the various interviews with each contractor, Farley had dropped the name of each union's chief organizer. Only Vada had slipped, only Ferrone had registered. It was not a dramatic breakthrough in the case, but it was another arrow pointing down a narrowing path. Since only two unions were involved with every burned-out contractor, Tom was down to the short list—but until the case was distilled to one man, one match, and evidence tight enough to make an arrest, nothing would stop the Normandy from becoming a flame-shrouded coffin.

* * *

Stretch had turned the "toaster principle" every which way. Burning a building the size of the Normandy posed a set of problems like a Chinese puzzle, and Stretch was forced to face the limitations of his experience. No angle seemed satisfactory, and the chances of killing tenants seemed overwhelming. On another level, the threat Sievers had made concerning Farley left him almost as upset as the danger to the Normandy's residents. He wanted to outwit Farley, not have him dumbly eliminated by a pair of thugs.

Stretch began to run scenarios through his mind—endless, imaginary conversations with his employer. Okay, I always said I could be a great salesman, he told himself. What I have to do is unsell Frank on the whole idea. There has to be a button in him somewhere. Some argument has to make him wake up.

Stretch was neither a weakling nor a coward. He had seen some royal battles fist-to-nose. If it came down to a good thrashing by Henry and Ben, he was ready to take his chances. But he knew Sievers wasn't kidding. Not only was he looking at a garbage can, so was his family in West Alton. He desperately sought the button. Frank had to have one—everyone did.

Stretch dreamed of a perfect sales pitch to Sievers, scrapped it, dreamed again. Button, button, who's got the button? Finally, in despair, he decided that the most promising approach seemed to be the difference between the charge of arson versus that of murder and the evidence necessary for each. A cool, relaxed conversation. Don't get his back up. Sell him, for God's sake!

* * *

Frank did not move to the couch. He sat behind the desk, relaxed and listening thoughtfully. Stretch's hopes rose as he delivered his concluding argument. He felt he might have made a sale.

"You've lived a very sheltered life, Stretch." Frank's tone was almost paternal. "You aren't up on the history of life in the modern American city. Now, you're dead right about the evidentiary differences. I hope you don't think I didn't know that. What you're insufficiently informed on is relationships. Who owes who what in a town like this? Like, who's on your back? I don't have anyone—at least, no one's left—who's after my job. A rival's one way to get shot down. A Jimmy Hoffa or a Yablonski—now, they had guys gunning for them inside the organization. I don't have that. If I did, maybe someone out for my hide would feed a cop or a D.A. inside evidence. But I don't.

"Now there's another possibility. Say some cop or even someone in the D.A.'s office got the funny idea that I was somehow involved in burning the Normandy. Pretty unimaginable, even if someone gets hurt, but just suppose. I'd have thought you realized by now the kind of company I keep. You know what kind of leverage I've got on George? And on my big-shot attorney who's thinking of running for Congress? There are guys from the legislature to City Hall to the police force who I could have out looking for jobs as garbage collectors tomorrow if I wanted to lean on them. I mean, I've got long arms around here. I support a lot of people—the right people. They *owe* me—and they know it.

"Some flunky fire investigator or city detective can scratch his head all he wants, but no one is going to dare to actually accuse Frank Sievers of anything if they don't have a perfect, airtight case. And how are they going to get that, Stretch? You aren't going to tell them. I'm not going to tell them. And they won't get any airtight case, will they? 'Cause Stretch Jackson may leave a *suspicion* of arson behind if worse comes to worst, but he doesn't leave any tracks. Not even for the rules of evidence on a murder charge. If they don't find me with a match in my hand, there's no one around who'd dare open his mouth. *No one!*"

Not with anger, but with an icy, verbal bullwhip, Sievers leaned forward. "Now, you bring that subject up one more time and you are going to go for a swim in the bay wearing cement shoelaces. Let me explain you a fact of life. You are very, very good. I trust you. That is why you and only you are going to do this job. I got connections in every city and town in the country. You back out or you screw this up, I will find you and everyone connected with you and make you all *permanently* sorry. Do you hear me?"

"I hear you, Frank." A taste of acid rose in his mouth. No sale.

"*No one crosses me!* You bust your brain. You find a way not to hurt people. Then, hurt or not hurt, you leave no trace, no clue, no pointed fingers. I'll take care of anything else—*if* there is anything else. And there won't be. Once and for all, is that clear?"

"It's clear, but it's a goddamn dangerous game," Stretch said with the remnants of his defiance.

"Sure it is! You damn well ought to know you don't get to the top if you're not ready to play some dangerous games. This ain't no fucking lily pond." Sievers stood up with finality. "And you're in the wallow as much as me, Jackson."

* * *

The next day the president of Amalgamated Building Trades had another visitor who needed convincing. Theirs was a friendly, businesslike discussion without any hint of threat or menace. After being almost excessively cooperative, Frank leaned toward his caller and said with earnest sincerity, "Look, Mr. Farley. Anything that threatens the building trades threatens us. We live and grow on our good reputation. Everything here is an open book. That's the way we run this union and I, personally, won't have it any other way. If there's anything at all we can do to help . . ."

"The information you've already given here is very useful." Tom rose to go. "Say, how's Mel Ferrone? Is he still your chief organizer?"

"Know Mel?"

"We met. Got a good mutual friend."

"Mel's fine, still top dog on our organizing side. Sure is. I'll tell him you said hello."

"He may or may not remember me by name, but please do." Farley had what he came for. He extended his hand. "Thanks for the offer. If I need you, I'll call."

Frank gave his smile all the warmth that was in him. "You feel free to do that." In his book Tom Farley's standing had risen. His business card said: *Private investigator—Specialties: Arson—Fire Causes; Insurance Fraud.* That meant he would be less in the docile class than a straight insurance man, but nowhere near as tough as a police detective or a P.I. who handled *real* criminal cases. Sievers had found out that Farley had an excellent reputation, but bright and bulldog tenacious did not make him "tough"—not in Sievers's league. Besides, it was clear from the interview that Farley was only on a fishing expedition and had undoubtedly left disappointed. A private detective was not likely to risk much of his hide on any given case, especially not for the lousy fee some insurance company was going to pay on a suspected arson file or two. Nonetheless—

As soon as the door closed, Frank picked up the receiver and dialed a mobile phone.

The elevator floated down from Amalgamated-Executive and Reception past an impressive number of floors: General Administration, Accounting, Pension/Health, Membership. While Tom's body descended, his spirits rose. He had played a long shot. If it really was a union involved with the construction fires, if it really was a matter of sweetheart contracts, and if it really was one of the two unions he suspected, then who would be more likely to contact the builders than the union's head organizer? Mel Ferrone was evidently still there and active. As Tom pondered that and a few other bits of information Sievers had inadvertently dropped he felt the case building.

But on the way to Oakland his thoughts hit another snag. His interview with the head of the other suspect union had gotten him nowhere. There was still nothing that ruled them out for certain, and no concrete evidence that definitely put the finger on Amalgamated. Farley's elation tarnished a bit. Intuition, intuition. Where are the hard facts hiding? How could he find the handle to start unraveling real evidence, the kind he could present to the D.A.'s office?

But first things first. His priority, of course, was to stop the Normandy from actually burning. Saving lives was at the top of the list, catching the toaster man in the act was a close second, and then tying him tight to his employer was third. Tom heaved a sigh of frustration.

He eased the Pontiac into a parking space at the Normandy. Before he could stop the fire and catch his man, he had to have the method of the burn figured out to absolute perfection. Working out the electrical methods of the toaster in a building of this size was proving to be a major headache. Tom grabbed his clipboard and headed again for the apartments. He needed a diagram of all the circuits in the building.

In the lobby Tom stopped a workman. "How you guys coming along?" he asked.

"On schedule. We finish here tomorrow. Second floor gets moved out—that takes two days. Then we set up. What floor you on?"

Tom ducked the question and headed for the electrical mains in the basement. He studied the control box, then started following the main cables. Like a trolley car on its tracks, his eyes were glued to the heavy overhead wires. One set veered into the furnace room. He followed the cable around the corner and walked straight into a hard blow on the chest. His clipboard clattered to the floor. His arms were wrenched up behind his back. Pain stabbed through both shoulder sockets.

Henry held him immobile. "What the hell you doing wandering around the basement, chum?"

Ben frisked his victim. "He's got nothing."

"We're security," Henry snarled. "Guys wander around, no business here, get arms and legs busted."

"I'm an insurance inspector, you idiot!"

Henry twisted, damaging Tom's elbow a little more. "How'd we know that?" he growled.

"Let go, you son-of-a-bitch, and I'll show you I.D."

"I.D. my ass," Ben snorted.

"And you'd better have yours!" Tom shot back.

Ben slammed his ham hand around Tom's neck. "Shall I do this creep?" he asked Henry.

Henry shrugged his shoulders. "Maybe he's legit. Too many junkies and rapists in this area to take chances, buddy." He twisted Tom's arms again to emphasize his point. "We usually shoot first, ask later. You get what I mean?" He looked at Ben. "Go on, show him your badge."

Ben flashed a phony security card. Henry let go and pushed Tom away with a shove.

"We catch you in here again and you won't walk out. That's a promise you'd better remember."

"What about my work?" The picture was quite clear.

"You got no work in this building without clearance from the chief. He tells us. We'll know if you get it. Now clear out!"

"Who's the chief?"

Henry blinked a moment. "Huh," he grunted. "You don't know that, really means you got no business here. Get your clipboard and git."

Tom obeyed. It was a new ball game.

* * *

Back at the office Henry and Ben were pleased with themselves. "Scared shit out of that peanut from the insurance," Henry said, smiling.

"Yeah," Ben added gleefully. "He got the message loud and clear."

"What was he doing?" Frank asked.

"Checking something with the electricity," Henry replied. "But don't worry—he won't be back."

"You guys check the building from time to time just in case. If he comes back, give him whatever's necessary for twenty-one days' bedrest."

Henry looked at Ben and grinned. "Two broke legs. Four to six weeks guaranteed minimum." The prospect apparently made him wish the "peanut" would come back.

* * *

Tom left the Normandy and headed for Station House 1, where he found Jonah in the back lot. "Jesus, what's that?" Tom asked.

Beaming, Jonah pointed skyward. "Ain't she a bitch!" he exclaimed proudly. "We're just taking delivery. Salesman's running her through the ropes for us. Emergency One makes it in someplace called Ocala, Florida. She doesn't miss a trick. A hundred-three-foot snorkel with an articulated three-section boom, aluminum cherry-picker cage on top with the works: asbestos cover, oxygen for two operators up in the basket, a thousand GPM jet/fog monitor, heavy spotlights. If it gets too hot, you can run the whole thing from down below like a tele-squirt. God, she's beautiful!"

Sighting up the boom to the basket suspended a hundred feet above them, Farley agreed. It was an impressive sight— slick, new, powerful, the latest in firefighting technology, available to anybody with one-third of a million dollars to spend. No doubt there had been a lot of bitching at the Oakland budget department. The unit was more than a high-rise hose, however; it was a major improvement for the city's rescue operation prospects.

A sober look came over Jonah's face. "Wouldn't Mannie have loved to captain that?"

Tom nodded. "She may get baptized sooner than I like to think—on a seven-story building. I just got part of the hunch confirmed, Jonah. The Normandy *is* scheduled to be burned.

All I don't know is when and who'll do it." He described the nasty encounter in the Normandy's basement. "They're ready to play rough," Tom said. "Of course, anyone willing to burn that building has to be cold-blooded. They don't give a damn about murder. I'll do my best to see to it that the place never gets lit, but, God help us, *if* I can't stop it, your job is even tougher. You have to have a perfect rescue plan set up and ready to roll instantly."

Jonah scratched his head. "Depends on what floor they're working when they do it. People on the first floor can usually get out. The second or third will have the scaffold. The bitch is everyone above. With that instant flame business, it means every hall, living room, and bedroom will break out simultaneously. Hardly leaves us time to move."

"Could you form a special task force for this job?"

"I'll talk to the Chief. I've been by the building a couple of times and I have a plan pretty well set. Rescue will have priority. The department has nine ladders. This new snorkel makes ten. We can ring the building with them and spray water at the same time, but . . ." He put his hand to his forehead. "Jesus! Every time I think about getting over two hundred people out of a building in a few minutes at three in the morning I get the shakes. Tom, can you meet me here at eight tomorrow morning?"

"Sure."

"I've got an idea. See you then."

* * *

Reaching for his office doorknob sent jabs of pain up and down Tom's arm. The thug really knew his job—the reminder would last. As he started to slip off his jacket, all four joints made him audibly wince.

"What's the matter, you getting old and creaky?" Charlene asked.

"Uh . . ." He didn't know if he should tell her or not. "I just had a demonstration of joint-stretchers. Gave me premature arthritis."

"Now exactly what does that mean?"

So he told her.

Charlene went pale. "You haven't had a Mafia-style case since that bottling plant last year." She stood up nervously. "Tom . . . this thing is getting awfully rough. Will you do me a favor and be careful?"

"Come on—don't mother me."

"I am not *mothering* you."

Tom gave her a look that said, What is it then?

Charlene hesitated. She lowered her voice almost to shyness. "I'm *caring* for you." She walked over to him and put her hand on what she knew was an aching shoulder. "You haven't let anyone be concerned about you for so long, maybe you've forgotten what it is."

A distant, cloistered bell sounded in him. True, it said, too true. He felt Charlene's warm hand touch his shoulder. So it wasn't purely his imagination, those flashes of wanting her. There was an action—or reaction—that came from her. It made no difference now whether he had been drawn to some subtle signals that she'd sent or if she was responding to his feelings. That the possibility had lain dormant (or had it really?) for all these years made no difference either.

"You're right," Tom said. "Maybe I have forgotten." He cupped his hand around her lower ribs, just where they curve from front to back, leaned forward, and breathed in the smell of woman face, woman lips, then touched her mouth gently with his own. Charlene responded. Their hands slipped to each other's backs and held—tightly held the fine cloth that separated flesh from flesh.

Tom stepped closer, felt the fit from breast to thighs. Charlene *was* warm and wonderful, given half a chance. He wanted to make love with her, to close the office, forget the Normandy, and take Charlene to *Sapphire II*. He felt they should shake off the chains to everyday and lose themselves. As quickly as the feeling came, he tempered it. No—that would have to wait. He reluctantly drew his head back, separating their lips. For the first time he wished he wasn't so goddamned responsible! Perhaps if he were still in his twenties he would not have the conflict—although, in the style of youth, he was still unsure of what was happening to his emotions, of how he had lost his grip on them.

"What are we getting into?" he asked gently.

Charlene was melted. "I don't know, Tom," was the soft reply. "I don't know, but it's nice."

"Can it wait?"

"Does it have to?"

"Mm-hmm."

"Then it'll wait."

Tom went straight to his office, fearing one more word would break his resolve.

* * *

Jonah introduced the young man with the funny face and huge mustache as "Lieutenant Roger Gitter, locally known as Buzz. You show him a dime and he'll put a helicopter down on it."

"That's about what we've got, Buzz." Tom shook hands.

The three men climbed into the chopper and rose from the Alameda Naval Air Station into Oakland's bright morning sky. "Want to see the scenery while you're at it?" Buzz yelled over the noise.

"Damn right!" Jonah yelled back. He did not get a trip like this every day.

The crinkled coastline stretched away as they gained altitude. Tom spotted the docks where the *Sapphire* and *Sapphire II* were moored. He could see all the way across the brilliant waters to where his office was in San Francisco. Brooks Island, Treasure Island, Angel Island were all in view. The bridges, streaming with traffic, to the east the mountains, cloaked in the peace of protected parks—all the grandeur of nature and the hustle of urbanism lay below.

Finally Buzz whirled the bird toward Lake Merritt and the Normandy. "It's got the usual problems, those tanks and antennas. Choppers hate them."

"We'll tell the tenants it's part of the remodeling job. Get the antennas moved in a couple of hours with a couple of off-duty firemen."

"Yeah. You'll have to do something to relocate that one water tower, too. Fortunately, it's a little one."

"Okay if we cluster the antennas in the corner?" Tom asked.

Buzz nodded. "See the football field at Laney College? I could drop evacuees off there. No, wait. The empty lot over there would save about two minutes a trip. You mark it, Jonah, and we'll check it from the ground."

They dropped back to the Alameda Naval Air Station, which was only a few minutes away, and climbed out to the shock of silence.

"Buzz, you tell the captain that we appreciate all this. I'll have the last of the details worked out by lunch and come back and see him." Jonah turned to Tom. "The captain is ready and eager to pitch in, if they're needed. Buzz is figuring on a two- or three-copter relay."

The pilot looked at both men. "Can't you just arrest somebody and stop this?"

Tom answered, "If you really want to look like the village idiot, try accusing some respectable bigwig on the mere suspicion of conspiring to commit arson. If you don't lose your P.I. license, at the least you won't find anyone in the business who'll talk to you for a year or so. No, I've got no factual proof. I hope we don't need you, because if that place goes, it'll be a massacre. I think, pray God, we're going to nail him, but we have to have a backup rescue plan, just in case."

On the way back to the station in Tom's Pontiac, Jonah reviewed the details of his other arrangements. "Starting tonight, I've got volunteers lined up. Four men in their own personal cars. They'll be walkie-talkie connected and parked about a block away from each approach. They go on at midnight and stick till five-thirty. No tan Pinto wagon will get within a block of the place—OUX 829 or otherwise, just in case he changes plates. They'll be delighted to grab him. Is this guy likely to carry a gun?"

"I've never seen a pro torch who did, but this character's not in the mold so far as anything else goes either. You'd better tell your men to notify me or the police before doing anything themselves. We'll have time. I'll be at the station late at night from now on. I don't want to see any of your men stop a slug. Anyway, we want him to get into the building and under way— that way he's caught in the act. If we get an open-and-shut case, *that* will make him sing about where his checks come from!"

"The guys will be disappointed if they can't tackle him themselves, but they'll understand."

"I'd like to know where that damn car is! Lieutenant Boskowitch sent out a general Bay Area pickup on it, but so far no results."

"Maybe he stashes it in his garage."

"Maybe. I don't like to think about that as a possibility. Let's hope he goes shopping with it every day in some very public mall."

"You know he wouldn't do that," Jonah said unhappily. "He's a smart son-of-a-bitch."

Farley shot an odd look at his passenger. That was his line. "Well, he's about to run out of rope, smart or not." He gritted his teeth, momentarily shot through with doubts.

* * *

A red ball with white stars came bouncing down the stairwell. Stretch stopped it and froze. He did not want to be clearly identified by *anyone* on his trips to the Normandy. He looked up tensely. The face of a six-year-old boy came into view, peering down through the railings.

"Hey, mister. Bring up my ball?"

"Yeah, sure. You all by yourself?"

"Yep. Jeannie wouldn't play. And I have a cold, so Mom won't let me go out to the playground. So I'm just me. Want to play?"

Stretch came upstairs and handed the ball to the boy and moved on upward. "Well, I've got work to do. . . ."

"You an electrician?" The boy trailed doggedly behind.

"No."

"Plasterman?"

"No, why?"

"They won't play either."

"They're fixing up your building."

"You fixing the building, too?"

Stretch turned and looked at the towheaded child. "Well . . . well, I guess. Sort of. Where do you live?"

"Seven fourteen."

Panic clawed at him. He did not want to see *them*, talk to *them*. "Right . . . right up top?" he stuttered.

"Yep."

At the seventh floor he was about to unstick himself from the boy when the landing door opened and an attractive young woman rushed onto the landing with a bag of garbage.

"Hi, Dee—he's fixing the building."

"Oh?" She hoisted the bag to the garbage chute.

"Want to play?"

"I can't, Wayne. My boyfriend's coming by."

Stretch turned and bolted down the stairs, exited on the fifth floor, and called it quits. Maybe he could deal with it the next morning. Why did the boy have to have his dead brother's name? A surge of nausea swept through him.

* * *

Eddie Barker was in the middle of organizing a major job in Atlanta, but he could not turn down the request. He took the next plane out—twenty-four hours would not make that much difference.

On the road from the airport to the Normandy, Stretch explained the toaster principle.

"Holy Christ, Stretch! That's got to be the greatest advance in arson since they invented safety matches!"

"That's why I asked you to come. I need someone to bounce ideas off of."

"Start bouncing, cowboy."

At that very moment, Tom and Jonah were on the same subject, but while eating sandwiches in the station house mess hall. Tom had finally figured it all out. Drawings and diagrams were spread on the table in front of them.

"Before I forget it," Jonah said, "Bill Holland, my contact at the city engineer's department, hasn't yet had a chance to check the roof for bearing the chopper's weight. He promised to do it tomorrow. Want to pass the ketchup? Where were we?"

"Electrically, it looks like a complex unit, but this guy's not going to take risks he doesn't need. He just wants to get the whole building involved. The obvious toaster trick would be to not only put a bypass on the mains, but the subs too." He pointed to parts of the diagram. "Here . . . here . . . and here."

"How much time would that take?"

"Well, it's not so much the time of each operation, but these would make him shut down the juice in each section of the building. I've practiced till I'm pretty expert. I can do what's necessary in each place in about two and a half minutes."

Jonah whistled. "That's not much."

"No, but it's still a total of ten minutes of people's lights being off. That's risky even at three in the meaning."

In the Normandy basement an identical conversation was taking place between the two arsonists.

Tom continued. "So I figured, if he skips the subs, in two, three minutes he can do just this one main."

"But then he doesn't have the fire spread."

"I don't need it spread," Stretch was saying to Eddie. "I only need it where I need it. This set of breakers controls all the hallways."

Eddie got the idea. "That means all the outlets . . ."

"Switches and lights," Stretch finished.

Tom was adding, "Now, he couples on the elevator shafts here."

"That means we can't get in to fight the fire. The bastard has all of the air shafts involved." Jonah looked up. "Tom, that'll fill the morgue."

"It could, but it won't. He's making another mistake like the Quonset. He's using a great idea on the wrong situation. Because what he doesn't know is that *we* know. He's got to come *right there*." Tom jabbed his index finger at the building plan. "When we finish these sandwiches, I'm going to see Boskowitch and guess who else is going to be *right there*? Cops, that's who! If he gets past your guys, which isn't probable, he's got a two-man welcoming committee— complete with guns, badges, and pretty blue uniforms. Nobody's going to the morgue, and one cold-blooded, smart-ass torch is going straight to jail. We can't let up on any of it, including evacuation plans, but I'm damned if I see how we can miss him."

Stretch turned and said to Eddie, "Come on, let's get out of this basement. It gives me the creeps."

They headed upstairs.

"The trouble with this plan," Stretch continued, "is that firemen can't get in to fight the fire because all the hallways are involved. And people can't get out either."

Eddie glanced sideways at his protégé. "You said it."

"So I've got another plan I want to try out on you."

Eddie stopped, face to face with Stretch. "So you *are* the guy I thought you were!"

An embarrassed grin spread across Stretch's face. "Yeah. I couldn't fry all these folks, Eddie."

A beam the size of Texas spread across the cowboy's face. "Technically it would have been a perfect touch-off. Perfect!" He wagged his head, slapped his buddy's back, and moved on. "Man, you sure had me worried for a minute. You're one smart son-of-a-bitch, Jackson." He could not have been more proud if he had figured it out himself. "Boy, you have made it to the top!"

"I still need you, creepo. Now you've got to tell me if this other plan will work. It's a bit weird, and I can't take any chances."

* * *

In midafternoon Tom was recounting the day's activities to his father and Charlene. "When I finished explaining it all to Lieutenant Boskowitch, this jerk desk sergeant pipes up, snottylike: 'All that on your femi-nine intuition, dearie.' I could have slugged him. He thought he was working Polk Street. Anyway, we went through it all again with the captain. Boskowitch was on my side. They'll give us two men in the basement from one to five every night, hooked by radio—one to the cop shop, one to the dispatcher at Station One. The four firemen in their cars will be hooked to the two police-men to warn them when the Pinto comes. It looks foolproof to me."

"Tom," his father said, "I hardly ever give you orders any-more, but I'm giving you one now. You got that thirty-eight Chiefs Special with the two-inch barrel. Wear it! I know your arguments, but I'm *telling* you—*wear it*! And if I was you, I'd put a second one in an ankle holster. But mule-headed like you are, if you just wear one, put it up top."

Charlene looked grateful. "Thanks, Pat."

Tom grinned at her. "You put him up to this?"

"She did not! My common sense did. Now use some of your own."

"Okay, Pop—orders are orders." He sighed in resignation. He hated carrying firearms. They're for the phony private eyes on television, he would insist—in real life it just begs for trou-ble, except in rare emergencies. He shrugged his shoulders. Maybe this was a real emergency.

* * *

Stretch and Eddie had returned to the concrete nightmare Stretch called home. "Some spread!" was Eddie's reaction to the place, but by now Stretch knew better. They talked by the pool.

The sun was setting as they went out the door to head back to the airport. Eddie refused to stay over. "If I go both ways in one day, I figure I won't even have jet lag."

Stretch paused at the threshold. "Remember something you said to me? 'It's kind of a secret, lonely life.' Well, it's et me up."

"Yeah, I can tell. That's the second time you've said it. Why don't you come to New York? At least you'd have me to talk to. I could even find you work."

"Naw, I think I'd hate the place. But I want you to know I appreciate your flying all the way out here for me—I really do."

26

The room was dark—not pitch black, but cast in charcoal shades, with only a hint of light filtering in from the city. The silence was absolute. The window was open, and from time to time a curtain trembled. Stretch was seated in a chair, black on black, like a Reinhardt canvas, waiting, silent as the room itself.

He had entered by the open window before midnight, done what he had planned, and finally had installed himself in the chair to wait. Midnight passed, then one. He was not worried. At two o'clock he became alert.

Soon after, a key clicked into the lock. The tumblers turned—once, twice. A silhouette passed through the entrance, then closed the door. Karen fumbled slightly for the switch and flipped on the light. Her fright came out half gasp, half scream.

"I thought you were never going to get back," Stretch said.

"Oh! Oh, my God!" She spun toward the voice. "You frightened me! What . . . what *is* all this? What are you doing—"

The living room was festooned with flowers—flowers hanging, flowers in baskets, flowers in vases, flowers everywhere.

"I had to see you, Karen, I just had to."

"You, you . . . Stretch Jackson, how did you get in here?" She was torn between anger, pleasure, and the remainder of her fright.

"By the window. Why'd you have to live on the second floor?" He got up.

"Too bad I'm not on the tenth! Now look—" She pointed to the door.

Stretch grinned. "I sure hope you haven't got hay fever."

"Listen—"

"Do you have any of that special bourbon left? It's okay, Karen," he soothed. "I only want to talk to you."

The gayness of the flowers, the tenderness of his voice, and the flamboyance of the gesture drained her anger. She took off her coat and dropped it over a chair. No one else in the world would have thought of it—or cared enough to have done this for her. She moved to open the cabinet with its lonesome bottle. No one had touched it since his last visit.

Karen handed him a glass. "Thanks for the flowers," she said grudgingly. She tucked her lovely legs under her and backed into a corner of the sofa, thoroughly unapproachable.

His eyes twinkled and drank her in. He carefully kept a respectable distance. "I really fell in love with you, you know. Hook, line, and sinker. I guess I never loved anything before— except a Chevy, maybe."

She couldn't help but smile. That was so West Alton. Involuntarily, her brown eyes sparkled.

"And all these months it's been getting worse . . . or better . . . or stronger. You know what I mean."

Karen nodded slightly—not to help him over the rough spot, but because she knew exactly what he meant and could not hide it.

"I thought making money was the answer to everything. I built myself a money machine, honed it, polished it. You get on that track and you can't quit, win or lose—even when you've found out that money's not enough and you hate the crowd at the casino. I've got *you* in my head." He was not so far away that he couldn't finger her long brown hair. "I always thought I'd fall for a blonde." His hand dropped to her shoulder, intimate, without menace.

All of the good feelings she had ever felt for him surged up around her heart. But apprehension still knotted the pit of her stomach. Karen really did not want to ask, but she had to. "Are you still lighting fires?"

"Yeah. That's why I'm here. The more I loved you, the less I loved fires—as well as money, I've decided I'll quit, Karen, if you'll give me a chance." He swallowed hard. There. It was all out on the table. He felt vulnerable—and scared. Scared because he had bared his feelings, and because she could rip them to pieces with a no.

The fear was mutual. Marie had nursed Karen back to health again. When she had recovered from sheer depression, there was only a dulled state of floating, like life in a deprivation tank. Not one good thing had happened in all these months except the recurrent, bittersweet remembrances of her moments with Stretch.

Karen turned her head and rested her lips on the back of the masculine hand lying gently on her shoulder. "The minute you quit, I'm ready."

At least he was not cut to ribbons. Stretch lightly squeezed her shoulder. "I don't know why I can't lie to you," he said with a sense of resignation. "I have one contract I can't get out of. It'll all be over in two weeks at most. Please," he pleaded. "Just see me. I need you, Karen."

No one had ever "needed" her before. What she wanted to do was hold him, ask him why and how and give him whatever she could, but the pain came back. She flushed with its recollection and set her jaw. "When it's over, Stretch."

"Karen. I need you . . . now."

"Karen Canfield. Litchfield. A principal named Sweeney. Remember?" she begged. "Remember me? Don't, Stretch." She was reduced to a whimper. "Please don't."

Stretch took a deep breath. Most of the battle was won. His fear subsided. "All right, Karen, but I promise you, I *am* getting out of it." He jumped up. "Whew, I was scared silly you'd flat out say no. Can't I have another short one before I go?"

The confession charmed her. The spell of her own fear was snapped. She got up and poured him another drink.

"Jesus, I hope you've got a watering can." He looked around at the flowers. "I almost killed myself getting half a nursery in here. The guy thought I'd gone berserk."

There was no way she could resist a light laugh. "He wasn't far off, was he?"

The combination of her innocent face and womanly body seduced him all over again. "Can I sneak into the Silver Doll and watch from a back table? Easy won't remember me."

"You do and I'll remind him," she said and laughed again.

"Well, can I at least phone you?"

"Can't you wait two weeks?"

"No."

"You're really impossible, you know."

"That's why I'm here! 'Love makes the impossible possible.' Walt Whitman. Or Shakespeare—or somebody."

"Stretch Jackson's more likely!"

"Can I?"

"Oh . . . Christ." The hunger in her took the edge off her resolution. "Oh . . . yes."

He swept her up with joy, swung her around, then stopped and kissed her—not seriously, not for long, but they both got a vibrant message.

"Sorry," he said, setting her down.

"You get out of here."

"Do I have to go by the window?" Actually, he felt as if he could leap out and land on his feet unhurt, or fly home, or walk across the San Francisco Bay to Alcatraz and back.

Instead Karen opened the door, pecked his cheek, and prodded him out. For the next hour he slowly cruised up and down Van Ness Avenue formulating his next surprise for her.

* * *

The firemen posted near the Normandy routinely got a two-thirty visit from Tom Farley every morning. He glided alongside a parked car, turned off his lights, and waved through his open window.

"What's up, Tom?" Bud Pyle inquired.

"Just checking. Any action?"

"Dead calm tonight." Bud picked up an ax handle from the seat. "But, man, are we ready for him. Dan Branch is on down Lakeside, Owen Pavitt's probably got his mustache twitching over on Seventeenth, and Les Black's fading natural-like into the night the next block over. We're all on our forty-eight off. I don't see how we can miss the bastard."

"I don't either. I'm going to check in with the two cops."

Tom pulled the Pontiac into an inconspicuous curbside parking space in front of the building. He didn't want to risk alerting his prey by using the regular parking lot. When he opened the basement fire door, he stopped, satisfied. The policemen were following instructions: no smoking, no conversation. They had made seats behind a pile of stored furniture. The view of the electrical mains was clear. The arsonist would proceed with his work and get caught red-handed and well into his act by a pair of men who had been completely concealed from view. It would be one of those rare and marvelous open-and-shut cases arson investigators dream about. Faced with murder charges on Rojas and Runyon, as well as arson on all of the other fires, the torch would surely be ready to turn state's witness in return for a reduced sentence. Then they could nail the brains behind, this operation. Anyway, that was Tom's scenario.

* * *

Late that morning. Bill Holland of the Oakland city engineer's office popped by the Normandy as he'd promised Jonah he would. The Normandy architecture had a facade that hid the fact that the building's roof was flat. There was easy interior access to the roof by stairs which came up to a covered landing at the corner where the two wings of the L-shaped building met. Immediately adjacent was a large, clear area where the helicopter could land if the small water tower were displaced.

There were several large, steamship-style, L-shaped attic ducts that stood four or five feet high, but they did not obstruct the clearing in the middle. From the top the roof seemed sturdy. Holland headed down to find the entries where he could get into the attic. Because these old buildings were built to last, he expected to find at least four-by-sixes on eighteen-inch centers.

The manager had told him where the two pull-down ladders to the attic were. When he got to the second one, Holland stopped short. The ladder was down. Now who the devil would be up in the attic? he wondered. "Hello," he called as he climbed up. "Hello. . . . Anybody up there?"

Stretch heard the first "Hello" and dropped flat into the dirty old asbestos insulation. He pressed himself down, invisible between the joists, far from the ladder.

Holland shined his light around, called out once more, and shrugged his shoulders. Must have been kids. Flashing his beam again, he made a quick check of the roof structure. He gave a grunt of satisfaction. Four-by-twelves on sixteen-inch centers, bridged and posted! Ah, for the old days. It warmed the cockles of a building inspector's heart.

Unseen by Holland, Stretch peered above a joist, following the inspector's movements. The flashlight played around the space once more, then lit the way back down the ladder. Orderly, as engineers are, Holland pushed the ladder up and the scuttlehole automatically closed behind it with the sharp bang of the lock snapping shut.

Stretch felt a shiver of fear. He was sealed in the attic and knew of no other way out. He didn't dare move for a moment. In addition to the problem of getting out, other questions boomed into mind. Who was that? Why was he inspecting the roof? Stretch got up and brushed the filth off himself, then nervously followed his own little tunnel of light to where the intruder had been. He hesitated by the door. It could be a trap. Someone—or several people—could be waiting by the exit, waiting to see if he had actually been up there.

Stretch dropped to his hands and knees and gave the lock a careful inspection. With an almost physical feeling of relief he realized that he *could* get out with no great problem. If some designer had not anticipated such a predicament, he would have been forced to rouse the seventh-floor tenants—who might well have called the police when they heard him banging in the attic. God knows where all of that could have led.

He decided to determine what the man had been doing. But when he looked where the stranger had looked, there was no particular significance—no meaning or menace so far as Stretch could tell. He assumed the visit had something to do with the remodeling—a building inspector, perhaps. Stretch went on about his business. It was fully forty minutes later when he pulled the latch, looked out furtively, and sneaked away.

Stretch saw the black-and-white Pontiac as he wheeled his Mustang out of the Normandy's parking lot, but he didn't notice who the driver was. His pulse rate would have jumped if he had.

Tom was sitting in his car in the parking lot, lost in thought. He picked up the mobile phone to call Charlene, too preoccupied to observe either Stretch's Mustang or the inconspicuous black car that slowed by the lot's entrance and then parked in front of the apartment building.

The office phone rang. Charlene answered. "Tom Farley, Private Eye."

His mouth dropped open. "What the hell kind of a way is that to answer the phone?" He was dumbfounded.

His secretary giggled. "I knew it was you."

"How'd you know that?" he demanded, more than dubious.

"I don't know. I've just known every time you called lately. Intuition, maybe. Vibrations, telepathy? I almost know what you're going to say each time."

"Okay, if you're so smart, what was I going to say?"

"Going to bed at five thirty in the morning and getting up at noon is killing you. You were going to apologize for your baggy eyes and short temper and say you got short-stopped on the way in, so I should go on to lunch."

"Jesus! Well . . . forget the apology. I think I've been very nice to you. Going soft in my old age."

"Hmm."

"But do go on to lunch. I'm at the Normandy."

She didn't like that. "Whatever for?"

"Actually, I got up at eleven thirty and while singing in the shower it dawned on me that if our guy—"

"Yours. I don't like him."

He snorted. There was no stopping her this morning. "If *my* guy decides to put a bypass on the elevator sub-mains we'd have two points to watch. I need to check where they hook in to see if he needs to or not."

"Are you following Pat's orders?" Charlene asked soberly.

The Smith & Wesson felt all too obvious in its shoulder holster. "Yes, my dear," he said mockingly, "I'm following all instructions, fatherly and motherly."

"Has anybody ever told you you're a—"

"Go to lunch," he interrupted. "I'll see you after."

There was a pause. "Aren't you going to say anything nice to me?"

A tightening in his chest was partly confusion, partly unfamiliar emotion. Tom was no longer used to all of these feelings. After being bottled up for so many years, they would still have to wait for a few more weeks! "No, but if you'll promise never to answer the phone like that again, I'll try to make up for missing lunch with you. What if your wavelength was wrong and it had been some sourpuss like Vic Whitlock?"

Charlene gave him his messages, they chatted a minute, and then said good-bye. Tom jumped out of the car and strode light-footed toward the building. He smiled to himself, troubled but not unhappy with this unexpected twist in his life. Unfortunately, the sinister quality of the Normandy basement quickly destroyed his lighthearted mood. To work, he said to himself, and began tracing the wiring from the elevators to the mains.

"Stop right there, friend." A nasty little snubnosed revolver reinforced the order. Henry loomed up from behind a pile of boxes and stepped into the dim light. Beside him, Ben held a three-foot length of metal scaffold pipe. "This thing makes very large holes," Henry snapped.

Adrenaline suddenly made Tom's mind as razor sharp as if he had tapped into electricity. "You fire that down here and fifty people would pile in to see what exploded."

For a split second Henry hesitated. "Smart, aren't you? Try again. The sound would never go through that fire door." He sneered, confidently. "Don't make me prove it, wise-ass." He moved the gun right against Farley's chest. "Just back up nice and flat against that wall. That's it. Now," he said to Ben, "didn't you say something to this guy about legs?"

"Broken legs?" Ben gloated.

"Yeah, something like that."

Henry stepped slightly aside so that Ben could take better aim. The revolver remained pointed at Farley's heart.

"Just hold still," Henry said in a poisonous growl. "This'll hurt a lot, but it won't leave you dead like the gun would."

Ben started to raise the pipe. Henry prodded Tom's ribs with the gun. "Move your legs out a couple more inches!" He looked down for an instant to check their distance from the wall.

Lightning struck right then. Tom's right hand flashed. His foot hooked out, up, returned. His left hand grabbed the rising pipe and pulled it forward, Ben with it. Tom—a Black Belt and T'ai Chi master—moved in an impossibly swift, powerful sequence.

Quick as thought, the switch was completely unexpected. The gun was suddenly jabbed against Ben's nose, just under his eye. It was still in Henry's hand, but that hand was doubled by Farley's. The trigger finger was Henry's, but his wrist nerve was semiparalyzed by Farley's right hand, which kept a viselike grip on a nerve pressure point.

"Pull it, you fuck! Go ahead, pull it!"

"Don't, Henry! Jesus!" Ben pleaded. Tom's left hand squeezed Ben's neck nerves, pushed his head against the gun's cold steel.

Tom's leather heel dug into Henry's instep, pressing, painful. "Slowly, now, buddy boy. You are not going to move if you don't want to smear your partner's brain around." He increased his weight on the instep. "You're going to very, very slowly transfer that trigger pressure from your finger to mine." Tom felt Henry's resistance. "Tough, huh?" He bounced on his heel. There was a cracking sound. Henry was hard as nails, but that made him jerk, tense. "Now? Or you want it powdered and permanent? Gently, goddammit! That's it. That's better."

With the gun firmly in his grasp, Tom also pulled out Ben's pistol and stepped back, a gun in each hand covering the two hulks. "Show me your ankles." They had no other weapons hidden. "I hate these secret meetings in the cellar, fellows," he mocked. "We'd better stop seeing each other like this."

"Next time, you'll never know what hit you," Ben said with sullen menace.

For a second, Tom had wondered if he could get the name of their boss out of them. Ben's threat was the answer. He wouldn't, unless he did things that were against his principles—not with this pair of brutes. They'd have only the phony I.D. and shut mouths that mark men in their business.

Anyway, he would see these two *and* their boss in a courtroom. "I doubt there'll be a next time—for your sake," he said. "You might really get hurt."

"You'll see, asshole," Ben snapped nastily.

Farley kept one gun on Henry, put the other in Ben's stomach, and leaned his heel on Ben's instep, grinding it in hard, pressing until an involuntary tear came from the hoodlum's eye. Tom backed off. "Now, stop crying and get out, scum!" For an instant he was tempted to add, "Say hello to Frank," to see what reactions he got, but he held his tongue. That might give *his* game away.

His training as a Green Beret, and having stayed in practice ever since, had paid off once again. He finished tracing wires and concluded that the torch would indeed do it all on the one set of armored cables.

Tom Farley was not bent on dying. He kept a hand on one of the guns in his pocket and decided he would step very carefully until this case was wrapped up.

* * *

A high threshold of pain was one of the important attributes of a man like Henry. He refused to see a doctor, even though he surely had, at least, a fracture of the central metatarsus. Limp he did, although he carefully minimized it when he went into the president's office to give his report. One tough man recognized the other. Frank knew the signs and poured them each a drink. They relaxed on the couch.

"Dammit, Henry, I don't like it," Sievers said.

"Frank, in the twelve years we been together, it's my first screw-up."

"No, I don't mean your getting foxed. That can happen. This whole Normandy business should have been a simple job and it's beginning to get out of hand." He studied his drink. "First Vada goes spooky, then Stretch starts acting like we're running the Salvation Army. Now this guy comes butting in. I don't mind the high stakes, but there are too many wild cards around."

"Why don't we take some of them out of the game?"

Frank shot Henry a look of interest, then got up and started pacing. "I'm not about to fold my hand, but maybe it's time to reduce the odds. I'm not much on putting my neck in a noose."

"Well, Frank, you name it. I'm going to make up for this." He pointed to this throbbing foot.

"Maybe you ought to see a doctor."

"I'd rather start by burying that P.I. son-of-a-bitch."

Frank smiled coldly. "Maybe that would be part of the doctor's prescription." He thought for a moment, then pulled out one of his business cards. On the back of it he wrote, "Marty Martin," then handed it to Henry.

27

Pickles watched Tom from a distance before curiosity got the better of him. He walked across the parking lot. "You sure must have a hot thing going, Tom, what with these crazy hours you've been keeping."

"Not exactly." Farley looked up from bending over the Pontiac's engine. "Just got a late-night case."

"Too bad," Pickles chuckled, his saltwater-taffy face crinkling. "Thought maybe it was a late-night dose. Why don't you take that machine into the garage? You been going over her every morning for days now. She won't start?"

"She'll start, all right. Just wants some pampering."

"Give her a little boot in the rear. That always gets 'em out of bed. Used to do it with my women and my boilers."

Tom slammed the hood down. "And look at you now. No women, no boilers. Times are changing. They don't build them like they used to. Engines have gotten delicate—and women, too." He opened the car door and winked. "Got to go with the times, Pickles. Treat them gentle."

"Holy bilge! Guy gets out of bed at eleven thirty in the morning and starts spouting philosophy. You sure that's an arson case you're working on, Tom Farley? Sounds like you're stoking up the fires of love!"

Tom's grin was the size of the steering wheel. He started the car and shot off to the office, leaving Pickles behind, more curious than ever.

* * *

It took five minutes of nudging and cajoling to get Karen to agree to "just go for a ride" to someplace mysterious. He swore he would bring her back immediately after she had seen something really special. Stretch promised it was important to both of them.

Loneliness was not her only reason for giving in. However reluctant the yes may have been, Stretch had that something that drew her like a moth to a flame. She recognized that part of it was sexual, but that came after the other click, after the seduction by Stretch's naiveté, honesty, and openness. She would long ago have taken back her violent reaction at the Buddha if the chance had arisen, but it had not until he climbed through her apartment window. She had meant what she said the night she walked out and still felt the same way about Stretch's torching, but she had also reproached herself a hundred times since for overreacting. Once she had left and entered the cab, it was too late to return. Karen did not even know Stretch's telephone number. If she had found it, she would have said she was sorry and tried to nurse him away from the terrible work he did. Instead she had lived on a hard diet of remorse and depression. Now she did not doubt for a second that he had done on his own what she would have helped him do. In a way, that seemed even better, for it proved his strength, his morality, and his concern for her. Hardly a minute passed when she was not thinking of his profile or flashing blue eyes. The months of separation did not seem wasted after all. She wondered how many relationships were broken and lost forever because someone went further than they meant to and never found the bridge back. Thank God, she repeated, thank God, he had returned.

San Francisco was awash with midday sunshine. On the pretext of having forgotten something, they detoured past Stretch's house. He wanted to demonstrate his affluence.

"It's gorgeous," Karen admitted, "but a little short on soul."

He could not restrain himself from giving her a hug. "Bless you," he whispered. "It took me months to realize it and you got it right away. We *are* on the same wavelength."

341

They drove across the Golden Gate Bridge to Mill Valley. In a couple of miles the temperature changed from Frisco comfortable to Bay heat. The convertible top went down. The Mustang peeled off miles through the pine forest, past the land of flaky chic that stretches from Mill Valley to Inverness. Stretch doubled back through the soft piney hills toward San Rafael. He wanted her to feel the country—so close to the Bay's millions, yet so remote. Her every reaction was in perfect sync with his. They were like the complementing parts of a fine-tuned engine, action-reaction, action-reaction. They rediscovered the feelings of the days they had spent in love and harmony. Karen leaned over, kissed his cheek, and confessed how she'd felt since she'd stormed out of the Buddha, hurt and frightened. She also admitted that she had decided she was going to leave the Silver Doll for higher ground.

In San Rafael he drew up to a curbside and pointed proudly. "There she is," he announced, directing her attention to a sleek white car poised in the front row of a car dealer's lot.

Confusion stammered off her lips. "You mean . . . we came all this way just to see a car? I don't even know what it is."

"Jesus, Karen," he said in half-real, half-mock mortification. "It's a Firebird!"

"Okay, so I don't know much about cars. You buying it?"

She had bitten exactly as he hoped she would. He turned and took her hands. "I'm buying the whole place."

"You're kidding!" It *was* true. She felt like a child who had just discovered ice cream.

"After I left you, I cruised the Van Ness car lots in San Francisco. Then I decided I didn't honestly want the hassle of the big city. I just want to be near it and on the Bay. I bought the trade papers, found an ad, drove up, and there was this Firebird! That's the sign, I said. A friend named Moe is going to help me on the credit rating." He went a bit shy. "I've got tons of money and a buddy in New York has even more, but, well, being an arsonist doesn't get you very far with a bank. I talked to the owner—that's okay. I have to pass the manufacturer's inspection, but that's Moe's department. Yesterday afternoon we went to his bank. That's taken care of. In about four weeks I'll be a major factor on the new- and used-car scene in San Rafael."

"I can't believe it, Stretch." She kissed him squarely on the mouth.

"You're my last hurdle. I mean, if you don't approve or don't like the town, I won't do it."

"*Ex*-torch? Never again? Promise?"

"Not for anything. Promise."

Karen looked down and shook her head, afraid to surrender herself, afraid not to. "You do it, Stretch." She looked up, tears welling from her eyes, her voice cracking with half a laugh. "I love you, Stretch Jackson. You do it and I'll love you . . . just forever."

All of Karen's barriers came down. She laughed and cried while they inspected San Rafael, through dinner in a little restaurant by the Bay, and late at night when their bodies joined their minds in making love. Neither of them had felt anything so deeply at any moment of their lives.

* * *

Pickles had been watching out of the corner of his eye. This morning's performance was even more odd than usual. Not only had the captain of the *Sapphire* lifted the hood of his car and poked around the engine, but now he was crouched on the ground, looking up the Pontiac's tail pipe with a flashlight.

"Well, Skipper," Pickles said, walking over with his Popeye smile, "I was in charge of sick bay on our minesweeper for a year during the war. If there's anything you want to know about tail pipes, I'm the expert." He slapped his knee. "What's she got up there, Tom?"

"A pipe bomb."

"A what?" The bravado vanished as Pickles involuntarily backed up a step.

"You want to pull it out? I'll stand over there and watch," Tom said nonchalantly.

"Not on your sweet life I don't!"

"Then you stand over there and I'll do it." Tom pulled off his jacket.

Pickles's eyes bugged at the bulging shoulder holster. "What's that?" he yelped.

"Come on. I know you sailors didn't get much training for hand-to-hand combat, but you have to know a thirty-eight when you see it!"

"Never saw you with . . . Hey, what're you into, with guns and bombs and all?"

"That's why I've been checking her out every time I crank up. I know I wasn't tailed last night. I've been watching. They must have waited until until I got home. See any strangers around here last night?"

"Nope."

Tom reviewed his options. He was sure he could remove the explosive device. Since the mechanism was detonated by heat generated by the auto's engine, there was really little risk. Handling and minor shocks would not normally set off a heat-sensitive detonator. Explosives more fragile than this one had passed through his hands in the army.

In the end, however, he left the bomb in the tail pipe and went back aboard *Sapphire II*. The possibility of fingerprints, the need to maintain the chain of evidence, and the opportunity to impress the Oakland police with the importance of the case won out. Someday, the bomb might prove handy in nailing its maker to a wall. There was even an outside chance that Tom might see the bomber himself in court before the Normandy Apartments case was over. Whoever was masterminding the operation had just upped the ante. Tom reasoned that the time for the fire must be drawing close, and the man in charge was becoming worried—even desperate—and a little careless. The thought brightened his hopes.

He dialed Lieutenant Boskowitch. The bomb would improve the officer's image with his superiors and give him a chance to get even with the snotty desk sergeant who doubted Tom's "intuition."

Next he called Charlene and sent her off to lunch alone once more. There was no need to worry her, so he chalked it up to a "problem with the car." Farley always preferred to tell the truth and, as far as it went, he had. There was nothing more to say about the Normandy case. From now on he would just *do* it.

As he hung up, he made himself a promise. The day after that son-of-a-bitch walked into his trap in the basement of the Normandy he would close the office and take a long vacation—*with* his secretary. He wondered if Charlene would like to sail to Puerto Vallarta.

* * *

Frank Sievers's fingers drummed a tattoo on the desk top. Weights without measure ricocheted in his mind. Sievers was in a dangerous mood.

Part one of his three-pronged program to reduce his risks on the Normandy had been to take out the arson investigator. That had failed twice. When he got the report that Farley was alive and well and still on his track, the boss decided that time was not playing to his advantage.

This was Friday. The second ploy to reduce his odds was his decision to send the Normandy up in smoke on Monday night, sooner than he had originally planned.

Now he was about to put the third change in tactics into action. That involved dealing with Stretch Jackson. Finally Hazel buzzed and announced that Stretch had arrived.

"Send him in." Sievers wasn't certain how he would play this. A lot depended on Jackson's reactions.

"What's up, Frank?"

"Sit down." It came out more gruffly than Frank had intended. "You know I wanted to get that investigator, Farley, out of the way." He watched like a hawk. There it was— Stretch went rigid and nervous. How could an arsonist not want to get an arson investigator off his tail? There was a flaw in his torch that he'd seen too late. "Henry and Ben dropped the ball twice. I've decided not to wait any longer. I want it to go Monday night. Are you ready?"

"I guess I'm as ready as I'm going to get on that burn."

That was a wishy-washy answer! It was exactly why he had decided on his next step. He pushed the intercom button. "Hazel, now, please."

A blond young man of the beach-boy variety entered.

"This is Marty Martin, Stretch. I want you to fill him and me in on how you're going to do the apartments."

Stretch was stunned. Then he jumped up, furious.

"What's this goddamn psycho doing here? Frank, I'm not going to talk about my burn with this crazy son-of-a-bitch! What is this?"

"Marty's the man who's been doing the torch work for George and Whitlock. He's a partner, not a competitor. I thought you might want a good assistant, somebody to back you up." Stretch's resistance was stronger than Frank had expected. It had never crossed Frank's mind that they might know each other.

"If I *did* want an assistant—and I don't—I wouldn't want one who had to set fires to get off!" Stretch was glazed with rage. "Do you realize every fire marshal in town knows this S.O.B.?"

"He's crazy, Mr. Sievers. My work—"

"It's not your work, turkey, it's your mind that's off!" Stretch spat.

"Well, listen, Stretch," Frank arbitrated, "you've got the weekend to think about it. Maybe we won't want Marty's help, but it won't hurt if he hears, now will it?!"

"He's liable to start pulling his pud just hearing it! I won't—"

"What do you feed this asshole? Wizard Wick?" Marty was losing his manners, too. "I have my tactics, he has his! So what?"

"Stop it, Stretch!" Frank commanded. "I don't know where you get your ideas and I don't give a damn what you think! Marty's been fine for Calhoun—he could help us out. I thought you were smarter than this. Now get the hell on with the outline. *I'm* the one who calls the shots around here—and don't you forget it!"

Every instinct told Stretch to walk out, but logic said he had no choice. "Give me that goddamn legal pad," he growled. Coldly, he began to diagram his new plan.

"But nothing's surer than the toaster," Frank objected.

"Now you listen to me," Stretch shot back, indignant. "You want this nut case to do your fire, you go right ahead. He'll fry everyone, burn the building—maybe—and land your ass in jail for sure, Frank Sievers or not! You want me for your torch, I'll do it my way. You tell me what to burn, it burns my way."

"It'd better be good."

"That's what I am! Remember? Now . . ." He got hold of himself again. "Usually when you want a total loss on a building you start your fire down below. The heat goes up and sets off everything above. But water's destructive, too. Monday afternoon I'll plant plastic bags of gasoline up both scuttle holes in the attic. There's old, blown-in, fire-retardant, rock-wool insulation that will slow the downward spread. First, I put this scuttle hole here on a fifteen-minute delay candle. That'll give me time to go to the second scuttle hole location, here, light that one with a short fire trail and get out down this elevator just around the corner. In about two minutes this set goes off and the first wing of the roof is involved. When I hit the lobby, I trip off the fire alarm so everyone can start getting out. Half the roof is burning, but the halls and stairwells are free for escape. Firemen should arrive in four minutes, five maybe. But by then the old timbers in that roof are unstoppable. Four minutes later, the top floor is evacuated. The firemen are just getting set up when the delay candle sets off the second wing of the building, this side here. By the time the water gets on it, the roof is ready to collapse, but everyone's out.

"The clincher isn't the fire, it's the water. I calculate they'll be pouring eighteen tons of water a minute on it. All the way down, the paint goes, the moldings split, plaster breaks from the keys, those old wood floors swell, carpets stain, and the wiring system's shot. No matter what you've got it insured for, the building is finished—absolutely totaled out. Fire's got the top of the building, water's got the rest. It's a clear torch job, all right, but the roof's collapsed so there's not a trace. No hard evidence and no link from the torch to anyone. Most important, no one's hurt, which means they're fighting the arson rules of evidence, not murder."

Stretch Jackson knew he had just laid out the plans for the perfect fire. He could not stand to stay and be degraded in this company any longer. He intended to see Frank Sievers just one more time—to pick up his thirty-two thousand dollars. As of Tuesday, he was a respectable automobile dealer who would marry a woman of his own kind.

Stretch wheeled and made for the door. He turned for one last word. "And keep that weird son-of-a-bitch out of my way! I'll tell *you* when I need help!" The door slammed behind him.

After a moment of stunned silence, Marty looked apologetically at Frank, "I'm sorry, Mr. Sievers. You know perfectly well no one has ever complained about my work. I really hate to say it after all that, but his plan is absolutely brilliant. All it needs is a match. He's a smart son-of-a-bitch. I'm sorry he's so crazy."

Frank's mind was elsewhere. He was listening to himself, not to Marty Martin. He's chicken, the inner voice was saying. The bastard's gone soft on me. And worst of all, he'd like to back out, even now. To Marty's embarrassment, Frank spun his chair around and ignored him.

Sievers stared out the window. He knows too much, he's lost his nerve, and he wants out bad. That's a lousy combination. Frank wondered whether Marty—a hardened professional even though he was neurotic—would not have been a better choice than a genius who developed scruples. Sievers frowned at the sky as though the answer might appear up there.

28

As the sun rose to heat the day, an S.F.P.D. patrol car was driving deeper and deeper underground in the cold and ominous Union Square Garage. The headlights of the slow-moving squad car flashed around the far post as the vehicle made a turn and began to inch along the row of parked cars; only the low hum of the engine broke the silence.

On a routine patrol, the two policemen automatically looked out the window from time to time, but their attention was locked on their animated discussion of whether or not the Chief's new secretary was a layable prospect. The patrol car rolled past a Pinto station wagon, then, almost as an after-thought, the driver halted, leaned his head out for a backward glance, and put the car in reverse.

"What's up, Mike?" his partner asked.

"Don't know. Where's the list?"

They consulted the mimeographed paper briefly, then stepped out of the squad car.

* * *

It was close to eleven o'clock that morning when *Sapphire II*'s phone began to ring insistently. With less than five hours' sleep, Tom Farley was a reluctant riser, but after four sentences of the conversation a thunderbolt could not have clapped him more awake.

When Tom hung up, he immediately dialed a number. "Sorry to bug you on Sunday morning, Jonah, but I think we've got him. . . . Yeah, really got him. Found the Pinto on a routine check in Union Square Garage. The space is rented monthly to the same MacDonald who's on the registration. They dusted the car for prints, but that takes a while. The important thing is, I got the captain who called to give me the precinct chief. He agreed to do a round-the-clock plainclothes stakeout on it. You can call off the firemen. . . . Yes, that's right, call them off! We'll get him at the source. That Pinto will never get out of the garage. He could change cars, but that's a one-in-a-million shot and, just in case, the two cops will stay in the basement on the mains—sort of a fail-safe plan. You stick with the rescue plan, too—although, thank God, that's a remote possibility now. The guy's stuck in a pattern. Sooner or later, he'll hit that car."

As of Sunday afternoon, an unmarked car with two plain-clothes detectives was parked at a discreet distance from OUX 829. The police do not usually muster much interest in arson cases, but, strangely enough, the bomb had impressed them. Tom was glad that Boskowitch was on his side.

* * *

A delivery truck pulled into a space behind the Normandy. The rear of the pickup was loaded with building materials ranging from two drums of roofer's asphalt to twenty buckets of white paint and several stacks of one-by-six lumber. The driver jumped out, dropped the tailgate, took the hand dolly down, and stacked it with bags of plaster. A small cloud of the fine white dust rose from the bags and settled on his baseball cap, plaid shirt, and faded jeans.

Stretch kept a nervous lookout in all directions, for this was the most vulnerable point of the entire operation. He had an alibi prepared in case he had been stopped in traffic, another if a workman inquired where his delivery was going, and yet a third should he be questioned on the seventh floor, above the remodeling job. But most of all, he did not want to be obliged to use any of his excuses. He didn't even want to be seen.

This hour of the morning had been carefully chosen because it was the low point of traffic in the Normandy's halls. Stretch pushed the dolly rapidly to the elevator. He was fortunate to be the only person going up. He made his way to the attic ladder, and finally carried the bags of plaster into the attic, one bag at a time, on his shoulder. Then he went back down to the truck. There had not been a single incident on the first trip.

He started loading the second cargo of plaster sacks. He treated them gingerly. If one of the plastic bags inside was to rupture, he would be in serious trouble. Sacks of plaster are not supposed to leak gasoline. He had spent days in the garage at his house, meticulously undoing the paper bags of plaster, emptying their contents, filling plastic bags with gas, sealing them, packing them into the paper sacks, and then resealing and dusting the now camouflaged load of inflammables.

He lifted the last sack onto the dolly. Stretch grunted. Marty Martin! Frank had his head up his ass! That psycho son-of-a-bitch could never have conceived the basic plan, to say nothing of working out all of these details. Would *he* have thought of putting enough powdered plaster on the bags to make them look authentic? Or of buying the one-by-six lumber and other supplies for a bona fide delivery truck look? Stretch burned with the insult. My assistant, my ass, he thought savagely as he humped the dolly up the ramp. If Frank wanted to eliminate someone, it shouldn't be Tom Farley, but an incompetent like Martin. Stretch had come to the conclusion over the weekend that he had overrated Sievers's intelligence. Guys at the top can be dumb, too. As dumb as anyone else! It had been a startling insight for a man who had always believed in authority.

He was headed for the elevator when he suddenly saw a man in a suit and hat with a clipboard in his hand. Visions of Tom Farley danced in his head. Stretch's heart jumped; all of a sudden the dolly weighed a ton. He forced himself to look again and found he was staring at some anonymous door-to-door salesman. He cursed himself for allowing his thoughts to wander. Damn Marty Martin and damn Frank Sievers! He'd be overjoyed to be rid of them both. He smiled with relief as the elevator rose. One more day!

That false alarm turned out to be the only incident during the entire delivery. Everything went off satin slick. Two trips in with plaster sacks, one with miscellaneous equipment—in and out in twenty minutes. He dumped the drums of tar, the paint, the lumber, and the rest in a portable bin at a San Francisco demolition site.

That afternoon Stretch returned to the Normandy in the Mustang, wearing different clothes, and went straight to the two scuttle holes. He set the bags in place, put the candle in one wing, the spouted jerrican of kerosene in the other. Everything was ready to make the final trail on the last fire of a short, brilliant, and lucrative career.

When he set the can down by the ladder and descended the stairs, his heart thrilled with joy. That was it—everything difficult was done. Stretch Jackson was ready for a normal life—and a lot of love. He stopped at a fancy food store, bought the largest jar of caviar they had and two bottles of their finest champagne.

* * *

There had been very little activity on Level C of the Union Square Garage to keep the two plainclothes detectives alert. Like most stakeouts, it was a very boring business.

It was Monday night, twenty minutes after twelve, when headlights rounded the bend. Both men came awake. The car approached the Pinto, swung into a space, and stopped. "Missed again," the detective on the right exclaimed as they watched a couple get out and head for the stairs.

* * *

Stretch had no intention of arriving at the garage before two o'clock in the morning. He was at his home where two bottles of champagne and a jar of caviar were chilling in the refrigerator. Everything else was being warmed—by a beautiful young woman with long brown hair and innocent eyes. Karen had Monday night off. Since it was the end of fires and the beginning of a new life for both of them, she had agreed to be part of the celebration. She no more wanted to wait for tomorrow than Stretch did.

The two lovers had spent the evening cuddling, kissing, and excitedly making plans. They mutually understood, without needing to say a word, that following the Normandy fire they would wallow in champagne and caviar, curl up and make love like never before, born anew. Karen had called the San Rafael Board of Education about openings for teachers. Stretch was trying to decide whether he would prefer to live on the bay or to the west in the wooded hills. They were ready to launch a life, a family. Tomorrow would not wait. It arrived early on the gossamer wings of love.

In timepiece terms it was already Tuesday. At exactly one o'clock the door chimes rang. Stretch checked his watch, startled. He squinted through his peephole, swore under his breath, and opened the door. Henry and Ben limped in.

"What the hell are you doing here? I've got company."

Henry knew about the lady. They'd been watching Stretch all afternoon. "That's too bad, Stretch, but Frank asked us to pick you up . . . just to make sure you didn't lose your way."

"You tell Frank—"

"Stretch! Now."

"Henry, your timing's off. It's too early!"

"Now." It was not a tone that invited argument.

Three o'clock was only a sentimental habit left over from Bert Morton's day. He shrugged his shoulders. Okay, he thought, let's get the damn thing over with. Stretch returned to the living room to explain to Karen. "Sorry," he said softly.

"Well, it's almost all over," she whispered, and gave him a kiss.

With a glance at his watch, Stretch recalculated his time. Everything was going to happen earlier. He had figured the timing from the house to the Pinto at Union Square to the Normandy and back down to the minute. He adjusted the total to allow a few minutes leeway for Henry's driving and then said, "I'll find a pay phone the minute it's over. That *can't* be later than twenty before three under any circumstance. Then you can break out the caviar. Okay?"

"Twenty to three and you're mine. I'll count on it. But don't you forget to call or I'll go crazy just sitting here waiting and worrying!"

"You kidding? I already can't think of anything but getting back to you." He kissed her gently on the eyes. "I love you, Litchfield." Then he went to the door to join Frank's henchmen.

Stretch climbed into the backseat. Henry backed his black Chrysler out of the driveway and headed east.

"Go to the Union Square Garage," Stretch said. "That's where I keep my fire car."

"Oh, no." Henry fixedly looked ahead. "Frank said we should take you straight to Oakland."

"What! Look, Henry, you guys have your way of doing your job, I've got mine. I'm used to using *that* car and nothing else!"

"My way of doing my job, Jackson, is to do exactly what my boss tells me to do. No ifs, ands, or buts. I don't think—he does. We're going to Oakland. Sit back and relax."

Ben turned around and stared at Stretch. "You're just not worth a shit at doing what you're told, are you?"

Stretch slumped back in the seat. It was true that he made a lousy flunky; he couldn't even argue with that. He was too relieved to be almost finished with this brainless mob to try. Stretch consoled himself with the fact that this change in plans would get him back to Karen a few minutes sooner. Over and done with, he repeated to himself. Over and done with.

They sped above the bay's dark waters, past the lights, like a string of glass beads, that lit the bridge. But at the northwest corner of Lake Merritt, the car turned left on Grand, away from Lakeside and the Normandy.

"Hey, Henry, it's down there!" There was no answer. Stretch snapped up to the edge of his seat. "Henry, goddammit, it's on the other side. This'll take you clear around the lake!"

There was practically no traffic on Grand Avenue when they swung into the deserted, dimly lit lane that went into the park and skirted the lake across from the apartments. Stretch was sitting bolt upright, outraged and confused. At the narrow point of the finger, the headlights pivoted toward the water's edge and flicked off as the car stopped. Another car was waiting in the adjacent space. Leaning expectantly against the fender was Marty Martin. Almost before the speedometer hit zero, all three doors opened.

Stretch jumped out first. "What the hell's going on here? I said I didn't want you around my light!"

"I been waiting for you, chicken shit! You've been bumped."

"Bumped, my ass—"

Stretch started to take a swing at the pretty-boy face, but Ben and Henry grabbed him and pinned him face up, spread-eagle on the fender of Henry's car.

"Not good enough for your assistant, huh?" Marty whined. "Frank figures you're a cop-out, two-bit punk, so he got a *real* torch. Make fun of me, you mother . . . embarrass me—"

Stretch tried to tear loose. "You'd jack off a chicken if you could burn its feathers. No other torch could've figured that light without killing someone—"

Martin's fist jabbed into the pit of his rival's stomach, just enough to shut off Stretch's wind. "Shut up!" Marty crowed. "Now it's *me* talking! You listen. Think you can be half a criminal in this business? Okay to be a capo's accountant, but not his hit man? A little fraud, no blood? Okay, huh? That's okay? Let me tell you, asshole, one hand wipes the other. They're both dirty. So who gives a damn you could have saved a couple of lives? I'm goddamned if *I'm* gonna risk getting caught by setting off a fucking fire alarm! The only skin that counts is mine."

"You psycho son-of-a-bitch!" Stretch lunged forward, but got slammed back onto the metal of Henry's car. "I'll kill you if you don't!" Marty got into his car. "I'll get you, Marty! You freaky bastard! *You break that glass!*"

"You got water on your wick, Jackson." His arm went back to deliver another punch.

"Okay, Martin," Henry barked. "We came here so you'd know he was out of your way—not so you two could get into a cockfight."

Marty glared, too, took the hint, started his car and pulled away. Henry and Ben relaxed their grip. Stretch straightened his clothes and shot a hate-filled look at the retreating taillights.

"Get in, Stretch," Henry commanded. "We got orders to take you home."

Stretch Jackson had become a major liability. "Home" was to be permanent—and watery: a small, totally isolated inlet south of Oakland. Three belts filled with lead diver's weights, waited in the trunk. By sunrise, Stretch would be twelve feet under—waterlogged and bloating.

Ben pulled Henry aside." Listen," he whispered, "we're not a hundred yards from the Normandy here. Why don't we sit and watch it burn a bit? Be a great show. And stupid there don't suspect nothing."

The idea pleased Henry. He had not seen a good fire in years and this one should be a beauty. They were perfectly safe and protected in the deserted park. "Sure. Ten, fifteen minutes, maybe. Why not?"

29

Station House 1 on Grove Street was quiet. The apparatus floor bristled with the polished, latent power of Engine 1, Ladder 1, and the spectacular new addition, Snorkel 1. Jonah had wrung a promise out of the Chief that, should the Normandy rescue operation become a reality, Jonah himself would captain Snorkel 1 to the fireground.

It was the Chief's night on duty. Tom and Jonah were doing what was by now their routine midnight-to-five vigil, and the three men were chatting.

"Thirty days straight of this graveyard shift's going to ruin my marriage," Jonah complained.

The Chief said, half-jokingly, "And it'll serve you right, if it's all your imagination."

Tom pushed the hat back on his head for the millionth time. "Funny," he muttered. "It's making me think about it."

"What . . . ? Marriage?" Jonah could not believe his ears.

Tom put his cup on the Chief's desk, checked his watch, and got up. "I think I'll go do my two-thirty, three-thirty hunker-down with the cops. Yeah, Jonah—marriage!" He shrugged his shoulders. "Did you think I was completely over the hill?"

* * *

No place in Oakland was more quiet than the Normandy Apartments. Only one light was burning on the seventh floor—the pretty young girl with the contagious urge had fallen asleep in the arms of a lover and had forgotten to switch off her lamp. Dee Hatford had said good-bye hours before to her boyfriend and was sleeping the sleep of the well-deserving. Although her apartment was right by the stairwell, it would have taken a troop of thundering horsemen to wake her. Six-year-old Wayne had recovered from his cold. Permanently attached to a soft and raggedy Peanuts doll, he was wrapped in innocent slumber.

The sole tenant up and about was an insomniac divorcee on the fourth floor. Well into her fifties, she tended to late-night boozing in the hopes of either sleep or obliteration. The alcohol had not yet succeeded, but a rerun on the tube was beginning to have a somnolent effect.

The two minions of the law Tom was coming to see sat in the soundless basement, their eyes dutifully riveted on the mains.

Far above them, the ascending elevator was going past the fifth floor. Marty's excitement was also rising. His eyes started to glitter, the pupils enlarged, his right hand could not help fluttering across his fly. He almost never got an assignment on an occupied building. He fought to control his emotions. Marty, he said to himself, don't blow your first job for Sievers. Don't blow it.

Marty let the ladder down gingerly. He checked the bags, the trailers, the candle, then went quickly to check the materials at the second attic entrance. Everything was exactly as Jackson had described it. He headed back to light the first candle in the south wing. Martin felt the surge of power. He controlled the destiny of all those people asleep in warm beds. They would feel him soon. His pace quickened toward the candle.

* * *

"Man, have we got a ringside seat for Marty's fire," Ben chortled.

"It's *my* fire! Just his matches."

"Listen, smart-ass, you are canned! Through! You are an ex-torch!"

For the first time there was a break in the clouds of Stretch's fury. The meaning of Ben's remark sank in. He beamed. "You mean Frank has really fired me? I've got to go back to selling cars?"

Henry shot Ben a knowing look, then twisted around to the backseat. "You're thick as pig shit. Yeah. You . . . are . . . fired! You got to your big one and went soft. Blew it, car peddler!" He turned back to look across the lake and didn't see Stretch slide low in the backseat to hide his ear-to-ear smile.

"Yeah, selling cars is about your speed, Jackson!" Ben was delighted to rub it in. "You should have stuck with it. Now look where you are. Play the uptown game, pay the uptown price."

Henry threw Ben a look that said, Shut up! They were not by the inlet yet!

Stretch missed the message, but the clouds returned and he lost his smile. His thoughts locked in on images of death across the lake. "Henry, you're no dummy," he said.

"Well, listen to that."

"That crazy bastard's going to kill somebody."

"That's not my business."

"Frank'll be mad. That's a murder rap."

Awkwardly, Henry turned around. Jackson's naiveté left him incredulous. "You think Frank ain't never put anyone away before?" There was no answer. He turned back around, catching Ben's eye on the way. "Look, Frank thinks, and I do. Frank takes good care of me. Anyhow, Marty was probably kidding. You make it sound like he'd get off at a weenie roast."

Both men in the front seat laughed.

"You can't trust a psycho. Frank doesn't know pyros . . . or perverts."

Stretch looked down at the Congril Zippo he was fingering. It brought back images of burning men and the psychotic-killer look that Sergeant Hager and Marty shared. Faces from the Normandy Apartments jumbled together with the horrors of the past. Like it or not, this *was* his fire and *his* responsibility. He couldn't start his life with Karen like this, with blood and burning flesh on his hands.

Henry pulled out a cigarette.

"Here, Henry." Stretch leaned forward. The Zippo flamed high. Henry leaned to accept the light. The blazing Zippo dropped squarely between his legs, then slid, flaming, down the seat to his crotch.

Instantly, Stretch was out the door, leaving panic in the car. He had spent hours sitting at exactly this spot while he studied the Normandy—and he knew the fastest way to reach it. He ran ten steps, did a flat, racing dive, and swam for his life. Running, limping, Ben pulled his gun. Henry was right behind him.

"Don't shoot, Ben! You'll wake everyone in the neighborhood!"

"I can't see him now!"

"C'mon! We'll head him off! Jesus!"

They ran back to the car. It was a long, twisting drive up and around the finger.

Stretch's head broke the surface of the water. He heard them, heard the motor start. As the headlights came on, he ducked and swam underwater, waiting for the bullets. When he came up again they were gone. He stroked flat out for the Normandy shore.

* * *

Marty struck a match in the Normandy's attic and applied it to the wick of a candle. Then he turned to head for the other attic ladder. He breathed hard just thinking about the other light. *That* one would be really exciting.

* * *

Breathless, Stretch had only one image in his head now: the red fire alarm. Not even a champion swimmer could have covered the distance faster, especially not fully clothed. Lakeside Drive was higher than the park side of the lake. A concrete embankment rose in front of him. He remembered stairs. They were to the left, barely visible in the streetlights, but he made them. At the top, he dropped behind some low bushes by the curb.

Ben and Henry careened around the lake, ran the red light at Grand and Lakeside, slowed in front of the posh Amington Hotel, where there were always taxis and occasionally a patrol car, then sped on. They approached the Normandy.

"Ben, when I say, 'Now,' you grab the wheel—we swap places. I'll do the roll, you close the door easy. Keep cruising slow. He'll be watching the car."

Henry was right. Crouched low, dripping wet, Stretch had his eyes on the approaching headlights. He did not see the front door on the far side open or Henry roll out of it and plunge into the bushes.

In Henry's mind Stretch could have been anywhere, but one thing was certain; he would head for the lobby. With unexpected agility, the gunman ran, unseen, from bush to bush, heading for the rear entrance of the building. Streetlights glinted dully off of his drawn gun.

Ben parked the car in clear view and turned off the lights. As Henry had said, Stretch would watch the car, not who was in it.

Over on Twelfth and Broadway, the stoplight was stuck on red. There was not much moving at this hour, but a befuddled, law-abiding citizen sat there, undecided whether to go through or wait forever for legality. He was holding up a black-and-white Pontiac, and Tom, becoming very impatient, began to toot his horn.

Stretch estimated that there was Lakeside Drive plus fifty feet of lawn between the shrubs where he was hiding and the front entrance. The trees would provide no cover. Obviously, the men in the car a bit up the street were waiting for him to make his move across the exposed lawn. He bit his lip. What he couldn't figure was whether they would come out running or shooting. If it was a running match, Stretch was certain he could break the glass before they stopped him. After that, he knew he was in heavy trouble, but he barely allowed the thought to skip through his mind.

* * *

Finally! Thoroughly irritated, Tom edged across the intersection at Twelfth and gunned it for the Normandy.

* * *

Martin discovered that there was far more accelerant in the jerrican than was needed for the fire trail. Originally, Stretch had intended for the trail to go down the pull-down ladder and stop. But when Marty looked at what was left, his emotions totally blocked his brain passages and a transformation occurred. Transfigured, he watched himself making the stream wiggle down the main stairwell. He dribbled it abundantly across the hall and in front of the door that was next to the stairwell. Finally the supply ran out and he splashed what little was left against the door itself and set the container down.

* * *

Stretch ran for it. His side that faced the car had a cold, numb feeling. He waited for the bullet's bite and didn't even look. He jerked the front door of the building open, thanking God that he'd made it. One foot was in the lobby when Henry stepped out of the alcove and jammed a blue-steel barrel straight into Stretch's chest.

"Freeze or you're dead."

Shattered, Stretch froze, his eyes on the red rectangle on the other side of the lobby. "Henry," he hissed in sheer desperation. "It won't blow his job. The alarm's just there."

"Frank gave it to Marty!"

"You got to be part human!" he said through clenched teeth. "Those are honest-to-God people sleeping up there! He's going to *burn them*!"

For a split second Henry hesitated—then hardened. "That's his decision. Frank gave it to him."

Stretch's eyes gave a hint that he might make a break for it. A negative grunt emerged from Henry, who grabbed Stretch's arm in his ham hand, flipped him around, and twisted the arm hard up behind Stretch's back.

"You almost cost me my job, you asshole!"

* * *

Marty struck the match and dropped it into the accelerant. For a moment, the flame burned slowly, then gathered force and moved up the door, and finally it flared in the puddle by the head of the stairs. Martin's hand slipped into his pocket.

* * *

Tom spotted the flash at the same instant he pulled the Pontiac up to the front of the building.

"Jesus Christ!" he yelled. "Jesus Christ!" He leaned on the horn and rammed the car over the curb, through flower beds, and across the lawn. He didn't stop the Pontiac until he hit the entrance steps. He jammed the horn down with his clipboard. Lights began going on as Tom jumped out, leaving the blaring horn behind.

It took a few seconds for Henry to collect his wits, what with the horn blasting and the headlights rocketing toward him. Stretch took that instant to violently slam the hand holding the gun against the corner of the wall where the alcove met the lobby. Something—or everything—split in Henry's wrist. The gun clattered to the floor and skittered toward the door just as Tom burst in. Both Tom and Henry dived for it. Tom only got a fleeting glimpse of another man's back racing toward the elevator.

Stretch slapped the UP button and almost simutaneously jerked the hammer on its chain, broke the glass of the fire alarm, and yanked the handle downwards. Bells clanged in every corner of the building, screaming their loud, anguished cry of warning. Not waiting for the elevator, Stretch bounded up the main stairway.

On the lobby floor, Tom and Henry wrestled viciously for the gun. One had brute strength, the other leverage.

* * *

On the seventh floor, Marty Martin panicked at the clamor of the fire alarm and jumped for the elevator just as its red light blinked—signaling its descent. A head appeared in a doorway. Someone screamed at the sight of the flames. For all of his fascination with flames, Marty Martin had an equal, insane terror of being burned. With this wing's elevator gone, he felt trapped. He cowered, flattened against the inset doorway of the utility room, paralyzed by fear, not knowing that there was a service stairway at the other end of the hall.

Bells rang in the basement, too. The two officers reacted at once. Running, they switched their radios on and SOSed for policemen, firemen. The Normandy Emergency Plan was put into action.

Fire hit the first group of gas bags. In mere moments flames roared through the south half of the building's attic.

Tom's hand sliced at Henry's collarbone and landed directly on the acromial nerve bundle. In addition to the upper-right paralysis, no gasp could express the flash of white pain that ripped through Henry's huge body, high pain threshold or not. Tom rolled away and grabbed the gun. The two policemen came flying out of the stairwell from the basement, guns in hand and immediately covered Henry. Tom raced up the main stairway after the other man he'd seen. The number of tenants hurrying down those stairs was changing from a trickle to a stream.

The long bell rang at Station 1. "Normandy Apartments," the intercom blasted out. "Captain West, it's your operation.

Special task force orders in effect." All nine Oakland fire stations with ladder companies got the same call.

"My God!" the Chief said, pale-faced, jumping down the pole ahead of Jonah. "What went wrong?"

Snorkel I raced out of Station 1, sirens ahowl, red lights flashing. Bud Pyle gunned it, foot to the floor. Jonah did not have to tell him the route. The flash of chrome and red tore a hole in the night.

Owen Pavitt had been promoted to captain of Ladder 1, taking Mannie's place. The ladder truck followed in the snorkel's tracks.

The Chief headed the screaming procession in his buggy. When they hit Lakeside, he could already see flames—and to his horror, they were all on the top floor. He grabbed the radio. "Hold the choppers—roofs involved! Send every squirt and tower available, and stand by all ambulances!" Every truck that the O.F.D. commanded converged on the Normandy, plus six heavy engines.

In the apartment next to the seventh-floor stairwell Dee Hatford woke from sweet dreams to a nightmare. She smelled smoke. Everywhere, voices, bells, and sirens were rattling the building. She ran to the hall door to see what was happening. When she wrenched the door open, flames rushed in. Every photo of charred buildings and burned bodies which had ever crossed her desk at Global Insurance flashed out of the neat filing system of her mind. The images came alive and blacked out her reason. She slammed the door shut and leaned against it, trying to catch her breath. Shock froze her tight in its grip.

Every truck knew its place. Ladders quickly ringed the building, plucking up the elderly, children, and, most of all, everyone who appeared at a seventh-floor window. Wayne's parents, on that floor, were screaming, "Over here! Over here!"

From the moment Stretch pulled the alarm, every thought was excluded from his mind, save one: laying his hands on Marty Martin. He knew that by pushing the elevator button he had trapped his quarry on the top floor. Working his way up the stairs, Stretch could not know that Marty had spread accelerant in the seventh-floor stairwell and the adjacent hall. He also could not know that Tom Farley was coming up after him, gun in hand, ready to kill if he had to.

Bud Pyle manned the thousand GPM monitor on Snorkel 1. Jonah was up in the basket with him. Flames had already found their way up roof vents. Bud only got in a squirt now and then, since their main priority was rescue. The engine companies would have to worry about the blazing rafters.

"Shut her down!" Jonah yelled, swinging the basket to a window where a pretty young girl and her lover leaned out, screaming for help. Smoke, unable to escape upward, was starting to back down from the attic and wisp lightly out of the windows. Heat, likewise, could not rise out fast enough and was also building up, banking downward to the seventh floor.

Dan Branch was top man on Ladder 1. "The window on the right," he called into his helmet radio. Fifty feet below, the ladder operator pushed levers. The ladder swung around toward Wayne's hysterical mother.

"Hold it, lady!" Dan yelled. The ladder went right to the sill. Dan jumped in, grabbed the child, and carried him down. The new recruit with the textbook memory had been assigned Jack Runyon's slot. He moved up to carry Wayne's mother down the ladder. Safely on the ground, the lady kissed her boy, then, tears of gratitude streaming down her face, kissed Dan Branch—much to his embarrassment. She gave the young recruit a hug, a teary kiss, and a stream of thank-you's. That moment made the new man a fireman for life. That moment of relief, of gratitude, and glory was the essence of a fire-man's reward. It's not a job one does for pay alone. Both men bounded back up the ladder.

Ten minutes had passed since Marty had struck the first match. As the fire gnawed its way through the roof structure, there were still many horror-stricken people trapped in apartments and others trying to get out by the main stairwell or down the narrow service stairs in the north wing. But for all of the south wing's flames, the candle in the north wing had not yet touched the matches that would make the bags of gasoline explode into flame.

The crush of people coming down the main stairs slowed Stretch's advance. He finally reached the landing on the fifth floor and looked up in horror to see the stairwell between the sixth and seventh floors ablaze. He studied the situation to see if he could get through. Above all of the other sounds, he suddenly heard someone just behind him yell, "Freeze!"

Stretch turned and found himself staring into the barrel of Tom Farley's .38.

"*You!* You son-of-a-bitch!" Farley could not believe his eyes.

"Tom, I—"

"Don't say a word! I should damn well make you fry in it!"

"Tom, I didn't set it. The guy who did is still up there!"

A lady in a housecoat saw the gun, gave a loud gasp, and jerked her way sideways toward escape down the stairs, overpowered by the multiple horrors around her.

"It's only half lit. There's a time candle on a pack of matches in the north wing. Tom, I can get to it! There are three minutes. Let me go!"

"You must think I'm really dumb."

"For Christ's sake! You know my fires! You think I'd do this? I didn't use the toaster so no one would get hurt. Then Sievers turned that psycho Martin loose on my job, *my job!*" He realized that Tom hesitated. "Who do you think broke the fire alarm? Me! I'll give them all to you—Sievers, that banker George Calhoun, the whole ring, the ship fire, Vic Whitlock—"

"*What?*"

"You heard me! They're all yours. I only want that son-of-a-bitch upstairs. *He's mine!* Tom . . . mine!"

"Okay, but we both go!"

Stretch in the lead, they flew down the fifth-floor hall to the service stairs.

* * *

Dee Hatford's paralysis suddenly turned to hysteria. She screamed. The scream reverberated down the seventh-floor hall and broke Marty's paralysis as well. He fled from the doorway where he had huddled and caught sight of a man running from his apartment to the north wing. Marty ran to follow the tenant, praying he was heading for a way out. Marty chased the man, past the north attic ladder and past the stairs that went up to the roof.

Dee flew to the window, her long hair flowing. Outside she saw pandemonium—red lights, spotlights, people milling, ambulances, firemen. Her screams pierced the apartment again. Heavy smoke backed down a vent and rolled into the living room. Heat. Heat. Boiling hot. She ran in an irrational frenzy to the bedroom and grabbed the framed picture of her new fiancé kissing it, clutching it to her breast, cooing to it dementedly. Then she raced to the window, threw it open, and climbed onto the ledge.

Dan Branch saw her as soon as her first foot appeared. "Seventh floor, on the left!" he ordered.

The ladder started to swing around. He saw the second leg come out. The woman sat, apparently secure, but instinct told him something was very wrong.

"Hey, lady, we're coming! Hey . . . lady!"

She looked completely unsteady. The ladder was thirty-five feet away, twenty. "Hey, lady—"

Dee Hatford slipped off the ledge like a drop of water on a butter mountain. Clasping the photograph, she hurtled down. Dan looked, unbelieving, at the empty window . . . ten feet away . . . five. He felt sick, unsteady. He clutched the beams of the ladder, dropped his head to a rung and wept—wept unashamed tears that threw the crumpled form below out of focus. He cried until Owen Pavitt came and helped him down.

Fed by the gasoline and the fresh oxygen rushing up the scuttle holes, the blaze chewed rapidly at the roof structure of the burning wing. Since the firemen's number-one priority was rescue work, the flames were doused with less water than they might have been ordinarily. Search-and-rescue parties were fanning through the building. The downflow of terrified tenants had all but stopped.

As he burst through the door of the fifth-floor service stairs, Stretch collided violently with the tenant who was running down the steps from the seventh floor.

"You okay, Stretch?" Tom asked.

"Yeah. Sorry, mister. You okay . . . ? Up here, Tom!"

Between the sixth and seventh floors, Marty Martin stopped in his tracks. He heard the name, recognized the voice. The footsteps were heading up the stairs, so he turned back, not taking the time to think which way was most dangerous. He flew through the door and to the north attic scuttle hole. Atop the ladder, the candle burned, millimeters from the pack of matches. Martin grabbed one plastic bag of gasoline and jumped back down the scuttle ladder. He sailed the bag down the hallway just as the door from the stairwell was pushed open, then hurled his flaming Zippo after the bag. Stretch saw the nightmare coming as he emerged into the hallway. He backed into Tom with a thud and pulled the door shut at the instant the bag split and filled the hall with a blast of fire.

"Six seconds and the heavy top's off the flame!" Tom said.

"Candle's got ten, fifteen. I'll get it."

"I'll get *him*."

"He's mine!"

"Now."

Stretch slammed the door outward. Marty had not expected to see them come at him right through the flames. He leaped toward the steps that led to the roof.

"Freeze!" Tom yelled, but Marty fled, disappearing up the stairs. Tom leaped up after him.

Stretch sprang up the attic ladder. He slapped his hand down on the flame at the instant the phosphorus matches flared. Pain seared his left palm, but he held it there. Nothing caught. He went limp with pain and relief for a second, then jumped off the ladder and dashed after Tom.

The stairs to the roof opened next to the parapet wall. Stretch darted out and stopped. The far wing was a surrealistic inferno.

The Fire God belched smoke and flame from the steamshiplike L-shaped attic ventilators. Spotlights cut round shafts out of the billowing black clouds. Jets of water drilled arcs through the night sky. The isolation of the fiery red light at the vents made the scene look strange, unreal, like a Dali landscape. A murmur rose from the crowd below. The distant droning of the mob, punctuated by sirens, added to the purgatorial vision.

Suddenly a shot rang out and someone yelled, "Out! Come out!"

Stretch squinted. He could make out Tom, crouched on the opposite side of the north wing. He stooped low and ran to Farley's side. "*I said he's mine!* You get everybody but him! Where is he?"

Tom pointed just as Marty streaked briefly into view. Martin ducked behind a more distant vent on the roof's south side. Stretch started toward him, but a monitor's stream swept the roof and knocked Jackson off his feet. Farley rushed to his side and helped him stand.

"Let go, damn it!" Stretch cried, racing after Marty again.

A tongue of flame lashed out of the roofs stairwell. The fire bag Martin had thrown down the hall was spreading flames upward. The fear struck Tom that this new fire source might reach the gasoline bags where the candle had been snuffed out. "Stretch!" he screamed. "It's enough. He can't get off here! Stretch! The roof'll go!"

Vengeance won the upper hand. Stretch continued toward the flaming vents.

"Leave, him! For Christ's sake, leave him!" Tom bellowed.

But he cried out too late. Stretch got a fix on Marty's hiding spot and sprinted to it. Marty vaulted from behind the attic's flaming nostril.

Stretch caught him. "You pig!" he screamed, "Look what you did!"

Martin lunged. "Yellow bastard!" His fist rammed into Stretch's shoulder.

They grappled, trading blows, until Stretch landed a right that flattened Martin on the roof deck.

"You slime! You're not worth getting blood on my hands." Stretch backed off in disgust. He turned to walk away, then stopped, dazed. Seeing Tom in the distance switched reality back into focus. Now what? He thought of West Alton and the gray granite soldier. What had gone wrong? Suddenly, he remembered his promise to Karen. He was late! And he would be even later! Much later. She had to be waiting, worrying already. What could he say to her now? San Rafael, the dealership, his new life crashed in ruins, ripping, clawing at the guts of his mind as they went. Vaguely it registered that someone was calling him.

Ever since Pat Farley had lost his leg on a burning roof, Tom had a horror of them. This was the first time he had ever been on one—and he wanted off. He also wanted Stretch Jackson. And he wanted to hear more about Vic Whitlock. Farley cupped his hands and called once more. Why was Stretch just standing there? "Stre . . ." He stopped in the middle of the yell, immobilized by disbelief as a volcano erupted before his eyes, thundering smoke and flame to the night heavens. The Fire God sucked the roof of the south wing into his bowels, rumbling roaring, regurgitating fire in return. In a flash Stretch and Marty were swallowed into the crater.

The cherry-picker basket of Snorkel 1 had just poked above the parapet wall. "Tom!" Jonah bellowed. "Tom!!"

Shaken out of the nightmare, Farley bolted through the rain of ash, along the north rim of the flaming crevasse. He jumped to the parapet and teetered. Snorkel I's basket was three feet away—across the void. A spotlight hit him. A roar came from the onlookers many floors below. There was no choice. He jumped. Everything fell: the pit of his stomach, his body, his hopes for a neat open-and-shut case. He reached out desperately for the Snorkel's rail.

Jonah braced and grabbed him, held him steel tight. Tom Farley was spent, as if he had just lived an entire lifetime. He leaned his head on the captain's shoulder. Slowly, wordless, he rode the Snorkel down.

EPILOGUE

Snorkel 1's basket was only halfway to the ground when Tom Farley's mind started functioning again. There had been a flaw in his analysis. The Normandy *had* burned, and the charges would include murder as well as arson. Had his case died with Stretch and Marty? And what had Vic Whitlock and a banker named Calhoun done? Tom rallied every cell in his tired brain and body. When the cherry picker came to rest on the truck bed, Farley had all of his possibilities calculated. He knew he would need a bit of luck to make a case, but he knew exactly where to look for it. He also realized that in some odd way he wanted to succeed for Stretch Jackson as much as he did for justice, his job, or himself. He hit the ground on the run.

From his car Tom telephoned Charlene. She dressed and raced to the office to get Marty's address from one of the case files in which he had been questioned.

Henry was sitting at the police station, sullen and still handcuffed, waiting to be booked. Lieutenant Boskowitch was on duty. He personally pulled the slip of paper from Henry's pocket that had his day's assignment written on it. It consisted of Stretch Jackson's name and address. The lieutenant made a call to the San Francisco Police Department to lay the groundwork for Tom to visit Jackson's home accompanied by police with a search warrant.

Tom broke the news as gently as he could. He could tell this girl was not the tough, sophisticated type he'd seen at lunch with Stretch. Karen tried to stammer out an explanation but collapsed into a catatonic state of shock. One of the policemen called an ambulance for her. Tom held her hand tightly as she lay closemouthed, open-eyed, and tearless on the stretcher, and continued to hold it as she was hurried to the ambulance. And then she was whisked away.

Another policeman would eventually find sketches and plans of the Normandy, Sievers's name, a box number at Calhoun's bank, and enough technical notes to build the bridges necessary for a court case.

Charlene was waiting at the office. When Tom called in, she told him that Marty lived in Daly City. But before she hung up the telephone, she had agreed to one of the year's fastest proposals of marriage.

Warming himself impatiently in weak early-morning sunlight, Tom waited outside Martin's apartment building. It took a little longer to get a search warrant in Daly City than in San Francisco. The wait was worth it. Sloppy to the end, Marty Martin had kept a full, dated, and detailed diary of everything he'd ever torched—including the names and addresses of who the clients had been for each job. It was bonanza time. The diary was just bluntly labeled FIRE and rested right in the top drawer of his desk. In a few minutes Tom Farley knew exactly what and who he was looking for. The police confiscated the evidence and sealed the apartment.

No moves were made immediately.

Two days later, in New York City, Tom was locked in conference with the President and the National Fire Loss Manager of Global Insurance Company. It took him three days in New York to get photostats of everything he needed. He had located each fire listed in Martin's diary, plus every one from Whitlock's office where there had been an uninvestigated major total loss or a change of ownership accompanied by an increase in the policy amount shortly before a fire. After finding the first few, Tom's "sixth sense" quickly discovered the pattern. He even tracked the case of a boat, the *Tania T.* The national fire loss manager was bowled over by Farley's astuteness, the president by the size of the company's loss, and all of them by Vic Whitlock's double life.

Back in San Francisco, it took Tom, Charlene, Pat, three Bay Area district attorneys, four fire marshals, and a number of police detectives exactly three weeks of ceaseless effort to wrap up the investigation.

Frank Sievers, after a moment of fright, had made the logical assumption that the death of both his torches provided him with an airtight screen. Two weeks after the fire, apparent calm reigned, and Sievers, with his usual self-confidence, began making the moves to rake in his profits on the Normandy venture. Even when Hazel announced the arrival of two detectives "on business," Frank was not alarmed. However, confronted by an arrest warrant and a pair of cold, steel handcuffs, Sievers went from apoplectic to sullen to apoplectic again. Hazel, Henry—who was out on bail—and even the union's "fancy attorney" were helpless as they scurried to follow Frank Sievers out of the building and to the police station for booking.

Not only was George Calhoun the first member of his prominent family to be accused of a crime (an indictable one, anyway), but the shame and disgrace of being led through the lobby of that august temple of banking with handcuffs on, like a common criminal, was more than he could bear. His face turned the color of the distinguished gray at his temples, his eloquence left him, even his dignified bearing was reduced to a slouch. By the time he reached the sidewalk Calhoun resembled any other captured criminal.

The only man who knew in his bones that something was going wrong was Whitlock—but he could not put his finger on what it was. He was moved by the death of Dee, but within a week that concern was replaced by a sense of personal foreboding. He was brooding in his arboretum, a little sloshed, playing hooky on a weekday afternoon, when the officers finally located him. As he was led past his wife and her car and her poodles, he knew exactly what he had to do. He confessed and pleaded guilty.

Vada turned state's evidence and was not indicted. The insurance agent in the Whitlock–Calhoun ring also agreed to be a prosecution witness in return for reduced charges.

Mannie Rojas, Jack Runyon, Dee Hatford, Marty Martin, and Stretch Jackson had died in the fires. Over forty people had been injured,

Tom and Charlene visited Karen as often as they could and in time, when she was released from the clinic, really took her under their wing. Eventually she became a teacher in San Rafael.

A long time and several appeals later, Frank Sievers, Ben and Henry, Whitlock and Calhoun, the insurance agent, and nine other people were found guilty and served time in prison.

* * *

With an impish grin Pickles cast off the *Sapphire*'s fore line with his left hand while his right hand reached into his bulging pocket. "Happy honeymoon!" he yelled. "And don't burn up the boat!" He rained rice from the stem to the stern. Tom and Charlene would still be finding a grain here and there in Mexico.

The *Sapphire* sailed out of San Francisco Bay on a fair wind.

"You know," Tom said with an air of amazement, "I'm actually looking forward to a month without fire."

Charlene kissed the back of the skipper's neck and asked, "Of which kind?"

ABOUT THE AUTHOR

Jack Siler's life has been constant contrasts: raised between a small farming town near St. Louis and the cultural life of the city itself, educated at the University of New Mexico, but graduated from the University of Illinois with several degrees, then living and working, literally, from one end of America to the other.

Siler was an independent investigator for insurance companies. Arson cases fascinated him, because they always included high drama. Eventually, he specialized in catastrophic damages, a 16/7 job that took him from Miami to Portland, LA to NY, yet that left him free to live large chunks of each year in Paris, the Kenya bush, Italy, or Mexico, learn 6 languages, and write. His passion is studying social diversities from nation to nation, from America to Egypt. And skin diving!

He is currently finishing both a new thriller and, after years of research, a history mystery exposing what the real fate was of Aristotle's Alexandrian Library.

CPSIA information can be obtained
at www.ICGtesting.com
Printed in the USA
BVHW041627160619
551042BV00034B/594/P